Enjoy !!

Fred

Whitson

D0814653

< 1 >

W.F. WHITSON | THE LIBRARIAN

This is a work of fiction. All of the characters, organizations, and events portrayed in this novel are either products of the author's imagination or are used fictionally. Any similarity to a real person is purely coincidental and not intended.

For permissions, write:
Blue Room Books
Attn: The Librarian/Whitson
blueroombooks@outlook.com

Executive Editor: Tom Whitfield

Cover design, interior layout, and editor:
Angela K. Durden

The Librarian
978-1-950729-11-1
W.F. Whitson
BlueRoomBooks.com

< 2 >

This book is dedicated to the memory of three GLCM'ites with whom I would love to have been able to discuss this book:

Carl H. Cathey
Lieutenant General, USAF
Retired after 35 years of service
1931-2000

George E. Cooke
Colonel, USAF
Retired after 30 years of service
1938-2006

Richard D. Bean
Lieutenant Colonel, USAF
Retired after 26 years of service
1940-2007

< 3 >

PRINCIPAL CHARACTERS

From the United States

1. Wesley Forrest, Lieutenant Colonel, USAF: First Ground Launched Cruise Missile Officer assigned to RAF Greenham Common AB, UK, the first of six GLCM bases in Europe
2. Tom Rogers, Colonel, USAF: RAF Greenham Common, 501st Wing Commander
3. Marlin Frazier, Colonel, USAF: RAF Greenham Common, Commander of Base Security Police
4. Brenda Judd, Lieutenant Colonel, USAF: RAF Greenham Common, US Vice Wing Commander

From the United Kingdom

1. Morgan Pritchard: Electrician, Northampton General Hospital, and master thief. His sister Mari is a leader in the Women's Peace Camp
2. Elliot Knight: Agent, Her Majesty's Security Service [MI5], K Branch
3. Glendon Brown: Recent transfer, Her Majesty's Security Service [MI5], K Branch
4. Andrew Tidwell: Detective, Thames Valley Police
5. Finley Mackay, Group Captain, RAF: RAF Greenham British Base Commander
6. Lila Kerr: Mackay's secretary (who spies for the Women's Peace Camp)

< 4 >

7. Iain McKenna: Crew member of Captain Ross' North Sea fishing boat (also used to smuggle drugs from Europe)

From the Soviet Union

1. Nikolai Sokolov: Spy, USSR. Ordered to stop the GLCM deployment. (Code name GOSHAWK)
2. Vasili Podgorsky, Lieutenant General, Head of the First Directorate, KGB
   [*Komitet Gosudarstvennoy Bezopasnosti*]

From the Women's Peace Camp

1. Mari Pritchard: Welch and one of the original members and supporter of the effort to stop the deployment of GLCM in the UK.
2. Katelin Nagy: Hungarian (who Sokolov blackmails for information—code name BIRCH).

< 5 >

ACRONYMS USED

1. APO – Army Post Office, located on both Army and USAF installations.
2. GAMA – GLCM Alert and Maintenance Area. Secure storage for the weapon system.
3. GLCM *(pronounced glick-um)* – Ground Launched Cruise Missile: Officially designated the BGM-109G Gryphon, was a variant of the Tomahawk missile, carrying a W84 thermonuclear warhead, with a range of 2000-2500 miles.
4. KGB (Komitet Gosudarstvennoy Bezopasnosti) — The Committee for State Security: Was the secret police force that was the main security agency for the Soviet Union from 1954 until the dissolution in 1991.
5. LCC – Launch Control Center: Housed two launch officers and was connected to from one-to-four GLCM TELs for launch. The LCC used satellite links to communicate with the National Command Authority. Towed by a large MAN 8x8 tractor thus capable of traversing rough terrain.
6. MI5 – The Security Service: the United Kingdom's domestic counter-intelligence and security agency. The US equivalent is the FBI.

< 6 >

7. MI6 – The Secret Intelligence Service – the foreign intelligence service of the United Kingdom. The US equivalent is the CIA.
8. MDP – British Ministry of Defence Police.
9. MOD – British Ministry of Defence. US equivalent of Department of Defense.
10. RAF – Royal Air Force
11. SAC – Strategic Air Command (USAF)
12. TAC – Tactical Air Command (USAF)
13. TEL – Transporter Erector Launcher: An armored erector mounted to a heavy-duty trailer, carrying four GLCM missiles in their containers, ready for launch. Designed for dispersal operations.
14. TVP – Thames Valley Police
15. USAF – United States Air Force
16. USAFE – United States Air Forces in Europe

< 7 >

< 8 >

< 9 >

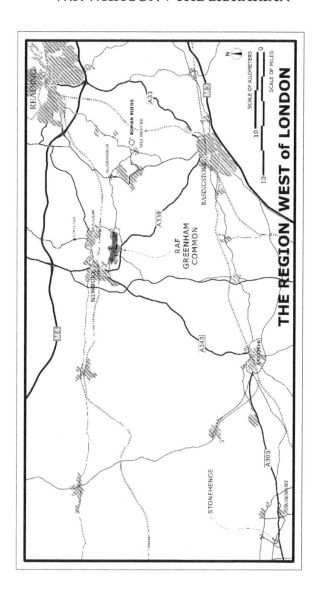

< 10 >

Maps courtesy Chuck Clark, Architect
Atlanta, Georgia

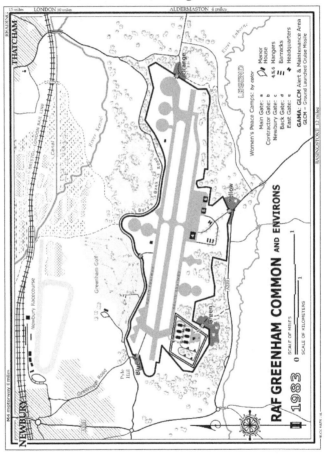

< 11 >

< 12 >

PART ONE

< 13 >

< 14 >

ONE

Moscow
15 November 1981

Nikolai Sokolov paced in front of the safehouse. His life was about to change. The black wool coat, Kashmiri scarf, and fur hat kept out the cold, but his mind was so focused he didn't feel the fragments of ice pelting his face.

Why had he been summoned from Budapest to Moscow for a conference with the Komitet Gosudarstvennoy Bezopasnosti general?

A KGB corporal drove him south to the Yasenevo District. Traffic was heavy at the dinner hour, but the black GAZ Chaika with official plates sped through the congestion. Thirty minutes later the driver turned down a narrow, empty road and entered a pine forest sprinkled with birch trees. Within one hundred meters they were stopped by a manual boom gate. A soldier in winter brown uniform tightened earflaps on his fur hat and walked around the car. An officer with a peaked hat fastened his overcoat when he approached the driver's window. His handler's identification and credentials were reviewed.

Exiting the woods, they were stopped at a high chain-link fence topped by razor wire for another vetting before being allowed to continue.

The headquarters of the KGB's First Chief Directorate — the Soviets' foreign espionage and intelligence arm — was an immense, seven-story, Y-shaped gray structure. It loomed over snow-covered lawns and flowerbeds. Sokolov tried to imagine them in full bloom in the summer.

Inside, a major introduced himself, took Sokolov's outerwear, and escorted him down green-walled corridors lined with pictures. They passed a bust of stern-faced Felix Edmundovich Dzerzhinsky, Iron Felix, hero Bolshevik revolutionary. Then through another security check and a not-so-well-hidden metal detector at an elegant executive elevator. On the fourth floor, they entered a drab, characterless room, where an immaculately uniformed lieutenant watched from behind an empty desk while the major knocked lightly on an inner office door. Following a command from inside, he opened it and motioned for Sokolov to enter.

"Dobryj dyen, Comrade Nikolai!"

Vasili Podgorsky, head of the First Directorate, laid down his reading glasses and came from behind a mahogany desk to shake Sokolov's hand. The tall two-star general, a full head of dark hair, looked down at him. "Tea?" he asked, pointing to one of two leather upholstered club chairs.

Sokolov ran fingers through his thin hair, nodded, and hesitantly took a seat. He'd seen Podgorsky in person, once, from a distance of fifty meters in Moscow during a military parade. He was considering a comment about that event when the general spoke.

"How is your father?" Podgorsky asked, nodding to the major who slipped from the room.

Taken aback, Sokolov asked, "You know my father?"

The general settled into his chair, seemingly lost in thought for a moment, then said, "Yes, from the old days. We dated sisters for several years. After university, Party service took us in separate directions."

Stunned by the man's unexpected familiarity, Sokolov searched his memory and couldn't recall either of his parents ever mentioning the general. He was about to speak when Podgorsky raised his right hand and squared his chair to face Sokolov.

"Nikolai, your job as Budapest rezident — recruiting, training, and managing operations — has been outstanding. The importance of the

< 17 >

intelligence you gathered has been praised by the Chairman, who, as you know, spent time in Hungary."

They were interrupted by the arrival of a sergeant delivering tea on a silver platter. The general poured for Sokolov, none for himself, and indicated milk, sugar, lemon, and bite-sized pastries.

"The Chairman is convinced the Americans want to eliminate Soviet leadership with a preemptive nuclear strike," the general said. "He further believes the British agreement to base American first-strike, ground-launched cruise missiles on English soil is a major step in that plan."

Podgorsky rose, moved to his huge picture window, and stared out at the Moscow city lights reflecting off dense clouds. "For example, a missile could be launched from a Royal air base. Wing low across Europe. Enter Russia under our radar. And, using terrain-comparing guidance, fly into the side of this building..." Glancing at the traffic circle below "...carrying a nuclear warhead."

He turned back to Sokolov. "The Chairman has convinced the General Secretary to continue our SS-20 *programma* as a deterrent, but he also wants to disrupt the Western preparations and to bring a halt to the missile deployment. If the first base

< 18 >

fails, he believes NATO will rethink its commitment."

The general refreshed Sokolov's tea and settled back into his chair, allowing Sokolov time to consider this information.

"That is where you come in, Nikolai. Because you spent three years in England as a teenager when your father served in the embassy, you are proficient in English, and better at improvisation than most of your peers, so I am sending you back for another tour. To London. To control this effort. You will be undercover. There will be no diplomatic immunity like you enjoyed in Budapest."

Sokolov couldn't control the grin that spread across his face. This would be more exciting than his assignment ten years ago in northern rural Cambria.

There he'd used a KGB "swallow" — an undercover prostitute — to conduct espionage. She used sex and alcohol to discover information about the British development of a new class of nuclear-powered submarines from the ship-builder's employees.

Podgorsky stood.

Following suit, Sokolov rose too quickly, spilling tea. Ignoring the *faux pas,* the general said, "This is important to the Motherland, Nikolai. You

< 19 >

must not fail." Podgorsky looked into gray-blue eyes. "Do I make myself clear?"

Without any signal Sokolov saw, the major re-entered the room as if summoned, carrying Sokolov's coat. The general continued: "The major has all the details you need, including a legend developed specifically for you, my boy." He smiled. "A librarian."

Podgorsky's smile faded and he grabbed Sokolov's wrist. "I'll give you all the support and resources I can," the general said. Then added in a cold, solemn voice, "But it's your job to stop those missiles."

After a few seconds, the KGB general released his grip and turned toward his desk, signaling the meeting was over.

The major led Sokolov to his office, opened a safe, removed a folder and handed it to him. "The general did not mention this, but before you go to England, you have to visit Western Siberia."

MAY 1982

The truck was one hour late and the railroad engineer was threatening to leave without cargo stolen from the Tomsk Nuclear Power Reprocessing Complex. It finally arrived and Sokolov inspected each wood-crated drum and

< 20 >

lead box to make sure all had survived the sixty-five-kilometer journey over treacherous back roads. Satisfied, he watched two men move the eight containers from the truck into the rail car.

Verifying they were securely fastened, the conductor asked Sokolov to sign the shipping order. The engineer was signaled and the train began to move.

Sokolov checked his watch and climbed the stairs to the observation deck atop the station. Twenty minutes later light filled the sky to the north, toward the Tomsk plant. It was as if an entire city turned on their lights at once then white-orange, flare-like projectiles were shot into the air.

Going down the stairs he heard a boom—no, like a crack of distant lighting. As he approached his car, he imagined the earth vibrated.

Sokolov raced his car to catch the train headed for the seaport at Arkhangelsk — then the UK.

< 21 >

TWO
Washington, DC
8 July 1982

The Pentagon's stairs were crowded with post-lunch traffic. Lieutenant Colonel Wesley Forrest moved along slowly. Oblivious to the noise around him, thinking about how things might have been, he reached the fourth floor, and slipped to the right out of the flow to decide which direction he should go. He was interrupted by shouting.

"Wes. Wes Forrest!"

It was Lieutenant Colonel James Olanski waving and rushing toward him.

"Ski, long time no see. How've you been?" They shook hands.

Olanski had worked on the Ground Launched Cruise Missile (GLCM) Program with Wes at Headquarters Tactical Air Command (HQ TAC) until eight months earlier when Ski was reassigned to Air Force Operations, at the Air Staff.

< 22 >

"Fine. Staying busy."

Wes noticed his wet hair and guessed Ski had just finished his noon workout. They were both a shade over six feet with wiry builds, similar stride, and enjoyed running together when schedules permitted.

"Heard your assignment to Plans was cancelled," Ski said. "Mixed feelings?"

"Roger that. Would love to have the Pentagon on my resume." Wes took a deep breath. "And Diane is not overjoyed by the change."

"Where you headed?"

"Air Force Intelligence," Wes responded. "To a Colonel Charles Wheeler's office."

"It's right around the corner off Corridor 10," Ski said, pointing to the right. "I'll go with you."

As they chatted and walked down the wide, florescent-lit hallway, they passed portraits of Army and Air Force flying aces and heroes. Ski said, "So, you're going to England?"

"Yeah. I'll be the first GLCM officer at the first GLCM base."

"Why's your wife not happy about the move?"

"One, our daughter. Lorianne is only in the second grade. We're reopening a base, so there's no close American elementary school and she'd have to go to a Brit school. Diane did some research and is not thrilled with what she found.

< 23 >

And two, her mother is ill, and she doesn't want to leave the States right now."

They reached 4E1070. Wes said, "Here we are."

As he departed, Ski said, "Best of luck, my man. If there's ever anything I can do for you, give me a call."

Colonel Wheeler's secretary told Wes the general's staff meeting was running long but would be over soon. Wes sat down to wait.

He shouldn't have told Ski so much about Diane, he thought. When he left this morning, she'd said, "You're a good guy with a lousy job."

What did she mean by that? He wondered, but his thoughts were interrupted when Colonel Wheeler came in. He approached with his hand out. "Wesley. Nice to meet you. Sorry I'm running late. Come on in the office."

It was a typical high-ranking military leader's office. Large desk, organized with files neatly stacked to one side, a credenza behind him stocked with manuals and books on leadership, the obligatory family photo, and a bank of telephones.

After Wes was comfortably seated, Wheeler got right to the point. "I can understand there may be disappointment with getting your assignment to the Pentagon canceled, but something has come

< 24 >

up. Two months ago, there was an explosion at a secret, closed Soviet nuclear complex near Tomsk, Siberia."

The colonel saw a puzzled look on Wes' face and stopped.

"A secret, *closed* complex?" Wes asked.

"Yes. Tomsk-7 doesn't appear on any Soviet map. It's one of several communities. Travel and residency restrictions are such that specific authorization is required to visit or remain overnight. There are about 100,000 permanent residents at Tomsk. Workers mostly connected to its clandestine purposes."

The colonel reached for a pitcher of water and poured himself a glass. Wes shook his head when the colonel raised it slightly in his direction.

After drinking, the colonel continued. "In addition to the power production plant, the complex contains facilities for the large-scale processing of plutonium and uranium for nuclear fuel and weapons, and for the reprocessing of spent fuel. There are also storage facilities within its secure fencing."

He leaned toward Wes. "Then on eighteen May, there was an explosion in the Tomsk-7 reprocessing plant. The Soviets never reported it and have stonewalled any European Commission investigation. But our satellites picked it up and the CIA is working it. They think that while using

< 25 >

acid to separate plutonium from spent fuel, an explosion occurred."

"How did they get that information?" Wes asked.

"I don't know, but you can ask. In a bit, we'll drive up to Langley for an extensive briefing where you'll get more detail and be able to ask questions."

Wes nodded.

"Then in late June," Wheeler said, "Turkish security services arrested four criminals attempting to sell nuclear waste on the black market, including Cesium 137. Materials are thought to have come from Tomsk. So, the real question for the CIA is, was the explosion a cover for a theft?"

As Wes processed the information, Wheeler continued, "Wesley, I'm giving you the basics so you'll understand why you were reassigned." He checked his watch. "Anyway, naturally there are concerns about radioactive materials getting into the wrong hands...which brings us to you. You have a degree in physics and worked for a short time at Oak Ridge. You were a member of a survey team that documented delays at Watts Bar power plant, right?"

Wes nodded again.

"So, you know something about nuclear power and related fuel isotopes. You have a military

< 26 >

intelligence and nuclear missile background, and that, coupled with your cruise missile system development experience, makes you the perfect choice to be sent to RAF Greenham Common and act as liaison with the Brits. You will also serve a clandestine purpose by keeping your eyes and ears open and reporting anything out of the ordinary."

"Report to whom?" Wes asked.

"The CIA will explain. Remember, all this information is on a need-to-know basis only," Wheeler said. "They will tell you about contacts and where to seek additional information once you're in the UK. At this point the only military person in England who knows as much as you is the Third Air Force Commander, General Hudson. I think you know him from HQ TAC?"

"Yes, sir," Wes said.

After checking his notes, Wheeler added, "Oh, so you won't be surprised, the CIA is insisting you attend the twelve-week federal law enforcement course in Georgia. You'll get firearms and investigator training."

Wheeler was sympathetic to the situation. "I'm sorry if you're disappointed with the reassignment. But Air Force needs come first."

Wes wasn't thinking about the Air Force, he was thinking about how this assignment might blow up what was left of his marriage.

< 27 >

THREE
Newbury, Berkshire
16 November 1982

Protestors' hostile stares prickled the skin on the back of Wesley Forrest's neck. Trying to drive near the demonstration was a bad idea — his bad idea. Against his driver's advice.

But his curiosity had forced the issue, and now they found themselves stuck in traffic in the middle of a Newbury public square teeming with a mob of angry women. All ages were represented, wearing every conceivable style and color outfit, filling the square, the sidewalks, meandering back-and-forth across the street…and surrounding their vehicle.

Punctuating the partly cloudy, noon-time sky were hand-held signs reading CRUISE MISSILES: A REAL BREACH OF THE PEACE, RELEASE THE INNOCENT, and DEMAND A NUKE FREE UK.

< 28 >

"Welcome to your new assignment, Wes," said Lieutenant Colonel Art Gilbert, painstakingly trying to edge the vehicle free of the town's turmoil and toward the regimented confines of nearby RAF Greenham Common Air Base. Greenham was selected by NATO for the initial deployment of the ground-launched cruise missile (GLCM) weapon system. GLCM and the US Army's Pershing II missiles were President Ronald Reagan's bold response to the Soviet Union's nuclear missile saber-rattling.

"What's in the briefcase?"

"What?" responded Wes, pulled from his thoughts.

"The briefcase. You haven't turned loose of it since I met you at Heathrow."

"It's for the Chief Civil Engineer from the engineers at the Pentagon."

"Good," Gilbert said. "My boss was expecting it by courier. That'd be you."

"What is it?" Wes asked. "They wouldn't tell me. Stamped the package Modified Handling."

"It's their follow-up suggestions on modifications of the munitions storage areas at RAF Greenham and Welford and how to approach the Brits with the changes. The British will treat it as Confidential, so put it behind your seat, out of sight. I'll drop it by the office later."

< 29 >

Gilbert had picked up Wes at London's airport to drive him the fifty miles to Newbury. Although Wes was the first GLCM missile officer to report, other specialists like Gilbert, a civil engineer, arrived earlier to prepare the base facilities and infrastructure for personnel and equipment.

"Where's Welford?" Wes asked.

"RAF Welford is about six miles northwest of Newbury. One of the largest ordnance depots in Western Europe."

So much to learn, thought Wes. Then, looking out the window, he asked, "What's Release the Innocent mean?"

"Thirty women, give or take, were arrested for blocking RAF Greenham's main gate last weekend," said Gilbert. "They come up before magistrates today."

"Do they shut down gate traffic often?"

"Too often. Especially when anything is happening that might attract the press," Gilbert said. "As you see, they don't hesitate to use any opportunity to show their asses."

A barricade manned by two policemen forced Gilbert to drive toward a corner that hopefully turned onto a less-congested street. "At the base, they focus on two different gates, but photographers like the main gate. That's where the initial women's camp is. It's a favorite spot to

< 30 >

conduct protests and stage sit-ins or chain themselves to the fence."

"How long?"

To Gilbert's questioning look, Wes said, "You said 'initial camp'. How long has it been there?"

"This all started last year, when a group of women marched here from Wales and set up tents outside the fence. Been there ever since. Another area has been occupied —"

Gilbert abruptly laid on the horn, shouting at two middle-aged women pressing dangerously close to the vehicle's right front fender. He hit the horn again. In response, the duo gave the Americans the British two-finger V salute with the back of their hands, and shouted what Wes assumed was a mouthful of obscenities, but he couldn't be sure because all the protestors close by were also yelling.

Conflict was not unfamiliar to Newbury. From the Norman Conquest in 1066, kings and queens battled here against popular uprisings. Combatants in the seventeenth-century English Civil War razed the city and destroyed the local castle. With the advent of the second world war, the town and country gave full support to establishing a large air base at Newbury for the Allies; and to United States Air Force bombers and tankers setting strategic alert in the 1950s.

< 31 >

And now a woman standing on a box at the edge of the square shouted into a megaphone denouncing any support for America. Spotting them, she yelled, "Yanks!" and the crowd swarmed the car.

"Dammit!" Gilbert twisted the steering wheel to the left to avoid a protestor who stepped in his path. "Get out of the way, you crazy bitch!"

"How did they spot us?" Wes asked.

"Chevy. Steering wheel on the left."

At that point Wes made a decision to buy a British automobile.

One woman threw an open milk carton at the car, another a half-eaten ham sandwich. A third smeared an egg and mayonnaise bun on the passenger's windscreen.

Wes heard shouting in the distance and the women ran. He assumed police were coming to assist. He'd spent ten years in US-based missile programs. Four years with Minuteman, then three with Titan. These systems had missiles at remote sites over the countryside. Sometimes trespassers climbed over silo fences but were quickly observed by electronic surveillance and detained. Rabbits at night set off more alarms and were a bigger pain in the ass.

The last three years he'd been engaged in the development of the GLCM weapon system, adapting the Navy's submarine launched

< 32 >

Tomahawk cruise missile to a truck-based platform, but had never encountered anything like this. He wondered: How violent will it get?

Demonstrators moved in closer, fist-banging and kicking the American vehicle. A tall woman about thirty five, Wes' age, wearing a light-green parka, blonde hair pulled into a ponytail, moved quickly toward their car. She pulled a spray can from inside her coat.

"Stop the car," Wes yelled.

When the red stream of paint started, he shoved open his door, knocking away the can and slamming her backward. He jumped out of the car to confront the assailant, but saw another woman drop to her knee beside the rear tire, attempting to puncture it with a long, thin blade. As he stepped toward her, she rose, knife in hand. Their eyes locked. Wes thought this might be his second bad idea of the day.

A Thames Valley Police (TVP) Sergeant grabbed her from behind. The woman jerked her knife-wielding arm free and jabbed it over her head in an attempt to stab the officer. Desperately trying to avoid her thrusts, the policeman lost his footing, and together they fell heavily to the ground. The woman screamed, using her knife hand to break her fall. The weapon skittered across the pavement.

< 33 >

She frantically reached for the blade but Wes jammed his heel into her wrist.

"*Fowking* bastard," she shouted.

Wes kicked the knife under the car. He had no time to reflect on his success because the pony-tailed blonde, hands still wet with red spray paint, jumped on his back with a shriek. She wrapped long legs and arms around him in a bear hug. A solid hardwood nightstick glanced off her head and hit his, dazing him, but the adrenaline-charged protestor released him and attacked the Bobby.

At that moment, a police support van screeched to a stop and out rolled four additional officers. Two pulled the blonde off the Bobby, and the other two rescued the Sergeant still wrestling with the woman on the ground.

After both women were in custody, Wes sat on the curb and rubbed his head, blood on his fingers. The sound of boots... two women stood in front of him. Wes braced for the onslaught, but none came. Struggling to stand, he staggered, and the women grabbed his arms.

"Most of us do not hold with violence," said one, who reminded him of Miss Wells, his fourth-grade teacher. "Sorry for your injury." She handed him a clean, white handkerchief and walked away.

Wes turned and saw Gilbert's passenger car door open. Fear surged through his body. Rushing

< 34 >

over, he saw the briefcase with its package had slipped under the passenger seat. He sighed with relief then chastised himself for having his attention sidetracked.

* * *

At the police station, Gilbert and Wes gave statements. Clothing and the cut on his head were photographed. Once they discovered Wes' wound was delivered by a London policeman, an on-call nurse attended to it immediately.

Gilbert needed to stay at the station a bit longer, but told Wes to go to the base. A TVP patrolman took him in a patrol car.

Finally reaching the Manor House Lodge, his temporary home, Wes was disappointed. The historic mansion located just off-base was undergoing renovation. Three years before, when he'd been part of a survey team's visit, the lodge had resembled a photo from a travel magazine with manicured grounds all around.

What in the spring had once been roses, evergreens, and flowering shrubs was now construction equipment and building materials. Scaffolding, wrapped around the two sides of the manor he could see, hid much of the eighteenth-century brick and limestone. Pushing through the weathered-oak front doors felt like traveling back

< 35 >

in time. He wondered how many American officers had passed through this entrance since World War II when the fabled 101st Airborne Division headquartered here and the night drops of the Screaming Eagles led the D-Day invasion of Normandy.

Back then the British public had welcomed those soldiers, but today was different. Very different, he thought, touching the red paint marring his shirt.

< 36 >

FOUR
Mayfair
8 December 1982

En route to the Cavendish Hotel's Tea and Coffee Room, Nikolai Sokolov traveled an unpredictable route through London. After walking through a heavy pedestrian traffic area, he cut through a street lined with terraced houses, stopping at a phone box so he could look back to see if he was being followed.

The hotel's excellent coffee and friendly staff stirred memories of the cozy ambiance of Cafe Blu Beke in Budapest. It served excellent Hungarian cuisine, which he preferred to British food. Located near the Budapest Opera, Sokolov dined there often. And of greater importance, it was where he met Viktoria. Six of the most exciting and sexually satisfying months of his life.

< 37 >

Getting the hotel barista's attention, he said, "Expresso, please."

"It'll take a minute, sir," said the smiling man behind the counter. "Would you like a pastry?"

"No, just the coffee."

Always fearful of being noticed by MI5, Sokolov took the booth farthest from the Tea Room's main door where high backs afforded privacy but allowed him to watch the two entrances.

Enjoying his cup, he patted the envelope inside his coat pocket. He knew the message was from his operative at RAF Greenham Common because she was the only one who used that mailbox at the Royal Mail Post on Albemarle. Curious, he finished his drink and headed for home and his codebook.

Being overly cautious was what kept him alive. There were several ways to make his exit and today, walking casually, he entered the kitchen and left the hotel by a service entrance. Within several blocks, he followed a group into a multilevel department store.

Browsing at the lobby newsstand, he noticed *The Oxford Weekly Review* included a headline: "Women to Encircle RAF Greenham Common Air Base". He purchased it, took the stairs to the second level where he paused long enough to ensure no familiar faces were following after him.

< 38 >

Sokolov took the tube, then made two bus transfers. Upon reaching home, he opened the envelope and decoded the message, which read:

GOSHAWK
UNKNOWN TO EMBRACE PLANNERS
STOP ON TWELVE DECEMBER WILL HAVE
CONFLICT AND ATTEMPT MADE TO
ENTER BASE STOP
BIRCH

Sokolov was glad to see the code name BIRCH spelled correctly. Being misspelled was a signal of security concerns. He put the kettle on his cooker and sat in his only easy chair to read the paper he'd purchased earlier. The article began with a brief history. Greenham Common being purchased by the Newbury District Council in 1939; the war; and the forty women who, in September 1981, walked the hundred miles from Cardiff to campaign against the impending arrival of American missiles.

A major part of the article was an appeal for women to join a large protest at RAF Greenham on Sunday, 12 December, the anniversary of NATO's decision to place US missiles in Europe. It pointed out that, in only twelve months, this horrible governmental decision was due to be implemented. The Women's Peace Camp wished

< 39 >

to demonstrate opposition by linking arms and encircling the base. They invited women from all over the UK and Europe to come and participate in a candlelight vigil.

When the kettle whistled, Sokolov poured boiling water over a Yorkshire tea bag placed in a mug. While it steeped, he read more. The article identified four assembly areas and associated parking. To show the joy of life, everyone was encouraged to bring and display personal items they loved and wear brightly coloured clothing.

Adding a bit of milk and sugar, Sokolov sipped his tea and mulled the information from both sources.

Later, he examined his trimmed beard in a mirror. He'd appeared clean-shaven for several assignments and perhaps he should now, or just colouring the gray might alter his looks sufficiently.

No need to decide now, maybe upon his return from Scotland.

* * *

At the prearranged time, Wesley Forrest called his daughter in the States. The five-hour time difference made random calls impossible.

"Daddy, my recital is Saturday!"

< 40 >

A huge weight descended upon Wes. Dammit, he'd been caught up in the activities at RAF Greenham and forgotten about Lorianne's first piano recital. A month before he left Virginia, her piano teacher had announced the recital date. He and Diane discussed it with Lorianne, but let her make the decision on whether to participate, and what to play. Their marriage had been strained for some time, starting in...

"Daddy, are you there?"

Scrambling to remember what she was playing — he'd heard it so often — *oh yeah...Beethoven's Für Elise.*

"Sorry, honey," he said. "I'll bet Beethoven is as nervous as you are."

No laughter from Lorianne. "I'm afraid I'll mess up, Daddy."

"Sweetheart, you are very brave to do this. You've been practicing and you're ready. Focus on the piano keys. Pretend you're alone, or with your mother. Don't look or think about anything else. It's okay to be a little afraid, even Donny Osmond has shaky knees when he goes on stage, but after the first few notes, it goes away."

"He does not!"

"Yes, he does. I read it in the paper. What are you wearing?"

"Mommy bought me a new top. White with ruffles, but no sleeves. I'll wear a black skirt.

< 41 >

Mommy says it'll be more comfortable and look professional. And my black shoes with the little heels."

"Have your mom film it for me. And don't make faces at the camera like you usually do." Giggles from the phone. "Sweetheart, I am so proud of you! Show them what you can do, kid!"

"Okay, Daddy. Miss you. Wish you were here."

Wes hung up and thought about his wife. They had met at the Cottonwood Brewery & Saloon in Park City, Utah. She was out west skiing with friends from the University of Tampa and he was attending the University of Utah in Salt Lake City. They had kept in touch when he worked in Tennessee and gotten together again when he was assigned to MacDill Air Force Base in Tampa.

Over time they learned they had less in common than they assumed, and that Diane had unrealistic expectations of a military marriage, which was nothing like her parents'. Military members put duty first; everything else came second. Missing birthday parties and not being home for anniversaries was the norm.

After their daughter's birth, Diane had found more and more reasons to visit and spend time with her parents in Tallahassee.

He couldn't blame her.

< 42 >

FIVE
Outside RAF Greenham AB
12 December 1982

Singing and chanting woke Mari Pritchard.
She listened proudly.

> We don't want your war
> We don't want your sham
> We won't fight your war
> Shut down Green-ham!

She stepped out of her canvas tent onto ground
wet from an overnight mix of rain and sleet.
Stretching her slender frame, she shivered, and
wondered briefly about the weather back home at
the farm in Northern Wales. Bundling up, she
grabbed her cup and headed for the Yellow Camp
centre and the warmth of the cooking fires, just
outside RAF Greenham's main gate.

In the background, buses from Edinburgh, Yorkshire, and Liverpool honked as they inched along. Women hung from bus windows yelling and waving signs: Stop The Missiles and Refuse Cruise.

Mari watched two women interrupt the chanting by stepping between the singers and the gate. She was concerned when they began shouting insults at a group of Ministry of Defence Police standing vigilantly twenty feet inside the base perimeter. The officers stoically ignored the disrespectful comments, and the women lost their resolve and moved to the stone pit where a fire heated water.

Making a cup of tea, Mari attempted to joke with one of the singers. "You're here bloody early."

"We were keen about this event and did not want to miss a thing. We drove all night by coach," said the woman in a thick Scottish accent.

"How'd you hear about the event?"

"Newspapers and chain letters."

Good. Time well spent, Mari thought. "Well, we're glad you could make it," she said. "Loved your singing, by the way. Hope your voices last the day."

The cold drizzle stopped by mid-morning. Mari stayed busy steering arrivals to covered information kiosks lining the left side of the road

< 44 >

that connected the main gate and the Basingstoke Highway. For many attendees this was their first protest. Leaving husbands at home to mind the kids was a break from tradition.

She smiled when she recognized a tune from Culture Club's Boy George blaring from a battery-powered radio. *Do You Really Want To Hurt Me?* resonated with a lot of women who had spent time in the Newbury and Reading jails.

Living conditions at the permanently occupied camps, Yellow and Green, were primitive and depressing. No running water, electricity, or telephones. Culture Club's Caribbean-flavored *I'll Tumble 4 Ya* added a touch of cheer and got some in the crowd dancing.

To encircle the estimated nine-mile perimeter and properly embrace the base, at least sixteen thousand persons were needed, but organizers hoped for twenty thousand today. That Julie Christie and Yoko Ono were coming would not only increase attendance but also the number of journalists covering the event.

Around eleven a.m., Mari nervously twisted her watch and wondered how her brother Morgan was doing.

* * *

< 45 >

W.F. WHITSON | THE LIBRARIAN

Seventy miles north, Morgan Pritchard opened the garage where he'd hidden the stolen tipper lorry. The smell of cut wood filled the air. He checked to make sure the paint covering the construction company's name and logo on the doors was dry. Satisfied, he placed two full cans of diesel fuel on the floorboard on the passenger's side and a pouch containing plastic explosives behind the driver's seat.

Everything was ready.

* * *

As the Campaign for Nuclear Disarmament was setting up its buffet lunch at Yellow Camp, Mari used her walkie talkie to check with the other assembly areas to find out where people were needed to fill spaces along the fence. She passed the information to volunteers because she was needed at Green Camp.

A local supporter taking several cardboard boxes of programmes to Green gave Mari a ride in her golf cart.

Green Camp, the first satellite peace camp, was the closest spot along the base perimeter fence to the alert and maintenance area under construction. While only a mile west of Yellow Camp, the environment was very different. Where polite

< 46 >

confusion existed at Yellow, Mari found an acute lack of organization at Green.

Demonstrators' caravans, trailers, and tents, many with campfires, were spread haphazardly around the clearing and among the trees. Hundreds of people packed the parking area outside the Contractors' Gate.

Many activists were socializing, some meandering as if lost, others proceeding toward destinations along the fence. Children played games while guitarists led pockets of singing women. One loud group sang:

> Hey, you gen'rals in the military
> We don't want a nuclear war
> All those dollars and
> All those pounds
> Could feed and clothe
> The poor of the world.
> What d' you need more
> Atom bombs for?
> You got enough to kill us all.
> We don't want Cruise.

Carrying a box of booklets, Mari picked her way through the mostly female crowd. The partly cloudy sky and chilly air weren't dampening anyone's enthusiasm. For some it was like a winter festival. But while the surface mood seemed

< 47 >

joyous, Mari noticed many furtive glances and that she herself was tense.

A peace demonstration next to a ten-foot-high chain-link fence topped with three strands of barbed wire was surreal. The guarded and chained double-swing gate added to the sinister aura. From the gate, the perimeter fence ran in both directions, disappearing into foliage, a ten-foot-wide strip clear-cut on each side. In preparation for the candlelight vigil, women were making their way to find vacant spots along the fence.

Posters, pictures of children, and toys hung haphazardly on the fence, adding personal touches to the protest. To show the word Peace and the message Down with Nukes, someone creative had woven coloured yarn within the grid of the fence.

At the military gate, a lighted sign read:

Construction/Contractor Entrance
GLCM Alert & Maintenance Area
(GAMA)
RAF Greenham Common
No Trespassing

Below it hung another, hand-painted with messy, errant fingerprints:
Women's Peace Camp
Green Camp

Mari found Katelin Nagy standing on a crate near the guard shack. Very much in charge, she was directing people and supervised tasks in English heavily spiced with an Eastern European accent. Her shoulder-length dark hair fell and covered her face when she glanced down.

"Hey, Mari. Good to see you," Katelin said, stepping down. "Everything on schedule?"

"Yes," Mari said tentatively.

Katelin touched her arm and whispered, "And the other?" There was a quick flash caused by one of the few moments of sun, and Mari noticed a beautiful silver ring on Katelin's left hand.

With the slightest smile, Mari nodded, though not sure everything was ready.

"Anything I need to do?"

"Just get people in place along the fence," Mari said, sounding harsher than she meant. "Here are some schedules."

The booklet welcomed the public on this, the third anniversary of NATO's decision to base nuclear missiles in the United Kingdom. The schedule indicated protestors were to begin opposition by surrounding RAF Greenham in a peaceful, symbolic embrace. At four-thirty p.m., they'd hold hands, face the base, and sing *The Spirit Song*, showing the world their solidarity against Berkshire County becoming a nuclear

< 49 >

target. At five p.m., they would light candles for a thirty- minute prayer vigil.

Katelin scanned one of the handouts. "*Köszönöm*. Thanks. Timing at Green may be a little different. Song's lyrics and base map are *nagyon hasznos*...very useful." After a nod to Mari, she stepped into the crowd to distribute programmes and answer questions from the attendees.

At three-thirty p.m., Mari found a chair and placed it where she could casually watch the construction entrance and the guards. Try as she may, she found it impossible to keep her anxiety in check. She bounced a foot, crossed and uncrossed her legs, and scrutinized activity on both sides of the fence. At dusk she checked her watch one last time, then moved, first to Katelin, then to two other women, patting them on the back.

"It's time," she told them.

Inside the small portable building outside the contractor gate, a stumpy Ministry of Defence Police officer rolled his swivel chair back and forth. Through small windows he watched the swelling crowd. A tall, skinny MDP sergeant stood near the guard shack, leaning casually against the fence and speaking to every good-looking female who passed.

At night and on weekends this area normally went unmanned. The gate's double wings and

< 50 >

guard shack were padlocked with random security patrols inside and outside the fence. However, because of today's significant protest activities, in addition to the two lethargic British guards, two US Air Force policemen were posted inside the fence, their black-and-white Ford LTD angled to observe the action. An airman first class, his cigarette glowing as darkness settled, stood between the car and the exit. The technical sergeant sat in the driver's seat, door open, his left leg hanging out, and used the interior light to read. Congregating protestors blocking entrances were becoming routine to base security. Anyone watching the soldiers, as Mari was, saw they were lost in their own thoughts.

The singing of *The Spirit Song* started. Suddenly, a fiery redhead shouted and pushed a smaller brunette to the ground, instantly drawing everyone's attention. Jumping up, the brunette, green eyes flaring, charged her attacker. Yelling and cheering erupted. Onlookers quickly encircled the battling women.

Laughing at the catfight, the skinny MDP sergeant walked toward the scuffle. "All right, ladies, break it up. Break it up!" But he was unable to make headway through the wall of females.

Red grabbed and yanked the brunette's hair, who responded by ripping open her opponent's

< 51 >

button-down blouse, exposing her bra and plenty of flesh.

No longer smiling, the guard signaled to the American security team for help.

Flipping his cigarette, the airman motioned for the guard in the shack to unlock the gate. This was the guard's second mistake; the first was not reporting what was happening to the command post before leaving his secure box. Later, at his hearing, the MDP gate guard would say there appeared to be no threat and he expected the Americans to escort the women to base security and summon police from Newbury.

Once the padlock and chains were removed, the airman, followed by the skinny sergeant, pushed his way into the circle toward the two brawling females. The technical sergeant left the keys in the car, closed the door to kill the inside light and moved around the Ford, then stepped through the gate and outside the base. To get a better view, the heavyset British police officer stayed outside his shack.

As all guards would later testify, they were focused on the two fighting women, none suspecting the fight to be a ruse.

Within seconds, each of the four security policemen was suddenly attacked by at least three women carrying shopping bags containing handcuffs, rope, tape, and pillowcases.

< 52 >

The fat Brit dropped to a fetal position and yelled, "You filthy bitches!" He was kicked hard in the ribs by protestors' heavy boots. A pillowcase was pulled over the technical sergeant's head. He yanked arms free of grasping hands and spun, quickly striking his attacker in the jaw with his fist. But his defensive moves were short-lived when his knees were buckled from the rear. So many women pounced upon him, he couldn't move.

After their mouths were duct-taped and heads pillowcased, the four men were searched, forced onto their knees, and cuffed to the fence right below a sign displaying the peace symbol. One woman attempted to steal a guard's wallet, but after a whispered reprimand, Mari tossed it into a plastic bag Katelin carried. When they had collected all personal belongs of the four, Katelin tossed the bag in the back seat of the American police car.

Mari placed the tech sergeant's side arm — the only weapon carried by the four — in her leather bag and slung it over her shoulder. After directing several women to open both halves of the hinged gate and move the black-and-white out of the way, she made a call on her walkie talkie.

< 53 >

SIX
RAF Greenham Common
12 December 1982

A half mile west of RAF Greenham, Mari's brother, Morgan Pritchard, steered the lorry into the A339 lay-by and shut off the engine. After fifteen minutes, worried a constable might stop and ask what a hospital electrician was doing with a stolen five-ton tipper lorry full of firewood, cans of diesel fuel, and plastic explosives, he asked himself, "Where the bloody hell are the others?"

He was not sure where Mari wanted him to park the truck, but as he considered how he might navigate the base without assistance, a car pulled in behind and flashed its lights. Within seconds, his passenger door opened and a tall, thin woman wearing dark clothing sprang into the cab, stringy blonde hair escaping a camouflage bush hat.

"Where the fuck you been?" he asked.

Closing the door, she said, "Well, good day to you too, luv."

"You could've made this whole thing a cockup," he yelled.

"Not the whole thing. Just the most explosive." Getting only a cold stare from Morgan, she continued, "But I'm here now, aren't I? And you swear a lot."

"And you have a smart mouth."

< 54 >

She turned away, stared out the windscreen. "It's my fault we're late. Those gents in the car behind us are more pissed off at me than you are. That prat reporter was really mouthy." Then after a deep breath: "I had car trouble —"

"Hey, brother, you there?" interrupted Mari on Morgan's walkie-talkie.

"Yeah," he answered, then glancing at his passenger: "We're finally all here. Ready to roll."

Her voice crackled over the air. "It's time. Good luck."

Laying the walkie talkie on the seat next to him, Morgan rolled down the driver's window and motioned the car behind to follow. An unseen helicopter thumped in the distance. "Looks like the BBC is up and at 'em," the woman said. "Good coverage."

Once on the gravel road leading to the Contractors' Gate and the missile storage area, both vehicles killed their lights. Morgan's heavily loaded lorry moved at a snail's pace. Construction equipment had created more potholes than drivable tracks, and ruts were still wet from the morning rain. He grunted and cursed with each jerk of the wheel. His passenger stayed quiet.

When Morgan approached the gate, he saw several women wandering around the entrance. He flicked his lights on for a second, signaling

< 55 >

them to move, and only then did they see the guards handcuffed to the fence.

"What the hell?" his passenger said with a gasp. "Wasn't supposed to be any violence." Before Morgan could respond, he saw Mari and gave a quick wave as she pointed to the gate. A flow of women followed the lorry onto the base.

He watched in his rearview mirror as the car tailing him pulled to the side and parked. Two men exited, one carrying a camera, the other a torch and pad of paper. Morgan reminded himself to be careful. He didn't want to be photographed anywhere near one of his fires.

The truck had advanced only sixty yards when moonlight revealed the incomplete sections of the two parallel GAMA fences. Once through the opening, Morgan's passenger proved her worth by pointing to the right and helping him maneuver through a maze of construction supplies, dozers, excavators, and graders inside the missile complex. She soon indicated a spot between six massive earthen bunkers in various stages of completion, the bombproof shelters for the missile and command vehicles.

After positioning the lorry, Morgan turned to his mysterious passenger. "What's your name?"

"Like you care," she said, glaring at him. "Just call me Kerr."

"Like a *cur* dog?"

< 56 >

Climbing from the cab, she said, "You are an arsehole, Morgan Pritchard." Their eyes held briefly, then she slammed the door and disappeared into the darkness.

Figuring he had less than ten minutes before police arrived, Morgan reached for the control levers. The lorry jumped and jerked as the open-box bed elevated. The truck inched forward. Falling wood banged out, leaving behind a pyramid of split wood logs. Killing the ignition, he climbed down from the lorry. From behind the passenger seat, he removed three pieces of gnarled knotty pine selected for high resin content. Placing the smallest in the driver's seat, the other two were inserted into the huge mound of wood.

Taking one of the two twenty-liter cans of diesel fuel from the passenger side, he doused the woodpile. Using the second, he sloshed fuel over the lorry's seats, crammed a rag into the neck of the petrol tank and soaked it, splashed the tyres and the ground alongside the truck, and tossed the can on the woodpile. After inserting a blasting cap with a four-meter fuse into the plastic explosive, he laid the bundle atop the exposed gas tank.

Warning the photographer to take no pictures of him, Morgan popped a flare and tossed it onto the fuel-soaked pile of wood, producing a whoomp and a wave of heat that blasted toward

< 57 >

bystanders. As air flow reversed, a plume of black smoke rolled upward.

Morgan watched his fire with a perverse fascination. He'd loaded logs of various varieties and thicknesses. The pitch in the pine knots burned nicely. Wood popped and sizzled, sending sparks and now-white smoke heavenward.

The photographer staged women to take advantage of the firelight background, directing the protestors to dance around the inferno, even run to the top of the nearest shelter, as he quickly snapped picture after picture.

Morgan saw his sister. At first, Mari had joined in the revelry, but now stood with hands over ears, tight-lipped, eyes closed. He ran to her, pulled her farther from the flames, turned her away from the fire, and held her as she sobbed and shook uncontrollably.

She was reliving their childhood nightmare. His heart knocked hard.

He and Mari watched from a second-story window. Mother and uncle poured liquid on a body... dropped a lighter...

The sound of sirens brought him back to the present. He held his breath for five seconds and slowly released.

< 58 >

The photographer gave Morgan a thumbs-up, then he and the reporter bolted toward their getaway vehicle.

"Time to leave!" Morgan shouted. As planned, many women ran, yelling and screaming, toward the main base facilities, disrupting fire and security responses, fully realizing they'd be arrested.

The hospital would sack Morgan if caught, plus he couldn't allow the cops to get his fingerprints and discover his nocturnal vocation. Leaving Mari, he used a piece of burning wood to light the fuse, then tossed it into the cab, creating an inferno. A trail of fire ran toward the gas tank and tyres.

Returning to Mari, Morgan found her slumped to her knees. He grabbed her purse and stood her up. Carrying some of her weight, he steered her to join the river of people flowing back toward the gap in the GAMA fences to escape from the base and the police.

Morgan helped Mari into the reporter's parked car. An ear-splitting explosion made them all jump. The PE-4 detonated and ruptured the tank, jetting the petrol which instantly ignited. A ball of fire lit the nighttime sky.

< 59 >

SEVEN
After Green Camp bonfire
12 December 1982

Wes sat in the crowded squad room at the base's Security Police Headquarters watching the news coverage of the "Embrace the Base" event. All indications had been that it was going to be peaceful, but the SP Commander had men and cars standing by just in case.

The BBC news showed close-ups of protestors surrounding the facility, interviews of several participants, and shots of singing groups standing near the gates or around campfires.

A moving helicopter circled and photographed the GAMA. "Those shelters look like the four-thousand-year-old mysterious mounds in Wiltshire," a reporter said.

"Reminds me of six piles of dirt removed from a coal mine," her companion responded.

Film of the barbed wire circumference, outlined by candlelight, with John Lennon's *Give Peace a Chance* as background music, was impressive.

BBC switched to a reporter near the front gate Yellow Camp sign. She asked a woman, "Does criminal trespass send the correct message?"

The woman responded without apology. "When you want to get the world talking about our children's future and the future of our country, any press coverage is good."

Then, when the explosion occurred, the helicopter moved closer and the camera focused on what appeared to be a woodpile and a lorry on fire among the missile shelters. Prompting the rhetorical question by the anchor: "Does this mark an escalation in protests at the RAF base?"

Colonel Marlin Frazier shot from his office and yelled down the hall to the dispatcher, "Send 'em." To the desk sergeant, "Call BBC. I want a copy of that tape." He pointed at Wes. "Let's go."

In a pre-planned move, twenty American security policemen opened the front gate and cleared a corridor through the protesting women. Ten patrol vehicles screamed through, sirens blaring and lights flashing.

On the way to the Contractors' Gate, Frazier listened intently to reports coming in on the car radio and barked orders outlining actions he wanted taken.

Groups of people were moving along the A339 toward the base's main gate and Yellow Camp. While they were yelling, laughing, and singing, they acted peaceably, not obstructing traffic.

The area outside the Contractors' Gate was filled with people, but here the crowd did not move aside, so Colonel Frazier pulled to the side, killed the siren and engine but left the roof lights flashing. Impatiently, Frazier remained seated, waiting for Wes to get out before locking the car then headed into the mob. Wes got mixed whiffs of differing odors: smoke, burning wood, rubber. And something else…couldn't place it.

Near the base fence, a Thames Valley Police officer shouted into a bullhorn, "Move away from the fence and gate. Remain here until questioned. Cooperate and we all get out a lot faster."

This was followed by jeers. "We've got all night" united them in laugher.

Guards who had been cuffed to the fence were now inside the perimeter with the gate closed and guarded, getting medical attention. Outside the fence, matters were becoming more organized as police sorted people into groups for interviews. Singing and yelling were replaced by the buzz of conversation.

Katelin darted toward her caravan. A female TV journalist, camerawoman in tow, stuck a microphone in her face and asked, "Have you been here all day?"

Remembering what GOSHAWK had told her: Stay in the background, avoid publicity, Katelin nearly panicked. Here she was, about to be caught on camera.

"*Nem beszelek angolul*," Katelin said in Hungarian, and kept moving.

< 62 >

The reporter stared at her for a second, then turned to someone else, asking about the assault and battery of the guards and the bonfire.

A policeman stepped in front of Katelin. "I'm Sergeant Harrison, United States Air Force Security Police. I need to ask you a few questions."

Walking through the throng, Wes neared a policeman talking to a protestor. The woman said, "Okay. *Magyarországról. Nem jó angolul.* From Hungary. Not good with English."

"Your name?" Harrison asked.

"Katelin Nagy."

Writing her name down and checking the spelling took several tries because of the crowd noises. Harrison continued, "How long have you been in the UK?"

"*Három hét,* ummm…three weeks," said Katelin, twisting her grandmother's silver ring.

"That's one of them," another woman said loudly, pushing by Wes and pointing at Katelin. She approached with a TVP officer in her wake. "She was handing out propaganda."

The British policeman grabbed Katelin by the arm, growling, "Come with me."

Sergeant Harrison interrupted. "Whoa, constable. I'm not finished interviewing this woman." Then, seeing Wes, Harrison explained

< 63 >

the situation. "Colonel, this woman says she has been in England only a short while. So probably not one of the organizers of this event."

After nodding to Harrison, Wes acknowledged the accuser, "Ma'am, I'm Lieutenant Colonel Wesley Forrest. Did you see this woman go onto the base?"

"No. She was standing by the fence passing out information."

Sergeant Harrison handed one to Wes.

After glancing at it quickly, "Like this one?" he asked, holding up a pamphlet containing the Women's Peace Camp schedule for the day.

"Yes. That's it."

"Did you see her talk to anyone who went on base or anyone associated with the vehicle that entered the base?"

"No...I don't know. She talked to a lot of people."

"You do know the prayer vigil had government approval, right?" Wes asked, then added, "But not the base invasion."

No response, so he continued, "Did you see anything at all that made you think or believe she was in a leadership role for any illegal activity?"

"No, only passing out those," she said, pointing to the booklet in his hand. Then she blurted, "She had on a yellow shirt then! Like those in charge. She musta took it off."

< 64 >

Katelin was very happy she had dumped that shirt.

Wes turned to Harrison, who shrugged.

"Ma'am, thank you for this information, Miss..."

"Nagy," the Air Force sergeant said.

"We'll question her about tonight's activities," Wes said to the constable, "and include anything she tells us in our report."

Wes noticed Nagy was deep in thought, staring through him.

"Hello?" Wes asked.

Embarrassed, she said, "*Mi?*"

Wes asked, "Are you one of tonight's organizers?"

"What means...organizers?" Nagy asked.

"The people who put together this prayer vigil."

"*Nem.* I have not seen these people before. Only asked to lot out papers."

"Lot out?" Wes said with another pleasant smile.

"Not good English?"

"It's 'hand out' but that's good enough. Did you see who drove the truck onto the base? Who started the fire?"

"*Nem.* I could not see," she said. She pointed back along the fence. "I...outside... over there."

"So you did not enter the base?"

< 65 >

"*Nem.*"

"Why are you here tonight?"

"My *nagyneni*...err, aunt...was to help...err...hand out papers but is sick. So, I come." She paused, then added, "I am visit, but against war...and nuclear power. So, I tell *nagyneni* I help."

"From where? In what town does your aunt live?"

"Reading."

Another American policeman approached with a woman in a mackinaw. "Colonel, this woman has a camera. What should I do?"

"Roll up the film and remove it. Take her name, address, and number." Then to the woman, "Ma'am, you may pick up your film in seven days at the Newbury Police Station."

Then Wes turned back, "Miss Nagy, do you have a camera?"

Shaking her head. "*Nem.*"

After watching her for several seconds and seeing no reaction, Wes said to the sergeant, "We've got a lot of people to interview tonight. Get her information. Especially about her local relatives. Then let her go."

"Sorry, sir. I can't let you do that," said the TVP constable, who had been listening.

"Colonel Forrest, what's the problem?"

Shit, it's Judd. What the fuck is she doing here? Wes thought. With her round face, downturned mouth, and reddish-brown hair, his Wing Vice Commander looked like the Chow puppy his uncle had once owned. Even dress blues did not improve her appearance.

Wes summarized the situation to Lieutenant Colonel Brenda Judd.

The British constable added, "My orders are to bring in anyone suspected of leading this event. In my opinion, handing out programmes is evidence of leadership. And according to my witness, she had on a yellow shirt like other leaders."

Without looking at Wes, Judd said, "I'm the ranking American on scene and I authorize you to take this woman."

Wes clenched his jaw, took off his camouflage cap, ran fingers through his auburn hair, but said nothing. *Bitch!*

Katelin Nagy was pulled away, shoulders sagging. She was crying.

< 67 >

EIGHT
Newbury
12 December 1982

Getting onto the A339 before police vehicles arrived, the reporter talked excitedly with the photographer on their way back to London. They were eager to get to *The Guardian* to file the base invasion story and the bonfire pictures for tomorrow morning's edition. Morgan and Mari said nothing.

Once away from RAF Greenham, Mari relaxed and felt better. "On your way to the paper, drop me off at Euston rail station," she told the driver.

She received a questioning look in the rearview mirror and continued, "Quickest train home. North Wales."

As Mari got out, she pulled a cloth- wrapped package from her purse and handed it to Morgan. He opened it to discover a .38 Smith & Wesson revolver. He slid it in his pocket then looked for Mari, but she was already lost in the crowd.

The reporter dropped Morgan at St. Pancras Station where he caught a train for the two-hour run to Wellingborough, the station nearest home.

He found the loo, locked the door, and checked the revolver. It was loaded. He hid it back in his jacket. By Borehamwood, when the last of the London passengers disembarked, the conductor turned off the overheads, leaving on only the night lights.

Trying to relax, he put his feet on the opposite seat and gazed out the window. However, this was not to be a routine trip. When the train passed the Shell Oil refinery, he saw a gas stack flare. His mind returned to the bonfire and Mari's haunted reaction. He remembered what had happened in his youth — in the summer of 1954, when Mari was nine and he was six...

Mum was baking cookies, and Mari was begging for one.

"No, dinner's almost ready and your father will be home soon. Doesn't the Indian food smell great? Spicy and sweet."

Mari and Morgan smiled and nodded in agreement. Standing at the cooker, Mum glanced at the clock with a pained expression. Dad was over an hour late.

"Mari, please plug in the iron. I need to press your school uniforms."

Mum smiled as she looked out the kitchen window. She often said how pleased she was by the view from their

< 69 >

secluded new house standing on the edge of the rolling hills of Greenham Common, the nearest neighbor a quarter mile away.

Mum said all her girlfriends had envied her for dating and marrying the star of Laugharne Rugby Football Club, Maddox "Maddie" Pritchard. She said the nickname referred to an inability to keep his head and manage his anger on the pitch. They were a happy family until, during a match, an opponent slammed into his left knee, shredding the ligaments. When told he would never play again, Maddox wallowed in self-pity and excessive drinking before an acquaintance got him work with a construction company. Mum said Dad had only a slight limp, but a big chip on his shoulder.

When the front door opened and slammed, Mum froze. Maddox stormed in, smelling of pub tobacco and alcohol.

"Hello, Daddy," Mari said, forcing a smile.

Scowling, ignoring his daughter, he went straight to the stove, lifted the pan lid, and barked, "What's this shite?"

< 70 >

"Curry. Thought I'd try something different."

Without comment, Dad marched into the living room. For a minute it was too quiet, then — Bloody Git! — followed by two loud crashes. The kids flinched. Mum inched to the doorway, shocked to see their table lamp in a pile on the floor, the glass from a broken ashtray in a corner.

Maddox's attitude had been improving since Mum's brother Glyn found him this job in Newbury — his third in two years. "What's wrong, Maddie?" asked Gladys softly.

"Got fucking fired. My boss is an opinionated Scottish pig. Bloody well telling me how to do my job. I've been building houses for years. What the fuck does he know?" After a moment, he said, "I shoulda cold-cocked him. He ain't got a better carpenter than me. Relegated to picking up scraps because I was late. Because we watched that rugby match on the telly."

"Come, let's eat dinner," Gladys cajoled.

In the kitchen, Morgan said, "Daddy, we had fun at the Indian grocery today.

< 71 >

They have lots of spices that smell really good."

Standing by his chair, Maddox glared at Gladys. "What! Better not be Patel's store. I told you never to go there again."

She bent her head and studied the floor.

"He just wants to get in your knickers. Is that what you want?"

With no response, his face turned red and he yelled, "You damn whore!"

Seizing a knife, he grabbed her arm and cut her blouse sleeve to the elbow, then twisted it to reveal the "Maddie" tattooed on her wrist.

"See that! You belong to me and only me," he growled. "If I ever catch you with another man, I'll kill you. I'll kill ya both."

Maddox dragged the point of the knife down her arm, leaving a long red welt. Blood came to the surface but did not run. "What's this?" he asked, pointing to stitches on her wrist. "Did you go to hospital?"

"It-it wouldn't stop b-b-b-bleeding," Gladys stuttered.

"I told you never go to a doctor after one of your lessons!"

< 72 >

He slapped her, then his voice went coldly quiet.

"What did you tell them?"

She did not respond. He punched her in the jaw. Mari and Morgan screamed. "Shut the fuck up," he yelled at them.

He spun Gladys around and began cutting her blouse. Mari hit him with her full weight in the back of his legs, buckling his bad knee. He dropped the knife and fell against the counter. Regaining his footing, he grabbed Mari and threw her at the refrigerator. Her head glanced off at an angle, her body motionless.

Morgan shrieked.

His father turned on him. "I told you to shut the fuck up."

Grabbing the hot iron, Maddox charged the boy. The cord ran out, yanking the plug from the wall. Morgan opened the back door, but the screen was locked. Before he could unlatch it, Maddox hit him in the back of the head with his fist.

The boy fell hard.

"I'll teach you a lesson, you Mummy's boy," he snarled, and with the hot iron at the ready, he pulled up the

< 73 >

boy's shirt. Gladys picked up the knife Maddox had used on her and rushed forward, stabbing her husband in the back. Maddox sprang up, forcing her away, the knife still in her hand.

He turned, swinging the iron backhand, barely missing the tip of her nose, but the momentum exposed his upper body. Without hesitation, Gladys shoved the blade into his throat.

Staggering, Maddox dropped the iron and grabbed the knife handle. As the point came free, he fell through the silver netting of the screen door and landed on the roofless back porch, ankles lodged in the door frame, his throat gushing blood.

Crying, Gladys ran to Mari and quickly examined her, thankfully finding her conscious, no broken bones. Morgan rose to his knees and watched his father's body quiver. Severe spasms at first, then slower and spaced further apart, until movement stopped.

Gladys phoned her brother. "Glyn," she gasped, "I need your help."

"Gladys, speak up, I can't understand you."

< 74 >

She screamed, "Dear God, I think I killed him."

"I'll be right there." The line went dead.

Gladys ran to Morgan, motionless by the back door, staring out onto the Commons. He had wet himself. She led the children upstairs.

Hearing Uncle Glyn's vehicle pull into the garden, Gladys laid Mari and Morgan on a bed and covered them with a blanket. "I'll be right back."

They heard talking and noises outside, so they went to the window and watched Glyn wrap the porch rug around the body. Then Mum helped drag her husband away from the house. Glyn removed items from his dead brother-in-law's pockets when air escaped from the lungs and the body groaned. He jumped and yelled, frightened.

Uncle Glyn recovered quickly and said something to his sister. He went into the garage and returned with a can of petrol and poured it over the body. Gladys flicked a cigarette lighter she'd removed from her husband's pocket. As if she'd burned her hand, the lighter

< 75 >

dropped and flames whooshed and spread.

"Burn, you son of a bitch," Glyn yelled, nostrils flaring.

Morgan and Mari wrapped arms around each other, watching in a catatonic-like state.

Morgan was pulled from his nightmare by the screech of the brakes and the train whistling approach of the next stop. He'd sweated through his shirt. Years of psychotherapy had kept his demons at bay.

But tonight they were back.

< 76 >

NINE

RAF Greenham Common
15 December 1982

The intercom buzzed. The wing commander's secretary interrupted Wes' updating of the daily status report, saying line two was holding for him. "It's a Mr. Elliot Knight from London," she said.

"Don't know that name. He say why he's calling?" Wes asked.

"No. Only that it was personal."

"Take a number," he ordered.

"He said it's important."

Resigned, he picked up the phone. "Lieutenant Colonel Forrest."

"Colonel. Not sure if you remember me. I attended your briefing to the American Ambassador yesterday afternoon about Sunday's events. I'm from Her Majesty's Security Service."

Wes remembered two men who sat behind the Embassy staff. They were introduced by name, but strangely their position or reason for being there was never mentioned.

"Yes, sir. I remember," said Wes.

"Excellent," replied Knight. "We need to meet, the sooner, the better. This is important. Unfortunately, I can't tonight. How's tomorrow for you?"

"Why are we meeting?" Wes asked.

< 77 >

"Sensitive. Can't discuss over the phone."

Wes remained silent. After a slight pause, Knight said, "I suggest Wokingham, about halfway between us. At the Chez Francis Restaurant. Good French food and we can talk without being disturbed."

Wes heard a shuffle of papers. "Here's the address and directions from the RAF Greenham Manor House."

How the hell does he know I'm staying in the Manor House? Curious, Wes took down the information.

* * *

On Thursday, Wes arrived at the restaurant fifteen minutes early. A menu rested on a stand in the lobby. Expensive. The dining room to the left had white-clothed tables for two. To the right, a mirrored dining area had tables for four. Nearness of the tables indicated it was popular.

But could they talk here about sensitive matters? Wes didn't think so.

No one was waiting for him, so he went to the bar, where he found pre-renovation pictures from when the building was a pub and inn.

"I'd like to develop a taste for scotch. Any suggestions?"

< 78 >

"Have you eaten?" asked the bartender. Wes shook his head. "Then we should start you with a Rusty Nail."

"A what?"

"A blend, add Drambuie, garnish with a lemon twist."

"Let's give it a try," Wes responded.

His drink had just arrived when the stool next to him moved.

"Good timing," said a dapper man.

Knight ordered a G&T as Wes took a sip of his drink. Experiencing sweetened, smoky-tasting alcohol, he made a face. He'd had medicine that tasted better.

The bartender laughed. "It's an acquired taste. The climate in every glen is different and creates a unique flavor. You should find a wine and spirits merchant and attend a tasting."

Wes turned his attention to his host, noticed the tailored gray suit and remembered seeing him at the Embassy. No way to forget that high forehead separated by a widow's peak. His thinning, gray-flecked hair made him look older than Wes guessed from his voice on the phone.

Carrying their drinks, Knight led the way from the bar, down a hall to a small room at the rear of the establishment. He took off his coat and placed it on the back of a chair at one of the four

< 79 >

empty tables. A slim, leather briefcase Wes had not noticed was placed on a seat.

"The better value is the three-course meal," Knight said.

From *du menu du dîner*, Wes selected crab for the appetizer, Knight goose liver. For the main course, Wes chose trout and Knight the roast duck. Cheese selections were served with both. They reserved dessert choices.

Checking *la carte des vins*, Knight said, "Since we're having fish and fowl, I suggest a dry white."

Out of his culinary depth, Wes said, "Your choice." But he was glad to ignore the Scotch.

During dinner they spoke about US and UK politics, the invasion and bonfire at RAF Greenham, the weather — every topic except why they were there. Other than the waiter's brief appearances to deliver food and remove plates, they were left alone. No one was ever seated at the other tables. After dishes were cleared and coffee served, Knight told the waiter, "Give us a minute before dessert."

The waiter closed the door when he left. Knight took out a card, wrote on the back, and gave it to Wes.

M. Elliot Knight

Her Majesty's Security Service

"Not a lot of information, Mr. Knight," Wes said. "MI5 or 6?"

< 80 >

"MI5. And call me Elliot. The necessary information is added when the card is handed out. I've given you my office and home numbers."

Wes checked the back of the card. "So, Mr. Knight, why am I here?"

Knight got up and locked the door. "Seversk."

Wes was temporarily speechless. This was the code word to use to identify other persons with a need-to-know about the explosion and missing nuclear materials from Siberia. "Just a second —" He mentally put himself back in the briefing at CIA headquarters. "Tomsk Oblast."

"Very good." Knight said, pulling a folder from his briefcase. "We're here for two reasons. First, there has been at least one death in Northern Scotland from radiation poisoning. We have little information currently — "

Wes interrupted, "Is this place secure?"

"Yes. Checked about two hours ago. On 1 December, a sick man…" Knight glanced at his notes. "…Captain Douglas Ross, was brought to a hospital in Wick, Scotland, but never regained consciousness. He was the owner of a fishing boat out of the village and is known to have done a bit of drug smuggling in the past. Local authorities discovered one of Ross' regular crewmen is also missing."

Knight crossed his legs. "Local police called in the Scottish Marine Laboratory, Aberdeen, who

< 81 >

determined his boat had been radiated and, to get it out of their harbor, had MOD tow it to a munitions dump site in the Irish Sea where it was scuttled. Initial radiation sampling on the boat by the Laboratory indicates Ross might have brought in radioactive materials. This tipped off medical staff who sent the body to University of Edinburgh, Pathology Department for evaluation. We wait for their report."

Knight scissored his arms. "Also, crews with sensors are moving to our less-frequently-used Anglo-Scottish border crossings. Our hope is that the death has complicated delivery of materials to wherever and to whomever. And that we can find it."

"Why only less-frequently-used border crossings?" Wes asked.

"We don't have enough equipment to cover them all, and the guess is they'll use backroads."

Knight uncrossed his arms, clasped his hands at the edge of the table. "We're trying to keep all this out of the press. The point for you is that RAF Greenham is a prime target. Defences need to be improved, seeing the way the peace women move through your fences."

Knight lifted the wine bottle and Wes shook his head. Refilling his glass, Knight said, "Which leads us to our second item of discussion. There is a Russian spy in the Women's Peace Camp at RAF

< 82 >

Greenham. At this point we think she has only played a minor role in the women's camps: observing what is happening on the airbase and reporting activities to her contact."

Knight retrieved a second folder. "I'd like you to keep your eyes and ears open and let me know if anything suspicious happens. I'll do the same."

"You say you'll do the same," Wes responded. "Did you know in advance about the taking of the guards and setting the truck afire on base last Sunday?"

"We knew something was being planned but had no details."

"Why the hell didn't you tell us then?" Wes asked loudly.

"Two reasons. The message was not clear enough to act on. And second, we didn't have a contact on base we trusted enough with the information." Knight pointed at Wes. "You and I hadn't had this discussion."

The MI5 agent handed the folder to Wes. "This is everything we know about her. Sorry, no name or picture. This information was deduced from two intercepted messages, so please keep it secret. Protect our source! Without telling them why, have your security keep an eye out for any suspicious or unusual behavior in or around the camps. Let me know if you learn anything about

< 83 >

this woman and, of course, if you see or hear anything relating to the nuclear materials."

Looking directly at Wes, Knight added, "I assume you told your commander about your confidential mission?"

"Yes. Of course."

"Then feel free to tell him about our talk. But him only."

No longer hungry, Wes stood up. "I really wouldn't care for dessert, and I've got a full day tomorrow."

Knight said he'd pick up the cheque. "You leave first, Sport. I'm going to try the Crème Brûlée. I'll be in touch after the Captain's body has been autopsied."

Swallowing his irritation, Wes left without another word.

< 84 >

TEN
RAF Greenham Common
16 December 1982

The next morning, Wes pulled into the Contractors' Gate parking lot to find Colonel Tom Rogers, cruise missile wing commander, already there. Earlier, a Command Post report said about twenty protestors were blocking the gate. By the time Wes arrived, Thames Valley Police had made arrests and a bus filled with screaming prisoners was leaving.

Wes saluted. Rogers returned it then pointed to five tents partially hidden in the woods. "They're talking about evicting these friggin' camps, but they'll just move down the road to some other property and remain a pain in our asses." Irritated, Rogers continued, "Local police ignore the women on the outside and the RAF fence is like a sieve."

He thought for a moment. "You know what the Ambassador told me the other night? That the State Department thinks the peace protestors are a British political matter in which the United States has no authority."

"Yeah, until they get inside the fences."

Rogers nodded in agreement with Wes and turned toward the Contractors' Gate. "When are the CIA and MI5 going to tell other agencies about

< 85 >

the possibility of nuclear materials loose in the UK?" Wes had stopped by the Colonel's house the night before, after meeting with Knight, and passed along that information.

"Above our pay grades, I'm afraid," Wes responded.

"Well, it's like everything else," said Rogers. "When the proverbial hits the fan, they'll start looking for a scapegoat. So, we best cover our asses. I want more surveillance on these camps and a plan in progress to secure the perimeter."

Picking up an empty water bottle, Rogers tossed it toward a trashbin, missing the shot. "Damn." He left it where it landed. "You have a problem getting on base this morning?" he asked Wes. "Those damn bitches that stuck around after the Embrace thing are blocking our entrances up to five hours a day."

Not wanting to add fuel to the Colonel's frustration, Wes said, "No. There were only six protestors at the back gate, and they were more concerned with staying warm than stopping traffic."

Art Gilbert, the base Civil Engineer, pulled into the parking lot.

"There were twenty or so at the main gate. I told the Brit security to leave them lying on the road," the Colonel said. "They'll get hungry and get up eventually. Pavement's wet, maybe they'll

< 86 >

catch their death. We can only hope. We'll let 'em have their day, and keep the other gates open."

Interrupting the conversation, Gilbert saluted. "Sorry I'm late, sir."

"Forget it," Colonel Rogers said. "What's the status of the damages?"

"Only minor damage to the guard shack and gate, sir," Gilbert replied. "They were fixed earlier this week. The perimeter fence is damaged in a couple of places." He pointed along the fence to where a crew was making repairs about fifty yards away. "Protestors cut the barbed wire on top and scaled over, using blankets to protect themselves. Inside the GAMA, a crew worked Tuesday and Wednesday removing the gutted truck and remains of the bonfire. Removing topsoil today."

"Everything was well planned," Wes said. "We were damn lucky their only goal was to blow up a truck."

Rogers gave Wes a nod.

The Ministry of Defence guard exited his shack as they approached. Wes asked, "Much traffic through here this morning?"

"'Bout average, sir. Some work cancelled 'cause the lorry cleanup blocks part of the site."

Wes said, "Thanks."

The guard started to open the gate. "Just a second," Rogers said. He walked to his car, taking a file folder from the front seat. Swinging by the

< 87 >

trash bin, he picked up the water bottle and tossed it in. Not hesitating at the gate, Rogers double-timed onto the base and charged up the gravel road the sixty yards to the GAMA fences. Gilbert and Wes jogged to catch up.

"Damn it. What happened last weekend is an embarrassment," Rogers said, addressing the ground while he walked, controlling his temper. "We're gonna be scrutinized, second-guessed, and..." Abruptly, he halted. "I expect you two to act like professionals. Don't get angry or defensive. That's my job. Help me fix this so it doesn't happen again."

Rogers resumed walking. Wes glanced at Art behind the colonel's back and arched his eyebrows. They stopped where the gravel roadway passed through a twenty-four-foot gap in the double fence surrounding the base's missile complex. Two parallel twelve-foot-high security fences ran southwest and northeast from this vehicular access to the current construction area. But there was no evidence of any ongoing work at this opening.

"This made it too damn easy to drive that lorry through here. Are these sections of the fence ever secured?" Rogers asked.

"No sir," Gilbert replied. "Since all the construction in this area is new, and none is finished, the contractors asked that these two fence

< 88 >

sections be the last things completed. Or at least until the earth movers, cranes, all the heavy equipment are out."

Rogers passed the folder to Gilbert. When he opened it, Wes saw it was a contractor's map of the GAMA with this gap circled in red ink. But the contractor's name had been cut off.

"Where did you get this, sir?" Gilbert asked.

"Police found it on one of the women arrested Sunday night."

"I'll check with the contractors," the engineer said. "Find out who it belongs to. Maybe one of them has an anti-American sympathizer who needs to be identified and fired."

"You mean arrested," Rogers corrected. Turning to Wes, Rogers said, "Wouldn't it be better to completely fence these sections? Force all traffic to use the GAMA's main entrance on base, along the runway to the north?"

"Sorry, sir, can't do that," Wes responded. "This will be the second egress point. Survivability of the weapon system depends on rapidly deploying to dispersed sites during a period of tension. The wing is required to get fifty percent — that's three flights — off base within six hours. Having only one exit would make it easy for a saboteur to tie up the flights in the GAMA. Can't afford a bottleneck. This will be the backup exit."

< 89 >

"Wes, remind me, how large is a flight?" the civil engineer asked.

"Twenty two vehicles. Sixty nine airmen."

Gilbert said, "That'll take time and space to organize and get off base. Colonel Rogers, do you want to look around inside the GAMA?"

"Not that much has changed since Monday," the Colonel said. "Let's talk security here and at the Contractors' Gate."

Turning to look at the area under construction, Rogers asked, "Art, when will the first GAMA facility be turned over to us?"

Gilbert consulted his ever-present civil engineer's logbook. "Intermediate Maintenance Facility, first one. Mid-April. About four months."

While the colonel and Gilbert discussed facilities, Wes wandered over to the closest GAMA fence to examine the security systems and found them nowhere near complete. Wire had been pulled through buried piping, but at connection points varying lengths were exposed and lay on the ground. No sensors were in sight, connected or boxed. Wes took a deep breath and shook his head at the thought of another surprise attack.

Rejoining them, Wes asked, "Art, what's the best guess as to when these two missing sections will have gates installed?"

"GAMA fences must be secure before mid-April."

< 90 >

"What if you put in temporary gates in only the outer fence's gap — with temporary lighting?" Wes asked. "We could at least lock it at night and weekends, like the Contractors' Gate. Plus, assign roving security patrols here during those times. That'd prevent — at least slow down — what happened Sunday."

Colonel Rogers studied the area where the sections were missing but gave no indication of his thoughts about the suggestions. Returning to the contractor gate, they continued to discuss damage control and ideas for additional guards, gate and guard shack improvements, and perimeter fence changes, to include adding razor wire to the top of the fence at vulnerable locations.

The gate closed behind the wing commander. He said, "Some of the improvements we're suggesting are better than our long-term plans. Because of Sunday's events, the Third Air Force commander assures me he can find more construction money. But...we need to act quickly." Turning to Wes, "Does he know about the latest threat?"

Wes nodded.

"You think the Ministry of Defence will fund additional guards?" Wes asked.

"The RAF will scream," Rogers said. "But Sunday was also an embarrassment for them. And we now have the additional threat. We're not

< 91 >

going to get more manpower out of the Pentagon, but they have agreed to host-nation participation. So, it's on Group Captain Mackay's and my plate to get RAF security personnel stationed here sooner than later."

The Colonel kicked a rock as if it were an extra point in an American football game, then checked his shoe to see if he'd scratched the toe. "What do you think, Wes? You worked with those Pentagon folks while developing the system."

"I like it. I'm sure Air Force brass will, too," Wes said. "Parliament has talked about more British involvement — if you call what they do talking. We add Brit security police to our GLCM flights earlier than planned. Get them here ASAP. Makes 'em available to augment base security. But RAF brass will resist the unplanned manpower drain."

"Tell that MI5 guy to help," Colonel Rogers said, starting toward his car. Then he turned back. "One last thing. Security police and MOD are preparing reports on everything that happened last weekend. Art, I want one from you on our infrastructure, especially the perimeter fence, with a revised timeline focusing on now through December. Add in the ideas we just discussed. Identify additional problems they create, especially costs and time. Need it tomorrow."

< 92 >

Rogers turned to Wes. "Okay, Exec Officer. Time to earn your pay. Get copies of all these reports — even if only preliminary. Explain the need to brief General Hudson. They'll bitch but comply. Read the whole lot. Play devil's advocate. Ask questions. Investigate where you think necessary. Then get back to me."

Rogers took a deep breath. "I want all problems identified, viable solutions proposed, and shortfalls pointed out by the time I report to Ramstein, London, and Washington."

"Yes, sir."

"Wes," he said solemnly, "we need to make sure State understands our status. Like MI5, the CIA needs to help. And Art," Rogers growled, "make sure all that bonfire crap is cleaned up. And the damn graffiti off shelter walls. I guarantee you the general will insist on a drive-thru. Soon. Surprised he's not already come."

The Commander gave a hurried return salute to Wes and the civil engineer, jumped in his car, and sped off.

Gilbert looked at Wes: "MI5? CIA?"

< 93 >

ELEVEN
Scotland
17 December 1982

Looking at the map, Sokolov said, "At Cumbernauld take A73 South to the A74."

"We're off to Glasgow, right?" asked the driver, Iain McKenna.

"Change in plans."

The normally chatty McKenna was suddenly quiet.

"Does that interfere with your plans?" Sokolov asked.

"I got a pickup in Glasgow."

"Money from drug smuggling?"

McKenna gripped the wheel but did not speak.

"I don't care, as long as there's no heroin in this truck now," Sokolov stated.

McKenna shook his head.

"We need to get across the border. You can return through Glasgow."

Once on the very busy, six-lane A74, McKenna drove the speed limit to the chagrin of many motorists.

< 94 >

"Tell me again what happened when Captain Ross landed. What was done and said," Sokolov asked.

"I already did, once. Ye know."

"I was busy then, concentrating on getting the VW loaded. Now I need to see if there's anything that requires follow-up."

"Well, th' cap'n called me when he arrived at th' boathouse. I find him alone, sick, red blotches all o'er his face. Peeling skin. He says they were takin' drums for a high-paying Russian, but that Roy, another crewman he uses, had opened one o' the drums and gotten sick. Said he was sweating, freezing, ye know. Dizzy. Th' next day, he started heaving o'er the side, filled with blood. Then shaking."

McKenna took off his newsboy cap, scratched his bald head, and continued. "Cap'n said he must have been in unbearable pain for Roy ta get th' boat's gun and shot himself. Cap'n throw'd him overboard 'cause he knew what it was."

"Only the two of them onboard?"

"Aye. My niece was getting married and I stayed home. Since they weren't fishing, two could handle th' Sorcha for a pickup and return."

"And then?"

"We — me 'n th' Cap'n — pulled th' drums into th' boathouse."

"How'd you unload it?"

< 95 >

"There's derricks on the boat for moving th' catch around and ta onshore. Moved them onto a platform. Power-winched them up the rails and inside. And ye saw the cranes in the boathouse."

He glanced at Sokolov. "How come ye ask?" Getting no answer, McKenna continued, "He said he was too weak ta navigate ta Wick alone and dump th' unsealed drum at sea, so I went with him. He had wrapped and taped th' thing in a lead blanket for protection. I caught a bus back ta Keiss. He was worried about taking a cut in money, but didn't want ta leave th' mess anywhere on shore either. He should have dumped it at sea along with Roy."

Hitting the steering wheel, he said, "He got sicker. Wife took him to hospital."

"Was there an investigation? Did he ever talk to police?"

"His wife said he was out cold when they arrived at hospital. He ne'er became fully awake." After negotiating a roundabout, McKenna continued, "I talked ta th' police."

This got Sokolov's full attention. "And?"

"I didn't really know for sure what Cap'n and Roy had been doing, where they'd been or anything. Was with family most o' that night. So, police didn't ask me much."

McKenna let a fast-moving car pass. "The took th' Cap'n's boat."

< 96 >

Sokolov turned to him quickly. "It's missing?"

"His wife said th' government got th' keys, took it out ta sea and sunk her."

For several miles, both were lost in thought. Then, breaking the silence, Sokolov said, "There are some loose ends. Including, I need to give the Captain's and Roy's families their earned wages. We need to decide on a story for you to tell them."

They crossed the Anglo-Scottish border and found a Cumbria Constabulary police van blocking the M6, and a policeman flagging vehicles onto a viewpoint turnout for Solway Firth.

"What should I do?" asked McKenna.

"Follow their directions. It may only be an auto accident ahead."

When they were on the turnout, they saw that every driver was being interviewed, with some cars moved aside for inspection.

"Stick to the cover story." Sokolov reached behind his seat, pulled a semiautomatic from his bag, and put it under his leg, out of sight.

McKenna lit his fifth cigarette of the day. Sokolov said nothing but rolled down his window. McKenna was stopped to allow a furniture company lorry to pass in front and pull out of the turnout.

An officer approached his window. "Where ye headed?"

< 97 >

"Northampton. Carrying a family's van home," McKenna said. "They were camping and blew a transmission ..."

Sokolov stopped listening as a second policeman stood outside his window and looked him over. He watched in his side mirror while the officer moved down the passenger side of the recovery truck, opening the storage compartment below the bed. After searching among the tie-down straps and tools, he closed it, then tugged at the straps attaching the VW camper's tyres to the flatbed and slowly walked around behind the truck. Everyone waited. Then, in a minute he approached his partner at the driver's window.

"Looks like a lot of stuff inside that ugly green van. What is it?" the second policeman asked him.

Without a beat, McKenna said, "Family's tent and other camping equipment."

"Move it on out," the first officer said. "We got a lot of vehicles in line."

A few miles south on the M6, McKenna spotted a service area and said with a shaky voice, "I'm needin' to piss...and smoke."

Once back on the road, McKenna asked, "We gonna have any more excitement?"

"Shouldn't."

"I have a question," McKenna said. "What are you going to do with the two packages we left in the boathouse?"

< 98 >

* * *

Wes walked anxiously out of the base post office. He ripped open his wife's letter the instant he got in his car and noticed the date, 3 December, two weeks ago.

Dear Wes,

I hope this letter finds you well and settled in your new assignment.

Just to let you know, Lorianne is very disappointed you will not be home for Christmas. I explained to her it was because of the important work you are doing, but girls her age miss their dads. I have not mentioned anything to her about our difficulties and ask that you not either for the time being.

Her Christmas wish is to visit England. I told her we couldn't afford it and she seems to accept that. If you agree, as a Santa gift, I'll buy the bike she wants. I'll also get the stocking stuffers, etc. Something from England, maybe popular with British kids, might just be a perfect present from you.

< 99 >

I know we've talked to Lorianne about attending a British school, but I have described the differences in the educational systems and how difficult it would be when returning home.

This brings me to us.

A lot has happened in the last several weeks and there hasn't been a good time to say what I need to say. I want you to understand my decision without being emotional. I'm taking a law school admissions test prep course in January; the exam is in February. If I do well Daddy thinks he can get me into FSU's law class starting next August.

You know I love you, but this is something I have to do. I have followed you for eight years, feeling trapped and unhappy. I'm just not suited to be a military wife. I need to test my own potential and have my own career.

Regardless of the exam outcome, I will not be coming to England.

Wes wadded up the letter and threw it into the back seat. Driving too fast across the flight line, he

< 100 >

was brought back to reality when a passing security police car bleeped its siren and motioned for him to slow down. At the Manor House, he spread the letter on his desk, smoothed out the wrinkles, and sat back to read the rest.

> Daddy is renovating one of his rental houses for us and will help me get a job with a good law firm in Tallahassee.
>
> I've spoken to a realtor here in Virginia, and our house can be rented out for enough to cover the mortgage.
>
> I still care for you, and you are the father of my wonderful child, but love and family are not enough for me. I know this now. I'm excited for the first time in years about going back to school! I'm sorry that this is happening so suddenly, but the physical distance between us has allowed me time to think independently. Please don't hate me.
>
> Lorianne sends her love. Don't forget her recital, Saturday, December 11th.
> Diane

Wes had expected this. Still, it hurt. Confirmation in writing was worse than speculation. He was frustrated, angry. He needed

< 101 >

to move, but pacing back-and-forth in his room wasn't enough, so he decided to burn some energy with a run. At Langley AFB, he had run two or three times a week to keep in shape and clear his head. He'd been in England for over a month and hadn't even unpacked running shoes; it took awhile to find them. The day was chilly, so he put on sweats, spent some time stretching, and headed east on Burys Bank Road, the letter constantly on his mind.

With the golf course to his left, Wes walked the first quarter mile, then broke into a slow jog. With little traffic, he increased his pace. But he couldn't stop thinking about Diane and his daughter. He loved Lorianne very much and would miss not having her near, but at the same time felt relief at not having the additional worry and stress of them so close to danger.

He thought about his last assignment at Tactical Air Command Headquarters. Developing a new weapon system had required a lot of planning and coordination with other offices, thus entailing a lot of travel. Wes thought about all the time he had spent on the road, when he went to the office on weekends, when he could have been with the family.

I chose my career path, which excluded her. Now she'd chosen hers.

< 102 >

He came to a hill, felt pain in his legs and lungs. This shouldn't be happening. Been inactive too long.

He focused on his movement, his arm motion, the length of his stride, the feel of his feet striking the pavement, and the steady, rhythmic breathing of the air entering his lungs.

He was absorbed in the activity, until a train blaring its horn blasted through an intersection, less than a hundred feet in front of him. *Whoa!* Regaining focus on his surroundings, he saw he was on a bridge, crossing over a river or canal, approaching the tracks, and realized he was in Thatcham. Having no idea of a cross-country return to the base, he retraced his path back to the Manor House.

* * *

Friday and Saturday nights, Wes slept the broken sleep of the depressed, filled with unpleasant dreams. Feelings of anger, despair, and helplessness kept him company during waking moments. Over the weekend he rarely left his bed except for trips to the bathroom down the hall.

But Sunday morning he felt like he was suffocating, so ran east along the North taxiway and back to the Manor House. After showering, he

< 103 >

felt the need for hydration and nutrition, grabbed bottled water, and went for a drive.

Wes drove the four miles around the east end of the base, then halfway to Basingstoke pulled into an empty field, exited his car, and screamed *Fuck*. That made him feel better, so he did it again. Near town centre, he found the Churchill Street Brasserie open for business and ate an excellent lunch of fillet steak.

His thoughts were interrupted by an argument from the next table.

"I tell you it's the *Moonlight Sonata*," a woman insisted.

"No, it's *Für Elise*," a man said.

Wes smiled as he listened to the background music playing in the restaurant. Leaning over toward the table, he complimented both. "You're both correct on the composer. Beethoven. It's the opening of his *Piano Sonata No. 14*."

The couple nodded and returned to desserts.

Only through Lorianne could he have known that. Remembering he'd brought Diane's letter with him, he reread it over coffee with a new perspective. The relationship had been great for the first six years, but during the last two he often felt a strain. And more of her going home to Daddy after arguments. At TAC Headquarters, he was on the road at least two weeks of every month — except December. All the contractors and the

< 104 >

Air Force tried to keep families together for Christmas. Diane didn't work or play golf. She found it difficult to make friends. And didn't like being left alone either. Homesick, she called her parents more often when Wes was gone.

He had already purchased and mailed their presents — a beanie-sweater combo and Christmas bears for Lorianne, and a kimono for Diane, all from Harrods. They should have them by now. Remembering the lateness of Diane's letter, he saw that she had transposed two numbers in the APO address.

"No one has ever died of a broken heart," he said to himself on his drive back to base. He smiled as he thought again about his daughter and her first recital — how well she did. She'd hit a wrong key but ignored the mistake and continued on as if it hadn't happened. He must have watched the video — which he received before the letter — ten times.

The idea of his daughter conquering adversity cheered him. *Maybe I can learn something from her.*

< 105 >

TWELVE
Northampton General Hospital
22 December 1982

Morgan finished replacing the wiring and wall receptacle, then went to the electrical closet and reset the circuit breaker. Lights came on all over the floor. *Maybe now the hospital will let us add another distribution panel.* Last year when a nurse left a curling iron on in a bathroom, the resulting fire had shorted out power to an entire wing, including a crisis care area.

Back in the Cardiac Unit, Morgan saw that most of the smoke had dissipated through a window he'd opened earlier. Dr. Young, standing over the treadmill, asked, "Will this stink last all day?"

Morgan answered, "'Fraid so. Melted wiring, burnt plastic, rubber, and ozone, all mixed together. I'll take out everything that is damaged except the treadmill; maintenance will get it later."

"What happened?" asked the doctor.

"The treadmill's motor overheated and the internal circuit breaker failed and burned. That's most of the smoke and smell. For some reason, the mains also overheated and smoked before the panel breaker popped."

Morgan could have told him that most of the hospital's wiring was old and its circuits overloaded, and that the Northampton General Hospital board annually approved only some of the repairs recommended by the inspection programme he'd developed.

"Crap," the doctor said. "We'll lose a whole day or more of stress evaluations. Not sure when we'll get a replacement."

Morgan knew there was an old treadmill in the off-site storage unit, but didn't mention it. The last hospital administrator put it in the doctors' lounge, hoping its easy availability would tempt physicians to use it. Like a lot of his stupid ideas, it didn't work.

Young headed out where a nurse met him and gave him a chart to sign. She looked Morgan over with obvious interest. The doctor, focused on the chart, paid her no mind. Morgan pretended he didn't see.

Morgan Pritchard was tall, good looking in a rough sort of way. He had an athletic build, thin and wiry, and a gravelly voice and brown eyes. Had a dazzling smile, too…when he chose to show it. He wore his dark curly hair longer than the hospital preferred. When not in hospital coveralls,

< 107 >

he frequently wore dungarees and motorcycle leathers.

Upon returning to the shop, his supervisor, Robert Bowen, asked, "How'd it go?"

"Another patch job," Morgan answered with a dismissive wave.

"Unless the board decides to spend some cash and upgrade the entire electrical system," Bowen said, "we'll have a real catastrophe on our hands one day." Picking up a file, he added, "Here's a complaint about problems with the security system in the radiopharmacy unit. I'll get Chris to check it tonight."

"I've got scheduled maintenance down here in the basement later this week, I can do it then," Morgan suggested.

"Good, I'd rather have Chris sort out the OR circuitry anyway. Been getting complaints of fluctuations."

* * *

When Morgan got home, he found a short voicemail on his phone: "Altar Boy. We need to talk. Tonight. Nine p.m."

Only Ronnie Bolnick called him Altar Boy. It stemmed from an episode at Wisbech Church of England School for Troubled Youth when they were caught stealing and selling church wine.

< 108 >

Ronnie was now an East End London hood who used Morgan from time-to-time when he needed an arsonist.

Anxiousness made him early; Morgan got to Ye Olde Cherry Tree at eight-thirty p.m. The pub, Morgan's local on High Street, Mears Ashby, is a rustic eighteenth-century former coaching inn with stripped floors, wall lamps, a long bar and a pool table, pool having become an obsession of the owner whilst visiting the United States. Morgan often stopped in for pub grub on his way home in the evening. Sausage with mash and onion gravy or gammon with eggs and chips. Sirloin steak on Wednesday nights, entertainment one Saturday a month and, weather permitting, a beer garden.

What drew Morgan were the quiet booths away from darts, dominoes, and pool players where he could enjoy a pint of Guinness and relax.

Tonight, he picked up a pint at the bar and headed for a quiet corner booth. Not hungry, he waved off the offered menu and waited for Bolnick, who walked in at exactly nine.

With no small talk, Bolnick tossed Morgan a copy of that day's *Daily Telegraph*. "Look at page two."

While Bolnick went to the bar, Morgan scanned the article. "Shit!" was his immediate response. The article read:

< 109 >

BODIES FOUND IN WEMBLEY FIRE DISASTER RUBBLE

Investigators discovered the bodies of two missing firemen yesterday, 21 December, within the gutted yet still smoldering remains of the GWS Warehouse and Distribution facility, which was totally destroyed over the weekend due to an explosion and subsequent fire.

The bodies of Wembley Fire Station firefighters James Coulter and Emory Lanier, among the first fire crew entering the warehouse, were found amid first floor debris, near the central stairway connecting the facility's three levels. Funeral services are pending.

Also injured were Park Royal firemen William Glover and Edward Wickson, both of whom are in stable condition and recovering at nearby Northwick Hospital.

Fire services' initial premise is that the fire started in the facility's cellar, rising through the upper two stories via the wooden stairwell. Bulk wine and whisky barrels stored in the cellar eventually reached boiling points. Once this happened, the barrels cracked and

< 110 >

released a cloud of flammable vapor which ignited.

The subsequent explosion blew out the building's entire south wall, sending tons of masonry onto the street and burying a fire appliance, which resulted in the injuries of the two Park Royal firemen.

Thanks to the quick work of the firefighting crews, the fire did not spread to nearby buildings.

Wembley Fire Station manager Lim Brooks said the fire is still under investigation. London Fire Brigade is assisting in the consideration of arson.

"Morgan," Bolnick said, pulling his attention back to the room. "I received word indirectly from George Saddler that since we fucked up the warehouse fire — killed and injured firemen — we will not be paid the rest of our money." Wiping moisture off his glass, Bolnick continued, "What happened at the warehouse?"

"You blaming me?"

Bolnick only returned his stare.

"For the most part, it went as planned," Morgan said. "I visited the site twice. Did a reconnaissance the Wednesday night prior, seeing what, if any, accelerants and combustibles were

< 111 >

available. Contractors were painting the first and second floors of the warehouse and had left paint, paint thinner, and turpentine everywhere. Wine and whisky barrels were in the cellar, stacked on timber tiers, three high. The first floor consisted of the small bottling and labeling room, which we were told to destroy. Cases of bottled wine and whisky stored on racks and large lockable storage lockers for up to twenty cases. The second floor had a conference room, offices, and small-volume individual lockers."

Morgan glanced at Bolnick to see if he had any questions. He didn't. "The warehouse closed at noon on Saturday, so I went in late afternoon, whilst still light. Again, no one was around. I found a stack of twenty-liter cans of paint thinner, as well as trash, cardboard boxes, and kerosene-soaked rags that had been used to clean brushes. There was an inside stairwell that connected all three floors, so I scattered these combustible items on and around the stairs, and also inside the bottling room.

"The idea being that with heat, the paint thinner cans would explode and spray flammable liquid in all directions — over the barrels in the cellar and the bottle and label equipment in that room — where I also opened all file cabinet drawers. Next, the heated bottles and barrels

< 112 >

would become over pressurized and blow with the alcohol vapor adding to the volatility."

Morgan took a large swallow, then continued, "I placed three charges — one, at the bottom of the stairs, another in the bottling room and because I needed air for the fire, placed an explosive at the secured cellar fire escape door."

After a moment's thought: "To help ensure an adequate air supply, I opened windows on the second floor before I left."

Morgan looked at Bolnick. "The vapor explosion was bigger than I thought might happen. Didn't expect to bring down a wall, but that was good, should have destroyed any evidence of arson. And work done by Wembley Fire is rubbish — they screwed up the evidence in last year's Bentley Auto fire."

Then with his first smile of the night, "Remember? One of my best-paying jobs."

"How did you set off the charges?" Bolnick asked.

"The cellar and first floor are — were — climatically controlled," Morgan said. "The outside air was minus one and the controlled temperature was 13 degrees Celsius. I left all stairwell doors and upper windows open, so over time the sensor could pick up a significant change and sound an alarm. That'd set off charges."

< 113 >

"Okay! Okay! You did the job right. But with firemen dead," Bolnick said, "the big guns from the London Fire Brigade will do an in-depth investigation." He leaned back and said, "I don't care so much about the fire crew, Morgan. Collateral damage. It's their job. But George Saddler? He's a loose end that needs tying up."

< 114 >

THIRTEEN
Holidays
1982

RAF Greenham Airbase was down to only essential personnel and activities for the holidays. Wes used the time to explore new routes to run and buried himself in two books by Ken Follett. He talked to his mom on Christmas Eve and Lorianne twice during the holidays. His daughter loved the stuffed momma and baby polar bears he'd sent her from England. But she was more excited about the Cadbury chocolates he had added. He endured her excited talk about spending Christmas Day at his mother-in-law's.

Close by at the Women's Peace Camp at Yellow Gate, the situation was just the opposite: festive. Many women had brought their kids and it was a continuous party with Father Christmas making a grand appearance.

* * *

On 27 December, Nikolai Sokolov received the latest message from his operative at RAF Greenham Common. Decoded, it read:

< 115 >

GOSHAWK
INFO REQUESTED STOP NAME IS
MORGAN PRITCHARD STOP
NORTHAMPTON GH STOP
BIRCH

Sokolov had requested the name or names of whoever had orchestrated the 12 December base trespass or the person who had driven the lorry into the GAMA. That appeared to be the work of one Morgan Pritchard, who had driven on base with criminal intent. Sokolov's operative seemed to be following his instructions a bit too closely: keeping messages short, like a telegram.

Was she saying that Morgan lives in Northampton? But what in the name of Mother Russia did "GH" mean?

Another puzzle from his newest agent. In her last message there was a Hungarian word without an English equivalent and she simply used the Hungarian word — *kódolatlan* — in the message. It had taken a while to figure out she meant "uncoded".

Walking to the rented garage he used for storage, an ambulance marked BGH — Barnet General Hospital — sped past and Sokolov had the answer.

Ah, Northampton General Hospital. That must be where Pritchard is employed.

Sokolov worked in the lower level of the Barnet library all afternoon organizing and cataloguing the family estate papers of a wealthy benefactor who had died. He actually enjoyed his undercover job and is title: Chief Librarian for Special Collections.

Arriving home, he realized he was tired, very tired. But he had several things to do before going to bed.

First, he decoded a message from Moscow. The KGB had pulled surveillance off her parents. His hold on her had evaporated — but Katelin Nagy didn't need to know that.

Now that he had the lorry driver's name, he revised his plans, made an inventory of supplies, and began his coded message to the KGB.

* * *

For the most part, Morgan spent the Christmas holidays alone at his home. He called his sister, Mari, and their mother, both spending the holidays in their respective homes in Wales. He rebuilt the frame of his Norton motorcycle and replaced a leaking brake cylinder on his Range Rover.

Morgan was lucky when George Saddler showed up at the closed GWS Wine Warehouse on his first day of surveillance. Saddler led two men,

< 117 >

he guessed insurance, around inside and outside the warehouse looking at damages. Later, Morgan followed Saddler to his home in St. John's Wood. Another day he followed Saddler to his solicitor's office in Kensington.

* * *

Colonel Rogers entered the building and motioned for Wes to come to his office.

"How did the meeting go?" Wes asked.

"The Newbury District Council made history today. Must want to start out the new year aggressively." He took off his coat and continued. "They are finally bending to the pressure of voters who are tired of the protestors, demonstrations, blocked roadways and related traffic congestion, plus paying for trash pickup. They voted to revoke the common law bylaws for Greenham Common. That makes them — the Council — the private landlord for most of the area outside the base fence."

"What does that really mean?"

"They can now claim eviction costs from those women whose address is given on the electoral rolls as the peace camps."

Wes shook his head. "Seems like poking a stick in a beehive to me."

< 118 >

PART TWO

< 119 >

FOURTEEN
RAF Greenham Common
4 January 1983

His radio buzzed. "Wes. It's Art. Where are you? I need you in the GAMA, like, right now."

"I'm in Newbury. Just left the Mayor's office. Can be there in ten, maybe fifteen minutes. What's up?"

"Get here! Come through the contractor gate. You'll see us."

It was not like the base civil engineer to act this impulsively; something important — or bad — must be going on. The MOD guard opened the gate and waved Wes through. Approaching the GAMA fence, he saw workmen standing in groups of two or three, many of whom had removed their yellow hardhats and held them under their arm or at their side.

< 120 >

Art Gilbert stood, hands on hips, near a backhoe that had apparently stopped mid-stroke at the edge of an excavation. A Thames Valley Police officer was stringing crime scene tape, another taking pictures.

"What's going on?" Wes asked.

Art pointed into the hole. Wes saw a bundle in a pack of rocks. Its black plastic wrapping ripped open, assumedly by the digging. Looking closer, Wes recognized a rib cage.

"Security police called Newbury Station," Art said. "Investigators and the deputy coroner are on their way. I'm leavin' it to you to tell the Old Man."

"Gee, thanks," Wes said. "He should be out of the Ministry of Defence meeting in an hour. I'll leave him a message. How'd this happen?"

"Guys were doing prep work for corner posts for the temporary gate when they hit an old foundation or wall. Backhoe driver jumped in to see. Found this."

"Any idea what to do?"

"I've stopped the work. Don't want anything disturbed until the police and coroner have a look. I'm sure they'll control what happens next."

"Yeah, probably not what we want to hear," offered Wes.

< 121 >

"I don't want the body, if it's human, to be further damaged." Art paused. "We don't want to be accused of destroying evidence."

The deputy coroner, Doctor Guy Peters, was already in the hole when a disheveled Thames Valley Police detective squatted nearby. Alerted by the shadow, the coroner looked up. "Detective Superintendent Tidwell," Peters said. "Sorry I couldn't wait. Have to get back to hospital stat."

"S'all right."

Peters carefully cut free the tape and black plastic sheeting damaged by the backhoe's bucket. Moving pieces of what looked like a burned rug, he peered at a charred chest cavity and a blackened human skull with grinning teeth. Some ribs and vertebra were still in place.

"Can you see?" Peters asked Tidwell.

Looking over the doctor's shoulder, the detective said, "All I need to." He studied the gray herringbone driving cap that Peters used to cover a bald pate. "I like your chapeau."

"From a patient. Donegal tweed." Then talking to himself as much as to Tidwell, Peters said, "Victim remains at old fire scenes are tough to investigate." Peters turned from the remains and touched his headgear.

< 122 >

But the coroner had a job to do and took a small tape recorder from his pocket, clicking it on. "The outside covering has no fire damage, nor is the dirt here scorched, as if this body was moved from the place of burning, then wrapped and placed here. Being moved means evidence may be missing. And because of the damage caused by the bucket, we'll have postmortem bone fracturing, and organs, if not fully putrefied, damaged."

The coroner stretched, then continued, "The majority of the body is still wrapped, so hopefully some biological tissue remains. With fire, bones discolor and become brittle. Makes for a difficult autopsy…"

Once Peters had completed his initial forensic examination, he climbed out of the hole. Stopping beside Tidwell, he asked, "Putting on a little weight?"

Tidwell nodded. "You been talking to the wife? She's been on my case. Stress-related eating."

They approached the group of military and contractors standing by in anticipation. He extended his hand to Wes and Art. "Doctor Guy Peters, Deputy Coroner."

Tidwell asked, "Were you first in the hole?"

"No. There were prints — work boots — already there."

"Damn," the detective said, and he stalked off.

< 123 >

Peters explained to Wes and Art why he thought the burning had occurred elsewhere. He turned the recorder back on.

"From the little I reviewed, it appears that an accelerant of some kind was poured on his upper body — soft tissue on the face, neck, and upper chest is burned away, with bone discoloration indicating that may have been the hottest part of the fire. There are also hard tissue modifications and pugilistic changes."

"Puge... what?" asked Tidwell, who had returned to the group.

"Pugilistic pose: characteristic body and limb postures caused by heating and shrinking of muscle tissue. Term comes from boxing. Means the making of a fist."

Peters continued to record his summary: "We have a middle-aged white male with significant burns to the anterior upper torso. Will examine lower at post. Can't determine cause of death until I get him in the lab. If it was fire, the lungs — if enough remains — might tell. But acid will sometimes look similar. There's a knife wrapped up with the body, so I'm withholding any opinion until after the postmortem." Peters stopped his recorder and tucked it away.

Tidwell yelled to a forensics technician: "Find and bag that knife and bring it to me straight away." Turning to the doctor, he added, "Any defensive wounds?"

"Decomposition is probably too far along to determine, but I'll let you know after the postmortem."

Wes asked the coroner, "How long do you think it's been buried?"

"Don't want to guess; will know more after post."

Art interrupted, asking Tidwell, "Can the contractors get back to work?"

"Not here. This is now a crime scene. Must be kept clear until our major-crime investigators do a proper job. Have to sift that surrounding dirt, locate any disturbed skeletal fragments, and take measurements and pictures."

"Crap. They'll bitch. Our commander will yell," Art said. "This means another delay because they'll have to drive around to the main GAMA entrance."

"Any idea how long this entrance will be blocked off?"

"Couple days at least. Maybe a week."

The ambulance had arrived, and Wes watched while two of the coroner's techs loaded the body and pulled out.

* * *

< 125 >

Sokolov decoded the message from his RAF Greenham operative:

RAF BASE FENCE MODIFICATION
DELAYED BY INVESTIGATION OF
DISCOVERED BURIED BODY STOP BIRCH

The delay in the fence modifications was great news. He'd been mulling over an idea, and this gave him time to work on it. Moscow was a little uneasy with US President Reagan's concentration on the USSR as the world's central problem and wanted to bloody his nose. Stopping the cruise missile deployment would be such an act. Kremlin analysts pointed out Reagan's willingness to sacrifice social welfare spending to support the increased military budget. That stoked Soviet leaders' fears about his attempt to alter the balance of military might between the two world powers.

< 126 >

FIFTEEN
RAF Welford
14 January 1983

Because of an increase in manpower and changes required for GLCM security training, the old wood-frame WWII building on the RAF Welford gun range had been replaced by a new facility complete with indoor and outdoor ranges. RAF Welford and RAF Greenham Common security personnel were competing today with their favorite sidearm: personal or government-issued revolver or semi-automatic. To reduce natural rivalries, no one was in uniform.

Inaugurating the new RAF Welford gun range, seventeen miles from RAF Greenham Common, Wes had been asked by the USAF Security Police Commander, Colonel Marlin Frazier, to chair a three-person jury for this friendly shooting match.

< 127 >

Ear protectors on, Wes watched seven competitors fire at their individually numbered ten-meter targets. After all sidearms were cleared and targets replaced, the range director announced, "Competitors will now move to the twenty-five-meter firing line."

Wes noticed one competitor twist slightly as he fired from the kneeling position, then appear to pocket something after the order went out to unload and show clear. He continued to watch the British RAF sergeant holster his weapon, retrieve his second target, and help police spent brass.

Wes immediately thought he's up to something. But what?

The director announced over the loudspeakers, "The next stage of the competition will be on the fifty-meter course. Please move to the outdoor range after giving your targets to the munitions techs to your rear. Make sure your name, weapon specs, and today's date are on the back of each."

They went outside into a mild but overcast day with only a slight wind, so perfect for shooting. Shooters lined up exactly as they had inside: USAF captain; RAF Corporal; USAF lieutenant; RAF flight lieutenant; the RAF sergeant, whose odd movement Wes had noticed; USAF staff sergeant; and a USAF technical sergeant. Wes knew the Americans and had met the three RAF members earlier in the day.

< 128 >

"This next stage consists of two courses of fire from fifty meters: five rounds from the sitting or kneeling position — your choice — reload, followed by five at prone. You will have ninety seconds. Any questions?" the shoot director asked.

There were none.

Wes focused intently on the British sergeant. Then zinging bullets barreling down the outdoor range jolted his subconscious. As fast as the crack of a violent whip, he was back in Vietnam eleven years earlier —

A shot hit a nearby tree and scared the living shit out of Wes.

"Maybe you was expectin' the little Viet Cong bastard to kiss your sorry flyboy ass?" Gunny scoffed, burning his ears in humiliation.

Gunny Jefferson Deloach was the Marine Corps sniper assigned to babysit Wes during sweeps of several South Vietnamese villages. Deloach had reason to be pissed; he'd told Wes not to be in such a damn hurry.

"Use the vegetation, son. Stay low and move slow."

It was the first and last time Wes chose not to listen to the wily grunt. He had taken two steps into the clearing

< 129 >

when the round screamed past his head. His ass puckered and he hit the ground.

Deloach's reaction was brutal. "Change your shorts and let's get a move-on," he laughed while Wes hesitantly pulled himself to his feet. Deloach then added, "Ah, meanin' no disrespect, sir, but I thought you was intelligence. You best start showin' some, or we be fitting you to a body bag."

Wes picked up food tins that had popped from his field pack. Gunny continued. "These VC snipers are tough little bastards. Raggedy-ass. Barefoot. Live on a handful of rice for three days. But they're like fuckin' leeches, sir. They latch on to ya, they ain't gonna let go 'til they get some blood."

The USAF range officer moved between Colonel Frazier and Wes. "Sirs, we have a problem. Flight Lieutenant Rawlins has one too many holes in his twenty-five-meter target."

Frazier grimaced. He hated anomalies. In his experience, unexplainable facts meant trouble,

< 130 >

trouble when you could least afford it. And why the extra hole got there was probably going to be more important than how.

Firing having ceased and targets collected, the jury headed for RAF Welford Commander and Range Director Major Ronald Driscol's office to evaluate scores. As they entered the building, Wes overheard, "Naw. No officer can beat me." Wes sensed Colonel Frazier hesitate, then continue as if he hadn't heard the insult. Then came derisive laughter and Wes saw the RAF Sergeant being patted on the back, followed by more laughter. He spun and faced Sergeant Landon Haskell.

"What'd you say, Sergeant?" Wes asked, coldly civil.

Haskell stood at attention. "My apologies, sir. I said an officer couldn't win, them spending so much time behind a desk."

Wes glared. The sergeant momentarily panicked. "Sir!"

"That sounds like a challenge," Wes said with a cold smile.

Haskell quickly gained his composure and also smiled. "Maybe. Shouldn't every member of the jury be a shooter?"

Colonel Frazier asked, "What's the holdup?"

"Sergeant Haskell has challenged me to a match," Wes replied.

< 131 >

Colonel Frazier looked at both, then said, "Sure. Why not?"

Turning to Haskell, Wes said, "Challenged gets choice of weapons and range. Right, Sergeant?"

Flustered by the turn of events and not sure how to respond, Haskell shrugged.

Wes turned to the range director. "Is the three-hundred-meter range open?"

Major Driscol smiled. "It's not complete, but it's useable."

Now it was Wes' turn to smile. "High- power rifles at three hundred meters."

The Welford Armory had only eleven such dynamic weapons. Sergeant Haskell grabbed a scoped Lee L42A1 Sniper rifle, leaving Wes to decide among the remaining models. He hefted a Remington M40, the revered Marine Corps sniper rifle. He smiled at Haskell. "Let's rock 'n roll!"

During the half hour the two adversaries were selecting guns and gathering the 7.62x51mm NATO-round ammo each required, the range officers checked the target frames at three hundred meters, raised a red range safety flag on the berm and, at two hundred meters, a red-and-yellow windage flag.

Arriving at the firing line, Wes found the land had recently been leveled. Range officers had busted cardboard boxes to use as ground pads at

< 132 >

shooting slots three and four, where bulldozer tracks were fewer.

Without hesitation, Wes declared, "I want more separation."

It had been a long time since Gunny Deloach had put him through the paces, improving not only his marksmanship but also his resolve. In Nam, his targets were shooting back and the margin between living another day and going home in a metal casket was nailing Charlie center mass.

The British range officer moved the cardboard to positions two and six. At position six, Wes tossed aside the shooter goggles provided and used his boot to make the tire-rutted ground under the cardboard as smooth and comfortable as possible. Frazier volunteered to serve as Wes' spotter. "By the way, can you shoot that thing?"

Wes smiled. "A Marine sniper, and a damn good one, showed me the basics back in Nam." Outwardly cool, Wes swallowed the lump in his throat, hoping he still remembered the drill.

Shooting tables were not available, so Frazier was given a Styrofoam pad to lay on, along with a German tripod-mounted scope for spotting duties.

Wes was given two targets to take to the number six frame. He hung one. The second he gave to the target pit team, who would hang it after the shooters sighted. Walking back to the

< 133 >

firing line, Wes recalled Haskell's unusual movements at the indoor range and the extra hole in Rawlins' target. He asked one of the line officers to count the number of rounds Haskell fired.

They were interrupted by the sound system: "May I have your attention. For safety, all spectators please stay back at least ten meters behind the shooters. Competitors — to repeat — you will be given five minutes and four practice rounds to sight your weapons. Then new targets will be hung and you'll shoot eight rounds at the prone position for score. It will be 'slow fire', so only one cartridge will be loaded at a time. You will have two minutes for that string. Questions?"

There were none.

"Take your positions on the firing line."

Wes placed the M40 gently on the cardboard with its bipod feet extended behind the firing line — an orange line painted on the dirt. He crouched behind the rifle and looked downrange to his target, a softball-sized circle with a V-ring surrounded by concentric circles — outside circles white; inner, black.

He aligned himself with the range and spread out on the cardboard, making himself comfortable, channeling discomforts — including the thought he had to pee — to the back of his brain. He checked as both range flags lay limp, then pulled the stock into his shoulder, closed his left eye and

< 134 >

moved the right eye to the scope. To anchor his position, he spread his legs, turned his feet so they were flat, and forced himself to relax.

He acquired the target through the scope. The fine crosshairs were dancing.

With the firing line ready, both spotters gave a thumbs-up and the shooters began sighting in their weapons with four live-fire rounds.

With a minimum of motion, Wes loaded the first round, breathed out, and relaxed. He felt his pulse at several points in his body, lagging his heartbeat. The crosshairs still hopped in a tiny circle. He let his shoulders go slack, breathed in, exhaled, held his breath, and opened his left eye — the crosshairs were still.

He squeezed the trigger.

"Not bad," Colonel Frazier said, "but you're high and to the right. Just outside the third ring at two o'clock."

Wes clicked elevation and windage knobs clockwise, moving impact point down slightly and to the left. Another shot, this one closer. His fourth round hit the left arm of the V, in the V-ring.

Thank you, Gunny! With the cease fire command, spotters policed brass and pit crews put up new targets.

"Give me two at a time, right here," Wes said, hitting the cardboard with his fist, making an indentation.

< 135 >

Frazier nodded. And then the competition began in earnest.

Wes became wholly focused on the target. Becoming one with the weapon and the round, he mentally sent the shot into the V-ring. He fired, then focused on the next shot, not concerned about the last. Confident the weapon would do its part, he did his. Frazier placed each cartridge perfectly, so Wes never had to think about them. Reach, load, acquire the V, and fire. A near-perfect team, as if they'd practiced together for years.

Breathe out, hold, crosshairs, squeeze, reload. If Frazier said anything, Wes didn't hear it. Only when he reached and no bullet was there did he become aware of his surroundings.

"Cease fire. Safe your weapons, police your brass. Pit crews mark and bring all targets to the firing line."

While Wes waited to find out how he'd scored, two members of the target team huddled with the range director, who confirmed to Wes that Haskell had fired the correct number of rounds.

Major Driscol approached the group. "We have a tie on points. But Colonel Forrest has one more hit in the V-ring than Sergeant Haskell, so he is the winner."

Haskell and Wes examined the targets, then shook hands, but made no comment.

< 136 >

"Colonel Forrest," said Driscol, "don't forget we have more targets to score."

Wes followed him to his office where twenty one targets from the pistol competition, in seven piles of three, had unofficially been scored by two munitions technicians while the two-man match was progressing. Score sheets for that shooter sat atop each pile. Wes noticed that two targets had a short red ribbon attached by paperclip. Judgment calls, he thought.

The official jury — Wes, as chief, and USAF Lieutenant Jerry Lynch and RAF Flight Lieutenant Rory Johnstone — looked at each target and preliminary scores, agreeing with everything except the two red-tabbed targets.

Wes laid the two targets in question on Major Driscol's desk, then pulled a third. He then addressed everyone in the room: "There are two issues here. First, Lieutenant Rawlins had eleven hits on one target — the kneeling target. The second problem is it appears one target of Staff Sergeant Vance only has nine hits, but there may be a double impact. If someone will get me a magnifying glass and an unspent .30mm round, I think we can resolve Sergeant Vance's dilemma quickly enough."

He ran the round thru several holes; at the third, however, the round could be moved around. "I think Sergeant Vance has a double." Everyone

< 137 >

looked closely and agreed one of Vance's rounds had entered a previous hole, elongating one side.

"Now, to Lieutenant Rawlins. It's clear he has eleven hits on his target," Wes said, moving to the piles of targets.

Colonel Frazier offered, "Simple. He should be disqualified."

Wes laid another target on the desk. "This is Sergeant Haskell's kneeling target. He was in the lane next to Rawlins. It has ten hits but note that one is high and to the left. Like he fired too fast returning to his target." Wes sat on the edge of the desk. "I saw Haskell make a furtive move during the kneeling stage, then pocket something — not sure what."

But somewhere, Wes almost said, there was an eleventh shell casing.

So as not to be distracted by the circles, they flipped the target over. Using a 7.62mm round, which Rawlins was shooting in his Browning, and a .38 special-load round, which Haskell was using in his Smith & Wesson M-15, they found one hole in Rawlins' target too large to be from a 7.62mm round, but consistent with a .38.

"What now?" Frazier asked.

"Is something going on between those two?" Wes asked.

"Humph," Major Driscol signaled. "Maybe I can shed some light on that. Rawlins is quite the

< 138 >

ladies' man. I've heard rumors, but no official complaints, about his — ahhh…his extracurricular activities."

Driscol took a deep breath. "I tried to talk to him, but he didn't listen. He's addicted to chasing skirts — married or not. Haskell had an opportunity and I'll bet was simply trying to embarrass Rawlins." Then a shrug, "Maybe Rawlins hit on his girlfriend."

Wes asked, "What sort of person is Haskell?"

"Contrary to his actions today, he's never done anything inappropriate. His Regiment evaluations are outstanding. Was a machine gunner in the Falklands. Well thought of by his peers."

Once results were posted, Wes watched both Haskell and Rawlins check their scores. Unconcerned, Rawlins cheered his second-to-last finish. "At least I didn't finish last."

Haskell, learning he'd beaten the six competitors, but only by a few points, asked to see the targets. Wes thought he'd love to be a fly on the wall to see Haskell's reaction when he saw correction tape over the extra hole in Rawlins' target.

< 139 >

SIXTEEN
St. John's Wood, London
20 January 1983

George Saddler, successful wine merchant and compulsive spender, walked out of his home earlier than normal. He had a seven a.m. appointment with his lawyer before going to work. God, I hate Monday mornings, he thought. Finding the car in the drive, he muttered, "Damn it. I forgot to tell Susan to park in the garage."

He knew that today he had several pressing decisions to make. One was when to tell his wife he was cooperating with law enforcement officials. He was aware of the things that were going to make her unhappy: changing their names, moving to an isolated place, lowering their standard of living. No more Versace labels or Tiffany trinkets.

As the arson inspector had put it to him, the government suspected an organized ring was responsible for numerous insurance-related fires over the last four years, but no conclusive evidence of arson had been found. The fact that each job was so cleverly done was sufficient to believe professionals were involved.

"Damn it," George said, opening the unlocked BMW's door and sliding into the leather bucket seat. His would be their first real lead, and he'd make them pay. No way was he going down for the warehouse fire and the death of those firefighters.

Total immunity and witness protection was his starting position. He'd have his lawyer so he wouldn't incriminate himself.

He began to insert the key into the ignition, then broke into a cold sweat. After a minute of reflection, his breathing slowed and he thought, Nah, I'm safe; only a few people know I'm meeting investigators.

He turned the key with a confidence he didn't feel. The car started immediately. Relieved, he barked a laugh, making his jaw pop. *It'll be a while before that arsonist fucker realizes he won't see the rest of his money.*

Saddler backed out of the drive and headed toward his lawyer's office. His gated community in St. John's Wood had installed speed bumps, much to his chagrin and opposition. The dipshit Association president had actually refused a bribe.

< 141 >

After he was past the exit arm barrier he exceeded the posted speed, turning left on the main road headed toward Kensington.

His mind was sorting out which details to divulge to the London Fire Brigade and what to withhold, when his left front tyre exploded — no, it was more, his steering was gone. He manhandled it to the side of the road and, cursing German engineering, got out and studied the car resting on the mangled wheel. Clueless what to do next, he kicked the tyre hard.

Fuming, Saddler looked up and down the empty section of road and mumbled, "Jesus, I'm screwed. Need to buy a car radio-phone."

He flagged down the next vehicle, a motorcycle, the rider dressed in black.

"Excuse me, sir, but I have a very important meeting," George said in his most pleasant manner. "Can you stop at the next garage and have them dispatch a tow vehicle?"

Instead of speaking, the rider got off his bike and walked to George's passenger door. "Can I have some sort of identification to give the station attendant?"

George thought this odd but got in the car and started looking for registration in the glove box.

Not finding any identifying paperwork, he turned to find the rider filling the doorway, setting his helmet on the roof with his left hand and his right behind his back. Startled, George said, "What?"

After waiting for a car to pass, but blocking George's exit, the rider said, "Get a good look at my face, Georgie. It's the last one you'll see. I'm the bloke you hired to torch your business. The one you was going to rat on — and not finish paying."

With that, Morgan Pritchard pointed to the front with a gloved hand and as Saddler looked out over the bonnet, Morgan pulled a revolver from behind his back, pressed the muzzle against George's left temple and squeezed the trigger. Then, leaning the body toward the console, he pressed the cleaned gun into Saddler's left hand. He checked the road to make sure no vehicles were coming and then, using George's finger, fired a shot into the nearby woods. He replaced one spent cartridge and dropped the weapon to the floor.

On his bike and heading out of London, Morgan thought that he had picked the perfect spot. Wonder what the police will make of the blown wheel assembly — if they even check!

* * *

The next morning's *Daily Telegraph* contained a short article:

APPARENT SUICIDE BY WINE
WAREHOUSE OWNER

The owner of the GWS Warehouse & Distribution, George Saddler of St. John's Wood, was found last evening in his car, dead of an apparently self-inflicted gunshot wound.

On Sunday morning, 19 December 1982, two firemen were killed and two injured, fighting a fire at Saddler's Wembley wine and whisky warehouse. Police and fire investigators would not confirm rumors this latest development was tied to their ongoing investigation of the fire.

A Telegraph inside source said the body was on the passenger side of his wife's BMW. The left-handed Saddler used a US-made Smith & Wesson .38-caliber handgun. This was not confirmed by police.

Morgan smiled after reading the article.
It will certainly stop any notion of that rat turning Queen's Evidence in exchange for witness protection. *Now maybe my life can return to normal.*

< 144 >

SEVENTEEN
Near Mears Ashby
16 February 1983

Morgan returned home late from work and parked the Range Rover in front of his garage at the back of the house. He walked to his back porch, noticing nothing unusual. His mind still on an electrical problem at the hospital, he stepped on the first porch step before spotting the blue airline flight bag, its handles hooked over the doorknob.

He froze, his mind clicking into gear.

Without touching the carrier bag or the door, he used a pocket torch and carefully inspected it for wires, finding none. Controlling his breathing, he put his ear close to the zippered tote to listen for ticking, whirring, or hint of vibration. Ignoring the bag's contents for now, he stood stock-still for five minutes at the bottom of the steps, watching and listening to his surroundings, then retraced his path to the detached garage.

Morgan entered his shop, filled with benches and tools, then walked through the regular vehicle

< 145 >

bay and the one with a grease pit, seeing nothing amiss. Behind a rollout-shelving unit, he opened a hidden door and entered a windowless room behind the shop, packed with electronics.

Going to the monitors, he checked his security system. Verifying a live feed from his motion-activated cameras, he found two recordings. He immediately rewound the tape for the front gate camera.

Three of his eighteen acres were surrounded by a fence with a gated entrance, and his house and garage were shielded by trees and hedges from passersby on the Mears Ashby Road, Wilby. But the only thing the tape showed was his departure this morning, and his return only minutes ago.

He next checked surveillance footage covering the back garden, and what he saw on the tape was perplexing. He watched a man approach the house carrying the blue bag currently hanging on his back door. The time on the tape read 15:47.

Morgan wondered what the hell this was all about. Brave bugger, in broad daylight — so he watched the tape three times. The visitor wore gloves and a dark, hooded sweatshirt. No distinguishable physical features, normal height and weight, nothing unusual about his gait. After quickly crossing the back garden, the man simply hung the bag on the door, left the way he came.

< 146 >

Possible scenarios ran through Morgan's mind, but none seemed plausible or made sense. Returning to the house, Morgan carefully removed and re-examined the exterior of the British Airways carry-on. Setting it aside, he re-inspected the door. Finding nothing awry, he unlocked and entered his home. Inspecting every room, he found everything as he'd left it this morning.

He took the flight bag to his shop and, wearing skintight gloves, cautiously opened it and removed a packet — a sealed yellow envelope, which he opened to find a folder of photographs and a note.

Scanning the photos, he gasped and loudly said, "Shit." The photos showed him at home near the garage; the back of his house; him in the hospital parking lot; one of his sister Mari in her garden in Wales; another of their mother at her school; one of him opening the boot of a Jaguar XJS and of the same Jaguar engulfed in flames; and another with him on his knees beside a BMW's left front wheel well. Saddler's registration plate showed clearly.

He sat down at his desk and thought about the photos. How had a photographer been at these scenes and him not notice? Was he getting careless?

Morgan had dealt directly with the owner of the Jag who could no longer afford the payments

< 147 >

and blown the car on 6 February. He placed the explosive in Saddler's BMW on 20 January. Today was 16 February.

So, someone had been watching him for a month. Fuck! *Where has my brain been?*

Whoever had sent the photos wanted Morgan to understand that he was dealing with a professional, and that Morgan's different skills were known. But why of his mother and sister? Was this blackmail?

Looking at the photo of his home, Morgan removed the gloves, got a pair of binoculars, walked into the back garden and looked toward the woods where he estimated the photographer must have stood. The same direction today's interloper had come and gone. Seeing nothing else obvious, he decided he'd wait until morning to examine the area.

Returning to the shop, Morgan put gloves on again and picked up the note:

Mr. Pritchard, I'm sure these photographs got your attention. Call this number, Friday, 18 February, at exactly 20:00 hours to discuss. Don't need to tell you to use public phone box.
020 9387 0425
GOSHAWK

Morgan determined 020 9387 were dialing codes for a London number in the borough of Westminster, probably Piccadilly Circus or Leicester Square, and no doubt also a public phone.

He grabbed his coat to drive to a public box and call Bolnick, then reconsidered. Maybe not a smart idea. Instead, Morgan grabbed a beer and sat in the living room, knowing that at times like this, his subconscious needed time to contribute. It amazed him that for the first time someone outside the game knew — really knew! — about his criminal activities, and obviously it wasn't the authorities.

Instead of fear, he was intrigued. Instead of panic, he was clearheaded. He decided not to call Ronnie and tell him about the package. Ronnie had as much to lose as he did. Instead, he'd call this guy, this GOSHAWK, Friday night and see what the hell he had to say.

Feeling better, Morgan went to the kitchen for another beer.

< 149 >

EIGHTEEN
RAF Greenham Common
17 February 1983

At noon, Wes, dressed in running gear, left the locker room at the gym and walked up the hill to Hangar 4. The fitness course was a mile-and-a-half lane running east along the south taxiway, around the end of the runway and aircraft parking pads, up the north taxiway, crossing the runway at mid-point and back to Hangar 4.

Wes jogged easily the first quarter mile. His mind settled on the Smith & Wesson used in a murder Monday morning. It was certainly the gun stolen from the American at the December Embrace the Base event. Wes felt sorry for the sergeant — no fault of his, really. However, he should not have walked off base armed without checking with command. In the excitement, could've happened to anyone — even me, he thought, remembering the almost-lost briefcase on his first day in England.

Wes moved along at a good pace. The sergeant was being rotated back to the States to face undetermined punishment. It was a sure bet the Air Force would have to wait until police were finished with the gun — and even closed their case — before it's returned.

Turning north along the end of the runway, a member of the British Regiment wearing combat boots and full backpack passed Wes and shot him the bird over his shoulder. Guess the word got out as to who instigated physical fitness testing.

* * *

Later that day, Wes pulled into the Wing Headquarters parking lot at the same time as Detective Andrew Tidwell. The twenty parking spaces in front of the one-story brick building were usually full, but it was the end of the duty day and several prime spaces were open. The old administrative office space now housed both the American wing staff and the British base commander's office.

"Afternoon, Colonel. Didn't see you at the coroner's jury hearing," said the detective.

"No. Sorry to miss it, but we had some big shots in from Ramstein — reviewing our bed-down status. They flew out an hour ago." Reaching the steps, Wes said, "I wanted to see the process and hear the evidence. I think your coroner system is much different than ours."

Shrugging his shoulders and brandishing a binder, Tidwell said, "There's something in the postmortem report you'll find interesting. Just got it. Can I get copies made for everyone?"

< 151 >

"Come on in. Let's find out."

Inside, Lila Kerr, the British base commander's secretary, met them and agreed to make the necessary copies.

"Summary and attachments only, please," said Tidwell as he and Wes entered the shared British-American conference room. Tidwell took a seat as Wes grabbed some coffee and asked, "I thought the jury briefings were to end yesterday?"

"Yeah, but the coroner, Sir Lawrence McPherson, likes to hear himself talk, so it rolled into today. Thank goodness for Doc Peters. He gets to the point."

"Art Gilbert, our chief civil engineer, thought he'd have to testify, but headquarters needed him so he couldn't leave the base. I heard the backhoe operator had to appear. Speaking of which, when can they restart fence work?"

Tidwell's reply was interrupted when British base commander Group Captain Finley Mackay entered. His outgoing smile and exchanging of pleasantries with several attendees led the way. Then, the US vice wing commander, Lieutenant Colonel Brenda Judd, oozing superiority, entered and swept to the head of the table taking the Group Captain's place. Mackay stopped in bewilderment. He's the one who had called this update meeting. Acting the professional that he

< 152 >

was, he pulled up a chair and sat to Judd's side as if nothing was wrong.

"Welcome, everyone," Mackay began and was rudely interrupted.

"Detective Superintendent Andrew Tidwell of Thames Valley Police has agreed to brief us on what happened at the inquest of the burned body found in the GAMA. You may begin," Judd said, nodding at Tidwell.

Wes looked away from Judd to hide his disgust. He had developed a distrust — no, a dislike — for this pompous woman.

Clearly addressing Mackay, Tidwell began. "The only new information presented was the postmortem report and Coroner Peters' testimony. He confirmed that the gender of the body is male and felt the age range was thirty to forty years. Victim's knees were damaged, one substantially, from an old injury. It's his opinion that the victim was dead before the burning — but I'll get to that in a minute."

Miss Kerr interrupted with copies of the summary and attachment. Several heads followed the slender young woman as she walked around the room passing out the copies.

Tidwell directed attention to a photo on page sixteen.

"See that nick? On the anterior of the fourth vertebra. Doctor Peters believes it was made by a

< 153 >

sharp instrument being thrust into the throat from the front. The notch, angling up and from the right, suggests a right-handed assailant standing in front of the deceased. Doc said the musculature is thin there, so the assailant can be either a man or a woman." Fixing his gaze at Mackay, he continued. "Doc said the nick could have been made by the knife found with the body. It'd have easily cut soft tissue and cartilage, then slid between the third and fourth vertebrae."

Tidwell paused. "We are processing the knife for evidence. See the photo at page eighteen. We found fingerprints, smudged but definable."

"Wow," said Wes. "That changes the investigation."

"Not the investigation, but certainly the scope," replied the detective. "No soot was found in the area of the throat or larynx — soot survives decomp — suggesting death occurred before the body was set afire. On page nineteen you'll see a picture of a lighter found with the body. Victim's pockets were empty; the lighter was wrapped in the body bundle. We're working to discover what we can about it."

He paused and checked his notes. "Doc Peters said there was copious blood on the clothing buried with the body, leading him to believe that an artery had been severed and death came quickly, followed by the burning. O-negative

< 154 >

blood was recovered and tested. Results indicate that the carboxyhemoglobin levels were lower than in typical smokers. Again, suggesting the victim was dead prior to being set on fire."

Now looking at Wes, Detective Tidwell summed up the postmortem report. "Looks like body mutilation by fire, preceded by a murder."

"What's next, detective?" asked Mackay.

"The inquest was opened to record all known facts and evidence as of today. In the UK," he said, turning to Wes, "Coroner's Court is a court of law, with one of its duties being to identify the deceased. Since that hasn't happened, the inquest stands adjourned, seeking further information."

"How long will that take?" Wes asked.

"Oh, it will continue until all circumstances surrounding this death are known. Sir Lawrence now has a good idea as to cause, but no name. Time of death also needs pinpointing, if possible. No need to call a jury at this time. In the interim we have evidence we can process."

"Estimation of time of death?" interrupted Judd.

"The deputy coroner would only venture 'more than twenty and less than thirty-five years ago'. The body was wrapped in a rug and then plastic sheeting — almost air- and water-tight — had good drainage, deeply buried in a relatively dry spot on the downhill side of a stone wall.

< 155 >

These are near-ideal preservation conditions, but still, decomposition is almost complete, even to the rug's cotton fibers. Testing continues."

Tidwell again turned toward Wes. "Back to your question, Colonel Forrest. Sometimes a case will be open for a year before we get a coroner's verdict. Since it appears to be an unlawful death, the coroner's office will be assisting Thames Valley Police in resolving this."

"Our contractors want to resume work," Wes said.

"Thames Valley Police have completed evaluation of the site, but I need to check with the coroner. I'll let you know tomorrow."

"That's good news," Group Captain Mackay said, nodding.

"Except that with the uncertainty," Wes interrupted, "they moved equipment to other sites. At least now they can start returning it."

"How long will that take?" Judd asked, drumming her fingers impatiently.

"They say at least a week to return to full speed."

After the meeting, Tidwell turned to Wes. "Walk me to my car. I've an extra copy of the Coroner's Report for you."

"And why," asked Vice Commander Judd, who unnoticed, was walking behind them, "do you rate a full copy, Colonel Forrest?" Wes

< 156 >

cringed at her tone, but she was already next to him. "I don't think we've met, detective. I'm Colonel Selectee Brenda Judd."

"Actually Colonel, it's my extra copy," Tidwell said. "Wesley has been helpful over the last month and he'll be more effective if he has all the details." Judd grunted and stormed off. "What's her story?"

"She made full colonel ahead of schedule and now commands more respect — even before she pins it on. Commanding it is the only way she'll get it. Sorry, you didn't hear me say that."

"Doesn't Mackay outrank her?"

"When she pins on her eagles, their rank will be the same, but as vice wing commander, she's in a higher position. More powerful."

"Makes things complicated."

Wes nodded. "You have no idea."

Wes watched Tidwell open the boot of his car and look reflectively at the report. "What's your story, Mr. Black?"

"Mr. Black?" repeated Wes.

"Yeah. I don't call an unknown deceased something impersonal — like a number. They had lives, friends, problems, family — so I give them a pseudonym until their true identity is established."

< 157 >

NINETEEN
Wellingborough
18 February 1983

No closer to solving the mystery of the photographs, Morgan drove into Wellingborough, found a spot in the town centre car park and located a phone box on the high street, now deserted because nearby stores were closed. At two minutes to eight p.m., he anxiously dialed the number provided in GOSHAWK's note.

"*Dobriy vecher*, Morgan Pritchard."

"Look arsehole, what's this all about?" Morgan's tension erupted. "Who took those pictures?"

"Good. Straight to the point. I like that. You use cameras to know what is going on, and I do same," Sokolov said.

"Why involve my sister or mother?"

"One good thing about your country, it is a short drive to Wales."

< 158 >

Suddenly claustrophobic, Morgan threw open the phone booth and started to rip out the handset. But his brain said: Stop. Relax. Can't lose contact with him.

After a few deep, controlled breaths, he asked, "What do you want?"

"I have a job. One for which you are perfect. Forgive my mention of Wales, but I need you in a position where you can't turn me down."

"I can turn down any job, you fucker."

"Not if the consequences are great. This job does not require you to kill anyone."

Morgan took another deep breath. "What consequences?"

"If I send those photographs to police — and I have more — you'd be implicated in many ongoing criminal matters — be in deep govno...shit. And there is always your family."

"You leave my family out of this. This is between you and me."

Sokolov now adopted a softer tone. "Let us be positive. I do not want to involve them unless it becomes necessary."

"Why should I trust you? Especially with a name like GOSHAWK."

Morgan heard a chuckle. "That's right. You don't believe in luck. More to the point, this is something you must do. A one-time thing."

< 159 >

I don't trust you and you know it. And when this is over, you arrogant arsehole, I'll hunt you down and...

"What's the job?"

"Like your sister and her friends, my friends want to stop the basing of nuclear missiles at RAF Greenham. I have a plan that will not kill people, but render the base useless."

"How's that?"

"You ever hear of a dirty bomb?"

"They're all dirty," Morgan replied.

"No, you peasant, a bomb that contains nuclear material."

"A nuclear bomb?"

"Wrong again. Standard explosives, but containing radioactive material. When it explodes, surrounding landscape becomes radioactive from fallout — unusable for many years. And in short term, causes panic, disrupts all those American plans."

"So, you want me to explode a bomb like that on the base?"

"Da," said GOSHAWK. "You, along with a few others."

"I've no idea how to build such a device. And I don't have nuclear materials."

"You will receive another package on Sunday, which has answers. There is some urgency because Americans are improving security weekly."

"Will it harm people nearby, the peace camp women?"

"No. It contains only small amount of material. Big unknown is weather, especially wind. Done in right spot, radiation stays on base."

"What's your real interest in the RAF base? Who do you work for?"

"Nice try, peasant. Leave your house Sunday morning…and don't stick around," Sokolov said, disconnecting the phone.

< 161 >

TWENTY
Mears Ashby
20 February 1983

When Morgan arrived home from his River Nene fish camp Sunday at noon, he discovered another airline bag at his door. He again checked the backyard video and gained no new clues to his visitor's identity. But then he checked the recording from his new camera — having installed it in the back-porch light fixture.

He now had several close-up photos of the deliveryman, including the lower portion of his face not covered by the hood.

Inside the bag was a small package containing a key and directions to an industrial estate in Northampton.

Morgan's Range Rover covered the ten miles in record time. The estate was large but nearly empty, so he found the correct unit easily. The personnel door was flanked on each side by rollup garage doors. The key worked.

< 162 >

Inside, Morgan stopped to look around. The unit's rollup door was to his left and parked inside was a two-tone green VW camper. In front, near the back wall, was a chair, and a desk with a large box on top.

He looked inside the VW, but a tarp covered all, and the doors were locked.

Next, he rifled through the box on the desk and found keys for the VW and design and technical information to build the dirty bomb. There was a list of supplies provided by GOSHAWK. And a list of items that Morgan would have to procure: the explosives; a transport vehicle; and a small amount of radioactive waste material from the hospital.

To get some of my skin in the game, Morgan thought. Does this spy know about the malfunctioning alarm system at the hospital? Or is this simply a coincidence?

GOSHAWK's documents explained that nuclear materials inside the VW had been stolen from a processing plant in Siberia. It was intermediate level toxic waste, following reprocessing of nuclear fuel, that had been packaged for burying between layers of impermeable clay. Active elements were primarily Strontium-90 and Cesium 137, beta and gamma emitters, respectively.

< 163 >

He enumerated the lead shielding's dimensions and weights. The Russian stated that a course of action had already been set in motion providing him the necessary cover to approach the base with a vehicle. Another operative — a Scot — would actually drive it onto the base. Those details and an escape plan to be explained later.

Thinking he might need help, Morgan contacted Ronnie Bolnick from an estate pay phone. Because of the importance and secrecy involved, they agreed to meet face-to-face.

* * *

At midnight, Morgan was waiting in a Milton Keynes Tesco Superstore parking lot when Bolnick's limo pulled in. Ronnie got out and jumped in Morgan's Range Rover. Ronnie's response after listening to Morgan's situation was, "I'm here to help with anything you need. But I don't know anything about radiation."

Morgan gave him the specs for a vehicle he needed.

Finished, they approached Ronnie's chauffeured Rolls and he said, "Heard something about the George Saddler investigation. The only thing out-of-sorts with a suicide was the explosive charge in the wheel assembly."

< 164 >

Morgan pursed his lips and nodded slowly. Before ducking into his car, Ronnie added, "Government investigators found out Saddler was behind in both his home and warehouse loans, plus owed money to the Kray Twins crime organization. Since they traced the explosive device to the East End, Saddler has been added to the list of suspected unsolved murders by the twins."

They laughed.

< 165 >

TWENTY ONE
RAF Greenham Common
8 March 1983

Terence Stewart, head of Newbury District Council legal services, gave Colonel Forrest his marching orders. "Remember, you're here only as an observer. You have no authority to act or give instructions. You have anything to say, say it to me," Stewart said.

They were sitting in the lawyer's car, parked to see both the RAF Greenham sentry booth and the main women's camp. It was not yet daylight, quiet, and cool enough for steam to be rising from his coffee. Stewart obviously had a lot on his mind. He initiated no additional conversation.

Be a nice guest, Wes said to himself.

The cloudy sky signaled a cold, damp, and gloomy day. As visibility improved, Wes noticed a large pergola covered with clear plastic sheeting.

< 166 >

Under the roof, several women worked over an open fire, making coffee and breakfast.

The pergola, a caravan, and several tents occupied the land to the right of the base's primary entrance road. There was no activity on the left side of the road where a collection of tents and lean-tos organized around fire pits made a ragtag but peaceful scene. Most of these tents were homemade, multi-colored fabric stretched over tree limbs into igloo and other motley shapes, and tightly arranged to form a core ringed by a bivouac of store-bought, pole-and-canvas tents, and three caravans.

Thirty minutes after sunrise, a forty-vehicle convoy of lorries, vans, and cars started to arrive and park along the Basingstoke Highway. Organized by the Newbury Council under Stewart's guidance, the convoy included one hundred officers and bailiffs from several neighboring constabularies. Their job: Evict the protestors. When officers filled the base entry road and lined up along the A339, Captain Peacock of the Newbury Police Station brandished his loudhailer.

"Morning. Please give me your immediate attention. As you may have surmised, this is an eviction. You have five minutes to gather your personal belongings and move to the other side of the highway."

< 167 >

A protestor exited her tent and yelled, "Hey, you knob heads, you can't do this."

"You were given notice of eviction on 12 January, this year," Peacock broadcast. "You are in violation of that order and will be removed."

The responses were: "Bite my arse!" "Go to hell!" "Fuck off, arsehole coppers!"

The captain watched the total disregard of his order. After checking his watch several times, he was finally able to announce, "Time is up. Officers, make sure everyone is awake and decent. Wear gloves and watch for needles from these hopheads." He wanted to get this done as quickly as possible. They had kept the plan secret, but with so many different offices involved, at least one reporter or photographer probably got word.

Police began to disrupt the campsite to the west of the entrance road, collapsing tents and makeshift huts, jerking plastic sheets off supporting poles, opening sleeping bags and yanking on blankets under which women were hiding or pretending to sleep. Some protestors in various stages of dress moved around assembling personal items and reluctantly following the captain's orders. Others sat defiantly on their kits. One artisan found a large piece of cardboard and wrote "You Can't Evict An Idea". Another penned "Evict Cruise Not Camp".

< 168 >

"How much force are they allowed to use?" Wes asked Stewart.

"As much as it takes. These women have been a pain in the backsides of a lot of people for far too long."

"Fire brigade, move in!" Peacock announced.

Men with fire extinguishers and shovels now moved through the camp, spraying fire pits and covering embers.

Up to this point, while vocal, most resistance had been peaceful — protestors locking arms and singing. But now dissenters clashed with police. One woman threw her blanket onto a still existing fire and its cotton flamed immediately; she was the first arrested. While the blaze was extinguished, three officers carried her, kicking and screaming, to a waiting van and cuffed her to a fixed metal seat.

"Well, I guess I won't be moving out of the Manor House today," Wes said to Stewart, who was intent on watching the proceedings and didn't respond.

In short order, a bulldozer and a payloader came to life with heavy-throttled rumbling and rolled off their trailers. Wes and Stewart got out of the car and walked closer to observe the action.

"If you impede or attempt to block equipment," Peacock announced, "you will be arrested."

< 169 >

Tensions rose at the approach of heavy machinery. Ten women linked arms to build a human fence to protect their tents and property. Two officers walked along the line and poked them in the stomach with a baton. If the protester stood pat she was hit on the side of the knee — bringing her to the ground. Many encamped women now saw the no-nonsense attitude of the police and began moving off the property, while others became more resistant, lying in front of the bulldozer or trying to climb into the cab.

"You bastard," a woman yelled, throwing soup on the nearest officer. Although the soup was cold, the policeman's temper boiled, arresting anyone who looked him in the eye.

"Leave my stuff alone or I'll sue," threatened another woman.

Yet another threw rocks and bottles at every nearby officer. She was subdued and arrested after hitting an officer in the back with a piece of tent framing.

Watching the clearing efforts, Wes turned to Stewart. "Why are they ousting campers on the left side of the road and not touching those to the right?"

"In a word, politics. The Newbury District Council revoked the bylaws of the Commons and is now the landlord of the western side of this road. But the Ministry of Transportation, which

< 170 >

controls the other side, is a massive bureaucracy and hasn't approved an eviction plan," Stewart said. "Today's left-side eviction is timed to coincide with clearing land for a new sewer line."

Women who moved across Basingstoke Highway, or to the tents on the right of the entrance road, were ignored. Protestors were warned, then arrested if they did not move along. Physical resisters were immediately carried to one of the waiting paddy wagons. When four or five women were cuffed inside, they were driven away.

"Where are they taking them?" Wes asked Stewart.

"Newbury Police Station. Most will be held, then released after we finish here today. Guards will be posted so they can't return. The violent and those with priors will be held over to go before magistrates. Probably tomorrow."

The dozer scraped everything into huge piles, then the loader dumped the refuse into waiting tipper lorries. Officers assisted by throwing miscellaneous items — dishes, cookware, stuffed animals, magazines and books — into the loader bucket. When the removal crews encountered a caravan, they cleared around its base, winched it onto a flatbed trailer, and hauled it away.

In front of a small, red-and-white trailer, two Buddhist nuns chanted prayers, beat drums, and

< 171 >

gently hammered bells. When a bulldozer approached, they moved to the main gate, blocking the entrance, and continued their percussive, irritating protest. Two officers attempted to remove the drums, but the women resisted. With assistance from other officers, they dragged the nuns across concrete and rocks to a police van.

Wes watched the nuns' caravan be winched and hauled away. "Where are they taking the trailers?"

"The Council's secure storage yard."

Mari Pritchard, along with two photographers, arrived that morning as the last of the caravans were being loaded. She spoke to several of the displaced women and found that, sadly, for many this removal was the last straw. They had been cursed, had rotten fruit thrown at them, been arrested. But when belongings were tossed in garbage trucks, that was the end of their dream of stopping the cruise missile deployment, of seeing the women's movement triumph over the authorities. The satisfaction they had derived from demonstrating and bringing this issue to the front page of the world's newspapers and the public's eye was not enough to carry on after this brutality

< 172 >

by totally insensitive government forces. Mari reminded them this was also about their children's future — but they didn't stay.

She approached Peacock and asked, "By what right are you doing this?"

Politely, the captain showed Mari a copy of the eviction notice. "If you have influence with these women, please have them go home."

Mari got in the captain's face. "They would love nothing better than to go home to their families," she said, spitting out the words. Then, backing up and softening her tone, she added, "But they are sacrificing their time to ensure a future for their children. And the way to do that is for England not to be a nuclear target."

Ignoring her, Peacock walked away.

"Why are you British men protecting American soldiers by arresting British women?" Mari yelled furiously, then walked toward Stewart and Wes.

"And who are you?" she asked.

Stewart spoke first. "A member of the Newbury Council. Observing."

"So, you are responsible for this civil injustice."

"No. You need to address your complaint to Mrs. Thatcher."

"She'll be standing election soon," Mari said loudly, "and basing nuclear missiles here will be the primary issue that'll get her defeated!"

< 173 >

Turning to Wes, Stewart said, "We're here about sanitary conditions and maintaining open access to military establishments, and they're here protesting basing of missiles. No wonder they don't understand what we are communicating."

Mari overheard and angrily replied, "That's because you are blindly following and hiding behind orders. You're incapable of thought. We're the ones worried about this country's future."

Glad he was in civvies and not his uniform, Wes asked, "What's your name?"

"Mari. What's yours?"

"Our names are not your concern," Stewart interrupted. "Please move along."

"What is your concern? Certainly not the British people," Mari said. Then she shoved him.

In response, Stewart stepped back and nodded to a group of bailiffs, who grabbed Mari. She immediately went limp and fell. A clumsy officer, stooping to get her up, accidentally bumped into another, who stepped on Mari's hand. She screamed and became a whirlwind, flailing, kicking and slashing at everything. She bit the hand of the bailiff who grabbed her wrist. Pulling free, the officer hit her in the face with his nightstick. Bleeding from her nose and mouth, Mari continued to yell obscenities as she was dragged to a waiting van.

< 174 >

Wes was disturbed by the brutality but held his tongue, because this was totally a British operation. Anyway, he was not sure of the right way to handle this situation, but felt brute force was not it.

After lunch, and the observation of twenty two arrests, Wes watched a protestor-free environment be cleaned of debris and vegetation, and surveyors mark a fifteen-foot-wide strip from the base fence to the road.

A Ministry of Defence sergeant approached. "Sir. What are they doing?"

"With the larger number of personnel and buildings being planned, the base sewer line has to be replaced with a new, larger pipe," Wes replied.

Over the next few days, protestors were prevented from returning to the now-cleared site. A backhoe opened a trench and workers removed and replaced the sewer pipe.

On Friday, while Wes moved to a house in the village of Silchester, tipper lorries arrived at the eviction site and dumped large rocks and boulders over the area, eliminating any flat space for women campers on the left side of the main entrance road to RAF Greenham Common.

< 175 >

TWENTY TWO
Northampton General Hospital
23 February 1983

Morgan moved into the hall once he heard the voice of Doctor Chung, head of the nuclear medicine department; this was the opportunity he'd been waiting for. The department offices were on the floor above, along with the medical library, clinical and treatment rooms.

Morgan had spent several hours in the medical library trying to piece together what GOSHAWK was trying to do at RAF Greenham. He now understood the difference between a nuclear explosion and a weapon combining radioactive material with conventional explosives. The explosion, *his* explosion, would disperse the radiated materials and contaminate the GAMA. The medical waste, while adding a small amount of radiation, was primarily to be visible evidence of the disaster, readily seen on TV and in

< 176 >

newspaper photos, causing psychological harm, but not physical unless someone was within the explosive's blast area.

The idea was to instill panic in the public, which in turn would pressure the government to kill the plan to base cruise missiles in Britain.

Walking out of the radiopharmacy, Lee Chung, MD, said, "Hello, Morgan." The greeting echoed in the basement hallway.

With degrees in both physics and medicine, Dr. Chung had been hired six years earlier to improve the hospital's medical physics unit. The idea was to create an enhanced radiation therapy programme for Northamptonshire and surrounding counties. He had designed and equipped three rooms in the basement, away from visitors and patients. First, the radiopharmacy where radioactive medications are prepared and dispensed, including liquid sources injected into patients as imaging agents. The pharmacy included a "hot" area where sources with short half-lives were manipulated.

Then across the hall, off an entrance foyer, two secure vaults had been constructed to his specifications. One, Storage Room Alpha, was for less dangerous materials: low-level radiation elements with short half-lives; lightly exposed items that can be cleaned; and non-reusable items exposed to low radiation awaiting destruction. The

< 177 >

second, Storage Room Bravo, was used for high-level radioactive materials.

"Sir," Morgan said, "glad I ran into you. I need to inspect the electrics in the nuclear storage rooms. It's been a year. You know of any problems or anything I need to be aware of before going in?" Let's see if he knows about the broken entry recorder, he thought.

"Nothing I can think of," Chung said. "There is a defective radiation therapy machine stowed away in Bravo, but it shouldn't affect your work. We've notified the company about it." Then, moving across the hall and into the storage foyer, he added, "But you may have to move the container to get to an outlet or something."

"Whoa! Will I need special protection?" Morgan pretended ignorance.

"No, no. The head of the cobalt-60 teletherapy machine is in a shielded, lead-and-steel container."

Moving toward Bravo, the doctor said, "Come on. I'll show you."

He entered his personal code in the keyless lock and opened the door. "There's the box with the teletherapy head. It's the green one, marked with radiation signage."

"How is it broken?" Morgan asked.

"The sliding drawer that holds the cobalt-60 pellets is stuck and we can't remove the radionuclide source. Normally we remove the

< 178 >

pellets after use and store them in those containers over there along the wall — marked CO above its radiation marker."

"So, I won't need protection in here?"

"You'll be fine. But do not open the container. Cobalt-60 releases gamma rays, highly penetrating electromagnetic radiation." Chung, known throughout the hospital as a practical joker, tried to keep a straight face. "There's about five gray waiting in there."

"Gray?"

"Yeah." Doctor Chung shifted into his pedagogical voice, "How we measure the absorbed energy of radiation. Named after the famed London hospital physicist, Louis Harold Gray. That much exposure is enough to fry you!"

Seeing Morgan's eyes widen, he smiled, "Just kidding. Whilst a full-body exposure to more than five gray can cause death, doses in much smaller amounts are given locally for cancer therapy. But seriously, everything in Bravo is shielded. You won't need protection for what you're doing. The cleaning crew goes in once a week without protective clothing."

Chung walked around the interior of Bravo. "There is a socket behind the machine head container. It weighs over a 150 kilograms, so if it needs moving, use the portable crane in the equipment room."

< 179 >

Needing more information, Morgan asked, "You say you notified the company about the broken machine. Will they come get it soon?"

"No. They'll send an inspector or two first. Since we have one working, it won't be a priority."

As Morgan nodded and began to exit, the doctor opened a drawer in a stainless-steel cabinet and said, "There is one thing more. The fridge in Alpha isn't keeping its cool like it should."

Leaving the doctor in Bravo, Morgan said, "I'll check it, sir."

Walking back to his office, he thought, Who the fuck does he think I am? His own people who use the bloody cooler should check it. But the machine head was a stroke of luck.

< 180 >

TWENTY THREE
Near Stonehenge
4 February 1983

Iain McKenna drove by Stonehenge where, in a few weeks, Druids and Pagans were set to gather around the prehistoric stone circle to celebrate the Vernal Equinox — the beginning of Spring. When a child, his father had told him stories of druids, witches, and human sacrifice. *If only to make me behave, God rest his soul.*

From the A303 he could see a lake of vehicles and caravans. He approached an open gate. A man held up his arm and stepped in front of his rental car. The old man looked like a homeless hippie off the streets of London.

Leaning and getting way too close, the vagabond said, "Hey, mate, you lost? Not many new cars around here."

Uncomfortable, yet resolved to show no fear, McKenna said, "I'm looking for H.L. Farmer."

< 181 >

The strange man laughed and asked, "You got an appointment?"

Someone he couldn't see spoke. "Chill, Skunk. Weeds is expecting him. How about a little less talk."

Skunk sulked away.

A huge man approached and said, "Hey, I'm Little Mac and I'll take you to Farmer. But you gotta park over there, near the copper's car."

After McKenna parked, a policeman climbed out of a vehicle and made note of the number on McKenna's registration plate. Good luck with that, he thought.

Approaching the centre of activity, McKenna saw that H. L. "Weeds" Farmer lived in a faded red double-decker bus, a psychedelic sign on the back proclaiming The Perfect Threesome, with pictures of a frosty pint of beer, a bikini-clad beauty, and a marijuana leaf.

A man he assumed to be Farmer stepped down onto a wooden box which served as the step for the open doorway. He motioned for McKenna to sit under a worn awning attached to the side of the bus. An automobile seat, used as a chew toy by a dog, held a stereo speaker, leaving him choices of a leather club chair, worn and cracked and whose next stop should be a rubbish tip, or either of two metal folding chairs next to a collapsible card

< 182 >

table. After shaking hands, McKenna chose what he judged to be the stronger of the folding chairs.

Weeds had the weathered appearance of a farmer, including the pale forehead. His long graying hair, dried from full days in the sun, was pulled back and secured with a rubber band. His salt-and-pepper beard had apparently not been trimmed since last spring.

Weeds said, "I cultivate, pun intended, the idea of being a farmer. I inherited the family farm, which proved to be worthless except for cultivating marijuana. Tea?"

"Nay, thank ye."

"Don't trust me?"

"Not really. Walking over here, I got high just from the fumes," McKenna said. *I'm a provider not a user*, he thought.

"Probably a good idea — I mean, not trusting me," Weeds chuckled. "Now, what is it that brings you out here?"

McKenna minced no words. "A mutual friend tells me ye be thinking about moving some o' your gang to RAF Greenham Common."

"And of what interest are our movements to you?

"Planned activities in Newbury th' weekend o' Nine April. Could use some strategic distraction."

Weeds studied McKenna. "They're not a gang, and certainly not my gang. They're friends on

< 183 >

holiday and independent travelers. However, as you can see, our allotted four acres are overflowing and some are discussing — with pressure from the local law — where to move."

Scanning ongoing activities, Weeds added, "I'm sure you've heard that the local community thinks we've worn out our welcome. Want us all to leave."

Weeds slowly pulled out a glass pipe and filled it. Taking his time getting it lit, he eventually said, "Let's take a walk."

Surprised, McKenna acquiesced. They wove through a jumping crowd, singing and clapping to a band playing on a makeshift stage. A Jimi Hendrix imitator played guitar, sending out electronic notes mixed with eerie screeching.

McKenna cringed. *How does a' body think that's music?*

Behind the flatbed trailer bandstand were piles of rubbish and a latrine trench. Three portable cabinets, one missing its door, and all probably stolen from construction sites, were supported above the trench by poles. A scantily clad female grabbed a few sheets of newspaper and a scoop of lime and headed into one of the Porta Potties. The smell made McKenna's eyes water. His senses were almost back to normal when they arrived at a trailer bearing a handwritten sign: Snack Shoppe.

"Something to eat?" Weeds offered.

< 184 >

"Nay."

"Trust issues again?"

McKenna turned away.

"How's it going, Cosgrove?" Weeds asked the dowdy person inside, then ordered a bacon sandwich with chips. He looked questioningly at McKenna and received a wordless frown and firm shake of his head.

McKenna, anxious to get down to business, followed Weeds as he moseyed back to his bus and grabbed two beers from a cooler, giving one to McKenna. Weeds eased into the club chair and dug into his sandwich.

"You here to negotiate?" he said between mouthfuls. "When and where we move?"

"I'm 'ere ta talk."

"Money talks."

"Money?"

"Yeah. Money will help pay for cleanup. Lord knows it needs it. This place is a pigsty." Weeds put his sandwich on the arm of the chair. "Establishing a firm departure date will make the government happy — keep cops off our backs. Money helps feed the bands; they entertain the crowd and keep them from rambling into the countryside. Money will also buy some Farmer's herb — the pot at the end of the rainbow, so to speak, to motivate people to wait patiently and then move quickly."

< 185 >

"Aboot what?" McKenna asked.

"I'm thinking three thousand pounds, cleanup, and three more for 'incentives'."

"No way my friend can afford that."

"Okay. I guess we move south to the coast."

"Damn it! Ye can't do that — that's extortion."

Weeds ignored him, taking a long, slow, large bite of his bacon sandwich. "And 9 April is a month away."

After studying the sky and considering the budget, McKenna said, "I can come up wi' thirty five hundred pounds and a bit of China White, but that's it."

"Forty five plus the smokable White stuff. No needles, and it's a deal."

McKenna nodded approval.

"The county wasn't expecting much in the way of cleanup help anyway — happy to be rid of us. But I need cash soon — at least one third by this weekend, or the deal is off."

"Okay, I'll be here next Tuesday wi' me camper and th' dosh."

"Good. We can discuss details when I have cash in hand." Stepping away from the awning, Weeds shouted to the neighboring trailer. "Mac. We're done here. Please escort our guest back to his car."

< 186 >

TWENTY FOUR
Silchester
12 March 1983

The Cricket Club had constructed a jogging trail around the ancient Roman town of Calleva Atrebatum, built around 45 A.D., and adjacent to Silchester. It circled the one hundred twenty acres of the ruins and grounds, visible earthworks, and extensive remains of the old city wall.

Wes finished a two-mile run, getting the kinks out following an all-day meeting in London, and was cooling down as he walked through the village. He was imagining an enjoyable life in this insular British parish.

He stopped suddenly when he saw the slender figure of the British base commander's secretary getting out of a car near the Red Lion, the local pub for Silchester's few hundred residents.

< 187 >

Lila Kerr. Why is she in Silchester? Wes watched, unobserved, as she made several furtive glances, and then entered the pub. Curious, he peeked through the front glass and saw her conversing with a woman with medium-length, bleached-blonde hair. Even though Wes was new to the area, he was beginning to spot the Silchester look — country-dressed gentlemen and ladies — and the blonde didn't fit. She was someone he'd not seen before and dressed like London.

Wes strolled home and showered, but couldn't get Lila off his mind. He'd noticed she'd been very aware of him lately, overly so, interrupting what she was doing to be pleasant. But the week before, he'd walked into her office to find her talking softly on the phone, facing the sidewall and so focused she didn't notice him. When she finally did, she hung up quickly.

"Ummm...how can I help you, Colonel?" she'd asked, sounding embarrassed.

When he left after his meeting with the base commander, she again acted peculiar. She was very attractive, but Wes had never had an opportunity to be alone and talk with her outside of work.

* * *

< 188 >

"Ms. Keating, it's good to finally meet you," Lila said to her blonde companion.

The women were shown to a table in the Lion's back dining room, where they ordered wine, then the reporter got down to business: "I want to personally thank you for the information you pass along. It has aided *The Guardian's* research immensely. And please, call me Ruth."

After wine arrived, Keating said she had a few things of importance to discuss.

"The Campaign for Nuclear Disarmament plans a revival of an old tradition," she started. "In the late 1950s and '60s, the CND organized Easter Marches from London to the Atomic Weapons Research Establishment in Aldermaston. But they grew too large, and the logistics became a nightmare, so the protests were abandoned."

After a sip of her wine, Keating continued. "They're going to revive the idea. As with last December's Embrace the Base, they'll get people to stand together in a fourteen-mile-long human chain, this time from Burghfield to Aldermaston to near RAF Greenham."

"That's a long way!" Lila said, wide-eyed. "When?"

"April First, Good Friday will be the day," Keating said, pulling out a poster and unrolling it. "I hear they're hoping Mari Pritchard would organize the Greenham effort."

< 189 >

"She's gone home to Wales for a while. Moving between her husband's farm and her mother's while she mends."

"Mends? What happened?"

"I guess you didn't hear. She was arrested and billy-clubbed during the Peace Camp eviction, then taken to hospital because of her injuries, later to Newbury Police Station. A CND attorney got her out on bail the next day, but she needed to heal — mentally and physically."

Lila stared at the reporter. "What do you want from me?"

"I want your eyes and ears on base. Let me know what's happening."

"I'll do whatever I can — as usual," Lila said. "When I agreed to help, it was with the assumption of nonviolence. I saw what happened to those guards in December and was relieved when none were hurt." After swirling her wine for a few seconds, she continued, "The bonfire was okay with me because we burned the lorry on property we basically gave to the Americans."

Lila took a sip of her wine, then said, "My boss went out on a limb to hire me — gave me a chance. I don't want to contribute to ruining his career."

Keating smiled and patted Lila's hand. "For the April First event, husbands and male supporters are being recruited to be along the

< 190 >

route and intervene in case of trouble. It'll be a peaceful protest — unlike the peace convoy."

"Peace convoy?"

"I assume you heard about the Travellers' Camp near Stonehenge?"

Lila nodded.

"Well, it's become a music and drug festival. The locals are sick of it and are trying to force them out, but the more they push the more entrenched the mix of Gypsy Travellers and drug dealers and users become."

"Yes, I read about it in the papers."

"What's not in the papers is that they have some financial backing and are planning a move — Newbury is on their list," Keating said.

"I thought the local police were discussing forcing them out," Lila said.

"They tried in years past and it didn't end well. Confrontations occurred, with photographers everywhere looking for a story. Besides, they have permission to camp on a small portion of that land. So, most charges were brought against the police — for brutality. Now they keep the press at bay, contain the hooligans, and hope they run out of drugs and move on."

Lila broke a minute of reflection. "Why are you staging the protest on Good Friday?"

< 191 >

"Easy. Politics and religion. CND leadership wants to make a nonviolent statement during a peaceful time for Christians."

* * *

Interest and curiosity overcame Wes, so he returned to the restaurant. Entering the Lion discreetly, he checked the bar and then the main dining room, not seeing Lila or the blonde. Getting a half-pint, he glanced into the back room and saw them at a corner table. Although part of him felt uncomfortable spying, the mystery compelled him. He took a stool at the bar, where he could watch the exit from the dining room.

Wes had been in the pub only a few times; nevertheless he'd seen several of the patrons around the village. It was built in the seventeen hundreds. Making it friendly were low oak beams and dark wood furnishings, intimate tables, and sofas by a large inglenook fireplace stacked with plenty of firewood in the recesses. He relaxed, had a beer, and watched. A few familiar faces smiled and nodded in his direction.

Eventually the blonde headed for the door. Wes got a good look at the mystery woman's face when she walked through the pub. Within minutes, Lila followed her. Wes reacted without

< 192 >

thinking, stepping toward her and gently asking, "Lila?"

She stopped and stared. Speechless. "I'm sorry," Wes said. "I didn't mean to startle you. Can I buy you a drink?"

"Yes," she stammered. "Yes, of course, but I need to go to the loo first," and turned away before he could respond.

Wes found a table with a view of the back patio and waved when he saw Lila looking around.

She walked over and he apologized again, but now composed, she said, "I was just surprised to see you here, and I have been drinking wine on an empty stomach."

Wes jumped on that and they agreed to have dinner at the pub.

When Lila ordered more wine, Wes asked, "Are you driving?"

"Why? Do you think I'm drunk?" Lila asked, defensively.

Apologizing again, Wes said, "Look, this has started out all wrong. Can we begin again?"

Lila seemed to relax. "Sure."

After ordering, she asked, "There is something I don't understand. You are a Lieutenant Colonel. But they say Colonel."

Laughing, Wes said, "That's us indifferent Americans — too lazy to say Lieutenant Colonel in

< 193 >

conversation, so we shorten the title. The full rank is used in writings or at formal events."

For the next hour, they shared a chicken, mushroom, and leek pie, and talked about safer issues — avoiding anything controversial. Lila volunteered that she had met earlier with a vendor who wanted to sell her product in the base exchange, and wanted to know the base commander's role and influence in such things.

"Normally, I get a free dinner out of these consultations. Only drinks tonight." Laughing, Lila said, "She doesn't have a chance."

Wes laughed with her, but what she said didn't sit well with him and he didn't know why.

< 194 >

TWENTY FIVE
Northampton General Hospital
16 March 1983

Entering the electrical shop, Morgan ran into his supervisor, Robert Bowen. "Morning, boss."

"Wh'cha doing for St. Patrick's Day?"

"Well, I'll wear a bit of green tomorrow to work, then later, have some Irish grub and a few Guinness."

"Did you hear that the Grand Marshal for New York's parade is none other than Michael Flannery?"

Morgan shook his head. "Selling 'The Troubles' in America."

Bowen dropped the subject and looked at the schedule chalked on the wall. "I see you've scheduled inspections in Alpha and Bravo on a Saturday. Why?"

< 195 >

"It'll be nice and quiet. I like to do those inspections when nobody's traipsing in and out and interfering."

"I'd want the whole world there if it were me — in case I got radiated. But I get your point. Anything you know needs attention?"

"Dr. Chung told me about a few things."

Bowen rolled his eyes and headed toward the door. Then he looked back over his shoulder, adding, "No money for overtime, so watch your timesheet."

"No problem, boss. But remember, I go on holiday after Easter."

< 196 >

TWENTY SIX
Northampton General Hospital
26 March 1983

Morgan was standing in the bed of his MAN truck, pushing the tarp forward, uncovering the metal framework, when a grit truck passed outside. He'd turned out the primary lights but was unsure if he was visible by the emergency lighting.

The salt-and-sand mixture had barely settled when Ronnie Bolnick pulled in and parked alongside him. They were in the basement loading dock for Northampton General Hospital, below area E that housed the Nuclear Medicine Department.

"Nice night for a theft," Bolnick said. "Everybody's bundled up at home. There's more snow predicted for the a.m."

< 197 >

He patted the side of Morgan's truck. "How'd this turn out?"

"Great, thanks to your contacts in military surplus. It's one of those VW and MAN collaborations."

In Morgan's tour of the nuclear medicine storage areas, he had located everything he'd need for the heist. He removed a hand pallet mover from the storeroom and rolled it to Storage Room Bravo. Bolnick pointed to the large yellow-and-black radiation hazard warning. "Do we have to do this?"

Morgan simply nodded. He annotated the sign-in sheet as a follow-up inspection and entered his personal code, but the pad started flashing. Stepping back in surprise, he read IMPROPER CODE. He felt sweat on his brow — a new sensation. GOSHAWK, you bastard, Morgan thought, when this is over, you're a dead man! Then he took a deep breath, relaxed, and slowly reentered his personal code. He heard a soft clink and Bravo's door unlocked.

"Why sign-in?" Bolnick asked.

"In case something goes wrong, makes it easier to explain why I'm down here."

Before entering, Morgan grabbed two radiation badges, clipped one to his coveralls and handed the other to Bolnick. He next checked the 24/7 monitoring meters which would send an

< 198 >

automatic warning to security if triggered by harmful radiation levels. Finding the meters working fine, Morgan sighed with relief. The graph paper printout showed no radiation spikes since the last inspection.

He measured the green lead-and-steel container thinking it would fit in the truck. Using the pallet mover, Morgan and Bolnick pulled and pushed the shielded cobalt-60 teletherapy head to the recessed dock. Next, they moved one of the three containers of cobalt pellets to his truck. Morgan's portable detector read slightly above normal background, which he didn't mention to Bolnick.

They returned to Bravo and this time moved two lead boxes, at thirty-four kilograms each, to his truck. Documentation said they held used syringes, needles, and wires contaminated with Caesium-137, a powerful radioisotope with a thirty-year half-life that was awaiting disposal. They secured the load with rope and covered the bed again with its tarp. Bolnick gave Morgan his badge and left.

Back in the foyer, Morgan altered the Bravo inventory sheet to show that a disposal company had taken possession of the boxes of nuclear waste and the vault only contained two containers of cobalt pellets. The machine head was not on the inventory, so that made it easy — for now. He'd

< 199 >

say it was not there when he inspected, figuring the hospital would assume it had been picked up. Besides, by the time they discovered otherwise, he'd be long gone.

After returning the hand truck to the equipment room, he replaced the device that recorded the date, time, and code for every entry into Bravo. It had been broken for over a month, but no one had shown any urgency to have it fixed. One would think having no record of the comings and goings of staff and the cleaning crew should've sparked someone's interest.

He ran a test which, as designed, recorded the date, time, and his code, then returned the two radiation badges.

In Storage Room Alpha, he checked the fridge, found a pinched and leaky door seal, making a mental note to put that in his report. Let someone else order parts and make the repairs. He locked up and drove off with his radioactive prizes. Next: the fun part — putting the puzzle together.

< 200 >

TWENTY SEVEN
London, MI5 HQ
31 March 1983

Agent Elliot Knight fumed in his MI5 office. He should have been thinking about what he was going to get his wife for their anniversary. But he couldn't get comfortable in his new ergo-something-or-other chair. The arm had broken on his old, red, cracked leather monster — that fit his bum ever so nicely — but then some twit ordered this new-fangled modern piece of crap. He wasn't sure whose spine it was supposed to fit, but it wasn't his. And it looked ugly next to his enduring, scarred, and welcoming wooden desk. There came a soft knock at his solid oak door.

"Wanted to see me, sir?" It was young Glendon Brown, new in K Branch.

"Yes, come in Brown. Have a seat. How do you like doing research?"

< 201 >

"Boring." Then remembering who he was speaking to: "Sorry, sir. Maybe it's just slow right now. Been vetting BBC employees. I'd like to get in the field."

"Vetting the BBC?" Knight feigned surprise.

"Yes sir, they gave us lists of organizations — subversive organizations in their opinion — and names. We look for any connections or adverse information. They use it when individuals are being considered for hire or promotion."

Toying with his pen, Knight nodded sagely. "Brown, I have a favor to ask. While you're running names, there are a couple I'd like to include." Knight handed him a list.

"Mari Pritchard and Katelin Nagy," Brown read aloud. "Anything I should know?"

With no response from Knight he asked, "Sir, may I ask what this concerns?"

"Don't want to know too much now, do we?" Knight said, raising an eyebrow, then continued, "Briefly, the women activists at RAF Greenham Common have an embedded Russian spy and the CND is having an event there on Good Friday. There are also indications that something is going to happen with those Travellers at Stonehenge and it might involve the base. I want backgrounds, any mention in reports — anything you can dig up on the two women. I already have files on most of the

< 202 >

pothead gypsies, but update the file on Henry Weeds Farmer. Weeds is probably a nickname."

* * *

By the next morning, Knight had decided to take his wife on a long weekend trip to Paris for their anniversary. She'd love another visit to the Musée d'Orsay.

Brown opened the door at the same time he knocked and dropped a file on Knight's desk. "Sir, you're not going to believe this: two reports dated within the last fortnight."

Knight skimmed the papers, one from his own K Branch and one from F Branch. K Branch was the largest department in Five, responsible for investigations involving Soviet operations. F Branch conducted surveillance of extremist political parties.

Mari Pritchard's name appeared in a CND phone tap report, mentioning activities at RAF Greenham Common. Katelin Nagy and a Morgan Pritchard — same last name as Mari — had been contacted by the same Russian controller who had been communicating with Nagy. The detail tying all three together was the mention of the Free Festival at Stonehenge.

"Odd name, GOSHAWK," said Brown.

< 203 >

Knight, tapping the top of the old desk with his index finger, said to himself as much as to Brown, "What connects those three to that sorry lot on the Salisbury Plain? I know Nagy has made prior contact with that Russian, but Morgan Pritchard's name is new. I forgot to mention, Mari Pritchard is, in fact, married. To a Myrddyn Griffith, Llanrwst, Wales."

Patting the reports, Knight said, "Good job, Brown — keep searching. You're earning kudos."

After Brown left, Knight stroked his chin and said to the room, "We need to find that spy."

< 204 >

TWENTY EIGHT
RAF Greenham Common
1 April 1983

At a little past noon, Katelin Nagy approached the cut in the RAF Greenham fence. The sky was cloudy, but rain was not forecast. She avoided detection by anyone inside the base by creeping alongside the thick shrubbery. "Opal. This is Krystal. Status?"

"Katelin...ah...sorry. Krystal. Two cop cars still at Orange. Over."

"Okay to move?"

"Roger that. Officers out of vehicles."

Another woman pulled the triangular cut open and Katelin sprinted the twenty yards to the back door of Hangar 6. It was unlocked, as promised. She signaled for the others to follow.

< 205 >

Contractors used this hangar for storage of supplies needed within the next few days or weeks. Katelin directed women to move boxes and equipment, clearing a place for the picnic. They found wooden sawhorses and sheets of plywood to serve as tables. Two photographers were already taking file photos, prepping for the big event. Katelin located a painting contractor's equipment stash — tarps, dropcloths, ladders, paint, and brushes. Then her walkie talkie crackled.

"Krystal, this is Jade. Got another group ready."

Katelin walked to the back door, looked out the small window and saw heads peeking over the bushes outside the fence.

"Opal?"

"All clear."

"Amber?"

"All clear."

"Okay Jade, send 'em through. But next time tell 'em to keep their heads down."

Katelin watched Joan, A/K/A Jade, run to the fence and pull back the cut section allowing eight more women to pass through and run to the hangar. One woman wearing a teddy bear costume didn't duck and the ear got caught in the fence. Others were carrying their artistic costumes, to be donned inside. After the slight holdup, all

< 206 >

proceeded into the hangar and Jade closed the flap in the fence, returning to the bushes.

A woman with long black hair, wearing an explorer shirt with all pockets stuffed, and carrying a bag of food, asked Katelin, "How many we expecting?"

"Maybe thirty in the hangar for the picnic, hopefully most in costume. Then maybe fifty coming over the fence to get security's attention."

Plywood tables were now in place and Katelin told the woman to place the food on a table and to find anything they could use for seating.

Katelin had been at Yellow most of the day and had not participated in the fourteen-mile human chain from RAF Greenham to Aldermaston to the Royal Ordnance Factory near Burghfield, but those who had were full of stories.

"Did you see Julie Christie? I did. Got close enough to smell her perfume."

"Did you see that small plane flying over Aldermaston? Trailed a banner reading CND – Kremlin's April Fools."

"Yeah. Bet the CPS fucks are behind it."

"CPS?"

"Yeah, Coalition for Peace and Security led by that arsehole Julian Lewis. He wants more nukes in the UK. He's in Thatcher's back pocket!"

< 207 >

TWENTY NINE
Barnet, North London, UK
Good Friday, 1 April 1983

Nikolai Sokolov awakened from a deep sleep, looked at the clock—1:33. Who the Hell is calling me at this early hour?

He snatched the phone from its cradle. "Hello?"

"Velikaya? Peter Velikaya?"

"Yes."

"This is Inspector Woods of the Metropolitan Police Department. There is a problem at the Barnet Library and we need your assistance. How long will it take for you to arrive?"

"Wait a minute. What kind of problem?"

"Too complicated to discuss over an open line. How soon can you get to the library?"

"Thirty minutes."

Sokolov only heard a click in reply.

A wary Sokolov/Velikaya found the parking lot filled with fire and police vehicles. Head of Library, Hillman Jackson, met him at the front door. "Sorry to call you in, Peter, but we have had a fire and a robbery."

< 208 >

Turning to another man, Jackson said, "This is Inspector Woods of the Metropolitan Police." After shaking his hand, Velikaya followed them to the manager's office where they took seats.

Woods got right to the point. "Mr. Jackson has been telling me you installed a secret camera security system."

Velikaya looked at his boss. Jackson nodded, then said, "Inspector, let me remind you that Velikaya is our Chief Librarian for Special Collections. Now tell Peter what we have."

Woods gave Jackson a nasty look, then said, "The simple truth is the library was robbed tonight. The thief lit an accelerant in a dustbin starting a fire that set off an alarm which summoned the fire service. During the excitement he must have escaped with the painting." He stared at his hands, and then continued, "Mr. Jackson thought your system might possibly have captured the thief."

After a few seconds of thought, Velikaya said, "I wanted to install a system on the lower level because I often store donated and purchased valuables there. Mr. Jackson concluded it was too expensive and turned down my request."

"What made it expensive?" asked Woods.

"The motion detector."

"Until," Jackson interrupted, "we had two valuable books taken from the Rare Book Room. I

< 209 >

suspected it to be a staff member and authorized Peter to set up his system. One in Rare Books and another in the hallway leading to the Board Room."

"So," Inspector Woods said, "I am assuming you collect what the cameras record on tape."

"Yes," said Velikaya. "I preserve the last four weeks worth of video."

"Is it possible for you to review the tapes now? It will help while I investigate and look for anything suspicious."

"But it's Good Friday!" Jackson complained.

"Do you want your painting found?" Woods snapped.

"Of course." Then turning to Velikaya, he said, "Peter, I will make sure you are reimbursed for your time."

"What time did the fire alarm occur?" asked Velikaya.

"At 11:07 pm."

"And what exactly was taken?"

Jackson answered. "The Lawrence painting from the Board Room."

In a small room off his work space, a curious Sokolov/Velikaya reviewed tapes for the approximate times and found footage of the intruding thief leaving the board room with a

< 210 >

painting. He knew it would be the Sir Lawrence portrait of Thomas Lister donated to the library by a thankful benefactor and valued at over two hundred thousand pounds.

The tape showed a thief, dressed in black with a hoodie practically covering his face, bringing the painting to the rear employees entrance, placing it inside a canvas bag, then heading back upstairs. The intruder moved a dustbin near the front door, very close to a heat sensor, took a small bottle from his pocket, and squirted a liquid onto the trash inside. He tossed the container into the bin and followed it by a lit match.

The thief then huddled with his prize near the rear door and waited until the alarm sounded, at which time he opened the door and left the building quickly, carrying the painting.

Sokolov used the edit/pulse functions on his machine to stop and review particular frames. The hallway camera had managed to catch a few images of the intruder's face as he looked around waiting for the alarm. Sokolov admired the thief's tactics. Not a bad operation, he thought. Using an attached printer, he printed a photo of the clearest shot, and went up to deliver it to the inspector.

Arriving at the manager's office, he entered and handed over the print to Inspector Woods. Woods looked at it, then took off, slamming the office door behind him.

< 211 >

Sokolov asked his boss, "Why do you think the thief set the fire?"

Mr. Jackson thought for a minute. "So he could get out at the alarm?"

"Exactly. At closing, he was inside, hidden. He had obviously cased the library. We need a camera covering the entrance."

Velikaya almost said, "Have you ever thought about a night guard?" But such a person would interfere with his nocturnal exploits, so he said nothing.

Mr. Jackson laid his head back and stared at the ceiling, thinking.

After what seemed a long time, Velikaya said, "Sir?"

Jackson, a devout advocate of civil liberties, sternly looked at him. "No. Using cameras in areas where we have valuables is one thing, but we will not watch the general public without cause."

* * *

RAF Greenham Common Air Base

4:00 pm: "Krystal to Yellow. We're set. Move 'em in."

"There's an issue. Stand by, over."

Issue was an understatement. Originally somewhere between twenty and thirty women

< 212 >

were to scale the fence, thus alerting security as they headed to Hanger Six to join the picnic in progress. But the insult on the plane's banner slandering the CND by saying they were the Kremlin's Fools, angered many into joining the base invasion. A hastily drawn plan sent people to the front gate and Orange and Green Camps, with instructions to obstruct traffic and cut or climb fences. And now, over seventy women were headed to the area behind Hanger Six.

* * *

The Wing Command Post called the front gate. "What are you doing?"

"Trying to stay awake."

"Can't you hear all the noise?"

The airman opened the guard house door. Only then could he hear yelling in the distance. "What the hell's that?" Then he heard sirens from several approaching police cars.

"The bitches are rioting," said the controller.

"Whatcha' mean?"

"They're coming over the fences behind Hanger Six. A group just arrived at the contractor's gate, another near the gate at the end of the runway. They will surely be raising hell at the main gate soon."

< 213 >

Just then a USAF patrol car pulled up to the gate. "Reinforcements," the sergeant said as he and two others got out of the car.

"Darndest thing," the cop said, as if nothing else was going on, "Charlie called me from Hanger Six a few minutes ago. He had gone to investigate a reported burglar. Said women were dressed as bears and Easter bunnies and chickens, sitting around eating, waiting to be arrested."

Taking off toward the front gate, the sergeant said, "Must have been in there a while."

Then, approaching the gate, he yelled, "Here they come."

Minutes later: "Krystal, this is Jade. Got a large group here."

Katelin looked out the hanger's back window to see women lined up all along the outside of the fence, making no effort at concealment. Some of whom, foolish enough to disregard the barbed wire, were trying to climb over. She directed women in the hanger to take ladders and tarps outside.

Police vehicles pulling in around the building with sirens and flashing lights increased the women's haste and confusion. Ladders were tilted against the fence, some even thrown over to women waiting on the other side. Seeing the police arrive, many turned away from the fence and headed toward the women's camp.

THIRTY
Reading
4 April 1983

Reading traffic was heavy and slow, but Lila Kerr finally found a spot in a car park three blocks away and walked to Cross Street. The narrow pedestrian road off Broadway was quaint: many small, brightly painted shoppes with fussy window dressings on one side of the street; the other side with an entrance to Marks & Spencer took up much of one block.

The cheerfulness ended at Number Nine, a three-story brick building with flats occupying the top floors. At street level, the decade-old dark green paint was now peeling, and window signage had been partially scraped away almost obscuring the word Hairdresser. Sheets of newspaper were taped on the inside of the glass so no one could see the interior. The space carried no indication it was the Reading office for the Campaign for Nuclear Disarmament.

Closed on Mondays, Lila opened the office door with a key given her by Winnie. When she flipped the switch, only half the overhead lights came on. The room was large with a high ceiling. Half-filled bookcases lined one wall and boxes and materials cluttered the other. Old campaign and marching posters, still attached to staves, leaned against the walls. Lila found it depressing.

Following a snakelike path through junk stacked on the floor, she wove toward the rear, almost stumbling over a hidden mop. As Lila turned on a desk light, the phone rang. She jumped and dropped her purse. Reaching for the phone, she saw this sign and stopped:

Let all calls go to the answering machine. Return your messages swiftly, then delete.
— Winnie Ashford, Office Manager

From the speaker, Lila heard a lady complain about the Good Friday and Easter activities that occurred near York. The faultfinder left a number.

Winnie had asked her to update CND membership information, and also listen to phone voice recordings and leave any comments for her.

< 216 >

She hit play on the machine and leaned back into the comfortable but well-worn office chair. Her mind wandered to Wes Forrest. He'd been cordial since they'd met at the Red Lion — but nowhere near as friendly as he had been there. Was he interested in her or not? She couldn't tell.

Then a message caught her attention:

> "Congratulations on the Good Friday demonstration. Very well organized, fun, and productive. Special thanks to the CND helper at RAF Greenham airbase, Mari something. She was helpful and knowledgeable. Need more like her.
> WELL DONE!"

Several more messages conveyed congratulations, a few of which mentioned Mari Pritchard by name. Lila was pleased; although she had not participated that day, she'd helped Mari prepare. Then she heard another female caller:

> Yes, hello? This is for the head of the CND office in Reading. I've been trying to contact Mari Pritchard for several days and can't reach her. I need to pass on some information I heard over the weekend. According to Bob, one of the Travellers at Stonehenge, they are moving to Newbury

< 217 >

and RAF Greenham soon. You may know that, but he also said "extra drugs are coming in on Friday", and "sledgehammers," and something about "invading the base" soon, possibly over this coming weekend. He mentioned "a big surprise for the Americans", but no details. Thought —

The message cut off.

Heart pounding, Lila replayed the incomplete message twice. Her boss, the British base commander at RAF Greenham, was in enough trouble because of previous destruction and violence at the base. Not knowing how to contact Mari, she rang Winnie for advice. Getting voicemail, Lila asked the office manager to call the CND office ASAP.

While she waited, "a big surprise for the Americans" was all she thought about, and caught herself chewing on her nails, something she hadn't done in years. She couldn't tell her boss, but she needed to tell someone. Wes Forrest!

She called his office. The American Wing Commander's secretary answered the phone. Lila said she represented a Reading merchant with information of compelling interest to Americans at RAF Greenham. The colonel was out of the office

< 218 >

and Lila was put through to his answering machine.

Later, Lila was unsure if she'd done the right thing, but she felt better. Someone is warned. What they do is up to them.

The CND rosters were very much out-of-date and contained errors, including misspelling her middle name — May versus Mae. She made pen-and-ink changes using information available. Winnie had not called by the time she had to leave.

* * *

"Forrest, why the hell didn't you bring this up at the staff meeting yesterday?" Vice Wing Commander Judd asked testily.

She had called Monday's meeting, ostensibly to thank everyone for the fine job they'd done over Easter weekend, but as head of security it was clear to Wes she'd really wanted to gloat. Praise to get praise! After Good Friday, no one had even tried to get on base. A line of peaceful women had protested near a remote section of fence, but traffic through the Main Gate went undisturbed. Judd's self-adoration made him want to puke.

Holding back sarcasm, he replied, "Because I didn't have the message until late yesterday."

< 219 >

She reached across her desk. "Let me see it," she said icily. Wes handed it over and found himself questioning his decision to come to her.

While technically the same rank as Wes, Lieutenant Colonel Judd was a fast burner, selected for Full Colonel a year earlier than normal rank progression, but still a Lieutenant Colonel until she pinned on the new rank. She was also the biggest ass-kisser he'd ever met. If that's what it takes to get promoted early, Wes would wait and do it on schedule.

Judd silently read the information he had jotted down; then read it aloud, as if Wes hadn't written it:

". . . for head of Reading CND... can't reach Mari Pritchard... heard over the weekend... Stonehenge Travellers moving to RAF Greenham... extra drugs... invade the base...big surprise for the Americans... no details." Judd looked up at Wes. "Is this the exact message?" she demanded.

"The highlights of a voice message left for me."

"Who is Mari Pritchard?"

"I don't know. But the person who left the message sounded British." All of a sudden, the name connected in Wes' mind. Mari. The woman hurt during the front gate eviction.

"Well, I haven't heard anything about those Stonehenge dope fiends moving here. Have you?"

"Well, yes, someone mentioned it."

< 220 >

Both her hands dropped to the table. "Who?"

Damn! Me and my big mouth. Wes shifted uncomfortably. Can't mention MI5. She'll want to know why I'm meeting with them. Piss on her.

"I'm not at liberty to say."

"Not at liberty to say? Forrest, you know I can order you to tell me anything and everything."

"Yes ma'am." *But you haven't got the balls.*

"So. Who. Was. It?"

"I was mistaken. It was about something else."

Judd's jaw tightened. After five seconds' glaring, she looked back at the note. "This is to the head of the Reading CND office. How'd you come by it?"

"An anonymous caller, ma'am."

Judd slapped the flat of her hand on the desk. "Damn it! Colonel, you brought this…this…whatever it is, to me. " She wadded the paper and threw it at him. "Expecting me to do what?"

"I don't know. Get ready for these… people to move in? Maybe prepare for something bad to happen this coming weekend?"

"You've got to be kidding. You bring a note from you-won't-say-who, about you-don't-know-what, won't say how you got it, and you expect me to react to it?" Judd stood, positioned her knuckles square on the desk, leaned into them until they were white, and hissed. "Colonel, I

< 221 >

don't know what your game is, but this is bullshit! We sustained minor damage on Friday and nothing happened Easter weekend and nothing will happen this weekend. I have my ears to the ground, and I have control of this situation."

Judd marched around her desk; Wes backed toward the door. "Forrest, you may have Colonel Rogers believing you're really smart — a golden boy — but you don't fool me. You're nothing but an opportunist." She raised her hand and pointed. "Get your ass out of here. I don't want to hear another thing about this."

Telling Judd had not been a good idea, he thought. Should've sat on it. Maybe gone to security police. Colonel Frazier. Or Thames Valley Police. Wes gave a half-assed salute that said without words exactly what he was thinking. *Fuck you very much. Been chewed out by better officers than you'll ever be.* He left her standing, eyes flashing. He was unsure what to do next.

But one of her questions got him thinking about the call. The person, a female, did not give a name, but there had been something about the voice. He'd heard it before. And why was he called?

Exiting Headquarters, he saw Lila Kerr's car and it clicked. Shocked at his thought, he said out loud, "No. It couldn't have been her."

< 222 >

THIRTY ONE
RAF Greenham
7 April 1983

Weeds Farmer walked the three rows to Tally's tent. "Magician, I want you to lead tomorrow's convoy. Put Doc at the rear with his walkie talkie. Let me know when you leave, and report any trouble along the way. Start early and if anyone drags their feet, kick ass and get 'em out of here. Make 'em do most of the preparation work tonight. Little Mac can help."

"Where will you be?"

"I'm going to Greenham airbase tonight to help the setup crew. I have an errand first, but can head back and meet you on the road tomorrow if necessary," he said.

"Will cops be out tomorrow?"

"Yeah. Soon as this lot gets on the road. That's my errand. I'm heading to a quick meeting with a deputy in Salisbury. They are so glad to be rid of us, they're blocking intersections all the way to Newbury. You should be able to move right through. A few well-placed quid the Scot gave us helped. And speaking of the Scot…" Weeds frowned. "McKenna and his wife have been no trouble, but keep an eye on 'em. There's something up their sleeve other than just selling drugs."

* * *

Vice Wing Commander Brenda Judd, in the middle of editing the third rewrite of her column for the base paper, paused to answer her phone. She snapped, "I thought I told you not to disturb me. I'm busy."

Karol, the Wing Commander's secretary, took a deep breath before saying, "Colonel, you said 'Unless it's important'. The command post is on line two, and they say 'It's important!'"

Hitting the line-two button, Judd barked, "What?'

Another deep breath from another subordinate. "Ma'am, Colonel Frazier says to tell you that at least seven vehicles are moving into the area outside the Contractors' Gate."

"What are you talking about?"

"It looks like camping trailers and trucks are arriving. Said he thinks they're part of that group at Stonehenge."

< 224 >

"Are they coordinating with the women protestors at the gate?"

"Can't be sure, but Colonel Frazier said they're setting up campsites away from the women's area, some distance from the contractors' entrance."

"What's his security people going to do about it?"

"Don't know, ma'am, the Colonel's en route to the GAMA. Said he'll call when he knows more."

Judd slammed down the phone. "Shit." Then she remembered the voice message that asshole Forrest had told her about. Where the hell was that note? She rifled through her desk. *Crap, I gave it back, actually threw it back.* Recalling his expression made her smile.

What was the note? Something like:

…Travellers at Stonehenge moving to RAF Greenham…a big surprise for the Americans…

"Shit, shit, shit," she screamed and threw her pen across the room.

An hour later the command post called Judd to tell her that Colonel Frazier reported the newcomers had settled in without any ruckus, and while a few were finishing installing latrines, the majority were at campsites cooking dinner over firepits. Thames Valley Police had posted men outside the Contractors' Gate.

< 225 >

< 226 >

PART THREE

< 227 >

THIRTY TWO
Newbury
8 April 1983

MI5 agent Glendon Brown waited patiently at the Hurstbourne Tarrant Primary School until a police cruiser slowly passed, lights flashing but no siren, leading a convoy of unconventional vehicles, mostly old, a few brightly coloured, a few needing paint. After twenty or so vehicles, there was a break in the parade of mavericks and he squeezed into the procession. His beat-up blue Humber Hawk Saloon, with gray primer in spots, pulling a teardrop travel trailer, blended in perfectly. He relaxed while local traffic on A343 unhappily honked their horns and recklessly passed the slow-moving convoy.

Where in hell did Knight find this heap? It was okay for the job, but the overpowering cigarette smell forced him to keep windows open. As part

< 228 >

of his cover, he hadn't shaved or bathed for a week, so he didn't smell all that sweet himself.

Once they reached RAF Greenham, Brown was unsure how the parking would work, but he was directed to the rear of the grounds. Good. An out-of-the-way spot.

He opened the trailer, smelled mildew, and left the door and window open to let in air and dry it out. He placed the black Geiger counter on the ground near the door. Sieverts. Grays. Roentgens. REMs. The thought alone gave him another headache. Fortunately, the engineers finally agreed he could use a device gauged in counts per minute.

Using a grill and kettle, he made tea and soup for dinner, adding crackers he had purchased earlier. Near midnight, he turned on the Geiger counter and watched for ten minutes to determine the local background radiation count. The gauge fluctuated between 27 and 42 counts per minute, well under the threshold warning level of 100 CPM he'd been briefed about.

Using a headphone so the clicks would not draw attention, he first walked the camp perimeter and down by the Contractors' Gate. A lone security guard sat in the guard shack reading. The guard waved and went back to his paper. An American security vehicle drove by inside the fence and tooted his horn at him.

< 229 >

Brown picked his way through the camp, heading back to his car, and noted that most had gone to bed, a few were cleaning up after a late meal, some sat around a fire, smoking — probably pot — but that was it. They seemed as exhausted as he felt and ignored him.

He tucked the Geiger counter under his coat, and slowly moved the probe near vehicles and campers, listening to the clicks. Only once did the clicking go nuts. When he checked the meter, it read 65 CPM. Afraid of being challenged by the owner, he moved on. Plus he'd been told to call MI5 only if he found radiation of over one hundred CPM. But curiosity got the best of him and he went back, locating the source: four gas mantle lanterns.

MI5's briefing had been skimpy on details, but except that one incident, nothing he saw unnerved him or seemed unusual. Feeling good about his first day of being undercover, oblivious to what was really going on, Brown walked back to his car, getting a good night's sleep in his four-foot-wide, slightly smelly, bed on wheels.

< 230 >

THIRTY THREE
RAF Greenham Common
9 April 1983

Pointing to the newspaper on her desk, Colonel Selectee Judd glared at Colonel Frazier and said, "Well, Colonel, what are you doing about this mess?"

Annoyed, Frazier, the head of Wing Security Police, answered, "Well, Lieutenant Colonel Judd, you may be the Vice Wing Commander — don't know whose ass you kissed to get here — but I still outrank you, so talk nicely. You don't have those eagles on yet, young lady."

"Sorry," she said, not meaning it. Her jaw tightened. *Yeah, you made it because you're black and were a big football hero at the Academy.*

"Thirty six vans, trucks, and vehicles with trailers pulled into the area outside the contractor entrance yesterday afternoon — getting a lot of publicity," Frazier said.

< 231 >

Belligerent again, Judd countered, "Tell me something I don't know." Assuming a stern expression, she eased back in her chair and listened.

"There are now about one hundred new campers there. This in addition to the fifteen women who were already there. Even so, everything was quiet last night."

"Lots of pictures in the papers," Judd said. "Those assholes at *The Guardian* support these women, and they love the free publicity."

"Nothing in the photos or articles was news to us, but they did exaggerate the numbers that arrived. Even that interview with one of the Travellers was self-serving — downplayed the drugs."

"Do we have someone on the inside?" she asked.

"Not anymore. The RAF policeman who was undercover at Stonehenge had some sort of a medical problem, I think appendicitis, which required admission to hospital. RAF Intelligence is scrambling to replace him."

They were interrupted by the arrival of the British base commander, Group Captain Filbert Mackay. Standing — making a point Judd missed — Frazier said, "Come in, sir. I was telling Judd about your spy at Stonehenge." He did not notice Judd's eyes flare.

< 232 >

Frazier flashbacked to the first time he'd met the Group Captain. They lunched together the week he reported. He recalled the exchange…

"We can surely use your security expertise," Mackay said. "I'm sure you heard of all our incursions. But you may find another layer of bureaucracy burdensome at times. We Brits try to get it right, which often means untimely. That's part of the reason I'm here. Short version: I was posted at RAF HQ. Had info I thought was important. Bypassed someone in my chain-of-command who was off station. I was correct and the situation was handled timely, but he added a note to my records that stopped any further promotion. I'll remain a Group Captain — equivalent to a Colonel, like yourself — 'til I retire. I was protected by others and posted here. Put out to pasture so to speak. Out of decision-making roles but also untouchable by that Air Vice-Marshal. Unless, of course, something bad happens here."

Frazier's reverie ended when the Group Captain began talking.
"… damned untimely. The word is we can't have anyone in there again until midweek. Our

< 233 >

man had been undercover with the Travellers for about eight months. It seems no one is immediately ready to replace him."

"That's just great," said Judd, sarcasm clear.

Looking sternly at Judd, Frazier said, "Let's focus here. Since we no longer have inside information, we need to discuss Rules of Engagement — decide at what provocation our men can open fire."

"What?" said Judd. "I didn't think we had authority to even arm our men!"

The Group Captain said, "Both your Air Force and RAF Command have authorized arming the men and allowing shots to be fired — but not the use of deadly force, and only within the GAMA and munitions storage area."

"Oh, my God, how can we walk that line?" she puzzled, more to herself than them. "Do not issue bullets until Colonel Rogers returns tomorrow night," she commanded.

Colonel Frazier looked at the Group Captain, then turned back to Judd. "Tomorrow may be too late. Besides, they've already been issued. We've got armed US airman and RAF troops standing by in one of the hardened shelters. Any security visible to the Travellers' camp will not be armed. This contingency plan was approved by Colonel Rogers before he left."

< 234 >

After Frazier and Mackay departed, Judd raked the newspaper off her desk. *Who the fuck left me out of the loop?* She knew full well only one person could do that: the Wing Commander.

* * *

Morgan pulled into the Flare petrol station south of Newbury. It was obviously a local, forgoing modernization in order to keep prices low. Filling up with diesel from one of the three pumps, he saw what he needed. Away from the pumps an air hose was coiled around an old wheel mounted on a fence. The sign next to it declared Free Air. He paid for the fuel and said, "Tyres are low. Have a small pressure gauge I can borrow?"

"Gauge on the end of the hose."

"Don't trust 'em."

The young lad behind the counter looked hard at his customer's beard, dirty shirt and soiled knit cap. Morgan noticed the skepticism when the kid sneaked a peek out the window and took in the MAN military truck. Its body camouflage was painted in broad black and green irregular bands, but the tarp covering the back was olive green — obviously new.

"Undercover," Morgan said softly.

Deciding, then reaching below the counter, he said, "Okay. But bring it back when you're done."

< 235 >

After five minutes a badly scratched Bedford panel truck pulled into the station and stopped at the pumps. Morgan was kneeling next to a front tyre when someone rapped on the bonnet and said, "Need some help, stranger? Maybe have a radiator glitch?"

Ah, we finally meet, Morgan thought.

Slowly getting to his feet, Morgan looked the Scot over, eyeing the flat, wide, dark gray newsboy cap. Then he gave the correct response: "No thanks. This one is air-cooled."

Extending his hand from a dark blue knitted sweater, he said, "Iain McKenna."

Morgan liked the firm handshake. "Morgan Pritchard."

While his wife was filling the Bedford, McKenna walked around the MAN. "Good. European specs. Some nice gadgets. Fits right in with the Travelers!"

He seems observant, that's good, Morgan thought, then asked, "Is the steering wheel on the left a problem?"

"Nope. I've owned 'em both. Travellers own a mix o' British 'n' European spec'd vehicles."

Patting the side of the bed, McKenna asked, "How heavy's th' load?"

"Good question," Morgan answered. "Your three packages — that's what GOSHAWK called them — were about four hundred and fifty

< 236 >

kilograms and I added three hundred. But this vehicle has the suspension and carrying capacity of over four thousand, so no problem."

"Dangerous?"

"Everything's shielded, with one exception. The parcels I added are protected low-level radioactive medical waste. The exception is the head of a therapy machine and it's in its shipping container as safe as your packages."

"Low-level?"

"It will not be much of a contaminant, but leave visual, photographable evidence of our work. Increases fear. Plus, small bits everywhere increases cleanup cost."

Morgan saw McKenna shiver. "Do I need special protection?"

"No. There is no danger until the covers blow," Morgan said.

McKenna was still not sure. "How far will th' radiation spread?"

"With the explosives I've placed in the truck and assuming no wind, like now, material should be blown a hundred to a hundred fifty meters in all directions. That's the reason it needs to be near the centre of those hardened shelters. GOSHAWK said you'd have the layout." That last part was not truly known. Morgan watched McKenna closely for a response and didn't get one.

< 237 >

Opening the driver's door, Morgan said, "Get in." Once McKenna was settled, he continued. "You must understand and remember what I'm about to tell you. To your right, mounted on the floor, is a digital timer. On the dash is a toggle switch. I'm sorry it's a long reach, but it was the only place I could connect all the wiring. The switch is a safety device. Unless flipped, explosives won't detonate."

For the first time, Morgan was pleased. He seemed to have McKenna's total attention. "The power for the toggle switch, which arms all explosives, goes through the timer. The sequence is simple but must be followed without error. You want to write it down?"

"Nay," said McKenna.

"Sure? There's a lot to remember and it must be done in sequence."

Begrudgingly, the Scot took out a pen and wrote on his forearm.

"After you are in position and stop the truck, put it in neutral, leave the engine running, then start the timer. Countdown will start immediately. It's set for four minutes…to allow you time to escape. Any longer and security may get to the truck and deactivate the charges."

Pointing, Morgan said, "Next, flip the toggle switch, which arms the explosives. Then run like hell. When the timer hits zero, explosives blow the covers off the isotope containers and the tops off the medical waste boxes, up through the soft roof. Five seconds later the entire truck explodes, so don't be impressed or hang around to watch."

"I'm no doaty dobber!"

"Yeah? Well then, don't act stupid and make sure you use those four minutes to get as far away as possible, at least out of the GAMA. Once explosions happen, fallout and radiation will be the next problem."

< 239 >

THIRTY FOUR
Newbury
9 April 1983

Driving to the base from Newbury, McKenna quickly learned the nuances of the MAN. Morgan said, "Repeat exactly what you have to do to set off the explosives."

McKenna glanced at his arm several times but got it right.

When they reached Green Camp, Morgan noticed a woman waving. After several seconds, he recognized Mari's friend from the bonfire. It was Katelin. After McKenna parked where she indicated, Morgan got out.

* * *

RAF Sergeant Landon Haskell lay on his belly on the closest missile shelter to the Contractors' Gate. He scanned the crowd outside the fence with binoculars.

"Anything?" asked USAF Technical Sergeant Abe Schear.

"Nah. Just drugs and music. Too cold for the women to take off their tops. Wasting our time."

With their two-hour shift almost over, Schear had just laid back and closed his eyes when Haskell said, "Abe, we got something.

Camouflaged military vehicle. Maybe a deuce-and-a-half. Just pulled into Green Camp. Call command post."

* * *

Remembering the MI5 file photos, Agent Brown recognized the woman walking briskly through the camp. That's the one they thought to be the spy, so he followed. She approached two men standing by a camouflaged military truck. Before moving closer, he took two quick photos. Sauntering by with his head down, trying to be unnoticed, Brown heard the guy in the newsboy cap say: "This is Katelin. She knows our friend."

"McKenna, I already know this man — I think," the woman said, turning to the other man and smiling. "Morgan, is that really you? Can't be sure with the beard and all."

But Morgan was all business. "The way we came in…is that the only way out?"

"It is. How is Mari?"

Morgan watched and waited until a passing stranger with a camera was out of earshot. "She's visiting family."

"Okay. Well, we've got an important change," said Katelin. "They've installed a temporary gate in the GAMA fence. That section was open when you drove through in December."

< 241 >

After a few minutes of conversation, McKenna, frazzled nerves obvious, pulled Morgan aside. "Don't ye think that since ye built that contraption, don't ye think ye should take it onto th' base?"

"Look, GOSHAWK blackmailed me into doing this much," said Morgan. "My part is done. I assume he's holding something over your head."

"Ah took the spy's dosh to Stonehenge, arranged —"

Morgan held up his hands. "Don't want to hear it. Don't care." Looking McKenna in the eye, he said, "If you don't do your part, you can answer to him."

McKenna did not reply, and instead began nervously reviewing a GAMA map with Katelin.

I don't trust that bastard, Morgan thought, as he climbed in the vehicle and changed the wiring so that when the toggle switch was flipped the timer was bypassed; explosions would occur immediately.

One problem solved, he thought, and then I'll find that son of a bitch Russian.

< 242 >

THIRTY FIVE
Dirty Bomb Day
9 April 1983

Sergeants Haskell and Schear were now using binoculars. "That's a MAN truck," said Schear. "Similar to what we'll use in our missile convoys."

They watched three people talk near the truck. "Wish I knew what the hell they were saying," said Haskell.

"What's your guess? About three twenty five to three fifty yards?" Schear asked.

"Well, it's two ninety three to the perimeter gate from here," Sergeant Haskell replied. "That truck's further and to the left. So, I'd agree. Three fifty."

"Two ninety three?" Schear's raised eyebrows showed his skepticism.

"Called the civil engineers."

< 243 >

"Smart."

After a pause, USAF Staff Sergeant Schear said, "Did you hear that they have identified the body found in January? That delayed the construction of the temporary gate?" Schear had spent a lot of time in the interim guarding the GAMA.

"No."

"Turns out to be a Welch footballer. Clue came from a cigarette lighter found with the body. Forgot the name, but he's been missing for years." Haskell showed no interest, so Schear simply added, "Thames Valley Police are investigating."

"Tell me again the US Rules of Engagement," Haskell asked.

Schear pulled a piece of paper from his pocket. "Complicated, so I wrote 'em out," he said, then read: "The rules are on a sliding scale, depending on the threat. We have a citizen threat. Since we have no missiles or aircraft on station at this time we do not — repeat — do not have authority to use deadly force. The only exception is self-defense. And the only area that gets special protection is the GAMA."

He continued.

"If anyone unarmed crosses the base perimeter fence, it's the responsibility of security at the gate and along the fence. If an individual circumvents them, we may discharge a warning shot. If that individual is carrying a weapon, we must first

< 244 >

shoot to warn; if not dissuaded, shoot to disable. Only if that individual is about to fire a weapon at someone can we shoot to kill. However, if an unauthorized individual enters the GAMA, shoot to maim, no need to warn. If armed, shoot to kill."

"That's supposed to be helpful?" Haskell muttered.

* * *

Standing outside the base on a small hill overlooking the construction gate, Morgan told McKenna, "Get in the damn truck and get moving. Now."

McKenna was about to object, but Morgan ordered, "Now!"

McKenna threw his cap into the cab, climbed in, rolled down the window, and listened as Morgan quickly repeated the arming sequence.

He turned the ignition too far, grinding metal, then gave it too much gas, flooding the engine. Morgan controlled his anger and said in a monotone, "You're panicking. Relax, Iain. Turn off the ignition. Take a deep breath. Refocus." After several seconds: "Now, pump the accelerator twice and take your foot off the pedal. Turn the ignition until it catches. Then give it a little gas."

< 245 >

The engine started. McKenna turned to Morgan and nodded. The MAN started to roll. He did not hear Morgan say "Don't fuck this up."

McKenna headed straight for the target. Skirting the guard shack, the two front ramming bars Morgan had installed worked perfectly. The Contractors' Gate's centre locks cracked apart and the wings flew back, one side busting its hinges and flying twenty feet, scattering observing officers. The MAN blasted through the gate effortlessly. McKenna looked right, where, about three hundred feet away, a security lorry began to move.

Timer then switch, timer then switch echoed in McKenna's head.

Policemen along the fence started yelling and waving. One stepped directly in the vehicle's path. McKenna accelerated straight at him, then laughed as the pig jumped out of the way. He smacked the steering wheel and, releasing tension, screamed like a wild animal.

He accelerated up the road toward the GAMA. His peripheral vision caught more guards rushing toward him, shouting.

McKenna hit the bi-parting, swinging, temporary gate in the GAMA outer fence at its centre, busting through with no perceptible slowing. The vehicle moved into the gap between the double fences and picked up speed. Suddenly, the passenger window shattered and holes appeared in the front windscreen.

Feeling th' wind. Hearing no sound. Juist soft roar.

He wiped his face, felt searing pain, followed by stinging. His fingers pricked shards of glass imbedded in his right cheek. Blood on his hand.

McKenna passed the gateless inner fence, trespassing onto the missile alert and maintenance area...then the rest of the windscreen exploded. More pain when the cold wind buffeted his lacerations. Suddenly his hearing returned. Wind whistled. People yelled and screamed. Bullets pounded the truck. Sounded like a tornado and hurt like hell.

His right eye filled with blood. He tried to wipe it away with his shirtsleeve and failed. Another sharp pain. A gash erupted above his right eye. Blood flowed from face to shirt.

Panicked, McKenna focused on the road, trying to remember where to position the truck. Then the right-side tyres blew. The truck lurched, its steering out of control. Another fusillade of gunfire, then the engine stalled.

He gripped the steering wheel so hard his hands and wrists ached and quickly scanned the area. Shit, short of where I need to be. Cops coming. Screw it. Blow the fucker and run.

< 247 >

McKenna pushed the button on the timer at his foot and watched the red digital numbers come to life —

4:00...

3:59...

3:58...

Reaching for the toggle switch with his right hand, he suddenly felt as if he'd been hit by a sledgehammer. Warm liquid splattered his face and chest. Only when he saw two fingers missing did he feel pain.

Reaching across for the switch again with his damaged hand, another projectile hit his right shoulder, slamming him against the driver's door. Unable to lift his right arm, he screamed, "This can no be happening!"

A desperate attempt to hit the switch with his right toe...only to be clobbered again by a bullet ricocheting off the windscreen frame, nicking his lower jaw, knocking him backward again.

He yelled, "Fuck!"

Using his left hand, McKenna opened the door and toppled face-first to the ground.

3:17...

3:16...

He managed to regain his footing and began to run toward the nearest building, a small contractors tool shed. After twenty feet, his right

< 248 >

leg was cut out from under him. He fell face-first feeling mouth and jaw hit a rock, then he ate dirt.

He was greeted by darkness.

* * *

Safely away from the fence, Morgan stood cross-armed, taking shallow breaths when the truck rammed through the perimeter gates. His arms and breathing relaxed when the truck broke free of the obstacles and headed toward the GAMA gates. He smiled as coppers tried but did not stop the accelerating vehicle.

But then he heard the explosion of gunfire, the sharp staccato of bullets puncturing metal, the guttural whine of the engine dying.

Where the fuck did that come from?

He had watched carefully all day: none of the guards within sight were visibly armed. Scanning the GAMA again, finally, on top of the nearest bunker, he saw two soldiers with rifles pointed at the MAN truck.

The echo of gunfire halted the excitement around him. Travellers froze, shouts of fear, many running toward campsites to pack and load — all intent on escape.

Morgan jogged to the perimeter fence, stunned when he saw a bloodied McKenna sprawled on the ground. No explosion. After two minutes —

< 249 >

still no explosion. Nothing happening except armed guards cautiously moving in on McKenna and the truck. A USAF security cop inside the fence yelled, "Move along. Clear the fence line."

"Mother-fucking-wankers," Morgan yelled back, spit flying. Picking up a rock, he hurled it toward the guard shack — nearly hitting a Thames Valley policeman, who yelled, "Hey, arsehole," and started after him, stopping when he realized Morgan was much faster.

On the run, Morgan's thoughts cleared: Must get to the backup detonator. Blow the MAN. Do the job. Destroy all evidence.

< 250 >

THIRTY SIX
Dirty Bomb Day
9 April 1983

Morgan, caught in the middle of a panicked mob, shouted for everyone to get out of his way. When he reached the spot where McKenna had parked his truck, it was gone.

"Damn slag," he bellowed. McKenna's wife was his ride out of here. Why the fuck had he left his bag in their truck with the backup detonator? Shit, she musta left early to get to the rendezvous point!

He quickly composed himself. Okay. He remembered leaving the detonator in the truck because the power supply was impossible to carry around. Besides, he didn't think he'd need it.

Regardless, his detonator and transport were gone. He felt defeated, tired, mind and body

< 251 >

failing him. Then he saw the guy who earlier had a camera, now carrying a Geiger counter like the one he kept in the Northampton storage unit when he built the dirty bomb.

The guy was in a hurry but moving in a straight line, easy to follow. Morgan watched while Camera put the radiation sensor in a detached trailer, then opened the rear of a car, and began talking into a handset.

Shite! A cop.

After a quick look around, Morgan picked up a rock and hit Camera on the back of his head. Brown slumped and he pushed him into the trunk of the saloon. Morgan saw a torch and used its light to examine the trunk, and found a gun, tucking it into his belt. But what momentarily stopped him was finding the badge wallet: Glendon Brown, MI5.

* * *

Hearing gunfire and seeing McKenna sprawled on the ground, Katelin decided it was time to leave. GOSHAWK had told her to help if she could. But there was nothing she could do. It was obvious the Americans had secretly increased security in the missile storage area.

Do they know about him? About me?

< 252 >

Arrangements for her escape were in place, so she sprinted to her caravan and grabbed a suitcase packed for such an emergency. After a frantic double-checking of clothes, tickets, different currencies, and false passports, she headed into the woods, walking along a secluded path the women used to get to Newbury. She heard sirens heading toward the base, but met no one to question her and caught a bus from Newbury to Oxford, then a train from Oxford to Glasgow, Scotland.

* * *

Sitting on the passenger side of a British automobile, Wes pushed his foot on an imaginary accelerator trying to get Detective Tidwell's car to move faster and urged him along. "Hurry up. Hurry up."

"Colonel, she's doing all she'll do," the detective muttered. "It's got a four-liter engine. Petrol costs, you know."

Tidwell downshifted and turned on two wheels onto the contractors' road, almost colliding with a blue-and-gray car going in the opposite direction.

"That one got away, but I got a good look at the driver," Wes said. Looking forward again, he

< 253 >

said, "Here comes more. Stop 'em before they all get out!"

Tidwell slammed on the brakes, sliding sideways on the gravel, ending up stalled perpendicular to the road, front end barely off the pavement.

Wes jumped out and watched helplessly as a blue splotchy Humber turned left on the A339 and roared out of sight toward the Main Gate, probably heading to Basingstoke.

Tidwell couldn't get his car to start and raised only static from the radio, so he stepped to the middle of the road, stopping all vehicles attempting to escape. Showing his credentials to the first car in line, he ordered, "Please step out of your vehicle. You'll have to be interviewed before you can leave."

Sirens announced a police cruiser and ambulance approaching from Newbury. The police vehicle sped by, going to the wrong gate. The ambulance made the turn, bypassed the roadblock, and headed toward the downed fence. A US Air Force vehicle barreled in, lights flashing, siren blaring, carrying four security police.

< 254 >

THIRTY SEVEN
Dirty Bomb Day
9 April 1983

By the time Wes arrived at the downed
contractor gates, armed USAF security stood about
twenty feet apart inside the GAMA fence. British
Ministry of Defence Police protected the area
where the perimeter gates were missing, keeping
away the remaining gawking protestors.

Moving toward the busted GAMA gates, Wes
saw two technicians in radiation suits inspecting a
camouflaged military vehicle which was leaning to
the right with both right-side tyres flat. Everyone
stood a respectful, safe distance away. He made
out busted windows and random holes punched
in the right side.

Seeing him looking at the MAN truck, a British
sergeant reported: "Sir. The driver was shot.
Medics whisked him off to the base infirmary
faster than you can say Tower of London."

"What's with the suits?"

"Security found a timer in the cab flashing
zero-zero, so they called in the bomb squad. Their
radiation detector went off, so this new team is
investigating."

Wes opened his mouth to ask another question
when someone yelled "Stop." Turning toward the

voice, he saw a woman running toward them, chased by a police officer. An MDP guard tried to intercept her, but she did a sidestep that would've made a college running back proud. When she got closer, Wes recognized Lila Kerr, the British base commander's secretary.

Seeing one of the policemen raise his gun, Wes yelled, "It's okay. It's okay, I know her." She ran straight to him.

"Wes…errr…Colonel Forrest," she said excitedly, out of breath. "I saw him. I saw him."

"Slow down. Saw who?" Wes said. "I'll help, but you need to talk so I can understand."

After several deep breaths, her anxiety decreased somewhat and she continued, "A man hit another, slammed him into the boot of a car, then drove off."

He remembered the car that had almost hit Tidwell as it exited. "What color was it? The car driven off."

"Blue. A beat-up blue."

"Have you told Detective Tidwell?"

"No. No one."

Taking her by the arm, Wes said, "Let's go find Tidwell."

As they walked, he remembered his suspicion that Lila had left the voice message warning on his answering machine and asked why she was here. She broke into tears, so he let it drop.

< 256 >

They passed disgruntled Travellers, unhappy because they had been told to return to their campsites and stay put until interviewed, a time-consuming process because more Thames Valley police had to be called in to help patrol outside the fence and conduct interviews. MDP and USAF personnel were ordered not to leave assigned positions at the fence. Fearing an inspection, a lot of unloading and repacking was going on at the campers' vehicles. Criminal evidence was fast disappearing.

They found Detective Tidwell standing next to a lady in jeans and a leather jacket being given first aid. "Can you describe the driver?" he was asking her. She had two crying kids wrapped around her legs, making it difficult to hear.

"No. It happened so quickly. I was loading the rear of Buggy when this car charged me. I jumped out of the way, hit my head, banged into my kids."

"Buggy?"

"Sorry. That's what we call the Ford van — our camping Buggy. Converted it ourselves."

"Detective," Wes interrupted. "Lila saw it happen."

"What?"

"The car was stolen. The blue-and-gray car that almost hit us!"

< 257 >

From the look Tidwell gave Wes, he knew the detective got the point and was immediately interested.

Observing Lila's disheveled condition, Tidwell turned to the lady in jeans. "Excuse me, can we borrow two chairs?" Then turned to Lila. "Would you like some water?" he asked, then sat in one of the chairs the woman brought. Lila shook her head in the negative but sat.

"Tell me exactly what you saw."

"I saw a man sneak up on another man standing behind a car, hit him on the head, toss him into the boot, then drive off, almost hitting that woman," she said, pointing to the van driver.

"Where were you when you saw this?"

Lila pointed toward a green Ford Cortina.

"Is that your car?"

She nodded yes.

"Why were you here?"

Lila took a deep breath and made a quick glance at Wes. "I was delivering toys and fruit — from our church — for the Travellers' children."

"What time did you arrive?"

"I'm not sure. I was emptying my car when I heard gunshots. Then everyone was running away from the base, scared."

By making her comfortable and his friendly approach with easy first questions, Wes saw that

< 258 >

Tidwell had noticeably relaxed Lila. He was not taking notes. *Better memory than me.*

"You know whose car it was?" Tidwell asked.

"Which car?"

"One we assume was stolen. The blue one."

"No. Maybe it belonged to the man who got abducted?" she responded.

"Can you describe the man who stole it?"

"He was tall. Taller than the second man. Had lots of hair under a dark knit cap. Wearing a brown shirt. Long sleeves. Brown pants. Didn't match. No jacket."

"Did he have facial hair? Beard or mustache?"

Lila paused, looking worried, as if she'd just thought of something. "I'm... I'm not sure." She shifted in the chair and tucked one foot under her. "Wait. He did have a beard. I saw it when he jumped in. He took the time to reposition the seat before driving off." Then putting hands to her mouth, she gasped. "And he pulled off the beard!"

"Ever see him before?"

Lila shook her head in the negative.

"Did you give the fruit and toys to the kids?" Tidwell asked.

Why is that important? Wes thought.

"No," Lila said. "One of the camper's wives moved the items to her caravan."

"You know her?" Tidwell asked.

"No, I never saw her before."

< 259 >

"Can you describe her?"

"I really didn't get a good look. Clothes were old and worn. Her head covered."

He looked at Wes. Lila had failed a truth test. "What can you tell me about the man who was abducted?" Tidwell asked.

"He was wearing a dark blue shirt. Maybe jeans or black pants. No hat, no coat," Lila said.

She sure remembers those details and not the woman she actually talked to, Wes thought.

"What about his physical appearance?" Tidwell asked.

"I didn't get a good look before… before he was hit on the head, but I think he was clean-shaven, short light hair. Brown or blonde. Young," Lila said, eyes unfocused, thinking.

"What did you do after the gunshots?"

"Everyone was running to their vehicles, packing and loading, so I decided to leave. I was turning my car around when I saw the man hit the other… "

"And left your car where it is?"

"Yes. I sorta froze. Then went to help the lady he almost ran over."

"Is this your first time to visit the Travellers' camp?"

"No." Then moving her hand to her mouth, she said, "I mean yes." For the second time, Lila seemed uncomfortable. "I mean, I haven't been to

< 260 >

the contractors' entrance in months," she said, shifting her feet back to the ground. "It's the first time since the Travellers arrived."

Tidwell ignored the contradiction. "You said the man was standing behind the blue car. What was he doing?"

"I don't know. I was watching the other man sneak up."

Wes saw what Tidwell was doing. By skipping around with his short questions, she responded immediately if she knew the answer, but took longer to consider her answers if she wanted to lie or distort the truth. He also wasn't allowing her to summarize or ramble.

"Did you see any women from the camp help the man in brown escape?"

"No, they were too busy…"

Then stopping, she went quiet and rocked back-and-forth in the chair, looking at the ground.

This statement brought back Wes' memory of Lila's meeting at the Red Lion. From photos, MI5 had identified the other woman as a reporter. Was that meeting about this weekend? Lila, Wes concluded, was deeper in this than she wants us to know. But how deep?

Before Tidwell could ask another question, Captain Walton of Newbury Police Station interrupted. "Detective, you going to handle some interviews? Our hands are full getting out

< 261 >

information to all police units to be on the lookout for the blue-and-gray car, plus interviewing all these Travellers and searching their vehicles. Wish we had more information on the stolen car."

Having noticed the repacking, Wes asked, "Searching for what? Drugs?"

"That and bomb-making materials. They found a bomb in the camouflaged truck that drove onto the base."

"Where are they taking it?" Wes asked.

"It's in one of your hangars. Where it goes next is being discussed. Your Air Force chaps want it kept on base, but MDP is asking London for guidance."

"Do you know what happened to the MAN's driver?"

"He's being transferred from your base infirmary to hospital in Reading. Don't know anything about his condition."

Tidwell turned to the captain. "This is a scene involving a missing person, maybe a kidnapping. I'm tied up here doing these interviews. Trying to figure out who saw what or knows anything. Maybe someone knows the make of the blue car. Got a partial plate number. Let's share information later."

Before Tidwell could explain what he wanted Wes to do, another Newbury officer came running

< 262 >

up. "I think we've located the missing man's camper. There's something you need to see."

Following the officer, Tidwell asked, "How did you find it?"

"A Traveller told us he noticed the guy acting strange earlier in the day. Then he said he saw him with a Geiger counter around midnight."

They walked over to a small teardrop camping trailer and the officer opened the door. Inside, the sheets were wadded up with pajamas and pillows. A Geiger counter was near the door, but of more interest, inside lay a camera and a leather briefcase. Tidwell picked up a file folder lying on the briefcase. Inside was a confidential MI5 report.

"Damn," Wes said. "That warning was for real. At least Colonel Frazier took it more seriously than Judd did. Glad I went behind her back."

"What warning?" Tidwell asked.

Wes ignored the question. "I need to see the inside of that deuce-and-a-half." *And call Colonel Wheeler at the Pentagon.*

"I'll catch a ride back to base in one of the security vehicles," Wes said. "Is Lila free to go?"

Without looking at Lila, Tidwell said, "No. I have more questions for her."

Wes left without even a backward glance in her direction.

< 263 >

THIRTY EIGHT
Wisbech, Cambridgeshire
10 April 1983

The phone rang and Morgan hurried to answer it. "Are you okay?" Mari asked with alarm.

"Glad you called. I was afraid your husband wouldn't pass on the message. You hear about yesterday at Greenham?"

"Only what was in today's paper, and that was vague. Typical declarations without facts. I left a message at the Quaker House, but no one returned my call. Were you there?"

"Yes, and I'm in trouble. Don't know how much," Morgan said. "I need help. I have a vehicle to dispose of. Quickly. But I'm stuck here in Wisbech."

"What happened? What do you mean *stuck*?"

"An uninvited guest. Can't talk on the phone. I'll explain later. Can you come?"

"Not until late tonight," Mari replied softly.

"See you then."

Morgan hung up and went to check on his prisoner. Morgan entered his garage only to have his senses assaulted. The bastard was piss wet, and had shat himself. Expecting this, he had taped Brown to a chair over a floor drain, each ankle independently shackled to the floor. But the smell was worse that he'd anticipated. Plus, Brown was yelling profanities. "Fuckin' cheap tape," Morgan castigated himself. "Didn't keep his mouth shut."

He grabbed a hose and shot a stream of cold water at Brown's chest, then moved to the black hood so that the flow went into Brown's mouth. Being strapped to the chair, Brown had little ability to move his head. The yelping stopped and the choking started. Morgan dropped the hose, went to his medicine cabinet and, once Brown's coughing stopped, gave him a shot of a sedative stolen from the hospital.

"You stink, but I'll fix that."

As Brown lost consciousness, Morgan moved his gantry crane over the chair, spacing the two pulleys a little more than shoulder width apart. He ran chains through the wheels and attached them to the leather cuffs on each of Brown's wrists and slowly pulled until Brown was in a standing position.

Returning to his medical supplies, Morgan put on surgical gloves and picked up a pair of scissors. Cutting Brown's shirt, trousers, and underpants,

< 265 >

he let them fall to the floor. Using the hose, he rinsed Brown and his clothes, putting the clothes in a plastic bag and spraying the floor until all debris was washed down the drain.

Before leaving the garage, he turned the volume up high on the music.

* * *

Regaining wakefulness, Brown shivered, realizing he was cold and naked. He heard an onslaught of sound. The constant beat of a drum, the interplay of a low-end bass and riffs and licks of rhythm guitars. He tried to move his arm and discovered both were secured over his head. Only then did he fully feel the excruciating pain in his arms and legs. His feet still anchored to the floor. He bet he looked like a grotesque marionette. A thought that gave him no relief.

There was not enough slack in the chains to bend his knees, but he could flex his ankle and rise up on his toes. The music seemed familiar. Heavy metal. But he found no other clues in his foggy mind.

< 266 >

THIRTY NINE
RAF Greenham Common
10 April 1983

Wing Commander Colonel Tom Rogers was on the phone when he heard his secretary say, "General Hudson." The general rushed into the office, banging his briefcase on the door, before the colonel could excuse himself and hang up.

"Do we have reservations at the Manor House?" the general asked. Rogers nodded. "Okay. Have someone tell my driver to go ahead. I'll get a ride later."

Rogers' secretary said, "Got it."

The general closed the door and turned to Rogers. He saw puzzlement in the colonel's face. *He thinks I came here to fire him; hope he never finds how close it was,* the two-star thought. *What the hell; tell it like it is.*

"Is everyone here?" the general asked.

"In the conference room."

"They can wait a minute," the general said. "Tom, your career got a lot of discussion last night. A Pentagon honcho insisted you be replaced, but

< 267 >

the Commander of US Forces in Europe went to bat for you and convinced the Secretary of Defense that the political and social environments in Europe are a lot different than in the States and you shouldn't be judged on those standards. SecDef called me this morning, not happy. He wants these on-base incursions stopped. If anyone else gets on, there'd better be an arrest. If more demonstrators get into the GLCM GAMA, we'll all be shoveling shit in North Dakota. Understand?"

Not waiting for a response, the general opened the door. "Let's get to work." He headed through the RAF Greenham Common Headquarters Building, and marched into the conference room with Colonel Rogers following.

The three waiting men snapped to attention: British Base Commander Group Captain Finley Mackay; Thames Valley Police Detective Andrew Tidwell; and Wing Executive Officer Wesley Forrest.

At the head of the teak conference table, General Hudson sat his briefcase down heavily then, seeming to notice the others for the first time, said, "At ease." He unbuttoned his coat, hung it on the back of his chair, and said, "Gentlemen, this is gonna be a working session."

Rogers sat down across the table from the three. No one else removed or even unbuttoned their coats.

< 268 >

"The group who attempted to contaminate Greenham yesterday failed," the general said. "But they will continue efforts to prevent the deployment of cruise missiles. We need defensive measures to protect the base as we offensively go after the bastards. First, updates."

Pulling several folders from his briefcase, the general turned to Rogers. "What's the status of that MAN truck?"

After a few seconds to crystallize his thoughts, Rogers said, "Sir, it's secured in a hangar here on base. Explosives have been removed. Nuclear materials safely stored. Security is going over the truck as we speak, looking for evidence — including fingerprints.

"Tomorrow a team is coming from the Atomic Weapons lab at Aldermaston to inventory the materials and try to find clues as to where they came from. Thames Valley Police are tracing the origins of the truck, but I'm not sure of the status."

Rogers glanced at Tidwell, who picked up the topic. "The truck was stolen from a dealer in Oslo three months ago. No record exists of it entering the UK. Plates are stolen as well."

Looking back at Rogers, the general continued, "We've successfully contained the fact that nuclear materials are involved. Third Air Force public releases have admitted to a bomb threat, quickly handled by alert security. But people on the

< 269 >

ground saw radiation suits." He paused. "We need to stop or short-circuit loose tongues. Can you handle that locally?"

Rogers stiffened and said, "Certainly concerning the US and RAF service members, and British Ministry of Defence Police that were present. But the Travellers outside the base? That's another matter."

After a moment of silence, the general, unconsciously tapping his pen on the table, said, "How about a joint press release, coordinated and signed by all authorities involved? It'll praise the officers for responding quickly, for using minimum firepower to stop the infiltrator — no... trespasser — who was wounded and is in hospital. Say a bullet ricocheted and struck a gas line, the suits were then used for fire protection. That should stop any rumors. The public affairs boys can polish it up."

Nods from around the table, so he continued, "Once that nuclear team determines what radioactive items are involved and how much, have them add a chart to their report showing probable contamination had the threat materialized. That'll, of course, make it highly classified and help keep a lid on this mess. I never want to see the word 'nuclear' mentioned in a newspaper. Understood?"

< 270 >

After a look at his notes, General Hudson asked, "What's the status of the two men who fired at the MAN?"

"They've been restricted to quarters and ordered not to discuss the matter until they meet with the base legal officer on Monday or Tuesday," Rogers responded.

"They're heroes, but that'll never be known publicly," the general barked. "Instead, they may be scrutinized for possible violations of agreements we have with the British. And that'd really suck. The good thing is that one of their own sharpshooters was involved."

Glancing between Rogers and Mackay, he continued, "This will affect us all, so I want Third Air Force and RAF legal involved. Colonel, tell your attorney to call them tonight."

Following a pause to glance at his notes, the general asked, "Next issue. What's the status of the dual fence around the GAMA?"

Again, Rogers jumped in. "They're physically finished except for the gates near the contractor entrance. Some sensors await installation and those in place are not fully tested."

He paused. "It'll be another two to three weeks before complete, sir."

Having opened a base in his career, the general understood, but said icily, "Put a boot to those

< 271 >

contractors' backsides. I want the GAMA secure as soon as possible."

Continuing in a stern monotone, the general said, "The contractors' perimeter gate nor that temporary GAMA gate didn't slow that lorry driver down very much." Looking at Rogers, he added, "I want that area secure...starting now. Get canine teams out there. Use security personnel you have for the missile flights to patrol inside the fence and have them visibly armed. Everyone is now on notice that we will shoot, so hopefully it'll deter other attempts. But, dammit, ensure no recklessness or cowboy foolishness by anyone."

Tidwell had a questioning look on his face, but the general ignored it. Turning to the RAF base commander, General Hudson said with obvious irritation, "Group Captain, what's with the perimeter fence? It has been abysmal for security. These people seem to come in and out when they want." He didn't wait for an answer. "Set up a meeting with the Air Marshal to talk about the status of the base fence and need for additional personnel. I want British Air Force troops permanently assigned here, under your command, to help with security. Let's get the RAF personnel that will accompany GLCM flights identified now and on location as soon as possible.

"Plus, discuss adding more manpower on weekends when we seem to have additional

< 272 >

problems. Maybe use RAF reserves and rotate them through three- or four-day weekends. I want that fence patrolled constantly."

"Where do we billet them?" asked Mackay.

"There are those old USAF bomb wing crew quarters. Have them cleaned and repaired. Can't cost much."

Pausing to chase a thought, the general continued, "I want those bitches stopped. Think about rolls of razor wire just inside every inch of the perimeter fence. I know with a good bolt cutter it takes a strong man about two minutes to cut a hole in the fence. But razor wire'll slow him down till security arrives. We still need to be alerted, so put on the RAF HQ agenda the possibility of installing sensors or cameras in major problem areas along the fence."

He stopped to let all that sink in, then continued. "Consider exactly what resources you will need and how you'll house and feed the additional manpower." Using his pen to point to Rogers and Mackay, he said, "You two talk. Get me estimates. In the meantime I'll look for extra USAFE billeting money."

Taking a deep breath, Hudson brought his point home. "I want this meeting ASAP. Clear? I can arrange to meet at High Wycombe. By the way, SecDef said he'd make a call if needed. He

< 273 >

also might be able to dredge up some additional DOD funds."

"Yes sir," replied the group captain.

But Hudson was already looking at the civilian. In his most relaxed manner of the day, he said, "Detective Tidwell, thank you for joining us. What's the status of the truck driver?"

"General. I stopped by the Reading-Berkshire Hospital on my way here. He's stable in the intensive care unit. We have been unable to interview him, but the doctor assures me he'll allow it as soon as possible. McKenna — that's his name, Iain McKenna — is in isolation to hold down infection. The high-velocity gunshot wounds caused considerable damage. Lost two fingers and his right femur was shattered, requiring extensive surgery. He's constantly under guard."

"What's his background?"

"He's from Northeast Scotland. Caithness County. The Chief Constable there was not available, so I left my number with a message that I needed to talk to him urgently."

Tidwell looked at Wes. "You asked about his profession. I found out that McKenna is a fisherman and has been arrested several times for smuggling."

< 274 >

Wes asked, "Are you going to mention radioactive materials when you talk to the Chief Constable?"

"No. I thought policy was to not mention it."

"It just dawned on me," Wes said. "McKenna was driving the vehicle with nuclear waste. What if he provided it, smuggled it into the country?"

"Could be important," the general said. "Detective, figure out a way to have McKenna's home and property searched. And checked for radiation, without alarming the neighbors."

After a quick glance at his notes, Hudson asked, "How about the man kidnapped? And his tie to MI5?"

Tidwell said, "We have identified the missing man as Glendon David Brown. Yesterday, a sergeant from Newbury station located his camper at the Travellers' Camp. We found a camera, and a briefcase containing confidential MI5 paperwork in the camper — which we're holding. He's twenty seven. Three years of agency service, mostly as a desk analyst. Five confirmed he's one of theirs."

Tidwell pulled an official photo of Brown from a folder and passed it to the general. "We want to know why he was here and what his undercover assignment was. The Security Service is not openly talking. They are as worried about the camera and briefcase contents as they are about him. A call

< 275 >

from Five's Deputy Director-General stopped our processing the film.

"We also have a witness that saw most of the event, but not sure how reliable her testimony is." He started to glance at Wes, then checked the movement. "She heard the gunfire and was leaving the area in her car when she saw Brown assaulted and kidnapped."

Shaking his head, Hudson paused to consider the complications, then asked, "Did Thames Valley Police find anything tying other Travellers to the bomb?"

"No, sir. Nothing suspicious or of a bomb-making nature was found in any on-site vehicles. We did find plenty of alcohol and marijuana. After they decamped, we located several bags of drugs buried among the bushes. Cocaine. Hallucinogens. Also found a revolver. Guess someone didn't want to get caught, so tossed it."

Since these were issues for the Brits to sort out, General Hudson moved on. "MI5's Director-General is also talking to SecDef. The timing is good, since our Secretary of Defense needs a favor from MI5, and now has a bargaining position. This morning they came to an agreement, with two provisions that affect us.

"First, Detective Tidwell, you will be the Thames Valley Police liaison during the investigation of this incident and will brief Five on

TVP findings...*all* findings. And you, Colonel Forrest, will quarterback the military side, US and RAF, and be involved in all aspects. There was a screw-up at MI5 headquarters. No disclosures will be forthcoming. Involving the missing agent. Anyway, you two are to be removed from other duties to work this and to keep MI5 updated through..." He checked his notes. "...agent Elliot Knight, with both written reports and oral briefings."

Turning to Forrest: "Wes, I think you've met with Knight, correct?"

"Yes, sir," Wes replied with some discomfort.

Hudson noted that and was going to comment, but then remembered Wes' Washington meeting with Colonel Charles Wheeler, Air Force Intelligence, and the CIA, and moved on.

Turning to the 501st Wing Commander, General Hudson mandated: "Tom, assign Wes to a special project for a while. I want him reporting to me, through you. It'll be confidential, but I see everything. It may be a while, so put in for another executive officer. I'll touch base with the military personnel center."

The general gathered his papers. "Any more questions? Concerns?" He sat back and took stock of the men in front of him. *I'm damn lucky to have this caliber of individuals working this.* Receiving no response, the general stood.

< 277 >

"Gentlemen, enjoy the evening."

When he walked out of the conference room, Hudson overheard Judd ask Wes, "Why were you invited and not me?"

"I can answer that, Colonel Judd," the general interrupted. "It was a need-to-know-only meeting." Then he looked her straight in the eyes and didn't speak. *You're doing some major Pentagon ass-kissing — and I don't trust you.*

She didn't respond. He turned on his heel and walked away.

< 278 >

FORTY
Wisbech, Cambridgeshire
11 April 1983

Glendon Brown awoke to a loud, merciless instrumental. His captors had put the album on repeat play, so he heard it nonstop. During MI5 academy training he'd been briefed about the use of sleep deprivation to weaken a prisoner, so his brain had been able to tune out the heavy metal noise to the point he could sleep. But periodically, this particular song — no, noise — would bring him out of his stupor.

It started out with a crying guitar, moved to a call-and-response between two electrics screaming at each other, slid into a bass solo, followed by the drummer trying to impress, then all galloping together, building in intensity into a final clashing crescendo.

< 279 >

Limited dozing here. Knowing he must keep his sanity, Brown tried to focus on his ordeal, but stuffed into the boot of his own car he got sick from the exhaust and passed out. Awoke, he found himself anchored to a wooden chair. Ankles secured to the floor. Arms taped to chair arms. Hips roped to seat, chest tied to chair back, head covered with a dark bag.

Taped mouth filled with saliva, but he managed to free a corner with his tongue and yelled until he was hoarse. A mistake because his returning captor had then added the loud music.

After hours of resisting, he had urinated and shat on himself. His captor chained him standing, cut off his clothes, then hosed him down with cold water. Restrained and wet, the cold had damaged his resistance far more than the music. At least he now had weight on both feet. Able to shift back and forth, raise an inch or two on his toes, gave some relief to his arms.

He tried to keep his mind active by counting album songs between the times the irksome instrumental played, but the count got different each time: ten, eleven, or twelve?

The song following the instrumental was a slow vocal — a mistake in album selection by his captor because it allowed Brown to transition to meditative mode, practice self-hypnosis, and ski his favorite runs at Zermatt.

< 280 >

Some time later, he didn't know how long, Brown jerked alert. Was that a squeak? A door opening?

The sound came from behind him and he tried to turn toward it. Attempted to talk but his mouth was dry and nothing legible came out. The music stopped. It was quiet. He only heard his anxious breathing inside the hood. Then from directly behind his left ear came a soft male voice.

"If you want water, do not move or speak, or else I leave with the water."

Brown stood rigid while the cloth covering his head was raised, exposing his mouth. Light from two intense lamps blinded him, but the silhouette of a hand holding a water bottle emerged and water poured over his lips and down his chest. He opened his mouth and his captor touched his dry, tender lower lip and slowly added water to his mouth.

When the bottle was empty, his captor said softly, "Very good. Remember, no sound." Then, the cloth was replaced, and Brown heard footsteps. The door closed. He did not move or speak, hoping his captor would return.

He didn't.

But the mind-numbing music did.

< 281 >

FORTY ONE
Barnet, England
11 April 1983

As he'd done since the failure at RAF Greenham Common, Nikolai Sokolov was seated at a table in the Barnet City Library reading room, perusing every newspaper that mentioned the debacle. There had been no mention of Morgan Pritchard or Katelin Nagy, nor had he heard from them. The stories spoke of the MAN truck driver, but not by name, so Sokolov — Chief Librarian for Special Collections Peter Velikaya — knew that Iain McKenna was in hospital at an undisclosed location. Authorities had also kept out of the papers the fact that nuclear materials were involved in the invasion of the base.

Sokolov had slept little. He understood waiting. Often it took days, even weeks for an operation, once set in motion, to complete. But that didn't make it easier — especially since this one had failed. He considered going to Newbury, but understood that was a bad idea.

Maybe to Pritchard's home?

* * *

For a second time, Claire McKenna put her hand on her knee to stop the bouncing. She'd been

< 282 >

sitting in the pale-green waiting room for over thirty minutes, trying to figure out how to find her husband's room without betraying herself. She learned the hospital name by calling *The Guardian* and identifying herself as a reporter for *The Caithness Courier*.

She learned nothing new listening to the conversations surrounding her. The hustle and bustle of the hospital only added to her confusion. The siren of an arriving ambulance echoed into the nearby emergency room, accompanied by shouting of nurses and attendants. Weary patients sitting near her complained about their plight in life and the intolerable National Health Service.

Iain had gotten in way over his head this time. *Dammit, how come th' Americans can't go home?* Claire couldn't get Saturday's scene out of her mind: her husband stumbling out of that bullet-ridden vehicle, falling to the ground after being shot, then unsuccessfully trying to crawl to cover. She had tried to rush to his aid, only to be stopped at the fence. Other security guards had immediately surrounded him. She panicked and ran. Drove away in their truck, leaving the wanker who built the bomb without a ride. She worried all the while.

Was he searching for me?

Finally, thinking of no other option, she approached the reception counter. "I'm 'ere ta see

< 283 >

Iain McKenna. Kin ah hae his room number, please?"

The clerk pulled the file, fingered a note on the cover, stared at Claire for a second, and said, "Just a minute." As she consulted with her supervisor, both glanced at Claire and spoke in whispers. Claire almost ran, but with heart pumping, stood her ground.

"What is your relationship with the patient?" asked the supervising nurse.

Thinking fast: "A relative...family."

The nurse paused, then said, "Mr. McKenna is scheduled for surgery today and cannot have visitors. May I have your name and number? We'll call when he reaches recovery."

Claire took a deep breath. "No number. Thank ye." She wiped away a tear, headed for the door.

As fate would have it, at that moment Detective Superintendent Tidwell exited the elevator. In no hurry, he had learned from nurses that McKenna was on his way into an estimated five-hour orthopedic surgery; he'd be immobilized for twenty-four hours following.

When Tidwell ambled through the hospital reception area, the duty nurse ran over. "Detective, a woman was here asking to see your prisoner." Pointing toward the door, "Just left."

< 284 >

FORTY TWO
Wisbech, Cambridgeshire
11 April 1983

Mari opened Morgan's door from the kitchen to the garage and flinched. Frozen for several seconds, she slowly closed the door and leaned onto it with both hands. Looking down at her feet, she said, "What in God's name have you done?"

Morgan did not respond.

She turned but avoided his gaze. "How long have you had him hanging like that? It's cruel."

Unfazed, Morgan said, "Since last night. Didn't plan on him being here, so had to make use of what I had, the chain hoist. Had him in a chair originally, but he crapped all over himself. Standing makes him easier to clean. Also, the cold may encourage him to talk."

Mari cringed and brushed by him, entered and slammed her bedroom door.

< 285 >

After thirty minutes, Mari reentered the kitchen, finding Morgan preparing breakfast.

"We have to figure out something else," she said, disgust in her voice. "I can't be a part of this inhumane treatment. It's totally unacceptable. I assume we're holding him for ransom?"

"We?"

"Yes, we. I seem to be in the middle of this. Have you thought about ransom?"

"Not really. I've got other things to worry about. I need to find out what he knows. Probably have to kill and dump him at some point."

Concealing her surprise, she said, "Receiving money is better. Enough for all of us — you, me, and Myrddyn — to leave the country...start over."

Ignoring the obvious problem of her husband, Morgan said, "I suppose. But then don't they always catch the bad guys at the exchange?"

"There's another option," Mari said. "Ransom him to stop the cruise missile deployment."

"I don't think the government will care about him that much. At least not enough to turn up its nose at NATO — rejecting its defense plans, its money."

Morgan took a sip of coffee, raised his cup to her. She shook her head.

"Now that you're here," he said, "I've got to get rid of Brown's car. By now it's probably been reported as stolen with all cops on the lookout.

< 286 >

Since I'm not sure of his training or capabilities, I've been afraid to leave him alone for more than a few minutes."

"You know his name? What do you mean training?"

Before answering, Morgan went into the garage and returned with the hostage's ID card. Mari, who had sat down at the table, looked at it, raising both arms in the air. "MI5. What the hell are you thinking?" She glared at him. "Improve his situation *now* or I won't be a part of this."

"All right. I've been thinking, treat him rough, then offer kindness and question him. Figured the fear of more rough stuff, you know…loosen his tongue."

Walking over to the window, he said, "I'll lose the car tonight — after midnight."

"Where is it?"

"In woods nearby and covered."

"What will you do?" she asked, glad to focus on something else besides the garage.

"Clean it. Wipe off fingerprints. Drive into East London and park it on a side street. Put the keys above the visor. Some laid-off dockworker will find it. In two days, it'll be in fifty pieces."

"How will you get home?"

"Pre-position my bike at the Wisbech bus station. I'll park his car near a twenty-four-hour

< 287 >

tube, take underground to Kings Cross, catch the bus back to my bike."

"What have you fed him?"

"Nothing. Just water," said Morgan.

"What? That's despicable. I'll do it right now," Mari said standing up quickly.

"Slow down," he said. "We need to do some prep work first. I need to know what he knows."

* * *

Brown did not hear the door open, but when the music stopped, he became fully alert. The smell of bacon from the kitchen, the potential for food, overrode the discomfort of the cold hosing he'd received. But this time he was wiped dry to his waist, where a towel was then wrapped and secured. The chains extending his arms were loosened. He felt unsteady as his weight was placed on his legs and feet. Something bumped against his legs from the rear and the male voice said, "Sit."

Pain replaced numbness in his extremities. He sensed rather than felt his wrists again being taped tight to the chair. He heard a fan, then felt warm air blowing from his right. The wet hood was removed and replaced by a blindfold. He looked around in the seconds he had, but was unable to see anything because of the bright lights.

< 288 >

The male voice said, "There is a nice lady here to give you tea and oatmeal."

A pause, then, "Feel this?" Brown felt something tap his shin and nodded.

"You can speak softly."

"Ye...uh...yes."

"It's a ball-peen hammer. If you become violent or verbally abusive, I will break your fuckin' tibia, rehang you and it will be a long time before you get food or water. Understand?"

Brown nodded.

"What?"

"Eh...understand," Brown said, voice straining.

A chair scraped the floor and a female said: "I have warm tea and oatmeal. You want both?"

Brown nodded, then felt a slight tap on his leg. "Yes-mum."

Following several attempts at being fed and watered, Brown was soon eating and drinking successfully. After about ten minutes, he sensed one captor leave. Then the female asked, "What is your name?"

Brown froze. What did training say to do? Shite, can't think. He labored to remember. It was in Sir Howard's class. Tell them little but include a grain of truth. You don't know what they know. Watch out for the Bad Cop-Good Cop routine.

< 289 >

"Did you hear? I asked your name." Short pause. "No answers, no food."

Finally, he said, "Glen."

"Very good. Glen. Please pardon my brother's attitude," she said, then gave him a large spoonful of warm oatmeal. "What do you do for a living?"

"Administrative work."

"Where?"

"London" got him a drink of warm Irish tea.

"How long have you worked for MI5?"

Startled, Brown choked on the tea, projecting a spray forward.

The woman gasped. Her chair moved.

"That ends today's meal," she said and left.

< 290 >

FORTY THREE
MI5 Headquarters
12 April 1983

Upon arrival at MI5 headquarters in his newly acquired civilian suit, Wes entered with Tidwell into a sixth-floor conference room. Their escort indicated where they were to sit by pulling out two of the five chairs on one side of the oval table. The wall behind them was mostly glass and Wes looked down on the busy traffic on Euston Road.

They'd been cooling their heels in the conference room for twenty minutes when the door finally opened and two men entered. If they smiled it'd crack their faces, Wes thought. The pair, followed by a subdued Special Agent Knight, did not offer hands in greeting, instead marched to the opposite side of the table.

< 291 >

Wes opened his mouth to greet Knight, yet hesitated when Knight didn't acknowledge his presence. Never looking up from the floor and obviously not enjoying himself, the agent took a place at the table.

"Gentlemen, I'm MI5 Deputy Director-General Clive Walker and this is head of K Branch, John McFarland. You've met Elliot Knight."

Looking intently at Wes and Tidwell, he continued, "Welcome to this investigation. I have talked to individuals high enough in your commands to know there will be no problems with coordination between our agencies."

DDG Walker aimed his attention at Wes. "Colonel Forrest, tell me what you have discovered, to this point, regarding the contents of the MAN truck."

"Yes, sir." Wes glanced at Knight, who was studying his hands. "Documents found in one of the containers removed from the truck suggest it was last delivered to Northampton General Hospital. I have an appointment with the administrator tomorrow."

"Are any of the nuclear materials from there?"

"Don't know at this time, sir. I'm told hospital paperwork shows nothing missing, but they're doing a physical inventory. Should be complete tonight."

< 292 >

Rubbing his chin, the DDG looked thoughtfully toward the window. "I'm really concerned about the strontium-90. That's usually under heavy security and tight control."

Since they had not discussed strontium-90, the statement told Wes that Walker was getting information from other sources. Probably the lab at Aldermaston.

Walker next turned to Tidwell. "Have you interviewed the MAN driver?"

"No, sir. Been to see him twice, but he is in isolation because of his wounds. Extensive surgery has been done to his leg. His doc says I'll be able to interview him by the end of the week. Has Five searched Agent Brown's home?"

If Walker felt Tidwell's question bordered on impertinence, he didn't show it. "We found nothing unusual there."

Yeah, right. Like you'd tell us if you did, thought Wes. So much for cooperation.

"Let's see if we can provide you some assistance for when you talk to McKenna," the DDG said. He nodded to McFarland, who moved to the head of the table and manipulated a series of buttons and switches. The lights began to dim, a curtain closed over the window, and a photo appeared on a drop-down screen.

"We processed the film from Agent Brown's camera, the one found in his camping trailer at

< 293 >

RAF Greenham by Thames Valley Police." By way of thanks, DDG nodded toward Tidwell. "We'd like your input on what we found."

When they went through the slides, Knight identified Katelin Nagy in several photos, explaining they thought she was a Russian spy. When a picture of two men and a woman appeared, Knight pointed out Katelin. Tidwell said the man in the newsboy cap was the MAN truck driver, McKenna.

The one in the knit cap looked familiar, Wes thought.

"We have been able to obtain copies of photographs made on 12 December last," Walker said. Shifting his attention to Wes, "The tipper lorry fire and explosion. It took a while to convince *The Guardian* it was in their best interest to share certain information."

When a photo from December — a man standing beside a tipper lorry holding a petrol can — popped on the screen, Wes shouted, "Wait." Embarrassed, he added, "Sorry sir, but isn't that the same guy as before? The one with the knit cap, standing by Nagy?"

McFarland displayed the two photos side-by-side on the screen and, after study, all agreed it was the same man.

Wes said, "I got a good look at his face when we almost collided with what I assume was your

< 294 >

agent's car the night of the dirty bomb. The knit cap and beard were gone. And now that I have seen him with and without a beard, I'm sure the beard was fake."

Deputy Director Walker asked to zoom in on the face in the photo without the disguise. "So, we may be looking at the man who blew up the lorry at Greenham in December and kidnapped our agent the other day." Staring at the photo, he added, "Bet we'll find he was involved with the dirty bomb as well."

Turning to Knight, the DDG said, "I want his name."

When the lights went up, McFarland gave packets to Tidwell and Wes. "Here are copies of the photographs you just reviewed. For your interrogations and interviews. Use them, but do not divulge their origins. I'll leave how you employ them to your expertise and experience. Please do not make copies or distribute a single one of them. And keep us informed of anything you turn up."

After looking at McFarland, who shook his head, the DDG asked, "Is there anything else?" Everyone remained silent. Exiting the room, Walker said, "Colonel, please personally brief me about what you find at Northampton General Hospital. And Detective, I want to know how that interview goes."

< 295 >

FORTY FOUR

Northampton General Hospital
13 April 1983

Wes hadn't known the route to Northampton General Hospital, so he stopped by a WHSmith bookstore and bought a set of Michelin maps. He was driving his newest acquisition, a 1978 Jaguar, British racing green, four-door sedan, twelve cylinders and a 5.3-liter engine, which never passed a petrol station it didn't like. He had gotten a real deal. Seventeen hundred British pounds, a little over twenty five hundred US dollars, but it was British specs and he wouldn't be able to ship it home. Still a high price to pay to drive on the other side of the road. But it was riskier trying to pass on English roads in an American car.

Traffic was light and once on the M1, he turned to a soft-rock music station, then sat back for an hour's comfortable and luxurious ride.

* * *

< 296 >

Wes was fifteen minutes early for his appointment with hospital administrator Jacob Berkovitz. He was impatient and, pacing, noticed two men in an adjoining conference room. One man saw him and closed the blinds.

At two-thirty p.m. the secretary escorted Wes into the conference room. He took a seat. Berkovitz remained seated and seemed edgy as he introduced himself. He had a pale complexion, a round face, and short, thinning gray hair. He wore a dark suit, a light blue shirt, and a coordinated tie, and had the air of someone who thought himself important. The other gentleman was introduced as Mr. James Knowles. Knowles sat to the Berkovitz's right, in a monitoring position rather than a participant — portly, yet professionally dressed and groomed.

Must be their lawyer.

Refusing tea, Wes got to the point. "Does your inventory show any nuclear materials missing?"

Glancing at Knowles, the administrator said, "I was asked by the Ministry of Defence to conduct an inventory, but why is an American visiting me and asking for the results?"

"I'm working on a special team with MI5 and the Thames Valley Police," Wes responded. "Detective Andrew Tidwell was to accompany me today, but had to attend an important meeting at TVP HQ. They authorized me to come alone."

< 297 >

Wes looked from one to the other. "MOD is also part of the on-base investigative effort. I'm sure you are aware of the attempt to bomb RAF Greenham Common on Saturday. But what is not public knowledge is that the person — or persons — attempted to use conventional explosives to spread nuclear materials over an area of the base in order to make it unusable."

Getting no response, he continued, "To determine who did this, we need to know origin of the materials and how they were obtained."

Taking a few pieces of paper from his worn leather briefcase, Wes handed one across to the administrator.

"This document was found in a box with nuclear waste." The administrator drew back and Wes added, "Away from any radiation."

As Berkovitz read, he thumped his right forefinger on the desk and breathed loudly. He then passed the document to Knowles and waited while he read it twice. Knowles looked at Berkovitz, nodded slightly and returned the document to Wes.

"As you can see," Wes said, "it's a shipping label, containing the words Radioactive Material Package addressed for delivery to the Medical Physics Department of this hospital."

The administrator spoke nervously. "I'm not sure what happened with our records. Some

< 298 >

nuclear waste seems to have been misplaced. But more importantly, the radioisotope portion, the head, of a teletherapy machine, as well as a container of cobalt pellets, is also missing."

"Well, the good news is we have several boxes secured at the base that we think belong to you," Wes said. "The bad news is that it may be some time before you get them back."

"What do I tell the military and the government...the National Health Trust?" the administrator asked.

"Nothing for now. We need to keep the fact that materials are missing on a need-to-know-only basis. So, until MI5 tells you otherwise, limit the number who have access to this information."

Wes sat back in his chair. "In the meantime, I must learn how and when the boxes were removed. Not to place any blame, mind you, but to determine who took them." Looking directly at the administrator, Wes added, "This information is essential to our investigation."

Seeing a look of consternation on Berkovitz's face, he continued, "Sir, I'm not here to criticize. And I can't offer you any advice, but I'm sure your lawyers can help." Noticing Berkovitz's quick glance at Knowles, Wes continued, "I'm sure your full cooperation will go a long way in any future proceedings."

< 299 >

They didn't know that there were other radiological materials in the truck besides theirs, and they wouldn't hear it from Wes.

Checking his notes, Wes asked, "Did you have any strontium-90 in your vaults?"

Giving Wes a questioning look, the hospital administrator said, "MI5 asked the same thing. The answer is no. We did use a small amount last year testing it as a radioactive source for therapy on some types of cancer. But none since then."

Knowles removed documents from a folder lying in front of him, sliding them toward Wes, and spoke for the first time. "Colonel, as you perceptively assumed, I'm the hospital's solicitor. Storage rooms Alpha and Bravo are where the hospital stores radioactive materials. We have found nothing missing from Alpha. Here are documents, including the last two inventories of Bravo — one being the latest, just accomplished at MI5's request."

Knowles cleared his throat. "As you can see, one box is not on the lists — the container with the cobalt-60 teletherapy machine head. The hospital is looking into discipline for the individual who did not accomplish the required documentation. Such an item was removed from Bravo."

Knowles lifted a paper-clipped packet of about ten pages. "Here is the log for Bravo for 1983, to date, which includes sign-in and -out dates, times,

< 300 >

and signatures. Our investigation determined that two nuclear waste boxes were not picked up by the transport company as indicated on the log... another concern. We are continuing our inquiry."

Glancing at Berkovitz, he continued, "In order to be as cooperative as possible, I...we...are allowing you to review these documents. However, at this time we cannot allow you to make copies or remove them from this room."

Wes shook his head. "This won't work. MI5 and Thames Valley Police may need to see this information. I can't tell you what might be important to them; even if I could, I'm not prepared to dig through this tonight. I also need to review other documents, for example, a list of employees who have access to both storage rooms — Alpha and Bravo — and their work schedules for the last...oh, let's say, the last four months."

Knowles said, "We understand, Colonel, and we want to help you with your investigation, but we have our own liabilities to worry about. We can't release any of these documents quite yet." He glanced at Berkovitz. "Just a second."

The two went into the administrator's office and Wes waited, getting angrier by the minute. After some time, they returned and Berkovitz said, "Okay, we will get together the other documents you requested, and you can review them here tomorrow morning."

< 301 >

"What?" said Wes, jumping to his feet. "This is not a theft of a patient's record. This is the theft of materials that can kill people. Do you want me to call MI5's director-general and tell him you are stonewalling?"

"That won't be necessary," said the lawyer. "We just called MI5."

Then after visibly trying to relax and taking a deep breath, Wes said slowly, "Mr. Berkovitz, if we don't catch this man or these persons immediately, another incident may occur. At this point, neither we nor you know if all your missing materials were transported to RAF Greenham. And we will not know until we compare your documents with what we found in the MAN military vehicle. Do you want to read in the papers that your refusal to cooperate prohibited an early end to this matter, or worse, that it contributed to a massive exposure in the UK that could have been prevented?"

The administrator looked at his lawyer. Knowles nodded and responded, "Okay, we will get you what you need tonight. But I still cannot allow anything to leave this room or be copied. You can start with what's here while we collect the others."

Standing a little taller, Knowles looked into Wes' eyes. "There is speculation within the hospital about what is going on. I cannot allow

< 302 >

you to interview any employees until the hospital determines the facts. If unsubstantiated information escapes, we might face multiple lawsuits. As you can see, I'm willing to share documents with you. I suggest you have one individual from MI5 and one from Thames Valley Police join you here to assist in reviewing the documents." Then, to Berkovitz when they walked out, "Jacob, have Ms. Cameron get paper and pens at the ready so the colonel can make notes."

Within minutes the secretary brought in a stack of paper pads and a box with a mix of pencils and pens. When she left, the conference room door clicked. Wes looked around the lonely room. *Where do I start?*

In comparing the two Bravo inventories, Wes confirmed what he'd been told earlier, one box — the cobalt pellets — was clearly missing with no notation of its removal. Assuming the information about the waste not being picked up was correct, this accounted for three of the boxes at Greenham. Plus, making it four, the piece of the teletherapy machine. But to make a detailed comparison, he needed to see the Atomic Weapons lab's inventory of materials.

He looked over the Bravo sign-in log and couldn't tell much. He didn't know the personnel or department codes. Handwriting was terrible.

< 303 >

When the secretary brought in the other documents, she rolled in a tea cart, with a pot, cup, and some warm buns. She was pleasant this time, asking if he needed anything else and provided directions to the loo. She had a typed list of nine hospital documents he'd been provided:

Earlier inventories of Alpha and Bravo
      Qty: 2

Yesterday's inventory of both
      Qty: 2

A list of hospital employees with access to each of the two rooms
      Qty: 1

A list of non-employees with access
      Qty: 1

Sign-in and -out logs from Alpha and Bravo from January 1983 to today's date, 13 April 1983
      Qty: 2

Work schedules of employees with access for the last 90 days
      Qty: 1

< 304 >

Wes was asked to verify that the documents were in his receipt and sign the sheet accepting responsibility. There was a place for the administrator's signature when the documents were returned.

Along with the document from the box of nuclear materials he had shown the two men earlier, Wes pulled from his worn briefcase: a document from the box with the teletherapy machine head, that he'd not shared with them, and a list of the photos from MI5. He had left copies of the actual photographs in the car.

He worked for the next hour, reviewing and double-checking documents, and finding nothing new. He went to the bathroom, then called MI5 and TVP, reaching neither Knight nor Tidwell.

The secretary returned to tell him that she had to go home soon, but when he was finished, the security guard would escort him out, locking the documents in the conference room.

Wes had a thought and went to his car to get the photographs. Upon his return he asked the secretary to go through the bonfire and dirty-bomb photos, assembled by MI5, to see if she recognized anyone.

"Oh my," she said. "Why would Morgan be where these were taken?"

Wes did not interrupt, but saw she was looking at the man standing by the lorry with a

< 305 >

petrol can. She went through the stack again. He asked if she saw the same person anywhere but this time wearing a fake beard.

Pulling out several photos, she said, "This is Morgan Pritchard. He works in our electrical department."

Wes found his name on the list having access to Alpha and Bravo, then on another document saw Pritchard was on vacation.

"I need to talk to Berkovitz. Now!"

Then looking up from the files, "Also, Ms. Cameron, can you suggest a good, close hotel?"

< 306 >

FORTY FIVE
Northampton General Hospital
14 April 1983

It was still early morning when Morgan got off his motorbike in the hospital parking lot. He stood back, admiring his black '73 Norton Commando 750. Purchased after it had been wrecked, he spent many hours rebuilding the machine, especially the engine. Attaching his helmet to the bike, he entered the hospital through the lower-level employee entrance. Several people asked how his vacation was going.

As Morgan approached the electrical department, he heard voices — and those voices were saying his name.

< 307 >

Wes and the administrator found Morgan's boss at his desk in the electrical department. "Is Pritchard on vacation?" Berkovitz demanded.

"Yes, sir," replied Bobby Bowen. "He's ta be back at work next Sunday." Glancing at the calendar on his desk: "The 17th. Easier to return from vacation on a weekend — get back in gear on a slow day. A lot of staff not here, so usually only routine maintenance to do. What's up?"

"This is Colonel Forrest. The United States Air Force has found several items from the Bravo storage area and we're trying to find out how they were removed without the hospital's notice," said Berkovitz. "On review of records, it looks like Pritchard was in the vault near the time the items disappeared. We need to talk to him to see if he noticed anything amiss."

Bowen said, "He'll be here Sunday morning — 8 a.m."

Wes spoke for the first time: "Is it possible to get his home address?"

"I can get it from personnel," said Berkovitz.

"No need," said Bowen, "got it right here. Phone number, too."

"How long has Pritchard worked for the hospital?" asked Wes.

"He's worked electrical here for over eight years," replied the department head.

< 308 >

Wes took the piece of paper with the address. "Mears Ashby — Wilby Road."

Morgan froze.
Holy shit! What do I do now?
He ducked into an empty office as they passed, Berkovitz showing the American officer out. Luckily, they went out the same exit he just entered. Berkovitz disappeared up the exterior stairs. Morgan watched Forrest cross the parking lot and get in a green Jag. Morgan walked swiftly to his motorcycle and put on his helmet to conceal his face. He saw the colonel check a map. Followed him toward the exit. Kept back a good distance.

When Wes reached the address provided by Pritchard's boss, he found a classic gated entrance sitting about fifty feet off the highway. Six-foot-tall steel wings hung from large seven-foot rock pillars. Every other stake extended above the wing, topped with a spearhead, each pillar topped with a fashionable lamp. Metal fences ran north and south from the pillars. Beyond the gate, the curved drive disappeared behind shrubs and trees.

As Wes was getting out of his car, a black motorcycle blasted by without slowing down. Walking toward the gates, Wes heard a whirring

< 309 >

noise. Sitting atop one gatepost, installed below the light, was a camera following his movements. After punching the intercom button several times with no response, he said loudly, in case he was being recorded, "No one's home — still on vacation I guess."

Sensors detect motion and cameras record. Similar to what we're putting in the GAMA, he thought. Expensive and highly technical stuff. The iron bars in the gate allowed him to see some property inside, but the foliage blocked his view of a house or other structure that might exist.

Wish I had a camera with me.

Returning to the car, he said out loud, "Okay, Green Beauty. We need to find a place to call Knight and Tidwell — and I need to eat." Concentrating on food, he did not notice a motorcycle staying some distance back.

Not far down the road Wes found the attractive Swan Country Hotel & Restaurant. It had a large pond at the side, with children feeding swans and ducks. The entry and connecting bar oozed charm with their crooked beams and ancient brickwork. One sign proclaimed it was a renovated seventeenth-century farmhouse. Another, lunch would be served for another hour.

Finding a red call box inside the lobby near the front door, Wes updated Tidwell on the day's

< 310 >

findings. "I learned the name of the man who almost hit us head-on."

He left a brief summary of the day with Knight's answering service, and asked Knight to research Morgan Pritchard.

After such a successful morning, Wes decided to have a good lunch. He ordered tomato soup, and the Swan's beef stroganoff served with rice and garlic bread. His mother used cream of mushroom soup in her recipe. But not here; the fresh mushrooms were delicious.

By the time he had leisurely finished, most patrons had left, so he pulled paper and pen from his briefcase and reviewed his notes from his hospital visit.

Stopping at the phone booth, he tried Knight again, catching him this time. Surveillance of Pritchard's home would be set in motion. Wes approached his car and noticed it leaning to one side. On close inspection, he found that both tyres on the passenger side were flat. The passenger's window, on the opposite side from the restaurant's entrance, was broken and the contents of the glove box scattered on the floorboard. The trunk had been pried open and the contents of his overnight bag had been dumped out and probably gone through, but nothing appeared missing.

Providentially, Wes had taken his case in with him at lunch.

< 311 >

Police investigated the scene, took photos, and made a report.

"Looks like an ice pick to me," the constable said, gesturing toward the tyres. "Do you have any enemies up this way? Not anti-American. There'd have been paint, and a message."

"Enemies? Not that I know of," Wes said.

"Anything missing?" asked the officer.

"Only the auto registration." With the Manor House address. He hadn't found his new home when he bought the car.

From the proprietor Wes learned that a nearby garage could repair or replace the tyres, allowing him to drive home tonight. The replacement window would have to be ordered.

* * *

From documents in the Jag, Morgan knew the American was Wesley F. Forrest and lived on the RAF Greenham air base.

That arsehole will go to the cops.

Morgan rented a van in Barton. Thomas's Car Hire agreed to store his motorcycle for three days. There was no incriminating stuff in his Mears Ashby house; however, that was not true of his garage and shop. From his house he took two bags of clothes, photos of his mother and sister, and

< 312 >

locked up. Moving toward the garage, he noticed another airline bag on his back-door handle.

"Fuck," Morgan said loudly. That bastard spy is back. Once at his shop, Morgan read the short epistle:

> Pritchard, neither of us is safe as long as Iain McKenna is alive to talk. You know what to do. He is in Reading, Royal Berkshire Hospital. Here's 4,000 pounds for expenses.
> GOSHAWK

After throwing GOSHAWK's bag and the current and old security tapes from the house's front and rear cameras into the rental van, Morgan backed it into the garage bay with the grease pit. Climbing down into the pit, he pulled on the stairs, which moved back to reveal a hidden chamber. Morgan did not have time to remove everything, only taking what he thought he'd need over the next six-to-eight weeks. There was only a small amount of the plastic explosive left after building the dirty bomb, so he took that plus four guns, ammo, some stored arson supplies, and a stash of emergency money, then carefully stowed them in the rental.

< 313 >

FORTY SIX
Peterborough
15 April 1983

Mari was able to get out of the house for a while. The sky was clear and the air cool and she felt more positive than she had in months. Her injuries from the RAF Greenham eviction had healed, the Good Friday event had gone well and, after all these years, she and Morgan were communicating again — albeit focused on the kidnap victim they were holding.

She walked around Peterborough, window shopping, trying to relax. The only time she allowed herself to think about the prisoner was when she stopped by Boots Pharmacy for some lotion for his wrists and ankles. She splurged for tea at Tower Café, with the accompanying freshly baked scone served with a dollop of clotted cream and homemade raspberry jam. On the way out of town, she stopped at Sainsbury's for foodstuffs for the next week, then drove the thirty minutes back to Wisbech.

Placing the groceries on the counter, Mari heard a scream from the garage. Entering, she saw their prisoner seated, hooded, with wires running from a box on a stand to his body. Morgan was talking so softly she couldn't understand.

< 314 >

Brown shook his head and Morgan quickly twisted a dial on the electrical stimulator and flipped a switch for five seconds. Brown screamed.

"Stop!" Mari screamed and ran to the kitchen.

Morgan, who had not noticed her, was startled by her outburst. When he entered the kitchen, Mari was at the table with her face in her hands.

She looked up. "What the hell are you doing?" she asked.

"Remember the strategy? Be mean, then nice? It's back to mean. I need additional information."

"So, what have you learned?"

"That MI5 has files on both of us." That got Mari's attention.

"They know there is a Russian spy who worked the Women's Peace Camp. Our names, plus a Katelin Nagy, and one of the Travellers named Henry Farmer. They actually had started research on us before the dirty-bomb operation failure. I mentioned McKenna's name and Brown said he was not familiar with it. I think he knows more. I'll let him rest…if you want to feed him. Go after him again tomorrow."

Later, Mari got out a stack of newspapers and started cutting out individual letters, intending to make a ransom note and send it to MI5.

< 315 >

FORTY SEVEN
Irish Sea
15 April 1983

The sun was rising over the Irish Sea, yet it was still bitterly cold. Katelin Nagy's new parka kept out the wind, although she had to hold the scarf on her head. The rolling motion of the Sealink ferry and the whitecap-peppered water suggested a strong wind. She wasn't sure of their speed but didn't think these boats traveled all that fast loaded down with cars, trucks, and cargo. She found a seat on the forward deck and watched Ireland — and freedom — approach.

But freedom at what cost?

Walking from RAF Greenham into Newbury had been the riskiest part. After the MAN truck and its driver — that damned Scotsman — were stopped by gunfire, all hell broke loose. GOSHAWK had not told her what was in the military vehicle, only that McKenna was to drive through the gate and into the missile storage area.

Certain that police would quickly link her to the attack, she'd bolted and caught the next bus leaving Newbury station, destination Oxford.

< 316 >

Once on a train to Glasgow she'd begun to worry about Mama and Papa. She'd believed the Russian when he said they were constantly under surveillance, and if she didn't follow instructions information would be divulged and her parents arrested. GOSHAWK had papers indicating a warrant for her father's arrest for his participation in the ill-fated Hungarian uprising in October 1956. Papa had assumed Mama's family name, Nagy, about that time. Now she knew why.

Why did I come to England to study art? Could I have avoided this? The answer: It doesn't matter now; it's too late.

She had spent Sunday in Glasgow visiting a friend who she met earlier at Greenham's Peace Camp. The friend arranged for more clothes and a new travel bag for Katelin because she left almost everything at Green Camp, including her camper. There was only room enough in her escape bag to carry money, papers, and one change of clothes.

She tried to call her parents from Glasgow, but their phone was out of order, increasing her worry. Rising early, she rode the bus to Stranraer to catch the ferry to Ireland. GOSHAWK had told her to use her British passport in the name Margaret Brontë Cole of Newbury to leave the country. A reasonable scheme since she should be able to answer questions about that area. He instructed her to be prepared to tell Customs that

< 317 >

her mother was a big fan of the Brontë sisters —
thus the middle name.

"Tidbits like that reduce suspicion," he'd said.

Everything had gone smoothly on the way out
of Scotland. She'd flashed her British passport and
been waved onto the ferry without a second look.
Only thing to do now was get to Hungary as
quickly as possible. Hopefully, following the
katasztrofa — disaster — the Russian would be
engaged with other issues so she'd have time to
locate her parents.

At the Port of Larne terminal, she joined the
line for British citizens' ID checks, then panicked
when she saw each one pulled aside, bags
searched, and interrogated. It was supposed to be
a wave of her passport. She overheard someone
say that fourteen Ulster Volunteer Force members
were being held on trumped-up charges by the
British government and, in retaliation, all Brits
entering or exiting Ireland were being put under a
microscope. Knowing officials would find her
extra passports and packaged money of different
currencies, and ask unanswerable questions, she
looked for an escape.

The Customs line for visitors from the
continent was moving rapidly, with only a
passport check if you had nothing to declare. It
was time to jump lines. Katelin dug into her bag,

< 318 >

found her Hungarian passport, and went to the other queue.

"Passport, please," mumbled a disinterested functionary.

Shaking slightly, she handed it over.

"Destination?"

"Budapest."

"Why were you in the UK?"

"Visiting relatives."

"How long will you be in Ireland?"

"Just a day. Catching plane home."

He reached for his stamp and she began to breathe again, when an unseen voice said, "Excuse me, Flynn, I have a few questions for this woman."

Flynn turned with obvious deference.

"May I see the passport?"

Flynn handed it over.

Katelin's legs went weak.

After inspecting it for what seemed to Katelin an extremely long time, the man said, "Ms. Nagy, I noticed you changed from the British National line to this one. Why?" Not really expecting an answer — Katelin had none — he continued, "I see that your passport was not stamped when you left Scotland. Please gather your things and let's step into my office and get these minor matters squared away, shall we?"

He held her arm politely, yet firmly.

< 319 >

FORTY EIGHT
Reading
19 April 1983

On Tuesday afternoon, Morgan, dressed as an electrician, entered the Reading-Berkshire Hospital. It was packed with outpatients trying to be seen before the weekend.

"I'm from Berkshire Electrical, here to complete an inspection," Morgan told the overworked receptionist behind the desk.

The matron quickly shuffled through a handful of charts and papers on her desk. "Not on any of my schedules," she said, then took a good look at Morgan. "I've not seen you in here before."

"No. I'm Dan. Dan Benfield." Morgan handed her a business card as proof. "We have a work order to inspect a circuit panel. It was scheduled for yesterday, but Robbie, your usual electrician, is off sick. Got switched to me for today."

After being tipped by GOSHAWK, Morgan had visited the hospital and found the business card of C.H. Robinson's Berkshire Electrical LLC taped next to the circuit breakers in the basement.

"How long?"

"Depends on what I find."

< 320 >

A line was forming, so the receptionist acquiesced. "Sign in on that clipboard," she said, and turned her attention to the next patient.

Morgan took the stairs to the basement. After consulting the building's electrical diagram, he installed a small explosive charge on a wire bundle, then headed back upstairs.

Tidwell and Wes walked the block from their parked car to the hospital.

"What do you hope to get out of McKenna?" Wes asked.

"All I can about Morgan Pritchard. We need to find him to get information to locate Agent Brown," Tidwell said, holding the door for Wes. "He's stonewalling. But today I'll explain that we have his doctor's permission to move him to Her Majesty's Prison next week. Stopping all this comfortable living, be putting him in a harsh environment that we control."

Tidwell, impatient as ever, flashed his ID and moved to the front of the line. "Afternoon. I'm here to see a prisoner... patient named Iain McKenna. Room?"

She pointed. "Second floor, 204. You'll see the guard."

< 321 >

At the second-floor nurse's station, Morgan told the staff he was going to have to cut power for a few minutes. "The generator will kick in and emergency lighting will come on," he said, "but everyone should expect momentary darkness."

Nurses scurried to patient rooms, but only the security guard entered McKenna's room. In mid-hall, Morgan opened the door on the circuit breaker panel, then thumbed his remote signaling device, detonating the charge in the basement.

Lights died and all machines went quiet. Morgan slipped in McKenna's room.

"Is the problem in here?" asked the guard.

"Yes," said Morgan, then pulled his Taurus revolver from his waistband and clubbed the officer in the throat with the butt. He pushed the guard to the floor and pivoted to the bed. McKenna's eyes opened wide in recognition. His mouth followed suit. A gun barrel was inserted.

"Tell me how to locate GOSHAWK." McKenna gave a questioning look. Morgan added, "The fuckin' Russian agent."

McKenna tried to say something, but the gun barrel interfered.

Morgan whispered, "I'm going to remove the gun. Tell me what I want to know. You'll live."

"He always...he always contacted me." As the gun moved back toward his mouth, McKenna

< 322 >

shrieked, "Wait-wait-wait! I had to send him a letter once...went somewhere in London."

McKenna grimaced in pain when Morgan jammed the gun against his cheek. "Okay. Ah think 'twas Barnet."

"I need more," said Morgan. He heard the guard trying to sit up, saw him rubbing his throat. Morgan snatched a pillow from the bed, pressed his gun into the pillow. One bullet went into the officer's right eye socket with a muffled thump. Cloth and feathers burst into a cloud.

Tidwell and Wes were waiting for the elevator when the power fluctuated and failed. "What the hell happened?" Tidwell shouted.

The receptionist said, "There's an electrician in the building doing an inspection."

Acknowledging, Tidwell turned back to the elevator, but noticed the call button light was off. Frustrated, he hit the button several times and nothing happened. "I don't like this. McKenna!"

Taking the steps two-at-a-time, they found the second floor in semidarkness, with only the battery-powered emergency lights on; patients were in near panic, yelling for help while nurses frantically tried to reassure them.

< 323 >

When the guard's head exploded, McKenna's eyes opened even wider, then he whispered hysterically, "Yea, yea, Barnet. To a library in Barnet. Th' name he used was Russian. Starts wi' a V. That's all ah know. Ah swear."

Morgan nodded, grabbed another pillow, and fired two rounds rapidly — one straight into McKenna's throat, the other into his forehead.

Wes and Tidwell heard two distinct but muffled pops from a room down the hall. Wes saw the guard's chair was empty just as Morgan exited the room. "Pritchard!"

Seeing the gun in Morgan's hand, Wes pushed a nearby nurse against the wall, kneeled over and protected her as two more pops rang out, this time much louder. Tidwell grabbed his shoulder and dropped his gun. Knees buckled and he fell.

Turning back to Morgan, now at the door to the rear stairs, Wes saw the gun pointed directly at him. Morgan pulled the trigger, but nothing happened. Baffled, Morgan looked at the gun, then at Wes, and was out the door.

Wes reacted immediately. His rear foot was against the wall, so he was off like a sprinter leaving his blocks. He busted the hall door open and rushed through, but Morgan was there and tripped him. Wes fell hard, hitting almost every metal-edged step on his tumble to the landing. He came to rest with his head in the corner, but his arm was grabbed immediately and his body flipped over. He was face-to-face with Pritchard.

"You fuckin' Yank." Forgetting it was empty, Morgan jammed the revolver against Wes' head and pulled the trigger. Again, no explosion, only clicks. Above them, the stairwell door burst open, filled with a bloodied Tidwell holding a gun.

Morgan clobbered Wes in the face with his handgun when a bullet hit the wall above his head. He turned and fled.

Dazed, cheek bleeding profusely, Wes got up on an elbow in time to see Tidwell drop his weapon, slump to his knees, and lean heavily against the door frame.

The nurses would take care of the detective, so Wes ran after Pritchard. When he burst through the first-floor stairwell door, he heard a crash and found the rear door wide open, the glass broken. Looking outside cautiously, he caught a glimpse of coveralls disappearing to the right. Wes rushed forward but pain in his right knee slowed him down. By the time he reached the street, Pritchard was gone, leaving another bloody crime scene in his wake.

< 325 >

FORTY NINE
Barnet Library
20 April 1983

Morgan ran, dodging puddles and the few people who dared the downpour. Reaching the Barnet Library's covered porch, he jostled his way to a corner and scanned those huddled under the shelter. Not one was paying him any attention.

Vigilant, he entered the double doors into a vestibule filled with boisterous kids, their parents oblivious. Morgan slipped into the used bookstore and saw three employees, all female — one at the cash register, one stocking shelves, the third assisting patrons.

"May I help you?" an old woman asked.

"No, just browsing," answered Morgan.

"Let me know if I can," she responded and turned to assist others. He left.

< 326 >

Morgan cautiously entered another set of double doors into the main library. He headed to reading tables and rows of periodicals across from the main circulation desk, grabbed a newspaper and a seat. He pretended to read as he watched library staff go about their business. He saw three offices; no employees brought GOSHAWK to mind. After half an hour, Morgan walked thru the stacks as if looking for a book, occasionally stopping to pull a book and read the jacket.

On his way to the bathroom, he saw an enclosed directory board with staff names on a black felt background, and at the bottom: Peter Velikaya, Chief Librarian for Special Collections.

Morgan hurried to the reference desk. "A Mr. Velikaya called me concerning an inquiry I had made on an old edition. Where might I find him?"

The librarian said, "I'm sorry. Mr. Velikaya is on vacation. May I help you?"

"No, thank you. It appears he has already done research on the topic. When will he return?"

She checked a nearby clipboard and told him, "The 25th, next Monday."

< 327 >

FIFTY
Wisbech, Cambridgeshire
20 April 1983

In times of personal stress, Mari had found gardening an excellent escape. So, mid-morning, she drove Morgan's Range Rover to the Wisbech Garden Centre. There had been heavy precipitation in early April, with snow over the Easter weekend. But it had been warming since and forecasters said Central England had experienced its last frost for the year.

When she got home, Morgan helped her move into the shed behind the house all of the purchased pots, fertilizer, and trays of bulbs started in the garden centre's nursery. After Morgan left to visit a library, Mari tackled an area in Morgan's back yard that received full sun. She found ample gardening tools left by the previous owner. The grounds indicated that Morgan had not used them.

Turning and loosening the soil and removing weeds, she lost track of time, until her stomach reminded her that she had missed lunch. Going inside, she used the bathroom, washed her face,

< 328 >

and went to look for something to eat. She put on tea and heated a scone.

A bacon butty sounded good for dinner. She found bread, butter, ketchup, and brown sauce, but no bacon, so she went to the freezer in the garage. She forgot about food when she saw the MI5 agent hanging by his ankles from the ceiling. On the floor beneath him was a pool of blood.

Mari immediately lowered Brown to the floor. Blood from his feet and sides covered his body. She soaked towels in warm water and washed his face. Brown opened his eyes.

"I am so sorry. You do not deserve this," she consoled. Recognizing it was a lost cause to clean him in the garage, she removed the shackles, got him up on unsteady feet and, with her support, walked him to the bathroom.

In the warm shower, Brown seemed to revive and regain mobility. Water ran red in the tub from blood washing off his body and clothes. With the blood washed from his face, she saw a swollen and purple eye — reminding her of her nightmare at the Greenham eviction.

Damn you, Morgan. We don't need to act like them. "Dry off. I'll get you something to wear," she said.

She hurried into Morgan's bedroom, opening drawers and his closet, pulling out jeans, a belt, socks, and a flannel shirt.

< 329 >

When she reentered the bath, the water was running, but the shower was empty. Suddenly she was struck from behind and propelled forward. She was able to use her hands to prevent hitting her head on the wall, but immediately Brown was on her back, his hands around her throat. She picked up a glass shampoo bottle and swung it hard over her shoulder, striking Brown on the side of his head. His fingers loosened and she pushed back into his body, throwing him off-balance. She turned just as Brown's hands hit her in the chest. The next to last thing she felt was the sensation of flying backward.

Driving home from Barnet, Morgan considered a variety of methods to handle GOSHAWK. Arriving home, he didn't see Mari working in the garden, but noticed her handiwork. He shouted her name when he entered.

Other than a deep silence that didn't seem right, there was no response. Looking inside the garage, he discovered Brown gone, chains and shackles on the bloody floor. Panicked, Morgan rushed through the house, calling again for Mari. He found her lying on the bathroom floor, head at an odd angle against the toilet. Blood flowing from one ear. Touching her throat, he found no pulse. The front door slammed. He raced down the hall.

< 330 >

He recognized his shirt and his erstwhile prisoner running away. In a rage, Morgan gave chase.

Brown hobbled past the moored boat and headed north along the river, toward Wisbech. The narrow, rock-strewn footpath, used by birdwatchers and hikers, tore at Brown's shoeless feet, and Morgan quickly caught him. A sharp shove to the back sent Brown down the bank and into cold, slick mud. He struggled to stand. Overanxious, Morgan got too close and Brown gave him a head-butt. His own motion caused Brown to lose his balance and fall. Morgan kicked him in the side of the head, but the clinging mud reduced the force and in seconds Brown was up, brandishing a wooden stick.

Morgan saw a shiny tip, the end of a broken walking cane. Cloud-filtered light illuminated Brown's mud-covered face; his eyes were wild. Morgan saw the end of the cane when the agent charged, jagged point first. Morgan sidestepped, grabbed the cane, and pulled Brown into his striking right fist, hearing the nose break with a dull snap. Brown went down, turned, and crawled away. Morgan leaped on him, overcome with anger. He grabbed Brown by the hair, dragged him to the water, and held him under until all movement ceased.

Morgan dragged the lifeless body onto the bank and sat, exhausted, his jaw aching where

< 331 >

Brown had butted him. Looking around, he saw no one in sight. Only then did he remember Mari. After pulling the body away from the path and under a bush, he ran to the house.

Slumped on the floor, Morgan cradled her body. Tears ran down his cheeks as he said her name over and over. He imagined the future she wanted. Collecting a ransom. Getting lost on the continent for years.

Now gone.

Guilt filled him. He should never have involved her. Finally gathering his composure, he laid her in the shower, and went to move Brown.

There were no indications that anyone had heard or seen the confrontation. Morgan lugged Brown's body to the garage, wrapped it in plastic, and tipped it into his freezer.

He carefully washed the blood from Mari's face and hands, then sprayed her clothes to remove most of the blood. He got a wool blanket from the cupboard and wrapped her carefully.

Morgan lowered the rear seats in Mari's Mini and spread plastic. Rigor had not set in, so he was able to fold her body, place his sister in the back, and cover her with a second blanket .

The trip to Wales seemed longer than it was because his head was killing him and his hands, injured in the fight, made it difficult to hold the steering wheel.

< 332 >

PART FOUR

< 333 >

FIFTY ONE
Llanrwst, Wales
21 April 1983

Morgan had only been to Mari's husband's farm once, right after their wedding, but remembered at Llanrwst to turn left over the River Conwy and after two miles, a right. Setting back a hundred yards from the Griffith Sheep and Cattle Farm sign, in Welsh and English, shining in the moonlight, was an old farmhouse made with stones that matched the wall enclosing it. Two barns were in sight. The one in closest proximity to the house, made of the same gray rock, housed machinery and the occasional sick animal. The larger barn was used for winter supplementary feed — hay and silage. He knew from Mari that The Farm, as she referred to it, was over three hundred acres, home for about two hundred fifty Grey Faced breeding sheep and thirty Hereford beef cattle.

< 334 >

Her husband was the fourth generation to work this farm and he managed with the help of two part-time shepherds and three sheepdogs. He'd been disappointed when, after ten years, he and Mari had no children. No male heir to take over the farm. He loved the fresh air, the pure water and the mountain grass, and his breeding programmes improved the meat's leanness and taste. An introvert, he enjoyed the solitude of hills and dogs and didn't mind being on his own when Mari was gone from the farm supporting her causes. Their social life consisted of a once-a-month community dance in Llanrwst, where more talking and drinking occurred than dancing. The men huddled discussing weather, land, and animals. Mari enjoyed the work, the new life of lambing and calving, restoring old hedgerows, but after years and no children, she'd grown restless.

Morgan parked his car and lights came on in the house. A burly man looked out the window and a blue-gray bearded collie ran toward the gate when he opened the door. The man gave a soft whistle and the dog stopped, not barking, and watched. He recognized Myrddyn Griffith, Mari's husband, walking toward him.

"'Lo, Morgan." Nodding toward the dog, Myrddyn asked, "Ya remember me bitch, Bleu?" Morgan remembered; he'd asked Mari why a sheep farmer would have a rough-coated dog

< 335 >

whose hair matted and tangled, and stayed dirty. Mari had laughed and said the dog was fourth-generation Griffith, super intelligent with a wonderful temperament and character. Besides, the once-monthly bath was bonding time between dog and master.

Breaking Morgan from his reverie, Myrddyn asked, "What brings ya to our fair county?" Then, seeing Morgan's sad face and displaying a sense only those in tune with nature possess, he asked, "Where's Mari?"

Morgan felt he must tell the truth, and with a lot of hand motion — unusual for him — he did. As he told Myrddyn what had happened, Myrddyn moved through the solid wood gate and inched toward the car. "I brought her here to be buried — on your land. What she'd have wanted. She loved her time here and had no ties to Carmarthen anymore."

Looking at the dog and not Myrddyn, he added, "Also, I do not want her death tied to me or anything I'm involved in, nor with violence surrounding the anti-nuclear movement. Can you say it was a farming accident?"

Morgan watched Myrddyn approach the rear of the car. He stood looking in the rear window for a moment, and then, like a pile-driver, struck the window twice, cracking it, and shook the pain from his hand. Leaning on the car, he cried.

< 336 >

Morgan stood silently until the sobs subsided. Looking at the ground, Myrddyn turned to him and said, "Let's move her in t' the house."

Morgan lay her on the bed. The blanket fell away from her body. Morgan gently caressed her hair and ran fingers along her cold cheek.

Moving into the main room, Morgan watched this man who, for the moment, looked defeated. But he knew he'd be okay. He was a man who dealt often with death; fox killing sheep, leaving him to bury half-eaten and gutted carcasses after crows had eaten their eyes, and spring lambs abandoned by mothers, with bottle-feeding every two hours out of the question.

"Need help?" Morgan asked.

"Have ya told her mum?"

"No."

"Then, it'd be best if...I'll take care of it." Looking Morgan straight in his eye, he said, "You've done enough, don't ya think?"

There was nothing Morgan could say. The Welshman maintained an outward appearance of control, but the sadness in his eyes was evident. He'd miss her, but his life demanded he keep on; he would acknowledge the grief once he was alone with Mari.

They walked toward the gate.

"There is one thing," Myrddyn said, walking back into the house. He returned with two letters

< 337 >

and gave them to Morgan. "Mari believed in the anti-nuclear cause, but the violence was not in her nature. She hated it." Then, face hard, gaze fixed, Myrddyn ordered, "She spoke of you often and your life pained her. You put her in danger and now she's gone. Don't come here again."

Without response, Morgan put the letters in his pocket, turned and headed down the road. He didn't look back. He walked the four miles to Llanrwst and caught the early train north.

Changing to the North Wales Coast Line at Llandudno Junction gave Morgan an opportunity to get a seat in first class and some privacy. He pulled out the letters — both addressed to Mari.

The first was a newsletter from London, listing Campaign for Nuclear Disarmament events for the next three months. He scanned the list, looking for mention of RAF Greenham Common; a statement said that CND officials had agreed not to protest at the Air Show on 28-29 May, the weekend before the Americans' Memorial Day and the British Spring Bank Holiday: "The CND is not responding to political pressure, but simply wants everyone to enjoy a long-standing summer tradition."

The second letter was in a plain envelope, mailed from Newbury:

< 338 >

Wednesday, 13 April

Dear Mari,

The CND solicitor advised me to reduce my profile with the women's camp to avoid detection because my name was part of a membership disclosure, even though it had limited exposure. However, she suggested I provide you via mail information I deem significant. I want to pass on two things.

First: in spite of last weekend's near disaster, two United States spy planes may participate in the Greenham Air Show. Details are unsettled, but security is being increased for the missile storage area.

Second and more important: The US Air Force is planning to slip in a load of cruise missiles for training purposes. The flight is scheduled to arrive at RAF Greenham on Friday, 29 April, at approximately 6:00 p.m., hoping no one will pay attention to a plane arriving at that hour on a Friday.

Lila Kerr

With a start, Morgan remembered that's the woman who rode onto RAF Greenham with him the previous December. Showed him where to park the tipper lorry for the bonfire. Morgan reclined in his upholstered seat and drifted into sleep, dreaming of Mari. When he awoke, he was alone in his compartment. Slamming his fist against the window, he informed the moving landscape, "Bloody Americans! Myrddyn blames me for Mari's death. If your fucking missiles were not coming here..." Then he understood what he must do. "I'll make you pay!"

< 340 >

FIFTY TWO

Barnet, Greater London
27 April 1983

Sokolov had begun searching today's *Times*.
The library was busy and he was so focused that
he didn't notice someone had slipped into the
chair opposite until a card was tossed onto his
paper. He looked up into a stern face with hard,
cold eyes. The handwritten note said: *Nikolai
Sokolov. Нам надо поговорить. Частная.* Sokolov
was shocked but *We need to talk. Private.* was
understood immediately. This intruder had to be a
KGB sleeper agent. He had been expecting
something.

He led the stranger to his lower-level office
and closed the door. The man held up both hands
to show they were empty, opened his coat to show
he was not armed, then reached out to shake
Sokolov's hand.

< 341 >

"I am Michael, originally from East Germany. As you may have guessed, I come at General Podgorsky's orders. To say he is unhappy is an understatement. But quoting him, 'Failure is not an option. You are allowed one more attempt.' So, he sent me to assist." Taking a seat, the agent asked, "What is your cover?"

"On loan from Saint Petersburg University to work on exhibit of Eastern European artifacts. Title is Chief Librarian for Special Collections."

Michael nodded. "What do you know about the water treatment works in the UK?"

* * *

Mid-afternoon, Morgan located the deserted warehouse near Mersey Docks in Liverpool. Examining the exterior, he found all doors and windows secure, but saw it was empty. He climbed to a rooftop perch a half block away on the opposite side of the street and settled in to watch. At eight-ten p.m., a people carrier parked in front of the warehouse. Men emerged and carefully examined the exterior as Morgan also had done. Later, two vans arrived with more IRA. All drove inside. Doors closed behind the vehicles.

Morgan saw no movement for the next hour. Not sure what to expect, he wished he had four or five mates from school to back him up. But

< 342 >

dammit, he needed those rocket-propelled grenades. He climbed down from his perch, walked to his vehicle and, with extra money next to him and a gun under the rental truck's seat, cautiously approached the building.

As directed by the IRA, he flashed his lights twice and the doors opened. Morgan drove slowly into the dimly lit warehouse. Only one van appeared in his headlights.

He stopped. Two men got out. He recognized Patrick and Ryan. Ryan, a Liverpool bartender, had arranged for Patrick to travel from Ireland and get the advance money from Morgan.

Exiting the rental, he glanced back toward the entrance where five men stood beside the other two vehicles.

"Hello, Colin, or should I say Morgan Pritchard?" Patrick said.

Morgan nodded, not surprised by their investigation.

"Pritchard, we're used to dealing with associates using false names but, lad, your past raises suspicion. I've been asked to find out your purpose. How do you plan to use these two bleedin' rockets?"

Morgan had expected a haggle over money, not the questioning of his intent. "I thought this was simply a munitions deal. You sell, I buy."

< 343 >

"Not today, sorry. It's a little more than that. I'll be askin' ya to let Ryan pat ya down."

Finding that Morgan was not armed or wired, Ryan moved away several steps, spread his legs shoulder-width and unzipped his coat in a bodyguard posture.

Morgan lowered his hands. He heard footsteps behind him and his truck door open. Not the time for heroics, he thought. "I want to shoot down an American plane, landing Friday evening at RAF Greenham Common. It will be delivering the first cruise missiles for their NATO mission."

Patrick gazed at him and Morgan felt the man wanted more. Looking at his feet, Morgan said, "Eh…my sister was killed…trying to stop the American deployment." Then directly to Patrick, "Damn it, I want to retaliate."

Patrick did not move a muscle, continued to stare, and it dawned on Morgan that something was terribly wrong. "I'm willing to pay more! Those bloody Yanks have ruined my life. They'll ruin Britain. I want them punished!"

Patrick still did not move, not even blink. But Morgan regained his composure.

"I built a dirty bomb to contaminate the base, but because of a fuckin' idiot driver, the plan failed. They should burn in hell!"

Still no response. His eyes bore into Patrick. "What's going on here? I only want revenge!"

< 344 >

After a pause, Patrick said, "Git back in your truck. I be havin' to make a call."

Patrick returned to his van and picked up a radiophone. Ryan did not move until Morgan was in his rental, then walked to Patrick's door, still watching Morgan.

Morgan felt for his gun. It was gone.

Fifteen minutes later, Ryan walked to the entrance doors, had a conference with the men there, and came back. Only then did Patrick get out of his van, carrying a package. Again, uncertainty filled Morgan. Patrick motioned for him to join him. Morgan got close. Patrick handed him the package.

"What's this?"

"Your money. You'll be findin' it all there. The decision has been made not to sell you the RPGs and launcher."

Morgan was shocked. "What! Why the hell not?" He did not take the money.

"Politics. It's always about the politics, lad. Money comes from the Provisionals in America's New England. If it were ever discovered we'd aided in blowin' up an American plane or the killin' of American soldiers, that money would dry up. Worse, Irish-Americans would go against the cause." Morgan started to speak, then felt a gun touch the back of his neck.

< 345 >

"I'm sorry...not my call," said Patrick. "Please lay down on the floor and don't be movin' 'til we're gone."

When he hesitated, the gun prodded Morgan forward. It occurred to Morgan he could die here, so he did as told. Hearing van doors open and close, the warehouse doors open, and the IRA vans depart, he finally moved.

He was never sure when the gunman behind him left, but he found the money package on his driver's seat.

< 346 >

FIFTY THREE
Paddington Green Station
28 April 1983

MI5 agent Elliot Knight met Wesley Forrest at the Edgware Road tube stop, led him to the local Police Station, then inside to a very dark room. Two chairs sat in front of a window of one-way glass looking down into a small enclosure, sparsely furnished with only a metal table and two chairs. Lights shone brightly on a woman in prison garb sitting with elbows on the table, head buried in her hands, fingers working unkempt hair.

Knight and Forrest sat down in theater seats facing the window.

"I need to explain the situation," Knight said. "Remember I asked about the female spy on base?"

Wes nodded.

"I never followed up. Then, right before the dirty-bomb attempt, Agent Brown came to me wanting more exposure to 'the undercover life'. I explained about the drug festival that was about to happen at RAF Greenham and arranged for him to get an older car and camper to spend a few nights there. I specifically told him not to take a weapon." Knight sighed. "He must have got caught up in the scene because he was involved in a shooting, then disappeared. Kidnapped, we think."

< 347 >

Knight watched the woman through the window for a few minutes. Her anxiety only shown by the twisting of a non-existent ring on her left hand. "I feel terrible for what happened...for encouraging Brown."

He paused. "Five had me notify his parents. One of the hardest things I've ever done. Promising career. Fortunately, he was not married...no children."

After another thoughtful moment: "The only good thing that came from this misadventure are the photographs."

Pointing to the glass, "This is the woman I asked you to report on," Knight said. "She was arrested in December, the night of the Embrace the Base fiasco, but her solicitor got her off."

He took a deep breath. "She was arrested again on 15 April at an Irish Sea terminal trying to enter the country to catch a flight to Hungary. Immigration said the first day she didn't talk and maintained a forced calm demeanor. Then on the second day, she asked to talk to the American colonel at RAF Greenham. We concluded that must be you. From that they were able to figure out who she was and sent her to us."

Knight stood and walked to the window. "She has talked very little, but says you interviewed her after the bonfire."

< 348 >

"I don't remember her," Wes said. "I talked to a lot of people that night."

A door opened, interrupting; the light momentarily blinded them. Knight introduced Wes to Agent John Niles. "One of MI5's best interrogators. I'll leave you with him," he said to Wes. "And thanks for the updates, especially your visit to the hospital. I'll pass it on to the DDG."

Niles took a seat and Knight stuck his head back in the door. "Ask about Brown."

"You must be relaxed at the start," Niles cautioned Wes. "With experience, a good interrogator can act on his emotions, his gut. But this is your first time, so don't even try."

"Okay." *Unsure what Niles means.*

"When you start the interview, there will be a psychological distance between the two of you, so you must try to draw her in. Try to create a feeling of normalcy. Don't ever argue with her. As a spy she will be better at this than you."

Normalcy? Like that's going to happen in that room? Oh, and thanks for the lack of confidence.

"Reduce the adversarial nature: Lean forward a lot, look directly in her eyes — talk to her, not at her. She must feel that you are listening carefully to every word she says."

Looking intently at Katelin Nagy through the one-way glass, the agent said, "Picture her with her hair pulled back; try to think about how she'd

< 349 >

look coming out of a hair salon, made-up. She is actually attractive — nice eyes, good skin."

After a pause and a shake of his head, Niles said, "That hair is gonna be expensive to fix."

Then to Wes: "You don't have to remember any details; room is wired, we'll be recording the entire interview. Listen for clues on how to proceed, facts that she needs to explain and then draw her out. Again, not to worry; I'll be in your head. Speaking of which, don't respond to my voice. She'll suspect we're communicating; no need to advertise it."

Wes didn't understand until he was wired. Agent Niles strapped a battery pack and receiver/transmitter to his back and added a small earpiece. It took effort to get everything in place because he was wearing a fitted blue suit coat which he had to leave unbuttoned.

He walked up and down a back hallway, testing and getting used to the device and the novelty of a voice with no one around. Niles asked several questions, and it took Wes many failures before he remembered not to answer.

Niles offered Wes last-minute instructions: "Remember, you have no authority to offer or give anything, or agree to any demand. When she says anything of that nature, we'll work it and get back to you. Just stall."

< 350 >

Katelin had been sitting undisturbed for a very long time; her hands and ankles secured with cuffs and chains were hurting. She needed to pee but was not going to allow them to see any discomfort.

What are they doing that takes so long? Why are they just letting me sit?

She glanced at what she assumed must be a one-way glass wall. She felt like a *majom egy állatkertben*, a monkey in a zoo. Putting her forehead on the table, she thought she should be in Europe by now. Was she set up by GOSHAWK? The escape plan worked well at first, but —

She caught her breath when the door opened. Pausing briefly, Wes then entered the room. They had discussed taking in coffee but decided to wait until she asked for it, allowing Wes a chance to get out and take a break.

Katelin straightened when he entered. She watched carefully as he sat across from her at the anchored metal table and placed a pad of paper and pencil on it — then pulled the pencil back quickly, slightly dislodging his earpiece.

With Katelin staring at him, he put the device back in place.

A soft voice sounded in his ear: "It's okay, cowboy, she can't stab you with the pencil unless you lay it on her side of the table. If she had a question about whether someone is talking to you,

< 351 >

that's now clearly answered. But she did sense something...maybe vulnerability. Talk to her!"

"Hello, Katelin, I'm Wesley Forrest," he managed to get out. "I'm a lieutenant colonel in the United States Air Force, stationed at RAF Greenham." Looking closely at her, Wes saw something on her face. Was it fear? It seemed she didn't recognize him, nor trust him.

"Like she gives a shit, cowboy. Why are you in there?" said the voice.

Cowboy? Do all Brits have to always use a nickname? Wes thought.

Looking into her eyes, he said, "I'm not sure why I'm here, Katelin. The security service said you wouldn't talk to anyone but me. They say you remembered me from December twelfth — the night of the bonfire. That I had interviewed you."

"You look different," she said.

"Well, that night I had on camouflage fatigues, not a suit. MI5 has asked that I wear civilian clothing while working with them."

"Where are you from?" she asked.

He said, "I was born in a little town called Greenville, the one in Kentucky, not South Carolina. Lived there until college, then joined the Air Force."

"What is Kent-tuck-ee?"

"It's a state, located in the southeastern part of the States."

< 352 >

Again, the voice: "Okay, cowboy, enough geography, get on with it."

As if she'd heard his earpiece, Katelin said, "Not sure I remember you, but I've got to talk to an American. I cannot trust the British."

Now Wes was focused.

Katelin stared at Wes for several seconds. Then said, "I need help."

Her voice softened when, apparently, she made her mind up to continue. "*Utálom így élni!* Err…I hate living like this. I want to be artist. I was forced to spy on Women's Peace Camp and base. *Az oroszok zsarolták.* Blackmailed by Russians. They threaten to harm my parents in Hungary if I do not cooperate."

"Where are your parents?"

"Budapest."

"Their names?" he asked.

"My father is Mikhail Nagy, but he paints as Mikhail Ivanov. And my mother is Yulia Nagy." Looking at her hands, she said, "Before I talk, I need to know they are *biztonságos*…safe."

A door slammed behind the glass wall. The voice in his ear said: "Good job, cowboy. Tell her the interview is temporarily suspended. She can relax. We'll resume tomorrow or the next."

< 353 >

FIFTY FOUR
Wales
29 April 1983

Standing, rigidly facing the rising sun, Morgan said, "Lord, I have no right to address You, since we both know I'm doomed to Hell. But my sister who left this earth much too early…she deserves more. I loved her, now she's in Your arms."

Emotionally drained, yet resolved, he mounted his motorbike, leaving Wales, and headed for the Shell refinery north of Borehamwood.

* * *

At two-thirty p.m., flight-line activity at Greenham airbase increased. Road sweepers cleaned the runway, taxiways, and the concrete apron around the hangars. Around fifty airmen walked shoulder-to-shoulder down the runway and taxiways, picking up foreign objects that could cause damage by being sucked into an aircraft engine or ruin a tyre.

Three hours later, all base entry gates were closed to traffic.

< 354 >

* * *

On his way to Borehamwood, Morgan got lucky. A Shell articulated fuel tractor and tanker unit passed him going in the opposite direction. He turned and followed the rig to the Wild Rabbit Restaurant and Pub. Morgan saw a sign advertising a salad bar and went inside. He sat where he could watch the tanker driver.

At one-thirty p.m., seeing the driver ask for his check, Morgan went outside. When the driver approached his rig, Morgan asked for a ride. The operator was brusque. "Sorry, mate, against company policy."

Morgan flashed a gun, then secured the driver's hands and feet with rope. Morgan wedged him in the floorboard of the left-side passenger seat.

On the way to Newbury, Morgan drove back roads to familiarize himself with the unit. Near Henley-on-Thames, a car cut him off, forcing him to slam on the brakes, causing the trailer to sway from side-to-side. The tied-up operator banged his head on the dash and screamed.

"I don't think you want me to slam into a tree," Morgan shouted, "so shut up and give me some help." And the driver did by explaining the rig's gear ratios, and handling sensitivities.

< 355 >

"Seems top-heavy. How much petrol is on board?" Morgan asked.

"Over half full. Almost equally divided in three compartments. Started full. Had three deliveries."

"Should be enough to blow up an airplane," Morgan said.

The driver's eyes widened in fear. It was a slow, forty-mile drive.

* * *

In the Newbury Racecourse parking lot, vacant except for a few empty horse trailers because it was a non-racing day, Morgan opened the passenger door of the hijacked petrol rig and said to the bound driver inside, "Well, mate, it's time for us to part company." The man resisted being removed from the Volvo's cab until Morgan said, "I'm going to crash this rig and probably die. Sure you want to stay inside?" All resistance ended. Morgan half-led and half-carried him to the entrance gate, duct-taped his mouth and tied him to a railing.

"Thanks for the help," he said and left.

The American plane was late. Morgan couldn't relax. He paced the racecourse parking lot, checked his watch often, and periodically checked on his prisoner. Maybe the military had changed plans, but he had no choice but to wait.

At six-twenty-six p.m., engine noises told him a large cargo plane was overhead.

* * *

As the US Air Force C-141 cargo plane circled the field and began its approach, Wes sat in the back of the commander's staff car, immediately behind Colonel Rogers. The mayor of Newbury, in the passenger seat, asked without turning, "Tell me again what's on this flight."

Wes understood that she knew, desiring only to make sure she had the terminology correct if members of Parliament or the press started calling.

"Madame Mayor, arriving is our second TEL — transporter-erector-launcher…and six missiles. Two LCCs, Launch Control Centers, arrived earlier this month. Warheads will not arrive until November. The TEL will be disguised as a regular trailer; the missiles will be in twenty-one-foot, twenty-six-thousand-pound shipping containers, like coffins, but covered with a tarp."

The mayor shuddered. Wes touched her shoulder and she turned to face him. "Remember, the fact that any missiles have arrived is classified."

< 357 >

"I have real misgivings about lying to my constituents concerning the missiles," she said. "I know four of them are dummies, and the best answer is to say that all are such. But if the truth was ever revealed, my credibility would be severely injured. Just not sure —"

"No time left for political strategy, ma'am," Rogers said. Huge wheels touched down with puffs of smoke. They watched in silence while the plane reached the end of the runway, turned, and headed toward the hangars via the south taxiway.

* * *

From the racecourse, Morgan drove the eighteen-wheeler two miles up Pyle Hill, then turned onto Burys Bank Road toward the back gate. He'd made a recon of the base from outside the perimeter, but still were many unknowns.

Approaching the gate at seventy five kilometers an hour, the truck was moving too fast to make the ninety-degree turn to hit the gate square-on as Morgan intended. Instead, he found himself left of centre. The right front of the tractor hit the double gate midpoint, knocking the right wing into a group of security policemen. The left wing and post snapped off, forcing the rig into the empty guardhouse. The small building was knocked off its foundation, which was lucky for

< 358 >

Morgan since it bounced the cab back onto the northern taxiway.

The aircraft was now moving parallel to him, so he turned the rig south on the crossfield taxiway. Too late, he realized he was again travelling too fast. The trailer leaned left; the right tyres lost traction. Straightening the front wheels, Morgan took his foot off the gas and held his breath, very lightly touching the brakes. Within seconds he had the rig under control, off the grass, and back onto the tarmac. His hands molded to the steering wheel; he forced the thought — relax.

The plane loomed directly in front of him and he stomped the gas pedal.

Colonel Rogers and Wes stood next to the commander's staff car near Hangar 4 as the yellow flashing lights of the service truck led the cargo plane toward the concrete apron in front of Hangar 5.

The car radio squawked: "Mayday! Mayday! Mayday! Tanker truck busted through back gate! Now heading across the flight line. Repeat: Tanker truck heading toward aircraft on the ground."

The speeding rig zigzagged, turning south in Wes' direction, then corrected itself. Wes jumped into a nearby green RAF Leyland water lorry. Not used to shifting with his left hand, fortunately he

< 359 >

found the gear locations on the head of the lever, moved through them quickly, picking up speed.

The pilots, warned by air traffic controllers, accelerated the big aircraft down the taxiway toward the east end of the runway as marshallers dropped yellow light-sticks and ran to safety.

Intercepting the semi as it drove onto the ramp in front of Hangar 5, Wes recognized the driver and yelled.

"Pritchard! You bastard!"

Wes aimed his vehicle at the tractor's fuel tank and where the trailer attached to the tractor.

With the direct hit, the rig's fuel tank erupted, throwing diesel fuel in all directions; the screech of bending metal and squeal of tyres added noise to the chaos. Rubber rolled from the rims, the metal on asphalt sparking the fuel into a fire. Wes was helpless when the trailer swung toward him. Time seemed to slow as the Shell logo approached, crushing the passenger side of his truck. He instinctively raised his arms, covering his head and eyes, protecting them from flying glass.

The water tank on the Leyland lorry broke loose from its mountings and crashed into the cab, rupturing with water gushing in. The indention missed his head by inches.

Wes was struggling with his door when a suited fireman pried it open. Amid a rush of steam

< 360 >

and flames to the front, Wes scrambled out, immediately enveloped in a cloud of black smoke.

The fireman grabbed his arm and pulled him to safety. "Jesus. You okay, sir?" Instead of answering, Wes wiped his face and saw blood on his hands.

The base fire chief ran up. "Wes, you okay?" Engine noise of aircraft taking off drowned out conversation, so Wes only nodded.

After the plane passed the chief said, "Damn lucky the fuel trailer didn't rupture." Then pointing, "Got to get the tractor fire out, then..."

The chief turned, but Wes was gone.

Stumbling around the front of the tractor, Wes avoided rushing firemen with hoses spraying the area with foam. The passenger door was open, the cab empty.

Son of a bitch!

Wes tried to approach, but a silver-suited fireman grabbed his arm. "Stay back, dammit! Still dangerous."

"Where the hell's the driver?" Wes yelled.

Barely audible through his helmet, he shouted back, "No one was in there when I got here."

Wes looked around wildly: across the runway...down the taxiway...then glancing toward the base, he saw a lone figure limping toward the door of Hangar 5.

Pritchard!

< 361 >

An American police car pulled up, roof-mounted lights flashing. Wes recognized the driver, a shooter from Welford, and ran over. "Get out. I need the car." The driver frowned but opened the door and stepped onto the tarmac.

Wes pointed. "That's the driver of the gas truck...in Hangar 5. Tell Colonel Frazier."

After jumping in the car, Wes did a spinning one-eighty and sped in that direction. Entering the hangar, he slowed, allowing his eyes to adjust. The flashing blue-and-white lights on his vehicle created strange shadows throughout.

Unarmed, he stopped the car, then leaned forward to check the glove box. A burst of gunfire erupted, hitting his vehicle; the driver's window shattered, pelting him with shards. As he fell onto the seat, he floored the accelerator, without thought of where he might be headed. The car fishtailed and he sat up. A red-and-black forklift was in his path. He twisted the wheel sharply to the right. The forklift driver jumped for his life as Wes passed within a foot. Wes covered his face when he crashed into a three-tiered pallet rack, throwing supplies and cardboard boxes in all directions. The Plymouth's laminated windshield remained intact, but the roof lights didn't.

Camouflage netting covered the front of the car. Wes' door was blocked by wooden pallets, so

< 362 >

he slid across the bench seat and checked the glove box. Empty!

"Shit!"

Instinctively he grabbed the car keys and fell to the floor outside. After listening and scanning his surroundings for a few seconds...he heard nothing. He crawled to the rear, opened the trunk, and grabbed two small bags from inside — one black, the other orange. He moved quickly toward the relative safety of the wall behind the pallet rack. From across the hangar, the MPT door opened. Captain Perez yelled, "What the hell's going on?"

Wes shouted, "Gunfire. Lock yourself in. Call security."

The orange bag was an emergency first aid kit, from which he removed a pair of scissors and put them in his camouflage pants pocket. The black bag contained an unloaded .38 revolver and a plastic bag with a handful of rounds.

Gun and bullets in hand, Wes edged along the wall toward the entrance, staying in shadows created by the overhead lighting. He stopped and surveyed each aisle before crossing. At the end of the third rack, feeling far enough away from the car, he stopped to load the weapon.

He moved slowly down the aisle between two racks. Each rack was ten feet wide, sixty four feet long, and ten feet tall, running perpendicular to the hangar's centre aisle. Sudden banging, like

< 363 >

someone hitting a wall with a hammer, interrupted his search. Wes ducked out of view into one of the many empty spaces in the racks.

He waited, strained to hear. Nothing. He peeked out toward the wall and across the hangar centre to the ops trailers. Again, nothing.

Wiping bloody sweat from his forehead with the back of his hand, he inched out of hiding and slid on his belly along the concrete floor toward the centre, hugging the metal rack. His wet clothing picked up dirt and oil from the floor, making a scratching noise, heard only by him — at least he hoped so.

A crash like a chain falling on concrete echoed in the hangar, then footfalls, a muffled outcry, followed by unintelligible shouts and a gunshot. The sounds didn't seem close, so Wes ran to the end of the aisle, dropped to one knee, and looked around the corner. Toward the entrance, he saw nothing except floating specks of dust in the light from the setting sun. Only the silent forklift at the building's interior.

But then, Morgan Pritchard stepped from out of the shadows. He moved slowly past the forklift toward him — one hand holding the maintenance man's shirt collar, pushing him forward, and the other cramming the muzzle of a gun against the man's neck.

< 364 >

"Forrest, I know you're watching and armed. Do not force me to kill this bloke. You know I will." A few more steps. "It's you I want, Forrest."

Using the rack's metal frame for support, Wes took aim and cocked his gun. But Morgan smartly stayed behind his human shield.

After a pause, both clearly assessing the situation, "Okay, Forrest, let's play a game. I'll count to three. One. Two..."

Instead of three, Morgan shot the hostage in the back of the leg.

With the screams, Morgan let the man fall to the floor, knelt, and placed the gun against the hostage's head. "Forrest, I don't have time to bluff. Game over."

After uncocking the handgun, Wes yelled, "Stop!" and stepped out into the central corridor, raising the gun over his head, in surrender.

"That's better," Morgan said. "Weapon on the ground. Kick it away." Wes did so.

"Now put your hands behind your head and lock your fingers. Then walk toward me."

Morgan, singularly focused on Wes walking down the hangar centre, let the muzzle of his gun drift away from the maintenance man.

Wes was aware that the sunlight was at his back and was wondering how to use that to his advantage when he noticed movement behind

< 365 >

Pritchard and saw Captain Perez stealthily approaching him with a raised crowbar.

No, you idiot!

"Pritchard. Please don't shoot," Wes yelled, inching forward. "Let me get a vehicle and get you safely off base."

"Too late for that."

Approaching sirens made it difficult for Wes to hear. "What do you mean?"

Morgan seemed to stare at nothing for a second, then said, "You've lived a charmed life. Today it ends."

"Why kill me?" Wes asked.

"Mari," Morgan hissed. "You fucked up my plans. And Mari's death. All caused by your interference."

Morgan started to raise his gun, but his face tightened when he heard a noise, then turned and shot Perez, sending the crowbar clanging to the concrete. The maintenance man wobbled to his feet, and Wes lunged, knocking him into Pritchard, who lost his balance and his gun.

Searching for his weapon, Morgan didn't see a left fist coming. Wes hit him in front of his right ear and he staggered, causing the right hook to miss. Recovering, Morgan hit Wes square in the face, busting his nose, then slammed his right fist into his sternum, knocking him to the floor. Wes

< 366 >

staggered to his feet, nose pouring blood. Morgan picked up the crowbar.

They circled each other. Holding the crowbar like an overhead axe, Morgan lunged. Wes blocked the descending arm, but Morgan twisted inside and drove the end of the crowbar at Wes. Wes fell backward and collapsed so Pritchard's thrust became a glancing blow off his ribs. Morgan lost his grip on the tool and it went skittering across the floor.

Without hesitation, Morgan was on him, pelting his head with his fists. Flat on his back on the concrete floor, Wes pulled the scissors from his pocket. With a limited range of motion and in desperation, he swung them in an arc, driving the sharp end into Pritchard's shoulder.

Morgan's mouth opened wordlessly. In a daze, he pulled out the scissors and, ignoring the blood, raised them above Wes' head, both hands preparing to drive the instrument downward.

Wes crossed his arms to block the attack, but Morgan's head jerked violently with an explosive eruption, blood and brain tissue spewed in all directions. Morgan and scissors fell.

Morgan was roughly shoved off Wes and light filled his vision. Colonel Frazier followed Morgan to the floor, driving his knee into his chest, and placed the muzzle of his gun against his head. He felt for a pulse. There was none.

< 367 >

* * *

Reminiscing on a call with his daughter Lorianne, Wes laid back on his pillows, reapplying a cold compress to his nose.

"Daddy, you're in the news! They say you saved a plane from being blown up."

Wes gave her a simple and less scary version of what happened.

"Are the passengers okay?" she had asked, worried, to which Wes explained that it was a cargo plane, with a small crew, all unhurt.

She sounded proud of him, and that made him feel better.

A lot better.

< 368 >

FIFTY FIVE
Paddington Green Station
2 May 1983

Katelin relaxed on the bed in a small room that had a high window with bars, but still a window. A toilet and shower with curtain for privacy filled a corner, a thick mattress filled the bed.

Four hours earlier she'd been moved from a windowless six-by-nine concrete block cell that had a small steel toilet and a narrow bed with a thin, worn mattress. Still, guards routinely moved along the narrow hallway peeking through the bars, watching her every move.

She was being set up for something. She knew it but didn't care. The shower had felt great, hot water and soap. It was good getting out of prison garb and into a gray track suit. They told her she'd soon get some of her own clothes to wear.

* * *

< 369 >

John Niles met Wes at the station entrance to escort him to that day's meeting room.

"Made great time," Wes said. "Almost no traffic."

"It's a bank holiday," said Niles. "Heard you were in hospital."

"Just for a few hours. Our base doc didn't have confidence in his X-rays, so sent me to the hospital in Reading for something called a CT scan."

"And?"

"Fortunately, my ribs are bruised, not broken. And no internal injuries." He took a deep breath. "It'll be pain meds and breathing exercises for a couple weeks."

* * *

Someone tapped on Katelin's door. She was surprised when Agent Knight entered her room quickly and said, "We need to go. I have another meeting."

A female guard cuffed Katelin's hands to a belt around her waist. No restraints were put on her feet. Once the guard let them out of the cell block, Knight led her around the corner to an elevator. He placed a key in a slot beside the lowest level indicated, and hit the button marked P3. Katelin noted both top and lowest levels required keys.

< 370 >

As the elevator descended, Knight asked, "The last few days before you left RAF Greenham, did you meet or see a young man in a beat-up blue Humber Saloon, with gray primer paint spots?"

Katelin thought, then shook her head.

"His name was Brown? Glendon Brown?"

Again, she shook her head. This time vigorously and the chains rattled.

"Sorry about the cuffs," Knight said, "but policy dictates that all prisoners — and technically, you are still a prisoner — must be secured when being moved within the building."

They stepped off the elevator and were met by a security guard who checked the paperwork Knight had for himself and Katelin. A heavy door, like a bank vault, was opened and they walked into a large room, with concrete walls thick like a vault. In the centre, a huge, rectangular glass box appeared to be suspended in the air. It reminded her of a rail car you could see through. Knight led her to a door at the end, up a set of stairs, and into the glass room. Once inside, Katelin saw it was a small conference room with transparent walls, dark carpet, and a ceiling of soundproofing tiles. She heard the soft sound of circulating air that felt cool, yet smelled metallic. Near the centre was a rectangular table with six folding chairs.

Knight pulled out the middle chair on one side for her and uncuffed her hands. There was an odd-

< 371 >

looking green phone in the midpoint of the table. Odd because there was no dialing mechanism. Looking around, rubbing her wrists, she asked, "What is this place?"

"This is a fully secure communications room intended to prevent, as well as detect, visual, acoustical, technical, and physical access by unauthorized persons."

"So why am I here?"

"We are in a room-within-a-room. We are actually inside a concrete vault."

"So why am I here?"

"We have your parents in protective custody in Budapest. Hopefully, you'll be able to talk to them in a few minutes."

She froze.

"Bottle of water?" Knight asked.

"No," was all she managed to say.

Knight sat to her left. Her mind was a muddle of questions and concerns. She'd worried a lot about her parents since her capture. Before she could ask Knight any questions, two men entered the glass box: Colonel Forrest and a man who introduced himself as MI5 Agent John Niles.

Forrest nodded to her and slowly sat down opposite Knight.

Niles placed his briefcase on the table, picked up the handset from the green phone, and said, "Are we ready?" After listening for half a minute,

< 372 >

he hung up, sat opposite Katelin, and said, "Katelin. I'm sure Agent Knight told you that you are about to speak to your parents. There is a problem with the voice encryption device in Budapest, but it should be repaired in a few minutes. Once you begin, you will have only five minutes."

Sitting down, he continued, "I can tell you that they are in an MI6 secure facility in Budapest, in a room similar to this. All communication going out and coming into this room will be encrypted, so you can say anything you wish. The conversation will be recorded at both ends and available for you to listen to later, if you so desire. The purpose of this call is so you will know they are safe, and you no longer have to fear any threat from the Russians. You are free to speak in Hungarian, English, or Russian, whichever you and your family are more comfortable with."

Niles removed a pad and pen from his briefcase. "Your parents were only secured yesterday, and they were not aware of your situation — the attempt to flee and your arrest — so they may be in a bit of shock, and as concerned about you as you are of them. They have not been presented with options regarding their future. MI6 will take the lead on that issue. The point is don't waste time talking about the next step in this process...it's too early. You will be a part of those

< 373 >

discussions over the next few weeks. Any questions?"

Katelin's mind was blank, so she simply shook her head. The phone rang. Niles picked it up and said nothing, listening for a short while before looking at Katelin and handing her the phone.

"*Anyja?* Mama?" Katelin said with apprehension. Then she spurted words in broken sentences while tears flowed. Not interested in listening to one side of a conversation in a foreign language, and to give her some privacy, Wes and Knight moved away from the table.

Niles noticed Forrest wince when he got out of his chair and stood. Katelin and her parents were talking enthusiastically, and he guessed it was about each party's current situation. He'd see a translation this evening.

After four minutes, Niles wrote, "One minute left" on his pad and showed it to Katelin. She nodded and spoke more rapidly, then panicked when all she heard was static from the phone. She dropped her head and the phone, and sobbed. Wes found a box of tissues and gave them to an appreciative Katelin.

Without any discussion or questions, Knight took Katelin back to her room.

As he was taking off her restraints, she said, "I'd like water now."

< 374 >

After drinking the whole bottle, she cried herself to sleep.

The next morning at seven, Katelin was served a prison breakfast, with weak coffee in a plastic cup. A file folder lay on the tray. She picked up the transcript, in English, of her telephone conversation the previous evening. She longed for a super-strong espresso in a china cup relaxing with her friends in Budapest.

Would she ever see them again?

< 375 >

FIFTY SIX
Paddington Green Station
3 May 1983

By the time Agent Knight came for Katelin, she'd read the transcript three times, feeling peace of mind on one hand — her parents were safe — but fear and uncertainty of the future on the other. This time the guard's cuffing was gentler.

"I'm sorry we have to continue to use these," said Knight, "but you're being held for passport violations."

Instead of the concrete vault, Knight took her to a small conference room where Colonel Forrest and Agent Niles were waiting. Niles said, "Have a seat. Would you like coffee, tea?"

"Yes. Strong coffee."

Knight looked at Wes, who was standing near the wall. "Ribs?"

< 376 >

Wes nodded. "Forgot my meds. Feels better to stand."

"There are several bad people out there who failed in their terrorist attack at RAF Greenham," Niles said to Katelin. Then, tapping a file folder lying in front of him on the table, "They did not accomplish their mission, so we must assume they will try again. But we have a deal for you if you help us catch them. Tell us everything you know: names, locations, phone numbers — everything — and we'll place you and your parents into witness protection and drop all charges. You will have new names, new papers, new lives."

It was what Katelin was hoping for. "Yes," she said excitedly. "My parents?"

"We anticipated your cooperation and received a telex from Budapest — MI6 — this morning," said Niles.

Knight removed her cuffs and Niles continued, "Your parents were up all night discussing options. They prefer political asylum in Northern Scotland. Your father likes the cold."

Katelin almost smiled. She could hear her father saying, "The only thing I miss about the Russian Republic is the weather."

"Their decision hinges on your desires. Whatever they do, they want you with them."

Katelin thought of the pleasant day she'd had in Glasgow visiting a small shop that sold local art.

< 377 >

"Scotland would be nice." She hoped that northern cities had art galleries and museums. Maybe even an art college, where her mother could teach.

"I'll pass it on," Niles said. "But first I... we...need to understand what you know." Getting right to the point, he asked, "When and how and by whom were you recruited? Start with where you were when you were first contacted and when you came to the UK."

Katelin's nervousness returned when she told her story, massaging every finger and joint as she spoke. "I came to the UK in 1976 to study at Camberwell College of Arts in London. Graduated. Got job at Tate Gallery. In 1982, I applied to the Slade School of Fine Arts. Postgraduate work. Was accepted."

The coffee arrived and they waited until Katelin nodded her approval, and for her to continue. "About a year ago, a man came to me at the Gallery. He said my father was in trouble and I am the only person who can help. I don't believe him, but...I am scared. What he said made me remember...you know...from childhood. We go to a coffeehouse. He shows me documents and Soviet warrant for arrest of Georgiy Mikhail Ivanov. Charge of participation and treason in the 1956 Hungarian Revolt.

< 378 >

"I try to tell him I don't know this name. I try to explain my father's name is Nagy, and the man says 'It is now.'"

Niles interrupted, "He tell you his name?"

"He called himself GOSHAWK."

"Can you describe him?"

Katelin nodded. "He's a little taller — "

"Not now," said Niles. "Tomorrow we want you to sit down with a forensic sketch artist and give him every detail you can remember. We need to know what this guy looks like."

After a pause, Knight picked up the questioning. "What happened following your initial meeting?"

"There must be a mistake. I call *Anyja...* Mother. But when she hears my question, she hangs up. I get more scared. She never hangs up on someone, especially me. So, I took leave from Gallery. I say my mother is ill. I fly to Budapest." She continued nervously, massaging her hands: "That's when I discover many secrets."

She paused, deep in thought, cupped her hands around the coffee and took a sip.

"My mother was painter, sculptor, architect. In college, she worked for estate of Ilya Repin. She help make his home a museum. She's expert on his works and in 1948 she's invited to assist in collecting and moving works to the new Ilya Repin Institute...in Leningrad. Three years there, she

< 379 >

falls in love my *apa*...father. Stalin dies, *Apa* move *titkosan*...secret...to Budapest... they marry, but take *Anyja*...Mother's last name. I am born in 1954. Two years later, when Soviet tanks rolled into Budapest, *apám veszélybe került*...errr...my father compromised, and hid to avoid arrest."

She stopped, took her time with another sip, then reluctantly resumed her story. She related that her Grandfather, Peter Nagy, a pharmacist, assisted many elderly and sick during and after the Revolution. Even though he was reported several times for hiding people, including Katelin's father, the Hungarian Security Police turned a blind eye. By '58, the unrest had settled, and her father was able to get forged documents, including a Hungarian birth certificate, and a job as a custodian of a government building.

Niles interrupted again: "In what name was the fake birth certificate?"

"Gyorgy Mikhail Nagy. I thought that was his real name."

Wes eased into a seat at the table, inhaling deeply. "How many meetings did you have with GOSHAWK?" he asked.

Without hesitation, Katelin said, "Three, face to face. One near Tate, I say already, you know. Two, Budapest. Three, when I return England."

"Did he ever mention Morgan Pritchard?" asked Wes.

< 380 >

"Slow down, cowboy," Niles said. "Let her tell it chronologically...her way." Turning back to Katelin, "You were talking about your father."

"Yes, when I found out truth." She glanced at the ceiling, then continued. "There was some *probléma*...you say question, yes? Question of legality of warrant. But my parents fear going to authority. You understand this, yes? We agreed it was best to do as GOSHAWK asked. I get paid for only reporting on peace camp."

Then turning to Knight: "I must tell you. This man knows of my school plans and offered money — six hundred pounds every month. He deposited it in Newbury bank account in my name. It covered expenses and savings for Slade School."

Looking at her hands again, she sighed, "I won't be attending."

"Probably not," answered Knight. "Is that the money you had when you stopped in Ireland?"

"Yes." Katelin muttered. "I keep emergency money hidden in my camper."

"Wait, I'm lost," said Niles. "You saw GOSHAWK while you were in Budapest?"

"Yes." She looked at the table and swallowed. "The first week, I felt followed. Never see anyone. One day, he talk to me on street. We go to park and talk. He says he'll take care of my *Apa's politikai problémák*...political problems...and I can earn money helping in England. I hear of the

< 381 >

Women's Peace Camp at RAF Greenham, but no details."

"And when you returned?" Knight asked.

"Back in London for two days, he slips a note under the door. I am to go to the Campaign for Nuclear Disarmament sit-in in the central lobby of Parliament. He comes. Suggests coffee at a shop. We talk the Budapest trip. He says I am to go to Greenham for a long weekend. He gives me money to buy sleeping bag and other *példány*…items. Last time I see him."

Katelin finished her coffee, took a deep breath, and continued. "I visit RAF Greenham. It is all fine. I feel *kellemes*… comfortable…with the women. I return to the apartment and find a letter explaining *levelezési rendszer*…mail drop system, you know this? Yes? Okay. Two lock-box keys, one to post office in London and one to Newbury and two letter box addresses. And he gives combinations for each post office. Next day — "

Knight interrupted. "No phone numbers?"

Katelin shook her head and continued. "Next day I go to the box in Newbury. There is keys and book with *utasítás*…instructions. I decode. It is easy. It says my code name is BIRCH and that I have a used car and a caravan in a parking garage. And I am to use it at Greenham."

"Name of the book?" asked Niles.

< 382 >

"First, *One Day in the Life of Ivan Denisovich*. We are now on second book, *Jane Eyre*." Katelin took the time to explain how their code system worked.

"How did you get involved with Morgan Pritchard?" Wes asked again.

"Around Easter, GOSHAWK send message saying Travellers coming to Greenham from Stonehenge. He say two of his men embedded and attempt to drive vehicle onto the base. I am to assist. A few days before their arrival, he tell me one of the men is Mari's brother, Morgan Pritchard. And Scotsman, Iain McKenna."

"Had you met either before?"

"No. I saw Mari's brother at the Embrace Event in December, but I never talk to him."

"What was Pritchard doing in December?"

She answered Wes, "He *meghajtó teherautó...* drive lorry with firewood."

"Did he set the bonfire?"

"Don't know. I not go onto base."

"Did GOSHAWK give you instructions about the December event?"

"No. Embrace the Base and bonfire organized by Women's Peace Camp, especially Mari, and Campaign for Nuclear Disarmament. I only help."

Finally remembering Katelin, Wes asked, "Didn't we have a discussion about what 'organized' means?"

< 383 >

Katelin looked at Wes, blushed, and said, "Now I remember you."

Concerned, Wes asked, "Did you know what was in the military truck that drove on base on April 9th?"

"No. I don't. Why is everybody so *érdekelt*… interest. Why bullets?" She stared at him, waiting.

Knight changed the subject. "When did you last hear from GOSHAWK?"

"The message I just tell you, telling me names of two men I am to assist." She took a deep breath and added, "Plus woman he never mentioned."

"What woman?" Knight asked.

"McKenna's wife. She was there."

"Never found a camper we could tie to McKenna," intoned Wes. "She left early in it."

After a quiet moment, with everyone lost in their own thoughts, Katelin said, "I'm very tired. Can we take break?"

"Actually, this is enough for today," said Niles. "We can talk tomorrow. I need to telex Budapest."

Knight took her back to her room. "Why wasn't the base told more about what was occurring between Katelin and GOSHAWK and the dirty-bomb incident?" Wes asked Niles.

"Well, cowboy, you didn't hear this from me," replied Niles, "but your buddy Knight fucked up. A lot of information was there, and he didn't put it together."

< 384 >

FIFTY SEVEN
Barnet, Greater London
10 May 1983

It was still dark when Wesley Forrest joined MI5 Agent Elliot Knight at the coffee shop, Caffé D'Oro. Knight and four other agents were sitting at a window table with mismatched chairs. He had a pot of coffee and a cup ready for Wes. They were far enough away from the counter to be able to talk confidentially.

"I had difficulty getting into town, streets are blocked," said Wes. "What's going on?"

"Fire," answered Knight, looking out the window at thinning but still circulating smoke. "Locals are investigating. Does not seem to be related to our case."

Turning to Wes, "Where's the Thames Valley detective?"

< 385 >

"Tidwell said he had a suspect to arrest in Oxford this morning," Wes said.

Pointing to a three-story up the street, Knight said, "Our boy's flat is up there."

"How'd you find him?" Wes asked.

Knight explained that, last fall, a stranger had approached an engineer from the Atomic Weapons Establishment expressing interest in buying diagrams of the Trident submarine-launched ballistic missile. The engineer needed money to fund a nasty divorce. Though the stranger asked for unclassified drawings, he felt it was only the beginning and came to Five.

"They arranged a meeting in Basingstoke where the engineer was to hand over a set of proposed design changes in exchange for money. We put three men on it, but within minutes of meeting, the spy must have sensed something was wrong and walked out."

Taking a deep breath, he continued, "Unfortunately, it was late at night and very dark. We got only a few, poor photographs. One almost decent profile shot came from a security camera as the buyer walked past a nearby business. We lost him within a few blocks. At the time, the engineer could only say he was a white male. Dark hair. Average size. Scruffy beard. Slight accent he couldn't identify. That could've been faked," he added.

< 386 >

A bit defensive, Knight added, "MI5 has a limited budget. It's tough to get the necessary manpower to properly tail someone. It takes sixteen bloody agents, working in shifts, to watch one suspect."

"So, what happened?" asked Wes, not interested in Knight's budgetary problems.

"I think the engineer overplayed his role. The man hasn't contacted him since."

"How long ago was that?"

"November, last."

After ordering biscuits, Knight said: "The profile in the Basingstoke photos resembled the sketch Nagy provided. We showed her the photos. She was confident it was GOSHAWK. We had her send him a coded report. He never picked it up. But we've kept surveillance on that post office ever since. When shown the sketch made with Katelin's guidance, the engineer was certain it was the same man he met with."

Knight rubbed his finger over the table, picking at small bits of stuck-on food. "Last month the same spy tried to get misinformation into the Ministry of Defence. Correction, he did get it in. Bribed an undersecretary. It was a false report about the cruise missile warhead from an American laboratory...Lawrence something..."

"Lawrence Livermore?" Wes asked.

< 387 >

Knight nodded. "It said the cruise missile warhead might not be capable of safely handling the rugged, off-road environment the operational plan called for. It implied catastrophic results and recommended at least a year of testing before deploying."

He sipped coffee, then continued. "Caused quite a stir...all the way up to Heseltine...until someone conferred with the laboratory and found out the spy had interspersed old speculation into a classified evaluation report. Needless to say, a major security evaluation is ongoing at the laboratory and here. We have been looking and watching, but nothing happened until Thursday afternoon last."

"And that was...what?"

"Well, a member of our surveillance team had just gotten off post office duty. Stopped in the café at the Cavendish Hotel. And..." Knight smiled.

"And recognized the spymaster from the sketch and photos."

"Yes, indeed." Knight added milk to his coffee. "The agent was able to make a call and, fortunately, we were able to get a few people there timely and followed the spy to this neighborhood."

Wes perked up. "Here?"

Knight nodded. "Yes. Took us a day to arrange 24-hour surveillance and since that time he has not

< 388 >

been seen. Found out where he lives. Works at the library nearby. Alias Peter Zennia Velikaya."

Looking out the window into the night, Knight continued, "On inquiry last night at the library, I was told he is in Northern Ireland assisting the inspection and inventory of a collector's books and documents. Will be there all week. So, no rush, we'll go in after daylight."

"Did you call the Irish police?" Wes asked.

"No. Depends on what we find here."

At nine-thirty the next morning, the property manager opened the flat to MI5. He had leased the flat to one Peter Velikaya — A/K/A GOSHAWK and Nikolai Sokolov, but the manager didn't know those names.

There were no clothes in the closets nor personal items in the flat, no papers or forms of identification. Everything had been cleaned out.

< 389 >

FIFTY EIGHT
Thatcham, Berkshire
14 May 1983

The Thames Water supervisor answered his phone. "Peter Alyard."

"Sir, I hate to bother you at home and on a Saturday. But I have a pressing issue."

"And this is?"

"Thomas Simpson of the BBC. I'm calling because someone in upper management wants to see if a story about Cold Ash pumping station could be both educational and entertaining."

"You have my attention."

"I've been assigned to investigate. And of course, need a walk-thru," Simpson said.

"Exactly what are you looking for?" asked Alyard.

< 390 >

"Cold Ash is an old pumping station. The features producer heard it has a new mission. Monitoring the amount of lead in Newbury's drinking water and testing some control techniques?" Simpson paused for confirmation. Receiving none, he continued. "The story should probably include some history of the station and its ongoing preservation effort. Maybe who it serves, how it currently operates, and the newly designed testing. I will have a better idea after visiting the site."

"Will Wednesday morning at ten work for you?" Alyard said.

"I will make it work."

"Brilliant. Bring credentials."

* * *

After being tipped from the sleeper agent that his flat was to be raided, Sokolov accelerated his plans and visited the pumping station over the previous week. He'd even followed Alyard home, discovering he worked for Newbury District Waterworks as an inspector of sites that were not manned daily, checking on problems or issues.

Sokolov had taken numerous photos of the gate and lock, fence and as much of the inside as possible, but thirty-foot trees inside the perimeter fence blocked much of the view. He saw no sign of

< 391 >

security cameras but didn't want to risk an alert, so decided on a visit as a guest versus an intrusion. The Wednesday date allowed time for Sokolov to create a fake BBC ID card as Thomas G. Simpson and a vague memo purportedly written by the features producer at Broadcasting House.

Sokolov arrived at the Cold Ash gate fifteen minutes early to find Alyard waiting. "Tom Simpson," he said, sticking out his hand. "Thanks for meeting me."

"No problem," said Alyard. "Credentials." He did not shake.

Sokolov dropped his hand and gave the credentials to Alyard. He read the memo and inspected the ID card. Satisfied, he turned toward the entrance. "Follow me."

After they entered the compound, Alyard became more vocal, friendlier. "You will see there are several stories that can be written about this station. I suggest we start our tour with the reservoir in the rear and move back this way."

They passed a three-story, almost square, brick building with rows of tall, narrow windows along the side. Arched windows set even higher. The entrance was more ornate. Half-columns on each side supported a concrete nameplate of capital letters.

Alyard said, "This first building is the engine house, which is off-line."

Holding up a camera, Sokolov asked, "Photos?"

Alyard nodded and continued, "Inside are a pair of steam-driven, non-rotating-beam engines."

Glancing at Sokolov photographing the columns and COLD ASH STATION sign, Alyard said, "You've seen pictures of them, yes? Impressive fourteen-foot flywheels? Most late nineteenth-century water plants have them."

Sokolov nodded, "I think so."

Pointing, Alyard said, "You see it has lots of large windows. Natural light was necessary for engineer and staff who monitored and adjusted machinery around the clock. It was built in Victorian style in the 1880s and used until 1970."

They walked around the south side of the engine house. Alyard carried on. "The attached tower has the smokestack in the centre. Stairs circle and reach all levels of the engine house."

Continuing to walk west, Alyard said, "The attached rectangular building contains boilers. Which leads to an interesting story itself. The original renovation plan was to tear out the boilers and put in electric pumps, but a conservation group stopped the removal, formed a Preservation Trust, and started raising money to restore the engine and pump houses to the way they were fifty years ago. Eventually they wanted to use it as a working museum.

< 393 >

"Thames Water conceded…" Pointing south, he said, "…and built that building with piping, monitoring and control equipment, and three electric centrifugal pumps. One for each pool as well as a backup."

Sokolov heard the hum and buzz of motors through the walls and gave a questioning look.

Alyard said, "You'll see in a minute."

In front of them, a large field was surrounded by a barbed wire fence, enclosing a long, single-story brick building. Cows grazed on a flat pasture of grass. "Let's have a look at the reservoirs," Alyard said, "and the testing you mentioned."

They passed through an unlocked gate and, walking on a two-track road, approached the building. It covered what looked like a city block.

"Watch your step," Alyard said, stepping over a fresh cow patty.

Alyard opened the reservoir door with one of the many keys on a heavy metal ring. Sokolov saw no cameras or security system wiring.

Inside to the right, a set of descending stairs. To the left, a storage area about twenty feet square was filled with cardboard boxes of varying sizes.

At the bottom of the stairs, Alyard flipped a switch which lighted a concrete T with a walkway straight ahead that extended into the darkness. He flipped another switch and a large underground

< 394 >

pool and brick arched support beams were brightly lit.

"Wow!" Sokolov said, trying to impress. "That is really something."

Alyard smiled with pride. "You're seeing a pool holding one and a half million liters of treated water. That is a little over what the population of Eastern Newbury used daily in the early 1900s."

Alyard walked another twenty feet, opened a door in the wall, and flipped on lights. Sokolov saw another huge pool, but the ceiling was only ten or so feet above the water.

"In the 1920s," Alyard said, "there was a severe drought in this area and the populace demanded more water reserve. Combined with anticipated population increase, this second pool was constructed in 1935. The pasture you saw is above us."

Taking out his notebook, Sokolov asked, "What are the exact sizes of each pool?"

"Assuming your boss decides on a story, with your return visit I'll give you an illustration with exact measurements."

"What did you mean by 'treated water'?" Sokolov's camera kept snapping.

"Cold Ash is what we call a service reservoir. Until lately no treatments to the water were accomplished here. The filtration, disinfection, pH control and chemical dosing — chlorine and other

< 395 >

treatments to the water — are done at the Bradfield Water Treatment Works. Cold Ash was a reservoir to handle fluctuations in demand, and with pumps that added pressure to the system."

Turning to Sokolov, "Mr. Simpson, do you know about plumbosolvency?"

Sokolov shook his head.

"It is the ability of a solvent to dissolve lead. Believe it or not, water is a solvent. The water supply system in Newbury is old with a lot of lead pipes. The amount of lead in Newbury's water has increased over the last few years, not to an unsafe level, but still a concern. So, Thames Water is testing several ways to reduce the attack on lead piping. One way to prevent plumbosolvency is to keep the pH levels at seven-point-five. The treatment plant is working hard to do that."

Taking a few minutes to point to the bottom of each pool: "See those pipes?" Alyard asked. "That's incoming water from the treatment plant. See the boxes next to the pipes? They contain flow meters and where the test treatment — phosphates — are added. Cold Ash was perfect for treatment measures to minimize lead in the drinking water. No further questions? Then let's go outside and I'll show you."

Playing reporter, Sokolov changed rolls in the camera, took more photos, and recorded notes before they exited. Once outside, Alyard led the

< 396 >

spy to the right side of the reservoir building to a tanker trailer covered by a roof.

"This tanker holds orthophosphoric acid, which is added to the water at the box you saw at the water inflow pipes. A fixed dose is added in proportion to the flow."

"Are the phosphates harmful?" asked Sokolov.

"Sure, if there was an inadvertent overdose. But a person would have to drink ten liters of this water to equal the amount of phosphates in only one can of soda."

Sokolov took so many pictures of the tubular lines connecting the truck to the building that Alyard finally asked, "You need to see anything else here before we move on to the pumps and engine house?"

"No," said Sokolov. "I can't wait to step inside the engine house and get a few photos for my boss. Pique his interest."

< 397 >

FIFTY NINE
The Telegraph

Tuesday, 24 May 1983
LONDON

Local hospital sources say 62 Newbury residents, including 18 children under the age of 16, have sought medical assistance at Berkshire County Hospital Accident & Emergency units with primary complaint of respiratory distress. It has been reported, but not confirmed, that one child has died. Thames Valley Police are investigating amid suspicions of poisoning.

Thames Valley Water Utilities supervisor, Peter Alyard of Thatcham, was killed inside the Cold Ash Water Treatment Works on Monday. Police have made no announcements other than to say Mr. Alyard went there as part of the Newbury poisoning investigation.

Police are focusing on the Cold Ash facility. A source told this reporter that a message was painted on an interior wall in red paint. Police would not confirm or deny.

* * *

< 398 >

Wednesday, 25 May 1983
LONDON

A total of 28 Newbury residents, including seven children, remain hospitalized today after police authorities determined all 28 had been poisoned by consuming unknown quantities of paraquat , a toxic weed killer dumped into the Thames Valley water system at the Cold Ash Water Treatment Works.

An unidentified hospital source told The Telegraph that one adult and two children died as a result of exposure to the noxious chemical, all succumbing to severe complications due to multi-organ failure. The source feared the poisoning death toll will rise over the next few days and weeks.

A complaint filed by the Syngenta Industrial Plant, Huddersfield, on Monday stated an ISO tank container filled with Methyl Viologen, paraquat being the common name for the herbicide, was stolen from the port of Liverpool where it was being prepared for shipment to Brazil. Once they had that information, hospital personnel were quick to link the poisoning source to the

< 399 >

weed killer. Public Health contacted the corporate headquarters of the manufacturer based in Switzerland.

The company advised it was critical for patients to be moved to intensive care and placed on the recommended detoxification protocol for the poison.

< 400 >

PART FIVE

< 401 >

SIXTY
Gower Street
25 May 1983

Agent Elliot Knight escorted Wes to the sixth-floor conference room where they met previously. Deputy Director-General Clive Walker, no coat, loose tie, and sleeves rolled up, nodded to Wes, and hastened to the front of the room.

"Gentlemen."

Those not already seated did so. All chairs were quickly occupied, except for the two furthest away from the DDG, which Knight and Wes took.

Once seated, Walker said, "For those of you who have not met Lieutenant Colonel Wesley Forrest…" With the wave of a file indicated Wes. "…he's representing the States in these discussions. He'll be participating fully in this endeavor and, as such, is cleared by me for all reports and information gathered. And the rationale."

< 402 >

Walker made no effort to introduce the other eight at the table.

"Today is an overview. Each of you will be given an assignment in order to obtain answers concerning certain situations as soon as possible. I have received a preliminary report from the Thames Valley Police," he said.

He opened the folder in front of him. "It appears the terrorists entered the Cold Ash Water Treatment Works early Saturday morning to set up the apparatus allowing herbicide to leach into the water all of Sunday. Tainted drinking water was in homes by Monday. It took most of that day for hospitals to inform police of their belief of ongoing poisoning.

"As part of the investigation, Peter Alyard, a utility supervisor, went to Cold Ash early Tuesday morning and was killed by a hidden explosive device." Looking up, he added, "I presume probably planted by terrorists."

Clearing his throat, he continued. "I assume you've read all the guesswork from the press. Requires clarification. This information is need-to-know. It is *not* to be discussed with anyone outside this room. Contrary to yesterday's *Telegraph*, the terrorist did not write a message on the wall at Cold Ash. The erroneous assumption came from a photograph of red paint splatter on the

< 403 >

waterworks walls caused by the explosion. We have made no effort to correct the press error."

Walker looked up at the men. "However, a message was sent by a courier service to the Office of the Secretary of State for Defence. It has not been released."

He flicked a switch and a slide appeared on the screen. Wes noticed for the first time that the curtain had already been closed over the window. The message on the slide read as follows:

> You were lucky at RAF Greenham. You will not be so next time. You have until 24 June to announce publicly you are having second thoughts about the deployment of cruise missiles and will be seeking a delay while you debate the issue.

Several pictures delivered with the message flashed across the screen, including one showing a stack of lead boxes with a vintage nuclear materials symbol, and several more of Secretary Heseltine's children at home and at school.

"So, gentlemen, even with two of the terrorists dead and one accomplice in custody, this is far from over. I have set up three teams. You are each assigned to one of them. Team One: Help TVP at Cold Ash and see if we can find leads to the terrorists and the killers of Alyard. Team Two:

< 404 >

Follow up on the paraquat theft. Team Three: Assist in the Secretary of State for Defence investigation who sent the note and photos and their intent."

DDG Walker nodded to an assistant seated in the corner, who passed out a sheet of paper to each person. Wes saw it was a list of the three teams. Quickly glancing over it, he did not find his name.

"Gentlemen, you are dismissed to meet with your team leaders, where you will be shown copies of documents needed for your roles." Then looking at Wes, "Colonel Forrest, would you and Agent Knight stick around?"

As the room cleared, the DDG moved to sit near Wes. "Because of your friendship with Detective Tidwell, Wes, I thought I'd assign you to Agent Knight's team. Investigating the Cold Ash Water Treatment Works. However, I wonder if you have had other thoughts."

Wes had an answer ready. "When I interviewed Katelin Nagy, she mentioned the Scotsman's wife being at RAF Greenham. Has that been followed up?"

"Yes," Knight answered. "Scottish authorities interviewed McKenna's wife and determined she knew nothing about the dirty bomb. She was simply accompanying her husband to Newbury."

"At the interview," Wes said, "I felt something important was missing. In particular what, if

< 405 >

anything, McKenna's wife knew of the spy. I'd like to follow up that line of questioning.

"Second," Wes said, looking at his hands, "General Hudson suggested if we ever have the opportunity, we should check out McKenna's house." Then looking at the DDG, "Maybe now is a good time to visit the McKenna home in Scotland."

The DDG took a deep breath and thought about the request. "I agree." Turning to Knight, "Elliot, we'll cover his expenses. Please help with arrangements, including a letter with my authorization." Back to Wes. "I think you should take the Thames Valley detective with you."

"If he thinks it's important, wants to go, sure."

"Well, it can't hurt," the DDG said. "His badge may open some doors for you. Make sure he understands that it is an MI5 lead investigation. Report your findings to Agent Knight."

< 406 >

SIXTY ONE
Keiss, Scotland
27 May 1983

Wesley Forrest and Detective Tidwell arrived at the McKenna home at the scheduled time, three p.m. No sooner had Wes knocked than Mrs. McKenna opened the front door, looking at them through the screen. Holding up his badge, Tidwell smiled, stepped forward, and made introductions.

She let them in and Tidwell asked, "How would you like to be addressed?"

She seemed taken aback, but said, "Claire" and pointed to the front room, a comfortable snug where a small coal burner threw off heat remnants from dying embers.

"Please. Have a seat," she said.

< 407 >

"Thank you for seeing us," Wes said, after being seated. "It must be an inconvenience."

"Nay. I have questions." Turning to Tidwell, she said, "Mah husband was in yer protective custody in th' hospital and ye let him die. How come?"

Neither Wes nor the detective were ready for this opposition, but Tidwell put on his professional manner and answered, "The murderer came disguised as an electrician, responding to an actual documented problem. He carried full and proper identification. With that he got by the hospital security protocols. We're so sorry for your loss."

Claire nodded but remained tense.

After a quick glance at Wes, Tidwell continued, "There were no indications this was about to happen and we're sorry it did. The officer guarding your husband also died."

He's telling me not to say we were in the hospital when it happened, Wes thought. Wes picked up immediately, "Claire, like I told you on the phone, we are not here investigating you or your husband, but we are looking for the man who took advantage, put him in this horrible position."

Claire relaxed, but said nothing.

"Were you at RAF Greenham Common on Saturday, 9 April?" he asked softly.

She looked directly at him. Nodded.

< 408 >

"Did you ever meet or see the man who forced your husband to drive that day?"

"Iain was not forced. He was hired." Glancing out the window, she continued, "I never saw a farthing." She saw Wes' confusion. "No payment."

Tidwell, remembering that he'd barely missed her at the hospital, almost asked if she had ever visited her husband there, but felt she was being honest and truthful. He gently pressed on with Wes' line of questions. "And why were you there...at RAF Greenham?"

"I rode and stayed wi' him at th' Travellers Camp at Stonehenge, then on to th' base."

Before Tidwell could inquire further, Wes asked, "Did your husband meet anyone at Stonehenge? Or get information about Greenham or the military vehicle while he was there?"

"Nay. He was only given instructions regarding th' shift to Greenham."

"From whom?" Wes asked, frowning.

"Th' camp leader. Weeds Farmer. My husband did not mention th' military truck to me 'til we met up at Newbury."

"Met up?" Wes questioned.

"Aye, we met a guy. Iain called him Pritchard. He was driving th' truck. We met him at a petrol station; Iain drove from that point on."

"And you?"

< 409 >

"I drove our van and camper to th' women's camp and parked it."

"Did you talk to Pritchard?"

"Nay. But at some point, my husband gave me a map o' th' base wi' an X marked on th' fence on th' northwest side. He said, 'At the appropriate time, pick me up here.' Didn't know what he meant by appropriate time. He left afore I could ask."

Claire paused, then nervously added, "I assume th' map came from Pritchard or th' wifie?"

"Wife?" Wes asked.

"Maybe just one o' th' peace women helping them. I never met her, just watched them talking as Iain drove onto th' base." She took a deep breath and continued, "When th' shooting started, I figured that was th' appropriate time and drove to th' pickup point. But Iain never showed."

Tidwell wondered if this uncertainty was what Wes had sensed from Nagy and glanced at him. Wes asked, "Then what did you do?"

"Police were comin' from all directions. I panicked. Drove into Newbury. Then I just…just drove around. I was worried! And I heard some folks saying th' driver o' a military truck had bin shot and taken to hospital."

She looked down at her hands. "I thought it must be Iain. But I didna know a name or which hospital. It was days before I knew where he was."

Tidwell asked, "So, you only saw Morgan Pritchard with the military truck and never knew who provided the supplies in the truck?"

"Aye, but…some were saying the truck might be radioactive, based on rumors about suits worn by folk who examined and moved th' truck. I didn't see. Denied by th' government, o' course."

"And?"

Claire hesitated and, biting her lip, she said, "I thought it was awfully coincidental Captain Ross had died o' the radiation poisoning only a few months earlier."

"Captain Ross?" Wes asked.

"Aye. Iain often crewed on th' captain's boat and worked at his boathouse."

"Do you know where the boathouse is?" Wes asked, unable to curb his excitement.

"No. Sorry."

Wes and Tidwell asked several more questions but learned no more details. Mrs. McKenna gave Mrs. Ross' number to Wes and allowed him to use her phone. There was no answer.

* * *

At the Wick police station, Tidwell apologized for not telling them he was in town but explained their connecting flight had been delayed in

Edinburgh and they were running late for the appointment.

The Chief Constable introduced them to Kevin Rhodes who was part of the investigations of Captain Ross' death and of his contaminated fishing boat.

Rhodes explained that the captain died before accounting for anything. And the boat, The Sorcha Star, was scuttled at sea by the MOD after the Scottish Marine Laboratory found high levels of gamma and beta radiation, determining the boat was not economically feasible to salvage.

"At the inquiry nothing was said about a boathouse," Rhodes said when Wes shared what they had discovered. "Captain Ross' boat was docked at Wick harbor."

From the station, Wes finally made contact with Mrs. Ross and made arrangements for an interview the next morning. Constable Rhodes invited himself to attend.

< 412 >

SIXTY TWO
Wick, Scotland
28 May 1983

Forrest and Detective Tidwell, eager to interview the wife of Captain Douglas Ross, arrived early for their appointment, only to find Constable Rhodes was already there, parked on the street in his Wick police car.

The Ross home was significantly different than the McKenna home. Here was a detached, two-story brick with a large garden and a two-car garage, versus a small semi-detached, one-story, cement with a carport.

"So, how do we approach this witness?" Wes asked Tidwell.

"Do we know if her husband's body has been returned home?" asked Tidwell. "Or if it was disposed of?"

"No. Maybe we should ask Knight before we go in."

A woman exited the house and approached the car. "Either o' ye Colonel Forrest?" she asked.

"I am," replied Wes, getting out his ID.

"Then please, come on in. I'm glad yer early. I didn't sleep last night worrying about this

< 413 >

meetin'." Then pointing to the police car, "I'm glad ye brought th' constable."

Rhodes fell in behind them. Once inside, Tidwell said, "I am from Thames Valley Police, on loan to MI5. We read the reports of your husband's death and are sorry for your loss. You have our deepest condolences."

"Thank you," she said. "Let's sit at th' kitchen table."

"Thank you," Wes said. "So, Mrs. Ross, yesterday... "

"Please call me Sorcha."

"Sorcha. Yesterday Detective Tidwell and I interviewed Claire McKenna, Iain McKenna's wife," Wes said. "And we have follow-up questions about your husband's last trip."

"What happened to him was horrible," she said. Her eyes shifted to the bay window that overlooked a well-tended garden. "But I don't think McKenna was on that trip. I thought Roy Richards was th' only crew. And I remember they ne'er found his body," she said, glancing at Rhodes.

Rhodes nodded. "Aye."

Tidwell was quick to interject, "Mrs. McKenna mentioned your husband has a boathouse."

"Aye and nay," she answered. "He does not own it, only leases it. Which reminds me. I'm needin' to fin' out when that lease is up."

< 414 >

"Where is it located?" Wes asked.

"Not sure, exactly. Never seen it. But it's north, up th' coast." She rose from her high-backed chair. "I know th' estate agent he leases from."

She left the room, returning a few minutes later. "His name is Blair Campbell. 'Ere is his card." Handing it to Wes, she said with a half-smile, "He should be able to answer yer questions. But be careful, he is a solicitor."

She held up a six-inch boat paddle with a key hanging below. "I assume ye will want to visit th' 'potting shed', that's what Doug called it. I think this is th' key." She handed it to Wes.

Mrs. Ross sat down and again looked out the window, obviously in thought. Everyone waited.

"Something must be in th' air. Another o' Douglas' co-workers is gone missing. Sam Klooster's wife told me so. Wondered if I'd seen her husband. Evidently he disappeared again."

"Klooster disappeared?" Tidwell asked.

"He does that. Disappears when he's on a job. He worked wi' my husband doing secret stuff. I figured he thought what she doesn't know can't hurt her — or him."

"On a job?"

Knowing she had spoken out of line — her husband surely rolled over in his watery grave — she spoke quickly. "On a scenic flight tour."

"Klooster's a pilot?" asked Wes.

< 415 >

"Aye. He owns a plane and does flightseeing tours around Northern Scotland for small groups. I don't know how he gets punters — his plane must stink — he smokes all th' time, an American brand o' fags."

"Where is his business?" asked Wes. "His plane kept?"

"I don't know," she replied.

"I hesitate to ask," Tidwell said but resumed the questioning. "But have you interred your husband's body?"

"Nay. He was buried at sea," she said. "It took forever to get th' body released from th' university pathology department. Then th' government made arrangements for th' burial. We had a memorial service fur Doug mid-March, at our kirk."

She thought for a moment then, shaking her head slightly, said softly, "Maybe near his boat. He'd love that."

After a deep breath she said, "Government denied me any compensation for th' boat."

"Did the department determine cause of death?" asked Wes.

"Words I will ne'er forget. *Acute radiation syndrome*. They said it's commonly called radiation poisoning."

< 416 >

SIXTY THREE
RAF Greenham Common AB
Air Show
29 May 1983

Group Captain Finley Mackay sat in the VIP viewing stand with the family of Sir Douglas Bader, watching a flyby of a Lancaster Bomber escorted by Spitfire and Hurricane fighter aircraft from the Battle of Britain Memorial Flight. "Sir Douglas commanded a squadron of Spitfires and Hurricanes that played a significant role in protecting London from German aircraft during World War II," MacKay explained to a group of American tourists sitting in front of him.

The group captain was too nervous to enjoy the show. While it was true an accident had never occurred at a Greenham Air Tattoo, he was doing everything possible to ensure one didn't occur this weekend on his watch.

< 417 >

An American asked, "Why is it called a tattoo?"

Mackay paused to let the noise of the aircraft pass. "A tattoo is a military performance of music or display of armed forces in general. It became tattoo over time as a mispronounced version of the Dutch *doe den tap toe*, which meant 'turn off the taps'. A signal to stop serving beer and time for soldiers to return to barracks." Pointing toward the runway, he said, "And with a concentration of air arms, it's called an Air Tattoo."

Mackay constantly surveyed the Crowd Line, a fence stretching east to west, the full length of the base. Families and individuals were standing and strolling along the northern side, which was open to the public. This area included a taxiway lined with aircraft on static display. Over seventy thousand visitors were in attendance to view over three hundred aircraft, plus hundreds of exhibitors, merchants, and individuals manning concession stands.

To the south of the boundary was the operational portion of the base: the active runway, base administration, the secure cruise missile facilities, and parking for programme aircraft. The show included aerial demonstration teams for seven hours on Saturday, five hours on Sunday, followed by the departure of aircraft.

< 418 >

One potential headache had not materialized — confrontation with female protesters. Five or six were at top of Burys Bank Road holding signs, but they were being civil and not harassing vehicles approaching the base. This was because Lady Joan Bader, widow of Sir Douglas, had visited the women's peace camp earlier and asked for them to please respect her husband's memory.

* * *

During the aerobatic display by the RAF Red Arrows, Nikolai Sokolov walked through the viewing area, disguised with only a hat and sunglasses. But instead of watching the air show, Sokolov was looking for Lieutenant Colonel Wesley Forrest. He did take photos of the Lockheed TR-1 — the newer version of the U-2 spy plane which was shot down flying over the Soviet Union in 1960 — and the latest reconnaissance bird, the Lockheed SR-71.

Sokolov stood outside the exclusive Friends of the International Air Tattoo Enclosure when he heard a woman mention Forrest's name. "That jerk Forrest managed to skip-out this weekend, making someone else pick up his tasks. At the last minute, General Hudson had to conduct the bus tour Forrest was scheduled to do."

< 419 >

"I shouldn't say anything," the other woman responded. "But I heard General Hudson say that he's in Scotland."

The first woman whispered something that Sokolov did not hear, then she said louder, "See you tomorrow morning." They split, going separate ways.

Sokolov shadowed the officer who had first mentioned Forrest. When she stopped at a visitor information stand, Sokolov walked up and loudly asked an attendant if she knew where US Air Force Lieutenant Colonel Forrest was working. The attendant looked toward the female Lieutenant Colonel, with name badge Judd, who nodded, then spoke to Sokolov. "Why might you want to see Colonel Forrest?"

"I was to meet him today and discuss the purchase of a car."

"He is the last person on earth I'd buy a car from," she said.

"No. You misunderstand. I am selling, not buying."

"He has made many people unhappy this weekend besides you."

"Why would I be unhappy? We can meet another time."

Judd took a deep breath, stormed off in a huff.

< 420 >

"Don't mind her," the attendant said. "She's not a Forrest fan." With a polite excuse me, the attendant moved to help another visitor.

Sokolov was too startled to continue anyway. The sleeper agent had relayed the fact that Forrest was helping MI5, but not that he was going to Scotland. Why was he in Scotland? And where?

* * *

After Sunday lunch, Winnie Ashworth, the Campaign for Nuclear Disarmament office manager in Reading, found Lila Kerr at the Press and Information Centre.

With the engine roar of departing aircraft and intermittent crowd applause in the background, they walked east along the Crowd Line. Just two women enjoying an innocent stroll. Looking at the exhibition of search-and-rescue aircraft as crews prepared them for departure.

"Most of the aircraft will be returning to their home bases later today. Some have left already," Lila said. "But when the tattoo officially ends at three and the gates are closed and secured," pointing northeast, she continued, "they're going to move the new spy plane to that hardstand."

Turning north toward the perimeter fence, Lila asked, "Did you see the plane?"

"Yes. Dark as the night," Winnie said.

< 421 >

"Maybe why it's called Blackbird."

They walked along the perimeter fence behind parked cars, surveying the area, verifying the best invasion point was behind a metal storage building with an unobstructed path.

At a temporary gate opened for the air show, Winnie said good-bye to Lila. "I'm going to walk back to my car along Burys Bank Road and find spots with good cover for our vehicles."

* * *

Shortly before midnight, four women and two men slipped through dark woods toward the base perimeter fence. Storm clouds were moving in slowly from the west, blocking moonlight. All wore various shades of black, including their backpacks. Carrying two covered, heavy and cumbersome crates made travel difficult.

Seeing no close-by activity, they approached the perimeter behind the metal storage building. Oliver, tall, lean, and strong, opened his backpack and removed bolt cutters.

"Stand back," he said quietly, then, starting close to a post, he snipped across and down, creating a four-by-four section of fence that pulled out like a gate. After wiring it to stay open, Oliver and Paul maneuvered the crates through and onto the base.

< 422 >

Once inside, Winnie called them into a squatting huddle. "This is where we split up. Think about what you have to do and do it. But please be careful and be quiet. Any questions?"

Standing, she added softly, "This one's for Mari! For her leadership from the hundred-mile march from Wales extending through Embrace the Base, she gave her all. Thinking not of herself, but of a better UK for the next generation."

The men now moved one crate at a time along a line of bushes, using the building as cover from the airfield. Two pairs of women headed east toward the hardstands and their intended targets.

Because of an ongoing hangar modification at RAF Mildenhall, the SR-71 Blackbird — America's high-altitude surveillance vehicle — and its KC-135Q aerial refueler had to remain at RAF Greenham until Tuesday. It was rare for a SR-71, an advanced long-range Mach 3 craft, to be outside the security of its home base. Protestors had an irresistible opportunity. Lila, in her privileged position as the British base commander's secretary, knew about the repositioning to where trees and bushes provided sight screens from traffic on Burys Bank Road.

The women moved deliberately, avoiding detection by security patrols routinely passing along their side of the runway. Lila noticed that floodlights close to the aeroplanes were not on and

< 423 >

smiled. Her boss had unwittingly argued that to illuminate them would only draw unwanted attention. She noted three canine units, consisting of a handler and a single dog, patrolling around their respective aircraft. After a half-hour, both female teams were in positions west of visible targets, but far enough away not to risk being heard or smelled by one of the dogs. Fortunately, the slight wind was from the east, into their faces.

The women lay in a low place between the first pad and the perimeter fence to wait for the diversion. They remained calm, focusing on the planes. The SR-71 and the KC-135Q were both parked perpendicular to the runway, about fifty yards apart. Winnie crawled over to Lila and whispered, "They're not parked like we thought. Meg and I will take the refueler on the far pad. You and Amy get the nearer spy plane."

Lila nodded and wormed her way to her partner to relay the plan.

An American security vehicle passed approximately every ten minutes, making its rounds. Lila scanned the surroundings and reconfirmed the best way to escape was the way they'd entered. Impatient, she caught herself tapping the ground with her finger as she waited.

< 424 >

Awkward crates in hand, Oliver and Paul had worked their way to the front of the metal supply building. After a security patrol passed, they opened the boxes and tied ten-foot cords, with tin cans attached, to each drugged fox's tail. Paul poured a liquid that smelled like skunk spray — a strong, foul, chemical odor — on each fox, getting some on his pants and shoes.

"Gonna be a stinky ride home," he whispered.

"Yeah, in my van!" Oliver replied with no humor.

Closing the crates, they lugged them one at a time from the concealed location to the taxiway. They gave a wake-up injection to each fox, attached ropes to the doors, backed up and stretched out on the ground. Within five minutes, both foxes were scrabbling angrily, sounding like fighting puppies. Rattling cans increased their irritation. When the next scheduled security vehicle came down the taxiway from the west, Oliver said, "Now!" and the men pulled the ropes, opening the crates.

The foxes shot out, both headed east, away from the approaching headlights, but toward the parked spy plane. The clattering tin cans made the unnerved foxes run even faster.

From all directions, on and off the base, dogs started barking. Oliver pointed out one dog galloping down the taxiway at full stride toward

< 425 >

the foxes, forcing them to turn south across the runway. Team Fox abandoned the crates and ran.

When the dog and handler left the nearest pad pursuing the foxes, Lila and Amy crept toward their designated quarry. Approaching the rear of the Blackbird, Lila was surprised by its massive size — she could stand beneath the triangular body. It was wider than her parents' home. Running her hand along the undercarriage, she was astonished by its rough surface.

Hearing distant shouts, she crouched behind the wing-mounted wheel struts and protective panel. Nothing was heading her way, but the canine handler at the refueler was still fighting to control his dog. Trying to follow the other dog down the runway toward the commotion and commingled scents of fox and skunk, the huge German shepherd was dragging the short policeman away from his post.

Lila crab-walked under the plane to the nose, which looked more like a stingray than a bird, like something from the movie *Star Wars*. Amy began spraying paint on the side while Lila pulled the first paint-filled balloon from her backpack. She heaved the rubbery bladder high, but it bounced twice on the fuselage and flipped off, rupturing on the ground, leaving a large white splotch.

"Shite," she muttered. She backed up, focused on the windscreen, took a run at the plane, and

< 426 >

delivered a second balloon overhand like a cricket bowler. It went hard and straight, skipped, then ruptured.

"Okay!" she yelled, in her excitement forgetting where she was, and quickly covered her mouth. Luckily, the restrained dog at the KC-135 had broken loose and was running across the grass toward the runway and the fleeing, screeching foxes. His handler chased, yelling, but lost ground with every second, never looking back.

She splattered another on the windscreen and burst two on the spear-shaped snout.

Glancing at the other hardstand, Lila saw that Winnie had found exactly what she needed on the refueling plane's body. In front of the wing was an area two meters square, unmarred by words or symbols. Standing on her tiptoes, she had created a peace symbol with a spray can. Meg tossed white paint-filled balloons at the nose.

Lila's partner, Amy, moved to the rear of the SR-71 and threw her paint balloons. Lila moved quickly to the side, heaved one balloon at the US Air Force insignia and one more at an engine cover, then shouted, "Time to go!"

She motioned to the women and jogged toward the metal building and their escape gate behind it. They had been on the hardstand for less than six minutes.

< 427 >

At the metal storage building, the women dumped remaining spray cans and ran for the opening in the fence. As previously agreed, the first teams out were to leave something at the fence to signal followers that they had succeeded and headed home. Seeing one of Team Fox's crate covers, Lila knew they were gone.

Lila gave Winnie a questioning look when she pulled off work gloves and threw them on the ground. "Stole them from the rubbish bin behind the Camden Garden Centre. Let the government work with that!" Winnie replied.

When Lila and Amy approached the vehicle, they saw flashing lights and a man getting out of a police car parked behind it. The women ducked into a roadside drainage ditch and watched as officers walked around their car, trying to open doors and boot, shining torches inside. One officer returned to his car to use the radio.

"What are we going to do?" Amy whispered.

"Get out of here. Good we wore gloves in the car," Lila responded. "Let's move along the road toward Newbury. We can catch a bus or train."

"The car?"

"Forget it."

Whoever rented that car is in for a lot of questions, Lila thought. After a hundred yards, they hit the ground again when another police car flew past, its lights flashing and siren wailing.

< 428 >

Lila looked up and down the road, deciding. "I still think Newbury is our best option. But we need to travel on the opposite side — away from the base. More trees and places to hide. And we need to get out of these clothes."

They walked on the north side of Burys Bank Road, hiding successfully from the few passing cars, or so they thought. But after fifteen minutes, police cars converged from both directions.

"Run!" screamed Lila.

She headed across the Greenham Golf Course.

A police K-9 was quick to follow, its barking getting closer. She ran into a sand trap and fell, the animal instantly on her. With its teeth bared, low growl in its throat, it forced her flat in the sand. She felt the hot, stinky breath on her neck. Then a torch shone on her face. "Get up. Slowly."

"Lionel?" she asked weakly, but with relief when she recognized the British guard.

"Kerr?"

"Thank God, it's you..." Pleading, she added, "Please, let me go. My job..."

"Sorry," Lionel said gruffly. His voice showed his disappointment in her. He helped her up and cuffed her.

< 430 >

PART SIX

< 431 >

SIXTY FOUR
Wick, Scotland
29 May 1983

    Colonel Wesley Forrest and Detective Andrew Tidwell got out of their car when estate agent Blair Campbell unlocked his office door. After examining their IDs and credentials, Campbell said, "This had better be important. My wife is unhappy I'm not accompanying her to church."

    "It is very important," Tidwell said. "Several have died and more are in jeopardy."

    "What?" Campbell said in surprise. "Captain Ross' wife said ye wanted to visit a boathouse."

    "It is our understanding, from her," Wes said, "that Captain Ross leased a boathouse from you."

"My leases have a confidentiality agreement. See, I'm unable to discuss anythin' wi'out approval o' th' lessee or papers from th' court."

"Maybe I can be a help," came a voice from the doorway.

Surprised, all turned.

"I'm Constable Rhodes, East Caithness Constabulary, Wick Station. I'm carrying an important document." He continued talking as he handed it to Campbell. "I was part o' Captain Ross fatal accident inquiry. A boathouse wasn't mentioned 'til Colonel Forrest informed us yesterday, that is."

After a nasty glance at Wes and a minute reviewing the warrant, Campbell took a deep breath. "How can I assist?"

"Well, ye can take us to th' boathouse." replied Rhodes. "An' I'm needin' to phone th' Scots Marine Laboratory. They tested th' radiation levels on Ross' boat. There has been a radiated boat stored there, so they need to evaluate it before we get there."

Since it would take time for the Marine Laboratory to respond from Inverness, they decided to meet at "the potting shed" in two hours. Campbell gave directions to the Constable. He passed them on to the Laboratory personnel.

The Constable had invited Wes and Tidwell to ride with him, take a tour of the Highlands

< 433 >

enroute, and stop at the Reiss Cafe for a late Scottish breakfast with its excellent food and a view of the Sea.

"Nice car," Tidwell said.

"Aye. Fresh to th' force. A Rover SD1 Hatchback. Good pickup, good mileage for a V8. Seats five wi' room in th' back for equipment."

* * *

Just north of Freswick, Rhodes turned right off A99 toward Skirza and the North Sea. After ten minutes on a rough two-track lane, they approached an abandoned house with a dock area, all surrounded by a fence. Campbell was opening the gate.

"Good timing," said Wes.

They walked around the weather-beaten boathouse covered in gray shingles, trying to peer through the few dirty windows. The green paint on the personnel door to the rear and the large double doors on the water were split and peeling — should have been repainted years ago. They inspected the two rails, four-feet apart, providing a boat ramp from the sea to the large doors.

"Whin wull th' Scots Marine Lab be 'ere?" Campbell asked the Constable.

Rhodes checked his watch. "Soon."

"Shuid we open it...hae a keek ben?" asked Campbell.

"Nah," said the Constable.

"Absolutely not," said Wes.

Once the laboratory technicians arrived, it took only a short time for them to suit up. Campbell tried his key, but it didn't work. "Try this," Wes said, extending the key Mrs. Ross had given him. It worked.

Technicians found the radiation levels inside the building to be 110 times what the background level was. And mainly from Cesium-137. They instructed it be cleaned before anyone enter without protection.

To their disappointment, the boathouse was empty except for a box in the back corner. Wes asked the men to check the corner. The box turned out to hold two cans of inboard engine oil; but behind, on the ground, was an empty pack of Camels and a matchbook from The Marina Hotel, Port Ellen, Isle of Islay.

Wes and Tidwell left the estate agent and head of the laboratory team to sort out the decontamination of the boathouse. They told them the cigarette pack and match cover were evidence and needed to be bagged to protect them from picking up further fingerprints.

Once in Rhodes' police car, Wes said, "We need to get to the Isle of Islay pronto."

< 435 >

"Maybe, but remember it's MI5 picking up our tab," said Tidwell, "and I don't think an empty cigarette pack and a matchbook cover is enough justification." He looked out at the passing landscape for a moment then said, "When we get to the station, I'll call the police on Islay and see if there is something else."

We're moving too slow, Wes thought.

On a speakerphone, Tidwell explained who he was and the purpose of his call.

The Islay Police desk officer explained why they could not provide information on three unknown men without better descriptions or photographs. "Mind this scenic island is th' birthplace of Scotch, wi' seven distilleries and three breweries, so loads o' tourists visit daily."

"I'll call Agent Knight," Wes said. "They can be faxed this evening."

"There is one interesting thing," the Islay officer added. "Last week we find a scuttled fishing boat from your side. From Buckie."

"Buckie?" Tidwell responded.

"Yeah. From Moray Firth Fishing Charters. Boat's called th' Achieve. Interesting part is when we reported it to th' Scots Police, it came back as nicked."

< 436 >

"When was it stolen?" Wes asked.

"Aye...one sec." Papers shuffled. "Reported nicked on 5 May."

Tidwell, turning to Wes, said, "We got more evidence."

Before the Islay officer hung up, he told them that The Marina Hotel was very nice and of moderate price. When Wes stressed the urgency of securing a flight to Islay, a Wick officer called the airlines to check schedules, only to be told there were no direct flights to the island Isle of Islay. At least one stop had to be made.

"Let's drive to Edinburgh tonight," Wes said. "Fly out in the morning."

"I disagree," said Tidwell. "We should remain overnight and see what Islay uncovers, if anything, with the photographs."

Wes shook his head, but called Knight and updated him. Knight said, "I'll call Isle of Islay police, then fax pictures of Sokolov and McKenna to 'em."

While Wes was on the phone, the police department in Wick faxed an arrest photo of Klooster to the Isle.

The next morning, Detective Morrison of the Port Ellen PD, Islay called with information: "Klooster was in-fact on th' island and spent th' weekend in our jail."

< 437 >

Wes and Tidwell flew to Glasgow but missed the one daily flight to the Isle of Islay and had to remain overnight again for the flight to the island. Tidwell visited the historic Victorian city centre. Wes paced.

"A whole frickin' day wasted," Wes fumed. "Shoulda flown to Glasgow earlier. Coulda driven and used the ferry and got to Islay in hours."

"Look at a map," Tidwell said. "Have to drive north an hour to Loch Lomond, cross the mountains west, then south along Loch Fyne. Then catch a two-hour ferry to the Isle. Seven-to-eight hours total."

To quell his frustration, Wes went for a long walk. Later, he called Port Ellen for an update. Morrison said MI5 told them to do nothing until Forrest and Tidwell arrived.

"What the hell?" Wes said, and called Knight, leaving a message: "What are you doing?"

His call was not returned.

Shoulda left Tidwell in Oxford.

< 438 >

SIXTY FIVE
Isle of Islay
31 May 1983

The Islay Airport information desk explained to Police Detective Timothy Morrison that a storm was in their flight path and Forrest and Tidwell's plane had to fly north and west to get around it and would be almost an hour late.

After deplaning, both Forrest and Tidwell were pale and walked unsteadily. Wes was pissed at yet another delay but, once in the car, wanted to be caught up immediately. Morrison turned on the windscreen wipers and brought everyone up to speed.

"As I explained on th' phone, Sam Klooster got drunk and into a fight last Saturday night at The Malt House, a Port Ellen bar and restaurant. Spent most of Sunday sleeping it off in jail."

< 439 >

Morrison took a deep breath and watched a woman take four tries before getting into a handicap spot. "Klooster was released Monday mornin', but has a court appearance scheduled in two weeks. He can't leave th' island."

Morrison started his older, unmarked car. "After we acknowledged th' photos from th' Wick PD, we received these photos from MI5." He handed a file to Tidwell. "An Agent Knight requested we do nothing 'til yer arrival."

Shaking his head, Wes asked, "So, where is Klooster now?"

"Don't know. At his arrest, he gave us his address as a rental house up th' coast. Assume he's there."

"How far?" asked Wes.

"Not far. Three to four miles up th' A846. Do ye have a rental motor reserved?"

"No."

"Then ye won't get one. They're scarce out here. Th' chief will likely let ye use this motor."

* * *

They started with the owner of the rental house.

"Mr. Graham, I am Colonel Forrest, and this is Detective Tidwell." Tidwell showed Graham his

< 440 >

credentials, and Wes continued. "Detective Morrison gave us your name and address."

"You are kinda out o' yer jurisdiction," he said. The rain had taken a break, so he came out onto the front stoop. "Sorry, th' wife is sick."

"We were on the island. MI5 asked us to talk to a person of interest," Tidwell said. Pulling out his photos of Klooster and Sokolov, he showed Graham the photo of Klooster.

"They be rentin' my cottage for th' summer."

"They?" Wes said.

"Those two." Graham said, pointing at photos.

Surprised, Wes tried to speak, then managed, "Where is this cottage?"

Graham stepped off the porch and pointed to the left. "That's it."

"No cars?" said Tidwell.

"One is off island," he said, pointing to the Sokolov photo. "Th' other is either in a pub drinking or at the warehouse."

"Warehouse?" responded Wes, recovering from his momentary shock.

"Working?" Tidwell followed up.

"Usin' th' old Ardbeg Warehouse down on Lagavulin Bay. Workin' on something — not sure what," Graham said. "Th' Ardbeg Distillery went under in '81. Not a taste liked or acquired by youth, I guess."

Wes broke out in a cold sweat. So close! He rubbed the back of his neck. They left.

The rain had diminished, so when they topped a hill, they could see for a mile through the mist. Barren, not a tree in sight, gusty wind blowing from the northwest. The road below was level and widened from two lanes to four.

"Looks like a landing strip," Wes said.

Where the four lanes ended, a road angled to the right toward a small, arched, steel hangar and attached warehouse. Through the almost-closed hangar doors, they saw a small plane.

When they got closer to the dark gray and black stacked-stone warehouse, they could see windows covered with bars and a dock extending into the bay. A small red car was parked outside the personnel entrance.

"Klooster?"

Tidwell nodded.

"How do we handle this?" Wes asked.

"Same story. MI5 said talk to him."

"About?"

"We'll fake it."

After no answer to his knocking, Wes entered the warehouse, almost losing the unlocked door to a sudden gust.

"Hello," he shouted over the noise of the outside wind.

< 442 >

The south wall to their right was totally visible because a wide aisle extended the length of the warehouse. Midway were two large wooden barn doors that presumably opened onto the dock. From the north wall, heavy shelves made with oak six-by-sixes extended south. Designed to hold whisky barrels where contents aged, racks were empty, only holding dust and dirt.

Approaching the centre, they passed three piles of what appeared to be pieces of equipment covered with tarps. Tidwell yelled their presence, and a voice responded from the rear.

"Hello," a man said, cigarette dangling as he approached. "Can I hep ya?"

"Samuel Klooster?"

The man nodded. Klooster was a thin man, taller than either Wes or Tidwell. His unkempt brown hair and beard were spiked with gray.

Wes introduced himself and Tidwell again showed his credentials. Klooster said nothing. Offered nothing.

"We are on the island investigating a case," Tidwell said, "and MI5 requested we ask you a few questions."

Klooster's eyes widened and he looked from Tidwell to Wes and back. The cigarette dropped to the floor when he turned to run. Wes caught him by a rear door. Once stopped, Klooster made no effort to resist. There was an office in the rear of

< 443 >

the building with a desk and banker's chair, three file cabinets, and two additional worn wooden chairs. Wes pushed Klooster into one of the wooden chairs, where he sat, looking at his feet.

Wes glanced at Tidwell and raised his shoulders as if to say "What now?"

Tidwell pulled over the other wooden chair to face Klooster, who immediately blurted out, "I didn't do it!"

Tidwell leaned back in his chair.

"Ah did help GOSHAWK wi' moving th' the bomb stuff 'ere." He coughed. "Ah didn't wantae hulp, bit a'm needin' th' dosh."

Tidwell didn't miss a beat. "What is your role in his plan?"

"I'm a pilot 'n' I'm gonnae fly —"

Before Klooster could say another word, Sokolov stepped from behind the nearest shelf, gun in hand. Klooster jumped up; his face went ashen, eyes blinked wildly. He raised trembling hands and hesitantly approached Sokolov. "Ah have not tell thaim anythin'. 'onest!"

Sokolov paused, indecisive. Wes rushed forward, pushing Klooster into Sokolov. Sokolov's gun blasted and everyone froze.

Klooster grabbed his gut, blood running between his fingers, and slowly slid to the floor. Before Wes could close the distance to him,

Sokolov raised his weapon, pointing it at Wes, center forehead. Another shot rang out.

Wes thought he was dead. But the shot was not from Sokolov's gun.

Tidwell yelled, "No."

Wes turned to see Tidwell's gun pointing over Sokolov's head.

"You are not to kill Wesley," Tidwell said calmly.

"But the *mudak* killed our pilot. How am I to deliver this?"

"There are other ways," said Tidwell.

"Yeah, and they'll all fail!" Wes blurted out an instant before Sokolov hit him on the back of his head, knocking him forward. Wes outstretched his left arm to break the fall, heard his shoulder pop when he crumpled and hit the floor.

< 445 >

SIXTY SIX
Isle of Islay
31 May 1983

Head hurts…arm hurts…Don't move… don't move…don't move…don't move…

So Wes froze, stayed perfectly still. He heard scratching, whisperings, faint voices.

Focus. Is that Sokolov's voice?

He made out, "Why in hell did you not tell me Forrest was on to boathouse?"

A second person replied, "I didn't know about it and neither did he."

Is that really Tidwell talking with the Soviet spy?

"Forrest simply wanted to interview McKenna's wife," the TVP detective said. "Which led to Ross' wife — and the damn boathouse. We found the Islay lead on Sunday when we inspected the boathouse."

Wes remained motionless. Sokolov stomped around, opening and closing drawers, eventually finding a roll of duct tape.

Tidwell continued. "I didn't know you were here either." He checked on the seemingly unconscious Wesley, finding the head wound had oozed only a small amount of blood.

"I stalled him best I could. Sent you a coded telegram Monday when we were stuck in Glasgow!"

Sokolov shook his head. "MI5 was watching the pickup location. Couldn't get to it. When I found out Forrest was in Scotland, I came back here," he said, pulling Wes' feet together and taping them.

Wes kept feigning unconsciousness and remained limp.

"Well, by killing Klooster," Sokolov said, "I lost my *mudak* pilot and that prevents completion of the current plan. Not killing Forrest? Your cover is blown." He stared coldly at Tidwell. "You sure you want to do that? If not, I'll kill him now."

"No. He's worked well with the Brits. And like me, just doing his job."

Looking down, "KGB offered to recall me two years ago," Tidwell said. "Haven't been back to Moscow since I left school, but ready to go now."

"I don't give a *govno* if you are best mates — he is an enemy and a liability."

< 447 >

Sokolov flipped Wes on his back and taped his wrists together at his waist. Pain shot through Wes' arm and shoulder. Although he almost blacked out, he did not utter a sound. A tear ran down his cheek unseen.

Sokolov double-checked his work, exited the office, and moved to the sliding exterior doors. They opened to clearing weather, cloudy but no rain and only occasional light gusts. Without saying a word, he pointed to a small idling boat, with its running lights on, tied to the pier.

He then walked to the three covered mounds inside the warehouse and pulled canvases off to reveal pallets with lead boxes and casks.

"Move the pallets to the dock. I'm going to search along the coast for a bigger boat. Wish we'd kept the Achieve," Sokolov said. "I'll be back as soon as possible. If the American so much as moves, kill him."

Sokolov boarded the small boat, then headed out to the Sound. Wes continued to lie on the floor without moving, thoughts bombarding his brain.

Tidwell's a damn spy. A sleeper! Bastard played me, stalling and delaying our travel to the Isle, and refusing to move until talking to both the Isle of Islay police and then Knight.

As a boat started and pulled away, Wes listened carefully.

Holy shit! Did Tidwell warn Sokolov about MI5 locating his flat?

In short order, a forklift started and moved around inside the warehouse. Wes tried to pull and tear the duct tape. That hurt his shoulder. He slid over to a trash can and tipped it. It made a loud bang. He froze, but the forklift continued to move and was not coming his way.

He found an opened can of beans with its jagged tin lid sticking up. He cut his wrist twice as he severed the edge of the duct tape enough to be able to tear it. He used his bleeding right hand to free himself. To stop the flow of blood, he put strips of tape over his cuts.

Ignoring the pain, he struggled to his feet and moved falteringly to the open office door. Wes watched a focused Tidwell move a pallet of whisky barrels away from outside the dock doors.

Where the hell is Sokolov?

Wes crept to the desk, rifled through drawers, tossing aside papers, pens, a paperback. Prayers were answered when he found a Browning Hi-Power pistol.

The only thing that's gone right today!

He ejected the magazine, finding it full with 10 rounds. Searching the rest of the desk supplied no more 9mm ammunition.

One of his wrists was bleeding beneath the tape, so Wes wiped and pressed it against his pants. He slapped the magazine against his palm to unstick any cartridges, reinserted it and went again to the office door. His elation was short-lived when he saw that where the covered pieces of equipment had sat, now only one uncovered pallet with two casks remained.

Wes could still hear the forklift out on the dock. Quickly searching and finding no one else in the warehouse, he warily approached the dock's sliding doors. A split-second later, he jumped back as the forklift with Tidwell driving came blasting through the doorway. Tidwell did a double-take, then drove straight at Wes, elevating the tines to waist level as he moved.

Raising the Browning, Wes fired two rounds, heard lead strike metal and ricochet deep into the warehouse. But the bull continued to charge. Wes fired twice more.

Tidwell slumped. But now the forklift was almost on Wes. He jumped out of its way. The path of the forklift did not deviate from heading straight to the remaining casks of nuclear waste.

Wes sat up, put his right arm on his right knee, aimed and fired until the slide locked open.

Tidwell toppled off the forklift. Wes froze, holding his breath. Would the dead-man brake engage and bring it to a stop?

It did.

< 450 >

Moments later, there was loud yelling when an MI5 taskforce entered the building. Wes, still sitting on the floor, tossed the gun toward approaching agents with weapons leveled at him. He raised his right arm.

Knight hollered, "Hold your fire. It's Forrest."

Knight went to grab his left arm, but Wes blocked him, moaning, "Shoulder!"

"Where's the Russian?" Knight asked.

"I shot one and the other left by boat I think," Wes answered, cradling his arm.

"What? Two?"

Knight's men examined the crime scene and Wes quickly explained to Knight about Tidwell working with Sokolov.

They were interrupted by a short heavyset agent. "Agent Knight, we were lucky. The forklift stopped within inches of what we think is nuclear waste. Had it punctured one of the containers, this place would be contaminated for decades. Plus, there's another body in a back office."

"Thanks Charlie." Then Knight yelled. "Detective Morrison."

He was at Knight's side in seconds.

"I need your help. We need scene and medical examiners here *now!* Your office should have all the contact information."

He paused and looked toward the pallets on the dock. "While you are getting that started, I'll

< 451 >

call the Office of Nuclear Regulation and find out what we need to do with that stuff. And Charlie! See if you can find a first-aid kit for Wesley."

Charlie created a makeshift sling for his arm. Morrison was nowhere to be seen. Knight joined his men in the investigation, and Wes was left alone with no real task. He did not want to see Tidwell's body so, feeling the need for fresh air, he walked out into the dark, to the end of the dock.

I can't believe Tidwell did this. I trusted him completely. That asshole!

Wes noticed an inky silhouette moving on the water. Focusing, he saw a boat with no lighting, slowly turning. A flash, then his left arm felt like someone had punched him hard. Pain engulfed his shoulder. Then he heard the shot. He dropped behind one of the thick pilings and four slugs drove into it — thump, thump, thump, thump. Then silence.

Cautiously peering around the pile, Wes saw the cabin briefly illuminated by an interior light.

Sokolov!

The light flicked off, engines roared, and the boat made a ninety-degree turn for open water.

Wes turned toward the warehouse, all pain receptors kicked in and he collapsed on the dock. He shouted, "Knight! Knight! Call the Coast..."

And he slipped into darkness.

SIXTY SEVEN
London
1 June 1983

Wes awakened in a fog. Nauseous. Dizzy. Heard soft murmurings, hands gently touching his good forearm.

"Wesley. Wesley," someone kept pleading. "You need to wake up."

He tried to focus. Vague forms, ghosts, seemed to be moving around the room. He strained, but the darkness moved back and engulfed his mind. Wes next woke up in a brightly lit room. When he moved his damaged arm, alarms sounded. He was immediately surrounded by people in white coats. *An emergency department.*

"What's your name?"

The pain in his head increased while he processed the question. "Wes. Ah...Wesley Forrest," he whispered.

Everyone around the bed became cheerful, confusing Wes further. He felt the prick of a needle and darkness returned.

* * *

When Wes next awoke, he was thinking more clearly and realized he was in a hospital room. He vaguely remembered travel. Ambulances. Flying. Turbulence.

"Where am I?" he asked a nurse.

"St. Mary's Hospital, London."

"How long have I been out? What's the date?"

"Today is 2 June. Thursday."

"How'd I get here?"

"Her Majesty's Coast Guard. Search and rescue helicopter brought you from Scotland."

Wes took a deep breath and slowly released it, then muttered, "I'm starving. Got any food?"

Following a hospital breakfast and conversation with a trauma nurse from Austria, Wes finally relaxed and fell asleep. A noise disturbed Wes and he found Elliot Knight sitting next to his bed reading a magazine. "Good day...rather, good afternoon," Knight said.

< 454 >

Wes nodded, took a deep breath, and struggled to reposition the pillows so he could sit up. Knight was quick to assist, taking care not to bump his left arm still in a sling.

"This is the first time I've been able to visit," Knight said. "You were brought in last evening but had been sedated for the air ambulance flight."

Leaning forward, he asked, "How do you feel? I talked to a nurse outside —"

"The cute one from Austria?" Wes asked, glancing toward the door. He grimaced when he moved. "She brought breakfast and sat and talked while I ate."

Laying down the magazine, the MI5 agent continued. "She tells me, in excellent English, by the way, that you're pretty banged up. Some visual. Some internal."

"I don't know about all that, but this arm's messed up," Wes said, looking at the sling. "I understand the bullet grazed me. Above the elbow — didn't hit a bone, thank God. But they think my rotator cuff is torn. May require surgery. Will know later today after more imaging and tests."

Knight offered sympathy but quickly got down to business. "Can you tell me what happened on the dock?" he asked, getting paper and pen from a file folder.

"I don't remember much. Remind me what was happening."

< 455 >

"Well, after getting approval for you and Tidwell to go to Islay …"

"Tidwell!" Wes said suddenly. "Where…?"

"Everything related to Tidwell has been transferred to MI6, including the body. They sealed his office and home and are investigating. They believe he was a Soviet agent."

No shit, We thought, and leaned back on his pillow.

"He came to England from Australia to attend University," Knight said. "But they have not found an Aussie birth certificate." Knight took a deep breath. "They, MI6, are anxious to talk to you."

"Assuming it'll all come back," Wes said to himself as much as to Knight.

Wes was thinking about his shooting Tidwell, but Knight continued, "If you remember, Klooster, the pilot who owned his plane, is dead."

"Did you figure out their plans? How about Sokolov?"

"We never saw him," said Knight. "But I need to tap your memory about him. Let's go back to your arrival on Islay."

They talked awhile, but Wes had tired so quickly that Knight stood to leave.

"Well, I need to go," Knight said reluctantly. "Got to get to the office." At the door he said, "Keep me posted on your status." Then winking, "I'll summon that nurse on my way out."

* * *

After she was asked to check on the patient in Room 308, trauma nurse Jocelyn Kellner first went to the loo. She captured the few stray wisps that hung down the back of her neck and rearranged her bun. Leaning into the mirror, she took a close look at her face. She wore little makeup, as the hospital dictated. Blessed with smooth complexion, she wished she had inherited her mother's straight, narrow nose. She thought her eyes and high cheekbones were her most appealing assets.

It had been awhile since she'd been attracted to a man. She wanted to know more about this handsome American. She liked his looks, his smile, his temperament — everything. She felt a tingle of desire, which embarrassed her. Thoughts of her philandering ex-husband in Austria ruined her mood.

I would meet a nice man just as I am finishing my course here in London.

* * *

Beaming, Nurse Kellner rushed into the room. "Wesley! Great news." She stood next to his bed and continued. "As I walked by the nurse's station, your doctor was on the phone."

< 457 >

She called me Wesley.

"You only have partial tear of the rotator cuff. No surgery required. They can use conservative treatment. Recovery will be faster."

"What's torn?"

"One of four tendons that attach shoulder muscles that provide stability and support movement. Not sure which one is injured. The doctor will be in soon with details."

"Recovery?"

"Yeah. You may be able to go home tomorrow or Saturday. Take pain meds. Wear a sling for two to three weeks. Home programme of rest and physiotherapy."

"Wait. My car is at home. I took the train to London." Looking at his arm, he said, "Also, you know, if I'm on drugs…" He looked up at her. "…am I allowed to drive?"

A huge smile spread across Jocelyn's face. "I'm staying with my aunt in Reading. Maybe I can give you a lift?"

< 458 >

SIXTY EIGHT
Silchester
6 June 1983

Wes woke from a deep sleep, dreaming about a certain Austrian female nurse. A gray cloud circled the bedside lamp. He first thought he was back in hospital, but then he began to cough and rolled to the floor, landing on his good shoulder. The air above him was thick with smoke.

Holy shit, the house is on fire!

His reactions were automatic. Using his good arm, he belly-crawled to the hall. Standing and holding his breath, he bolted down the hot stairs, bare feet stinging, finding the front door already consumed in flames. Fighting panic, lungs about to burst, he rushed to the rear kitchen door only to find it barricaded from the outside and on fire.

I am not going to fucking die!

Swallowing panic, he barreled into the dining room. Fire danced along the wooden floor toward the curtains. Seizing a chair and ignoring the pain, he smashed the wide bay window and jumped out into the back garden. Falling to his knees, he vomited amongst broken glass. Still gasping, his brain began to function properly. He patted his smoking pajamas and ran toward his neighbor's house, yelling for them to call the fire service.

Got to move my car. Dammit, no keys!

Wes ran across the front lawn toward his car when a bullet whizzed by, popping when it hit flaming timber. Ducking behind his car, he froze, listening, hearing sirens in the distance. He peeked over the roof and saw a muzzle flash from between two houses. A round skipped off the car top beside his head. He dove to the pavement. More shots struck the vehicle. Left tyres blew.

Sokolov!

A Silchester police car passed him going too fast and slammed on its brakes, sliding to a stop in the street in front of his house. An officer got out of the driver's side. Wes heard his companion on the radio. A shot rang out and the blue flashing light was gone. The startled officer just stood there. Wes ran and tackled him, ignoring his shoulder pain. Now both were protected by the police vehicle.

"Shooter. Between the houses," Wes yelled. The officer understood, rolled and pulled his gun.

Unfortunately, the cop in the car panicked. He opened his door and ran toward the nearest house. Shots followed and he fell before reaching cover.

Wes jumped into the idling vehicle, popped the clutch, and drove the car toward the barrage. It promptly hit the curb and went airborne, a touch of good luck because he was met immediately with gunfire, which hit the bonnet and glanced off.

< 460 >

Now he was heading for the neighbor's four-foot picket fence.

Seeing a post directly in front of him, Wes yanked the wheel to the left, sent boards flying in all directions, recovered, and headed again toward the flashes of gunfire. His windscreen cracked but did not shatter, his one headlight flashing on a child's jungle gym. Wes saw the swings, the slide — and the shooter kneeling under the covering roof dressed in black firing a rifle at him.

He aimed the patrol car at the swing set and ducked. He felt it ram into the structure, more substantial than the fence because the posts were cemented deep in the ground, and come to a stop in the sandbox. Wes tried to open the door, but pain shooting through his shoulder stopped him.

Pow-pow-pow. The officer he'd left standing in the street ran by, firing into the darkness. Returning after a short chase, the officer helped Wes out of the car and from under the rubble. Once clear and on his feet, the pain in his shoulder intensified. This time he refused to faint, pulled his left arm in close to his body, and concentrated on his surroundings.

He walked toward his burning house. A high-volume pumper truck was spraying water. The fire crew was successfully knocking down the fire. The lady next door, who had been watching the action, brought a blanket to Wes and put it around his shoulders. Firemen circled what remained of his home, looking for hot spots.

The fire chief told Wes that the officer who ran from the car had been shot in the leg and taken to hospital. Not critical.

"The arsonist knew what he was doing," the chief said. "To block your escape, he squirted an accelerant under all exterior doors and ignited it. Then it seems, he hid away from the scene, waiting with a gun, in case you did get out."

A Hampshire policeman approached. "Colonel, we found where your shooter landed after you rammed the swing set."

The officer shifted the torch to his left hand, pointed it in the direction of the swing as he explained. "He fell over two meters, landing on a stump. Blood all around. Lost his gun. A Lee-Enfield military sniper rifle. He must also have a handgun because he exchanged a few shots with Corporal Keenen when he was running."

"Corporal was armed?" the fire chief asked.

"Yes. Keenen is an Authorized Firearms Officer. Anyway, the shooter climbed up on the platform because it afforded him a greater field of fire. He could see all your front yard, as well as a lot of your garden. Could lie in wait in case you survived the house fire."

As he walked away, the officer said, "A police dog is on the way. We'll get him."

< 462 >

SIXTY NINE
North Sea
14 June 1983

When the engines on the pelagic fishing boat Golden Plover came to life, so did the roosting sea gulls. Nikolai Sokolov watched the activity on the stern ramp.

"Smells good today," he said to Skipper Jessie MacTavish. "'Course, that's before the first fish are hauled in."

"You better hope that Soviet trawler shows up. The men hav' not taken kindly to your insulting comments about their livelihood," the captain said.

"*Idi Nahui!*" Sokolov swore. His ribs hurt day and night, so he didn't really care. "For what I'm paying you, you can control them — and their tongues."

Going forward to the wooden vessel's bow, Sokolov thought of his situation. He scanned the

< 463 >

distant rows of orange clouds backed by a curtain of blue. Fog blended with the sea at the horizon.

"I could enjoy this under different circumstances," he muttered to himself.

The open water was choppy. A crisp salty wind caused early morning whitecaps. Only a single boat was visible, another of the twelve-boat fleet, which had been on the North Sea since Tuesday. They usually departed Buckie on Monday mornings and returned to home port once the boats were full of fish or on Friday, whichever happened first. But this Monday there had been a city festival, so they left a day late. These devout family men — and a few hardy women — prized weekends in their own beds.

During his first day aboard the Plover, Sokolov attempted to help the four-man crew with fishing and chores. Limited by his injuries, he could do little. The smell of gutted fish and the dumping of entrails into the sea also made him sick, so he had spent time hanging over the side, much to the fishermen's amusement. On the second day, he'd watched from afar while the crew washed and gutted whiting, cod, and haddock along with a few sole and plaice, sorting them by type and size into shallow iced trays of wood, which were then stored below decks.

The boat's part-time cook explained that when they returned to Buckie, the trays go directly from the boat to a warehouse to be bid on by buyers.

Sokolov had first slept fitfully in the fish hold, wrapped in a worn wool tartan blanket. The meds he'd brought on board helped some. But after two days the iced catch filled that space, so last night, with a temp of seven degrees Celsius, he'd slept sporadically on the deck.

Early Friday, to the annoyance of the captain, he made himself comfortable in the warm wheelhouse, watching the radar scope for signs of an approaching ship.

"Fancy this weather holding," said the skipper. "Last week we had battering ten-foot waves. Had to head to port early."

By eleven a.m., the airwaves between the Buckie boats were full of chatter about heading home. The captain of the Plover radioed he had spotted a fish-run and was pursuing it, explaining he'd stay no more than an hour or so and then catch up with the rest of the fleet.

Thinking he was crazy, none of the other skippers followed suit.

MacTavish moved his craft around as if fishing, but his eyes were focused on the radar scope. All the Buckie boats had cleared the screen when he finally picked up a blip, northeast of their location, heading straight toward them. Sokolov triggered his electronic signal device and the Soviet trawler pulled up alongside the Plover about twenty minutes after midday.

Looking at the rust-covered steel hull twice the size of his boat, Skipper MacTavish said to his first mate, "My God, what a derelict." But he took note of four towers of shiny antenna and dishes, and guessed that below deck was the best electronic equipment rubles could buy.

Sokolov called together the crew and gave each an envelope containing as much money as they'd make in three weeks of the best fishing. "Remember, I have a friend in Buckie. If any of you talk or spend this money in a way that draws attention, you'll..." He paused, pursing his lips. "I'm not sure what the men my friend calls in will do...but it won't be nice."

Without a thank-you or a goodbye, he boarded the Soviet boat which sailed north.

* * *

Sokolov hoped that spare outerwear was on board. In his haste to escape, he had not dressed nor packed for a cruise around northern Norway to Soviet Russia. From his duffle, he gathered any item that could be linked to the librarian Peter Zennia Velikaya. Wrapping them with sailcloth and rope, he secured the package to a piece of rusted anchor. He dropped it overboard and watched it disappear under the ship's wake.

That evening, he borrowed a seaman's overcoat and went topside. He lit a Russian cigarette given to him by a crewman and considered the grim reality of the reception he get at home.

He had been born in Vladimir, one of Russia's oldest communities. His father managed the worker's cooperative there and led the local cell of the Communist Party of the Soviet Union. Nikolai Sokolov had a flair for languages and in the early 1970's, when his father was posted to the Soviet Embassy in London, attended British schools.

Before his successful tour in Budapest, his previous undercover operation in the UK had gone well. But all that would be forgotten because the Motherland only rewarded success.

He'd never meet the General Secretary nor have a banquet in his honor, as he might have, had he succeeded at RAF Greenham. Till now he'd been a hard-working citizen doing his native country's business successfully, that is until the dirty-bomb failure. Though the mission had come from high up the party chain, he'd certainly bear the blame alone.

Elbows on railing and chin in hands, Sokolov was concentrating so hard he failed to sense a carpenter's hammer descending toward the back

< 467 >

of his head. It tapped him twice, gently, before he could turn.

The captain handed him the hammer, saying,

"To say the KGB is unhappy with your performance in England would be an understatement," said the captain. "So, you deserve and are getting punishment. As of now you are banned from the Soviet Union until such time as you redeem yourself."

"How?"

"You figure it out. That is part of your redemption."

Pulling a Dutch passport from his pocket, he gave it to Sokolov. "New identity," he said softly. Then asked, "Never heard how you were injured."

"Hunting accident. The game started to move away, so I stood for the shot, the stand gave way, and I fell on a stump. Got a lot of scratches and cracked two ribs."

"Too bad," said the captain. "Losing the game."

Then as an official for the Motherland, he stood tall and delivered the final ruling. "We will drop you off in the Lofoten Islands — near Svolvær. You are never to enter the Soviet Union again without KGB approval."

He left Sokolov staring out onto the Norwegian Sea pondering how he was going to get to his safe deposit box.

EPILOGUE

< 469 >

Ramstein Air Base
Germany
End of February 1984

Wes Forrest was walking out of the Ramstein bank with enough deutsche marks to pay his deposit and first month's rent, when interrupted by a shout.

"Wesley."

Wes turned to see the Pentagon Intelligence officer who'd started his adventure at RAF Greenham. Saluting, he said, "Colonel...ah...sorry, *General* Wheeler. What brings you to Ramstein?"

"I transferred here last November." Then taking a quick breath, he said, "Wesley, I'd like to talk to you about Greenham. I've got to run. Please call my office — USAFE Intelligence — for an appointment later this week."

"Yes, sir," was all Wes got out before Wheeler rushed toward reserved parking.

* * *

In the Intelligence wing, Wheeler's secretary said the Headquarters staff meeting was running long, but the general had asked him to wait. Deja vu. Wes had just gotten comfortable when

Wheeler rushed in and indicated for him to follow into his private office.

"Something to drink?" the one-star asked.

"No, thank you, sir. Just had lunch."

Wheeler punched his phone: "Wanda, will you get me a sandwich, please?" He looked at Wes with raised eyebrows. Wes shook his head.

"That's all," he said and disconnected.

"Been a busy day," Wheeler said to no one in particular. He turned his attention to Wes. "Wesley, congratulations on making the Initial Operational Capability date at Greenham. Getting that first flight functional was a critical milestone."

Wes nodded. "Wasn't me, sir. The Maintenance Squadron Commander and his troops busted their asses in October and November to make it happen. And of course, after the plane was painted in the summer, everyone got serious about perimeter security, which helped."

"But you and Colonel Rogers were responsible for ensuring all the necessary people and equipment were in place to make it happen…when you were not jaunting all over Scotland," the general added with a wink and a smile. "Which is the reason we sent you to Greenham in the first place, and now, pulled you to Plans at headquarters."

"We?"

< 471 >

"Yes. Me and General Hudson. Who, by the way, has been tapped for his third star and will become the Vice Commander of USAFE and report here in about sixty days." Wheeler held up his hand. "Information that is not official yet, so you didn't hear it."

The general paused. "The Italians have left no infrastructure at Comiso. Thank God the Belgium government is one-hundred percent behind us at Florennes. And the Good Lord only knows what problems will be at the next three bases."

The general turned and pulled a bottle of water from a mini-fridge built into the credenza behind him. He offered one to Wes, who again refused. "Tell me about the next phase at Greenham. Deployment."

Wes began. "We're working it. We... uh...*they* have all the dispersal gear and equipment necessary for three flights. Secret arrangements have been made with the British government to have a first exercise in July, with one flight deploying to an isolated, undeveloped area on Salisbury Plains for three days."

After a brief pause, Wes added, "The crews are in training, especially the security police. Overall, they will carry the biggest burden."

Wheeler's other phone rang. He picked it up, listened, said "Okay," hung up, and turned to Wes. "The latest intel is that the women protestors

< 472 >

have lost an inside source of base information, so are doing general planning. They're setting up communication networks to block the base gates and highways, whenever and wherever a flight convoy leaves the base."

This was not news to Wes, so he asked, "What's the status of Colonel Rogers?"

Before he could answer, his secretary brought in a tray with a sandwich and salad. She left, closing the door, and the general continued.

"With Rogers's promotion potential gone, due mainly to the painting of the spy plane, it's been arranged for him to go back to the Pentagon for a year, then quietly retire."

"He's a good man, sir," Wes said.

Wheeler nodded. "Yes, he is. If you'll excuse me, I need to return a few calls. You will be a part of planning the GLCM deployment to the next four bases, so I'm sure we'll have a lot more discussions."

Wheeler rose from his desk, asking, "What are you doing this weekend?"

After getting to his feet and snapping a quick salute, Wes said, "Well, sir, I can't move into my house until next Wednesday, so…I thought I'd visit a certain nurse in Austria."

< 473 >

— the end —

< 474 >

AUTHOR'S NOTE

The idea for this historical novel was born while I was stationed with the United States Air Force in Europe in the early 1980s.

However, I did not have the time or inclination to pursue the endeavor until I retired from the practice of law in 2009.

In order to simplify organizational charts and reduce numbers of characters for the reader, I streamlined both Royal Air Force and USAF staff at RAF Greenham Common Air Base. The most obvious is no mention of an American Base Commander. Non-military readers constantly confused the roles and duties of the British Base Commander with that of the American, so in the rewrite I simply removed all references to the American Base Commander.

I also made some minor changes to the base property and geography for the same reasons. For example, I changed 3-digit hangar identifiers to single digit numbers.

The RAF Charitable Trust will be surprised to find the 1983 RAF Greenham Common International Air Tattoo occurred in May. I needed to change the date from July for my plot timeline.

< 475 >

W.F. WHITSON | THE LIBRARIAN

I served through most of Glick'em's (GLCM) life. I was in Europe in December 1979 when NATO made the "Dual Track Decision" regarding nuclear weapons, which included deployment of the American ground launched cruise missile (GLCM) in Europe. I was the first missile officer at the first GLCM base (RAF Greenham Common UK in 1982) and was privileged to play a small part in the development of the Intermediate-Range Nuclear Forces Treaty agreement that dismantled GLCM and Pershing II missiles, and signed by US President Ronald Reagan and Soviet General Secretary Mikhail Gorbachev in December 1987.

< 476 >

ACKNOWLEDGMENTS

I learned the craft of writing by working my way through many drafts of this story, which is why I am immensely grateful to family, friends, and acquaintances who gave generously of their time over the years to read, comment, and offer suggestions on my story idea centered on Royal Air Force (RAF) Greenham Common Air Base.

In 2011, I decided it was time to get serious about finishing that book and joined two critique groups, attending each part-time depending on if I had something to contribute.

The leader of the Eagle Eye Book Store Critique Group, **Jedwin Smith**, has become an ardent cheerleader and mentor over the years.

George Weinstein, organizer of the Roswell Group, has held many positions with the Atlanta Writers Club (est. 1914), including president, who opened my eyes to writing workshops, seminars, and literary agents. He was the key developer of a bi-annual Writers Conference in Atlanta.

In 2012, several agents read my initial chapters, and while all liked the concept, none liked my approach. In 2013, I started over again. At that time, I sought advice from both Jedwin and George and laid out a multi-plot plan. These details were discussed with:

< 477 >

- **Michael Keir, PhD, CSci, FIPEM** – In 2013 he was Research Associate and Honorary Lecturer, University of Newcastle upon Tyne. In 1983 Mike was the senior physicist in the nuclear medicine department at the Royal Victoria Infirmary, Newcastle. He explained what British nuclear medicine departments and storage areas were like in the 1980's, and the associated risks. He was also kind enough to review and comment on two draft chapters.
- **Ken Wells** – In 2013 he was Force Museum Curator, Thames Valley Police Training College, Sulhamstead, Reading. Ken was charitable enough to answer questions I had about TVP organization and operations, especially jurisdictional and coroner issues if a body were found on RAF Greenham. Also, what police thought about the ongoing Women's Peace Movement, as well as information about dirty bombs in the early 1980's.
- **Greg Niemiec, Lieutenant Colonel (Ret.), USAF.** In 1983 he was the Maintenance Supervisor for the 501st Tactical Missile Maintenance Squadron, RAF Greenham Common, and refreshed my memory on facility uses in the early GLCM Alert and Maintenance Area (GAMA) and on base.

< 478 >

- **Michael Wasylik, MD, orthopedic surgeon, Tampa, Florida (USA)**. Through email and phone calls, the good doctor offered me thoughts and ideas on the book's medical scenes and suggestions for changes to add depth and make situations truer to life.

I am indebted to each of the above. Any mistakes in this book are errors I made in applying their invaluable information and guidance.

The aforementioned writer critique groups were exactly what I needed. Developing friendships with others who were going through or had gone through the same stages as I, made me feel so not alone.

When able, I continue to participate in both groups. And I owe each and every member a debt of gratitude. Over the years their feedback provided me advice and guidance that not only proved to be instrumental in telling a cohesive and interesting story, but taught me the craft.

By 2015 I had a 130,000-word draft but still no agents were interested, so I put it away and started a novel about the Civil War. But by early 2020, the forces that wanted Civil War history to be buried had reached new heights and the COVID-19 virus

< 479 >

forced us all indoors, so I returned to the RAF Greenham military espionage novel.

My heartfelt thanks to a team of Beta readers who read the 130,000-word monster, plus this revised, shorter story.

Bob Peterson and wife Susi were stationed with me at RAF Greenham during the period of this book and later at HQ USAFE. When I had any questions about the Greenham location, personnel, or operations, they were my go-to individuals.

Jim Horton worked GLCM weapon system development with me at HQ. TAC, Langley AFB, Virginia (USA). He knows the weapon system development story, then with his follow up assignment to the Pentagon, knows the headquarters positions on GLCM.

Doug Livingston and wife Mickey were stationed at Dugway Proving Grounds (early GLCM testing) and later at RAF Greenham. Mickey was a Vince Flynn fan, purchasing his novels on their release date. As such, she was an expert in the thriller genre, and kept me straight.

Mark House, an attorney in Phoenix, Arizona (USA) who has an excellent eye for detail and errors, read and fact-checked my manuscripts.

I must thank my sister, **Donna Borden**, for her many questions, knowledge of Norway, and constant loving encouragement.

< 480 >

My heartfelt thanks go to the team at **Blue Room Books**. I am especially indebted to **Angela K. Durden** for her editorial skills and the great cover design.

Finally, and certainly not last, I am eternally grateful to **my wife, Jackie**, who discussed plots and themes with me and read every draft chapter. She is good at finding places I misused tense and misspelled words (I am a terrible speller). My debt to her is immeasurable, as is my love.

< 481 >

ABOUT THE AUTHOR

William "Fred" Whitson was raised in Kentucky. He graduated from the University of Utah in 1968 with a degree in Meteorology. After two years working weather at USAF bases, he changed career fields to nuclear missiles. After assignments at FE Warren AFB, WY, and Vandenberg AFB, CA (Minuteman operations), he attended the Air Force Institute of Technology, Wright Patterson AFB, OH, earning a Masters in Logistics Management. Following a move to Davis-Monthan AFB, AZ (Titan maintenance), he was assigned to Headquarters Tactical Air Command, Langley AFB, VA as one of the first missile maintenance officers in the Ground Launched Cruise Missile development program. Then was the first missile officer at RAF Greenham Common, UK. More at his website:

wfwhitson.com

< 482 >

The Librarian
978-1-950729-11-1
W.F. Whitson
BlueRoomBooks.com